Super Mensa

by

Larry Buege

Gastropod Publishing
Marquette, Michigan

Other books by Larry Buege

Cold Turkey (Political Satire)

Bear Creek (Humorous)

Miracle in Cade County (Mystery/Love Story)

Chogan and the Grade Wolf (Native American)

Chogan and the White Feather (Native American)

Chogan and the Sioux Warrior (coming soon)

Published by Gastropod Publishing, Marquette, Michigan
Copyright © 2013 by Larry Buege

Library of Congress Control Number: 2013938959
ISBN: 978-0-9892477-1-9

Preface

In 1946 Roland Berrill and Dr. Lance Ware founded Mensa, an exclusive social organization for individuals with documented I.Q.s in the top two percent of the population. Today there are more than 110,000 Mensans in over 100 countries. They come from all walks of life, from ditch diggers to university professors, from house wives to theologians.

Within this top two percent is an even more exclusive group composed of individuals with truly exceptional I.Q.s. The secret Supererogatory Society consists of thirty-four individuals with the world's highest I.Q.s. They are the Einsteins, Newtons, and da Vincis of our time. They are the Super Mensa.

Although the secretive Supererogatory Society is fictional (or is it?), there are individuals within Mensa with I.Q.s too high to accurately measure. They are geniuses among geniuses. They are the Super Mensa.

To learn more about the Mensa Organization see their web site at www.mensa.org/. To learn more about the capabilities of people with truly extraordinary I.Q.s, read Super Mensa.

Super Mensa

1

Dark cumulus clouds billowed up in the southwest as the Spaniard stepped onto the tarmac. His sun-stained skin evinced a man who worked hard for his living. But the years of abuse his body had endured had not come without cost. He now feared the deep ache in his left hip presaged incipient arthritis. Age was taking its toll.

It was just past five, and as he expected, most of the people who had business at the small airport on the outskirts of Palermo had finished their tasks—or postponed them until the following morning—and were heading home for dinner, leaving the airport almost deserted. The Spaniard wiped the sweat from his brow with his forearm and looked up at the approaching clouds. The forecast predicted thunderstorms with high winds and possible hail moving across Sardinia, heading toward Sicily, not an uncommon occurrence this time of year. Such storms in the Mediterranean were to be expected. It was a complication, but one had to allow for complications. The Spaniard had weathered worse storms in the North Atlantic. He had been younger then. Now he was pushing sixty. His skills were still sharp—perhaps sharper—but that intense drive of his youth was gone.

Perhaps he should retire. He could return to Barcelona, fish in the surf, go for long walks in the countryside. He wondered if he could adjust to such a simple pastoral life. That would be a decision for another time and another place. Now he had a message to deliver. He didn't expect the message to be well received.

The Bell 430 helicopter waited for him at the far edge of the tarmac. Other than an old fuel truck that had weathered far too many years and a partially dismantled Cessna, there was no aircraft or vehicles within a hundred meters. With briefcase in hand, Pueblo Riviera walked toward the waiting helicopter. The helicopter's four main rotor blades were motionless except for minor oscillations generated by the gentle offshore breeze. Riviera suppressed his anger. He hated working with Italians. He had told the pilot to warm up the twin Rolls Royce turbines and prepare to fly. The storm was approaching fast enough without providing additional advantages.

Riviera opened the helicopter door on the copilot's side and settled into the seat. "Let's get this bird in the air *presto.*"

"We can't, *Signor.* The radio is all static. Unless they radio their coordinates, we cannot find the ship." The pilot, a man in his late twenties, momentarily looked into the Spaniard's eyes and then averted his gaze. Without further comment, the Spaniard reached over and entered the *Chimera's* last-know coordinates into the automatic pilot. Although not a pilot, he had logged enough hours on helicopters during his days as a CIA field agent to be familiar with the instruments. If push came to shove, he could take over the controls. He had done it before.

"There are your coordinates," he said. "Get this aircraft off the ground. The GPS will guide you to your location. Do I make myself clear?"

"But, *signor*, the ship may no longer be there, and we will be heading into the storm. I have a wife and two small children."

He was right of course. The coordinates were eight hours old. If the ship were moving at maximum speed—which he doubted— they could be off by two hundred kilometers. The Bell 430's limited fuel capacity left little room for error. But every mission had its element of risk. There was always that ever-present set of random parameters for which no amount of planning could accommodate. The Spaniard pulled out a nine-millimeter Glock 26 from somewhere under his denim jacket. It was a subcompact version of the standard Glock, weighing less than three kilos even with a full magazine of twelve rounds. With a clean handkerchief he wiped down the pistol with a massaging, almost lascivious, motion. The pilot watched with obvious concern. At no time did the Spaniard point the weapon at the pilot, but the point was well taken. Within minutes the twin Rolls Royce engines were whipping the rotor at an ever-increasing speed.

The Spaniard returned the pistol to its secluded spot under his denim jacket and removed his Marine Corps cap revealing black, medium-length hair. He would have preferred closely cropped hair, but that would have been suggestive of the military. The small tuft of silvery white hair on the left side of his forehead already drew more attention than he desired. He had never served in the Marines, but the hat fit his personality and, for the most part, hid the tuft of white hair. The cap was replaced by the co-pilot's helmet with attached microphone and earpiece. Once the motor was revving at full RPM's, the noise would preclude other means of communication. The Spaniard didn't foresee need for extensive conversation; he wasn't one for idle chatter. Since the pilot's English was better than the Spaniard's limited Italian, they would speak in English.

The helicopter gently lifted off the tarmac and headed out to sea. The motion was almost imperceptible. The pilot may have been young, but he wasn't lacking in flying skills. When the altimeter registered eight hundred meters, the pilot switched to automatic pilot, allowing the GPS to guide them to their destination. A solitary thunderhead loomed in the distance. When they got close, the pilot would regain control to circumvent the obstacle. But for now, the sun was shining on a calm azure-colored sea. The Spaniard looked down at the crystal-clear water. Light green patches identified coral reefs, some of which were under twenty feet of water. He had dived in those waters more than once—but never for pleasure. Someday he would return to truly enjoy the beauty of the coral reefs. It reminded him of his childhood when he played with his older brother in the surf near their home in Barcelona.

"See if you can pick up the *Chimera* now," the Spaniard commanded when they were half way to their destination. The aircraft entered a small cloudbank and began bouncing erratically. This was the pre-storm turbulence; they had yet to reach the storm front.

The pilot turned a few dials on the radio console and spoke into his microphone. His demeanor didn't radiate optimism. "Inbound Bell 430 calling the *Chimera*." By previous agreement, no other call sign was to be used. The personnel on the *Chimera* would know who they were. No one else needed to know. The pilot repeated the call three times after appropriate pauses. His only response was the crackling from the surrounding electrical storm. That did little for his disposition. They were burning precious fuel on the way to nowhere. He was being well paid, although hardly enough for a suicide mission. He needed money to live, but he didn't live for money. His two children needed a father; his wife needed a husband. There were other jobs.

There was sufficient fuel for an uneventful trip to the rendezvous point and back, but flying around the storm clouds was burning fuel at an alarming rate. A glance at the fuel gauge revealed three-quarters of a tank. He would need a half tank for the return trip; his aircraft didn't fly on fumes.

"You'll be able to refuel on the *Chimera*," the Spaniard replied to the unasked question.

"Yes, that is good, *signor*, but only if we find the ship. We could return tomorrow when the weather is perhaps better. Then we might know the *Chimera's* location." The pilot looked at the Spaniard, his eyes pleading his case.

"My employer is not accustomed to delays. We will make it today." The possibility of a twenty-four hour delay had crossed Riviera's mind. Despite flying around the thunderheads, the ride had become turbulent. The storm clouds could coalesce behind them, boxing them in. They would soon reach the point of no return. They had life vests in case they ditched, but they would never be found in time—not in this weather. The Spaniard didn't see himself as a coward, but neither was he a fool. "Try calling the *Chimera* again."

Without enthusiasm, the pilot turned the radio to broadcast. "Inbound Bell 430 calling the *Chimera*." He listened to ten seconds of static before repeating his request. "Inbound Bell 430 calling the *Chimera*." Again there was static; but this time, mixed in with the static, were English words. They were indistinct to be sure, but one of them was "Chimera!" Maybe his wife wouldn't be a widow after all. "Bell 430 to *Chimera*, please give us your coordinates." The reply was still garbled with a recognizable word or phrase here and there, but there were also numbers. The pilot hoped he had heard them right. "Bell 430 to *Chimera*, please repeat the coordinates." This time the numbers were unmistakable. The pilot plugged them into his GPS. The *Chimera* was eighty kilometers to their port side. Communications would improve, as they got closer.

They were now racing against time. The weather was deteriorating; rainwater leaked in around the doorframe creating small puddles on the floor; and there was insufficient fuel to return to Palermo—not if they were to circumvent the thunderheads. The craft pitched and rolled at the mercy of the turbulence. He could handle the weather, the pilot told himself. He was a good pilot, and he had a well-constructed aircraft. Unless the weather deteriorated, they should reach the ship. Just the same, he crossed himself.

"*Chimera* is a strange name for a yacht, *signor*. I haven't heard such a name in the past," the pilot volunteered with incipient prolixity. "Does it have English meaning?"

"The Chimera is a fire-breathing, mythical beast that is part serpent, part lioness, and part goat. My employer is not one for cute names like *WaterBed* or *See Shore*."

The Spaniard didn't encourage further communication, preferring to keep his own counsel. They were close to the *Chimera*, but he now doubted the wisdom of pressing into the storm—the winds were greater than he had expected, and they would only get worse as they approached the ship.

The pilot turned off the autopilot as they approached the *Chimera's* coordinates. They would have to enter a dense cloudbank to reach the *Chimera*. The Bell 430 could handle mild wind and rain, but the weather report suggested hail. The aircraft manual didn't elaborate on the aircraft's handling characteristics during a hailstorm. The pilot had no desire to find out. As if on cue, hailstones bounced off the Plexiglas windshield. Pinging noises echoed through the cockpit, as the stones slammed into the aircraft. A spider web appeared in the windshield. That would be expensive to repair. The pilot lowered his forward speed to reduce further damage. It would burn additional fuel, but it was a risk he had to take.

It was still daytime, although it had the look of dusk. In the dim light, ten kilometers ahead, a rotating searchlight pierced the darkness. It could only be the *Chimera*. Finally, a light at the end of the tunnel.

"There she is, *signor*." The pilot readjusted his azimuth and headed toward the light.

"Notify the *Chimera* that we are preparing to land and will require help strapping down the chopper. You have done well, my friend, but it is too dangerous for you to return today. My employer will provide accommodations for the night and fresh fuel for the morning. I will have the *Chimera* radio your wife that you have been delayed and that a handsome bonus will be wired to your account. Send us a bill for any damages to your aircraft. My employer richly rewards those who serve him well."

The pilot circled the *Chimera* to gather his bearings. Landing safely on a ship bobbing in a thunderstorm wasn't a foregone conclusion, even for the best of pilots. He needed to know the location of all wires and protruding pinnacles before landing his aircraft. Rich rewards would be of value only if they survived the landing.

"The *Chimera* is very big, *signor*," the pilot said. "Your employer must be very wealthy."

Indeed, at one hundred and twenty meters, she could compare favorably with any yachts offered by wealthiest Arab sheiks. The superstructure was painted white, while the sides of the ship—for it was more ship than yacht—were painted navy blue. Even in the bad weather, decks of highly polished mahogany were visible. At mid ship, a large swimming pool with adjoining hot tub was visible. What couldn't be seen were the two-lane bowling alley, first class exercise room, ultramodern dispensary, and capacious ballroom. They were below deck. At the rear of the yacht, next to the skeet range, was a large black "H" in the center of a white circle, the universal symbol for helipad. A Panamanian flag flew from the stern.

The pilot cautiously approached the ship from the rear. The ship was moving into the wind at twenty knots, eliminating crosswinds. But there was always the possibility of an unexpected gust of wind or an unusually high wave under the ship's stern. Once he cut power, there would be no second chance. Even after landing, a slight tilt of the ship, and they could slide into the sea. There would be no rejoicing until the ship's crew lashed the aircraft to the deck. The pilot crossed himself again before committing his craft to a landing. The black "H" rose and fell with each swell of the three-meter waves. The helicopter hovered momentarily over the helipad. When the deck rose up to meet the aircraft's wheels, the pilot cut the engine, allowing the aircraft to descend with the deck. Several deck hands appeared out of nowhere and began lashing down the craft.

Riviera removed his helmet and replaced it with his Marine Corps cap as a deck hand opened his door. "See that the pilot is treated well and has a place to sleep." The deck hand didn't question the Spaniard's authority.

Riviera left the care of the helicopter and pilot to his minions and headed for the third deck. He would shower and change into dry clothes before reporting to Kaufmann. Riviera keyed open the door to his private suite and set his briefcase on the wet bar. His suite consisted of a spacious bedroom with walk-in closet, a small kitchenette, a lounge with satellite TV, and a study furnished with computers and encrypted telecommunications equipment. The bathroom was state of the art with first-class shower stall and a sunken Jacuzzi tub. Lamar Kaufmann treated him well. But then he could afford to be lavish; he was one of the world's wealthiest men. His father had amassed a small fortune brokering assorted weapons to emerging nations and revolutionary factions who wished to overthrow emerging nations. It was rumored even small; tactical nuclear devices could be procured for a proper price. The black market provided substantial profit margins for those with adequate social contacts.

Lamar Kaufmann not only inherited his father's fortune but also his business acumen, doubling his father's wealth many times over. His actual worth was unknown since the bulk of his assets were in untraceable, offshore accounts. He did have legitimate enterprises, the largest of which were his four hotel-casinos, two in Las Vegas, one in Atlantic City, and the fourth and largest in Monte Carlo. The large cash flows generated by the casinos were indispensable when laundering money. A bevy of attorneys and accountants purposely kept the flow of money confusing.

Riviera checked his e-mail. Most of it was perfunctory memos and notices—nothing that needed a reply except for the terse message from the head of security in one of Kaufmann's Las Vegas casinos. They had suspected a dealer of skimming the tables; now they had proof. Going through the courts would prove expensive and time consuming, and juries don't always look favorably on the gaming industry. No, it would be best if he returned to the States and personally leaned on the miscreant. He would recover the missing money and make an example of the individual at the same time. It wouldn't hurt to let other employees know what happens to those who cross the line.

It was just before seven when Riviera arrived at Kaufmann's private dining room. A large circular table covered with a white silk tablecloth had place settings for three. Riviera assumed the third guest would be Cordelia Kaufmann, Lamar's wife. Del, junior to Lamar by ten years, envisioned herself as a movie starlet. This was more in her eyes than those of Hollywood, although she did have bit parts in several low-budget movies. Providence had provided her with the proper measurements of a starlet. All she lacked was talent. She didn't have the keen intelligence or drive of her husband, but then he hadn't married her for her intellectual capacity. As long as her ego was pampered, she was quite sociable.

A waiter in a black tuxedo materialized carrying a small tray with a solitary goblet filled with white wine. "Good evening, Mr. Riviera. The Kaufmanns shall be here shortly."

Riviera was sipping his wine and staring out the window, lost in thought, when Lamar and Cordelia Kaufmann entered the room, the deep pile rug absorbing the sound of their footsteps. Again the obsequious waiter materialized, this time with two wine glasses on his tray. The waiter's motion brought Riviera back to reality, and he stood at polite attention.

"Ah, Pueblo, it is good to see you again," Lamar gave Riviera a firm handshake before accepting his glass of wine. "I trust the storm didn't inconvenience you."

"It complicated life, but it wasn't insurmountable." Riviera turned his attention to Cordelia Kaufmann. "I see we have the pleasure of your lovely wife's company."

As usual, Del was both overdressed and underdressed, all at the same time. She was wearing a pink evening gown with ultra-short sleeves that were pushed down below her shoulders creating a plunging neckline that appeared to end just short of her lower sternum. A slit on the side of her dress exposed a generous portion of her left thigh. Around her neck was a necklace composed of perfectly matched diamonds that terminated in a sparkling stone the size of a grape. The stone was presently lodged in her cleavage. Large rubies dangled from her earlobes.

Del raised her right hand displaying an emerald ring surrounded by diamonds. If diamonds were a girl's best friend, Cordelia Kaufmann was far from friendless. Riviera, taking Del's offered fingers, gently kissed the back of her hand. Tonight would be formal, almost pompous. Tomorrow Lamar Kaufmann and Pueblo Riviera would be simple businessmen. That was how Lamar Kaufmann liked the game played. Riviera, having been treated generously over the years, offered no objections.

The dining experience was superb. Chef Ansel Marseau had outdone himself as usual. Three candles in their gold-plated holders illuminated the centerpiece bouquet of freshly cut flowers, providing a subdued, almost romantic atmosphere. Mellow chamber music played softly in the background. Lamar Kaufmann was in good spirits. This, Riviera knew, would change at the end of the meal when business would be discussed.

Lamar Kaufmann leaned back in his chair after he had polished off the last of his chocolate crêpe. The obsequious waiter took that as signal to remove the dinner dishes and refill the wine glasses. He then left the room knowing what was about to be discussed wouldn't be for his ears.

"Well, Pueblo," Lamar said after the waiter made his exit. "I must compliment you on your fine work. I understand from your report we have selected the Brazilian girl for our project. What was her name? Jacinta Rios, I believe. She seems to be the perfect candidate. She's mentally sharp, of European decent, good physical features, and has the same blood type as Del. She is also a Nobel Laureate in economics. She's everything we could hope for. When will we start phase two?"

"There is a new development." Riviera paused to allow this to sink in. "We have a problem."

"A problem? Your report mentioned no problem. You said the Brazilian was the perfect candidate."

"We have new information. She has a brother in an institution with Fragile X Syndrome."

"Speak English, Pueblo. What is this fragile X stuff?" The agitation in Lamar Kaufmann's voice wasn't lost on Riviera.

"Males with Fragile X Syndrome have enlarged testicles, pronounced ears, a prominent jaw, and a high-pitched voice."

"Enlarged testicles? You call that a problem? I should think the individual would be quite pleased," Lamar chortled. Del laughed politely. Riviera did not.

"They can be profoundly retarded."

"So?" Kaufman asked as he refilled his glass from the wine bottle.

"It's a genetic disorder. It's hereditary. Our subject is likely a carrier and could pass it down to any progeny."

"Her child could be retarded?" Lamar Kaufmann stood up and threw the wine bottle high over Riviera's head where it smashed against the wall. The gesture was more to display anger than to inflict pain. "You said she was the perfect specimen. You said we could get started right away." Kaufmann picked up his wine glass and threw it against another wall, this time over Del's head. The waiter opened the door to see if he was needed and quickly decided he was not.

"It's a minor setback. We have others to choose from. All of them excellent choices." Riviera had expected the temper tantrum. He had expected flying glass. Now that that was over, they could get down to business and consider other options. He wasn't fond of failure either, but all great plans had alternate scenarios to employ in case of failure.

"And where do you expect to find these so-called excellent choices?" Kaufmann sat down, his anger now expended. "You won't find many people with the I.Q. of our Brazilian subject."

"Are you familiar with Mensa?" Riviera asked.

"Isn't that a group of snobby geniuses?"

"I don't know about the snobby, but you do have to have a documented I.Q. in the top two percent of the population to become a member. That's an I.Q. of 130 to 140 depending on the test. At two percent of the population, they're a dime a dozen, twenty out of a thousand." If the truth were known both Lamar Kaufmann and Pueblo Riviera would probably qualify. It was another award Cordelia Kaufman would never receive. "Mensa was founded in England in 1946 by Roland Berrill and Dr. Lance Ware to promote stimulating intellectual and social opportunities for its members."

"If they're a dime a dozen, why should I be interested? I don't shop at dime stores."

Riviera ignored the sarcasm. "Within Mensa is an informal group of thirty-four individuals with I.Q.'s above 170. They call themselves the Supererogatory Society. No one knows their true I.Q.'s because they're too high to accurately measure. They are the Super Mensa, truly geniuses among geniuses, one out of a million, perhaps even three million. They're the Albert Einsteins and Isaac Newtons of our time. Apparently, a Polish nuclear physicist by the name of Dorek Dolinski organized the group to exchange ideas that the normal genius wouldn't understand. They meet periodically at scientific conferences or discuss ideas over the Internet. It's a quiet group that shuns publicity. Admission to the group is by invitation only. I happened to stumble on the list of names when I was pillaging through the computer of a Dutch paleontologist. I immediately removed him from our list. The idiot didn't even have a firewall on his computer. I don't know how he qualified for Super Mensa status.

"Anyway," Riviera continued, "some on the list had to be eliminated because they were Asian or Black, but we still have some good leads. That's how we found the Brazilian girl. If it weren't for the genetic disorder, she would have been the perfect candidate."

"How many are still on the list?" Lamar asked.

"We have two American women and a Russian."

"Using someone from the United States could prove problematic."

"I totally agree," Riviera said.

"What do we know about the Russian?"

"She's twenty-three years old, born in Kazan. Her mother was a nuclear physicist working at the Chernobyl nuclear plant when it had the meltdown in 1986. The Soviet Union cited her for heroism during the disaster but she died years later from leukemia. Our

Russian candidate's father was a general in the military. He died of prostate cancer a couple of months ago. Our subject is an only child with no other relatives."

"That is a definite advantage," Lamar said.

"Her I.Q. is off the scale. This was noted at an early age, and the Soviet Government fast-tracked her through school. She received a Candidate of Science degree, which is equivalent to our Ph.D., at age fifteen from the Polytechnic Institute in St. Petersburg. She had planned to take her degree in theoretical physics but switched to nuclear genetics when her mother died."

"What's nuclear genetics?" Del asked.

"It's the study of how nuclear radiation interacts with the body." Riviera gave Del his intimidating stare. He didn't have patience for Del's foolish prattle. "She speaks six languages: Russian, English, French, Spanish, German, and a little Polish. She is also well versed in the arts. If she wanted to, she could play violin in any of the most prestigious symphony orchestras."

"And no genetic defects?" Lamar asked.

"That's the wild card. We won't know until the end of the week. We have her scheduled for a complete physical and psychological exam. She looks promising, perhaps better than the Brazilian. It'll take an additional week to analyze the data."

"I guess we have no choice but to proceed as you have suggested," Lamar said.

"Tomorrow I'll return to Italy with the chopper pilot and catch a plane back to the States. I have a minor problem at one of your Las Vegas casinos that I need to personally address. Then I'll fly to Chelyabinsk to supervise the exam."

"What kind of problem do we have in Las Vegas?"

"You don't want to know. You can assume it will be discreetly resolved."

2

Anastasia Petrova hit her alarm clock on the second try and lay quietly in bed, allowing her mind to clear. It cleared, but grudgingly in the matutinal darkness. Only the amber light from the numerals on her digital clock illuminated the one-bedroom apartment.

Anastasia forced herself out of bed and stumbled toward the kitchen. The kitchen was small and utilitarian, typical of the apartments in her price range. It did have the essentials: an old, but functional, gas range and a small refrigerator. She found some cereal in the cupboard and covered it with milk from the fridge. Normally she skipped breakfast, but with the reactor coming on-line, she would be working late into the evening and would need the additional nourishment. The nuclear power plant had been three years in the making. That was still rushing it, in her opinion, an opinion she had shared at more than one staff meeting. But the citizens of Chelyabinsk needed the electricity, and the politburo had guaranteed they would have it today. Some things never change. Political expediency always supersedes common sense.

Chelyabinsk, a city of over a million people, hugged the eastern slope of the Urals just north of Kazakhstan. The surrounding Ural Mountains were richly endowed with large iron ore deposits. If it hadn't been for the iron ore and the steel it produced, the city wouldn't have been worthy of a first-class nuclear power plant.

It was a well-designed facility, Ana had to admit, far superior to any other Russian nuclear power plant currently in existence. It had safety features that would have prevented the Chernobyl disaster. They had learned from their mistakes at Chernobyl. But those lessons came at a high price. Ana could still remember the pain her mother had endured in the final stages of her radiation-induced leukemia.

Ana placed her dirty cereal bowl in the sink. She dressed in the semidarkness of her bedroom, choosing a conservative skirt and a light brown, pullover sweater. She would have preferred jeans, but that wasn't to be. Chelyabinsk was more conservative than St. Petersburg.

Fortunately, she was near the end of her three-month assignment in Chelyabinsk and would be returning to the Polytechnic Institute. Establishing radiation standards and protocols for the new facility was a poor use of her talents. Any number of people could have done it. But the reactor was to be the showcase of the new Russia. They had wanted the best design, equipment, and personnel. It wasn't surprising her name had floated to the surface. Once the reactor went on-line, she could return to her research at the university. Research was and always would be her foremost love.

Maybe not her foremost love. There was Dorek Dolinski, another reason for returning to St. Petersburg. She hadn't seen Dorek since she left the university two months ago. St. Petersburg was closer to Warsaw than Chelyabinsk. With St. Petersburg being the Russian epicenter of scientific learning, Dorek could always find a scientific conference or other reason for visiting her. And occasionally, with the state's approval of course, she could visit him in Warsaw. They conversed daily by Internet, but it wasn't the same. Ana wanted Dorek to hold her in his arms and passionately kiss her on the lips. She was a young woman. She had physical needs.

This could change in the future. The Beckford Corporation, a large, scientific think-tank, had offered her a two-year sabbatical in America. It was the answer to her dreams. The state had even agreed, something that would never have happened in the old Soviet Union. In America she could travel. She could go places, indulge in a variety of new experiences. She could do much of her work over the Internet, she had been told—perhaps even from Warsaw. The Beckford selection committee had all but guaranteed her appointment. All that remained was the physical exam scheduled for the end of the week.

It was ten minutes past six when Ana stepped out of her apartment building and headed toward the bus stop. In the east a reddish glow foreshadowed the sun's arrival. Its rays were already finding the high-flying cirrus clouds, bathing them in a palette of reds, yellows, and violets.

Few people in Chelyabinsk took notice of the spectacular sunrise; the streets were deserted—except for a man across the street walking his dog. The dog, an ugly mutt that only its owner could love, was lying on the dew-covered grass. They were far from home. None of the apartments in the area allowed pets. In the old days, she would have assumed the man was KGB. They had a habit of monitoring the comings and goings of people in sensitive positions; but since the fall of the Soviet empire, they had become impotent. They no longer had funds in the coffer for senseless meddling in personal affairs. Now they had to be content with true crime. Perhaps there were drug dealers in her complex. It wouldn't be the first time. But there had been other men in other places that had made her wonder if she were the one being watched. This man was new. With his red bulbous nose, she would have remembered. A linear scar disfigured his right cheek. With his ugly dog, they made a perfect couple. Ana waved to the man, and he waved back. If he were observing her, she could at least be friendly and acknowledge him.

By the time Ana reached the bus stop, the sun had risen above the horizon and the colored clouds had morphed into white wisps on a background of light blue. In another hour Chelyabinsk would be bustling with people, all heading in different directions, all with different assignments in life. If nothing went wrong, they would have a new source of cheap electricity by the end of the day. She wondered if they would appreciate the effort that went into providing that electricity—probably not.

Ana took the bus to the main terminal in the center of town where she switched to a chartered bus. Unlike the other buses, the charter was red and had a Russian flag painted on the side. Just to the right of the flag was the inscription "Kazakov Nuclear Power

Plant." Pipe fitters, engineers, scientists, clerks, and food workers lined up to board the bus.

The charter bus had accommodations for forty-eight riders. Later in the day, when the clerical staff was scheduled to arrive, it would be full. This early in the morning only twenty-four workers vied for a seat. Ana claimed a bench seat for herself. As an added bonus, the previous commuter had graciously left the morning paper. Someone had bent the pages backwards with the sections scattered out of sequence, a major affront to Ana's sense of order. She assumed the previous owner had been male. She compulsively reorganized the sections before skimming through the pages. Chelyabinsk's paper was hardly comparable to big city papers. There was minimal if any international news, and all the editorials were concerning local issues, nothing of interest to her, but it did help while away the time. With the power plant seven miles north of the town, it was a twenty-minute ride, when allowing for city traffic. It would have been a frustrating twenty minutes without something to occupy her mind.

In the distance, the cooling towers of the power plant rose high into the sky. There were two of them, part of the redundancy built into the systems. Most of the major systems had backup components. It truly was a wonderful work of engineering, the prototype for a new breed of nuclear power plants.

A chain-link fence marked the facility's boundaries, and signs posted every hundred meters warned visitors they were entering a restricted area. The bus driver, ignoring the warnings, proceeded down the dirt road and turned into a paved parking lot. Ana disembarked with the other passengers and headed toward a cluster of buildings one hundred meters away. A second chain-link fence topped with barbwire surrounded most of the buildings. Only the administration building resided outside the fence. It had a façade of red brick that was pleasing to the eye. Newly planted shrubs graced the front, giving the impression of a home for the infirm. The other buildings were more utilitarian and framed in cement block or solid concrete. Most of the passengers headed for the administration building. Ana headed for the guardhouse. It was the only legal access to the buildings beyond the fence.

"Good morning, Ana." The uniformed guard noted the time and placed a check next to Anastasia's name on his clipboard.

"And a good morning to you, Nicola."

Nicola smiled back at Ana. She was one of the few top-level employees who made the effort to learn his name. "Here's your film badge." He gave her a small, green, rectangular piece of plastic containing two square centimeters of undeveloped film. Any radiation worth worrying about would pierce the plastic and fog the film. The amount of fogging would be proportional to the degree of exposure.

Ana pinned her film badge on her sweater and headed toward the central complex. The central complex was a sprawling single-story structure containing the control room and offices for the department heads. Behind the central complex, resting on a pad of reinforced concrete, was a labyrinth of steam pipes, shut off valves, and galvanized catwalks. The steam pipes terminated at one of the two cooling towers.

To the left of the control room and attached by a windowless corridor was the containment room, a dome composed of reinforced concrete one-half meter thick. Its sole function was to contain any radioactive debris generated by a nuclear disaster.

A dozen employees were checking monitors and entering data into computers when Ana entered the control room. From their disheveled appearance, she assumed they had been working most of the night.

The windowless control room wasn't large, ten by fifteen meters at most, but the entire perimeter was paneled with electronic switches and monitors, giving the appearance of a backdrop for a Star Wars movie.

Ana greeted several of the workers and headed toward her workstation. It was less sophisticated, having few switches or input devices. Two monitors displayed a variety of graphs and charts. Her job had been to calculate radiation levels in various segments of the power plant. It was mostly theoretical work involving quantum mechanics and high-level mathematics.

Now her input was limited to two toggle switches and a red button. A plastic cup covered each switch to prevent accidental triggering. Both were independently capable of shutting down the reactor should the need arise. One would dump large quantities of boric acid into the primary cooling system to absorb excess neutrons and reduce the reactor to subcritical stage. Since boric acid in such high concentrations was caustic and would seriously damage the reactor, it would be used as a last resort.

The second switch would reinsert twenty-six cadmium control rods. They were also capable of absorbing large quantities of neutrons. Since the control rods caused no damage, they were the preferred method for electively shutting down the reactor.

Pushing the red button, the doomsday button, was an admission of failure. It was an admission that her safety features and backup systems were nonfunctional. Pushing the red button sounded alarms throughout the complex. All personnel would evacuate the buildings and assemble in the parking lot to pray that the containment dome would hold. Only key players, including Ana, would remain behind. Once the evacuation was complete and all favorable courses of action had been exhausted, they too would evacuate the building. It was Ana's responsibility to ensure this never happened. She had used the button three times in practice, and it had taken ten minutes to evacuate the buildings. She assumed the time would be reduced during a true disaster. In her absence the administrator on duty would decide when to activate the button.

Ana booted her computer and scanned radiation readings from monitors dispersed throughout the complex. All were in order as expected. Reactor activation was still several hours away. The cadmium control rods were in place, absorbing stray neutrons and preventing chain reactions. Nothing needed her immediate attention. Ana headed toward her office to check her e-mail.

"Ana, I've been looking for you."

Ana turned around. It was Dimitri Tumanov, the operations director for the facility, with seven or eight men in tow, all of whom were wearing visitor nametags. Like Ana, Tumanov had taken his degree in nuclear physics from the Polytechnic Institute. That was many years ago, perhaps eons ago. Ana found him likable, although he did have his limitations. He now thought like an administrator and had allowed his scientific skills to deteriorate. Like most administrators, he micromanaged, a dangerous habit when you know less than those being micromanaged. Any suggestion that his knowledge might be limited was met with hostility. Ana waited for Tumanov and his entourage to catch up.

"Gentlemen, I would like you to meet Anastasia Petrova, our director of nuclear safety. She has personally developed our safety protocols, making the Kazakov Nuclear Power Plant one of the safest nuclear power plants found anywhere in the world."

Ana nodded to the men. Such profuse flattery had to mean Tumanov wanted something. The men nodded back. Tumanov placed his arm around Ana's shoulders and pulled her aside. "I need a favor," he whispered. "These are businessmen and community leaders. I promised them a tour of the facility. After what happen in Chernobyl, some of them are a bit nervous. I can't think of a better person to explain the safety features than you. Besides, one of them is an American and speaks little Russian. Your English is excellent I'm told."

Tumanov didn't wait for a reply. "Gentlemen, Ana has graciously agreed to give you a tour of the facility. I'm sure she can answer any question you might have." He gave Ana a wink. "They're all yours." He walked off before Ana could offer a protest.

It wasn't that she was above giving a tour—she wasn't. It was the underlying principles. He was patronizing her. He had picked her because she was young, female, and physically attractive. It was a crass public relations stunt, and she was both dog and pony in the dog and pony show. On the other hand, she wasn't sure Tumanov could be trusted to explain the safety procedures. If the community leaders didn't support the nuclear power plant, it might never become operational. Either way, it wasn't as if she had a choice.

"Well, gentlemen, I guess I'm your tour guide. We might as well start at the beginning of the energy production, which is the nuclear reactor. If you will please follow me." The American was easy to identify. His dress was casual, and his pants had two pockets in the back, definitely not European clothing. He appeared to be in good physical shape for his age, which she guessed was late fifties or early sixties. His hair was black except for a small tuft of white hair on the left side.

Ana led them through the windowless corridor into the containment dome. "Feel free to ask questions as you think of them." She stopped in front of a concrete structure about ten meters tall. "Inside this concrete vessel is the nuclear pile consisting of ceramic pellets of uranium oxide. Ninety-nine percent of natural uranium is U-238, which is quite stable with a half-life of 4.5 billion years. The uranium we need is U-235, a rare isotope that accounts for only seven-tenths of one percent of all uranium. In order to be useful, uranium has to be enriched to between two to three percent U-235."

"What prevents a nuclear explosion?" someone asked.

"A nuclear bomb has to be enriched to seventy or eighty percent U-235. The uranium in our core is only two-point-six percent U-235."

"The plant in Chernobyl exploded."

"That wasn't a nuclear explosion. The Chernobyl plant had an RBMK type reactor, totally different than the pressurized-water reactor we have here. Their reactor overheated causing the water in a reactor vessel similar to this," Ana pointed to the reactor vessel, "to explode releasing large quantities of radioactive material into the air killing many people. If you look around you, you can see we are inside a reinforced concrete dome called a containment structure. It's one-half meter thick. Should all of our safety features fail and the reactor vessel rupture, the radioactive material would be contained inside this structure. It would be an economic disaster, but no loss of life."

"How do we know you aren't saying that because you work here? We could still have another Chernobyl."

"My mother died from the radiation at Chernobyl. I would never permit another mother to die in a nuclear disaster. The worst-case scenario would be the loss of a facility costing a hundred and fifty billion rubles, but no loss of life."

"How much is that in American dollars?" someone asked in English. It was the American. He had a Spanish accent, not Latin American. He may be an American now, but he had grown up in Spain.

"About five billion U.S. dollars," Ana replied in Spanish.

"*Gracias.*"

"How do you control the day-to-day energy output?"

At last, a sensible question. "Uranium-235 has a special property in that it can split producing very high energy in the form of heat. It also emits two or three neutrons, depending on how it splits. The emitted neutrons can hit other U-235 atoms causing a chain reaction. Most of the emitted neutrons are moving too fast to be captured by an atom of U-235 and must be slowed down by a moderator. We use water as a moderator in our reactor. The water is pumped between the fuel rods slowing the neutrons and at the same time removing the heat. The water is heated to 325 degrees Celsius, that's 617 Fahrenheit for those of you not familiar with the metric system. Only the extremely high pressure, 150 times atmospheric pressure, keeps it from boiling. This water, which we call the primary coolant, never leaves the containment building. It is pumped through these large pipes." Ana pointed to a large pipe coming out of the reactor vessel. "The stainless steel walls of the pipe are two centimeters thick. The primary coolant is pumped over to that vessel, which is the steam generator." Ana walked the group over to another concrete vessel. "A coil of pipe containing the super-hot primary coolant heats up the water in the steam generator producing steam. The steam, now under high pressure, is pumped out of the containment structure and into a turbine that runs the generator. After the steam goes through the turbine, it is sent to the cooling towers to condense back into water."

"You never explained how you control the reaction."

"I was getting to that," Ana said with dwindling patience. Explaining nuclear physics to individuals who barely made it through high school trigonometry wasn't an easy task. "High pressure pumps are constantly flushing water through the reactor core. If we wish to slow down the reaction, we add a small amount of boric acid. It's the same boric acid we would use in large quantities during an emergency to shut down the reaction, only this time it's used in small quantities. This boron absorbs enough neutrons to slow the reaction but not stop it. By varying the amount of boric acid in the primary coolant, we can vary the rate of the nuclear reaction. Now if you will follow me outside, I will show you our cooling towers."

It was ten o'clock when Ana returned to her office. Dimitri Tumanov would owe her one for that. She didn't have the patience or the temperament for public relations. She was a scientist not a bureaucrat. Tumanov should have handled the tour himself. That's what administrators are paid for.

Ana booted her computer and checked her e-mail, finding several messages but none from Dorek. One of the messages was from Chiron, that would be Marsilius Rousseau, the French Canadian neurosurgeon. Everyone in their group of thirty-four had a screen name of a mythological god or beast. Chiron was the oldest and wisest of the Centaurs, a half-man, half-horse, mythological beast. Ana thought they looked ugly, but men preferred grotesque and ugly. The more repulsive, the better. She assumed it had to be a guy thing. She had chosen Pegasus, the white, flying horse, for its grace and beauty. Ana clicked on the message. It read: *Knight to Queen-Bishop, three.*

Ana looked at the small chessboard on her desk. It wasn't the move she had expected. It left his knight exposed and vulnerable. Marsilius Rousseau was a grand master and not one to make careless moves. Any advantage he gave her came at a price. Unlike Rousseau, Ana wasn't obsessed with chess. She, too, could qualify for grand master if she cared to apply—she didn't. To her, it was only a game, although it did provide mental stimulation when she could find a worthy opponent. Other than her group of thirty-four, such opponents were hard to find. She was currently behind in her series, three games to his five. His latest move was intriguing and would require some thought.

A sharp beep brought her attention back to the computer. A message box in the left upper corner announced an instant message from "Apollo." That would be her Dorek. Ana clicked on the box to accept the message.

Apollo: *How is my sweet lovely Pegasus today?*

Pegasus: *Ready to fly into your arms if only I could.*

Apollo: *What is keeping you? My arms are open.*

Pegasus: *We are bringing the reactor on-line today. It will take a week or so to fine tune it. Maybe then they won't need me, and I can return to St. Petersburg. I miss you. I wrote a love poem for you. I'll read it to you next time we meet. It's called "Dorek, Forever My Darling."*

Apollo: *I also have something for you. I have attached two pictures of us taken by a friend last time we were together in St. Petersburg.*

Ana clicked on the download and the pictures began downloading in the background. She would look at them later.

Pegasus: *When will I see you again?*

Apollo: *I have vacation time. You name the time and place.
I'll be there.*

Ana was about to reply when she heard the alarm.

Pegasus: *I have to go. We're having another drill.*

Ana signed off and shut down her computer. It was just like
Tumanov to call a drill at the most inopportune time. People were
preparing the reactor to go critical and didn't need distractions.
They had three drills. Everyone knew the procedures.

Ana stepped into the corridor and began swimming upstream
toward the control room. A steady flow of employees casually
walked in the other direction, toward the parking lot. There was no
sense of urgency, another problem caused by excessive drills.

The key players were at their workstations when Ana arrived
at the control room. Some were manipulating data on their
computer screens; others were drawing diagrams on yellow note
pads. No one looked up or acknowledged her presence. Dimitri
Tumanov, at the far end of the room, was talking on the phone. At
that distance, she couldn't hear the conversation, but from his
facial gestures, she assumed it was less than cordial.

Tumanov uttered a well-structured string of expletives and
hung up the phone. He was obviously in a foul mood, which
explained the lack of levity normally prevalent in the young
engineers.

Ana walked over to her workstation and turned on her
monitors, revealing another reason for lack of levity. The reactor
was hot! Not only hot, but the temperature in the primary coolant
was above normal operating temperatures.

"You activated the reactor," Ana yelled at Tumanov. "That
wasn't to happen for another two hours. It's also running too hot."

"You don't think we know that? We may not be the State's
prima donna, but we've been to school. We know it's too hot."

"Why was it activated early? And why wasn't I notified?"

"First of all, no one 'activated' the reactor. We were testing
the software and programmed the control rods to rise five
centimeters. We had a computer glitch, and the rods fully retracted.
Now they won't budge. Second, we did try to notify you, but your
phone was busy. You were probably on-line with your boyfriend
again."

"Did you add boric acid to the primary coolant?"

"That was our first thought. The valve's frozen shut. It appears to be purposely frozen. We're talking sabotage. Someone didn't want the power plant to go on-line. We can't add boric acid to the primary coolant, and we can't reinsert the cadmium control rods. There's no way to shut down the reactor. It'll meltdown in about two hours, and there isn't a thing you or I can do about it."

There was sadness in Tumanov's eyes. This was to be the culmination of his career, the final star in a long list of accomplishments. He was head of the management team. His career would meltdown along with the reactor. The State didn't like failures, especially expensive failures. Scapegoats would have to be sacrificed to the political gods.

"What are we doing so far?" Ana asked.

"What can we do?" Tumanov through up his arms in a gesture of despair. "It would be suicidal to have someone climb on top of the reactor and manually reinsert the rods, even with protective clothing. I've ordered all non-essential personnel out of the building. The containment building will probably hold when the primary coolant overheats and explodes, but I'm not taking any chances. We'll bleed off the water in the primary cooling system. The core will heat up faster, but it'll only melt and not explode. There's no way we can save the power plant, but we can prevent loss of life. There'll be no repeat of the Chernobyl incident."

Ana had to give him good marks on integrity. His career was in shambles, but he was thinking of others. His intentions were good; he just lacked imagination.

"Do we have access to plastic explosives?"

"This is a mining town. We can get enough explosives to level the facility, not that that would help us any." Tumanov's voice was soft, no longer hostile. He had worked hard to get where he was. It wasn't surprising he would harbor resentment toward a twenty-three-year-old female who had risen to prominence, not due to her hard work, but due to her chance intellectual gift. But now he was desperate. He needed hope. It was a commodity no one in the room had been able to offer.

"How about dry ice? Can you get me four hundred kilos of dry ice?"

"It would have to come from town. If we placed a call now, we could have it in twenty to thirty minutes. What do you have in mind?"

"Place the call. We'll need a pipe fitter, the best we've got, someone who can produce a good, quick weld." Ana grabbed a yellow pad from her workstation and moved over to an adjacent workstation where a schematic of the reactor room was spread out "The reactor's too hot to get near, but the radiation level is inversely proportional to the square of the distance from the reactor. We can safely have a man in protective gear work here for up to thirty minutes." Ana pointed on the chart to where the primary coolant pipe emerged from the steam generator.

"I've seen some ten centimeter diameter stainless-steel pipe somewhere that has walls three centimeters thick." Ana began drawing a diagram on her yellow pad. "We'll need about a meter length of the pipe with shut-off valves at both ends. The pipe will be welded vertically to the primary coolant tube. A quarter kilo of plastic explosives will be placed on the coolant pipe inside the attached pipe. This will blow a hole in the coolant pipe. Turn off the lower shut-off valve, suck out the water from the attached tube, and add boric acid. We then close the upper shut-off valve and open the lower valve to add boric acid to the coolant. If we do that enough times, we should get the reactor under control. That will buy us time to fix the control rods. If we have to, we could add enough boric acid to shut down the reactor; but at that concentration, it'll produce considerable damage. It'll set us back several months. That's still better than a meltdown."

"Will we need a pump to force the boric acid into the coolant tube?" Tumanov asked.

"That won't be necessary. Boric acid has a specific gravity of 1.44. It'll sink down by gravity."

Tumanov wasn't sure if Ana was pulling his leg, speaking as if the specific gravity of boric acid were common knowledge. It did make sense. Boron was a heavy element. Any boron compound should be heavier than water.

Several engineers were now looking over Ana's shoulder, some skeptical, others nodding in agreement. At least it offered a proactive approach to the problem, something other than defeat by default. Questions began to fly.

"How do we know the plastic explosive will blow a hole in the coolant tube instead of the attached pipe?"

"The walls are one centimeter thinner. The metal in the coolant pipe will also be much hotter. Steel loses strength when it gets hot. Remember what happened to the Twin Towers in America? When the steel frame got hot, the buildings collapsed."

"Welding is going to heat the pipe even more. Won't that weaken the pipe and cause it to burst?"

"That's where the dry ice comes in. We shut down the pump so the coolant is no longer circulating. Packing the tube in dry ice will cool it and prevent premature rupture. There's no guarantee, but does anyone have a better plan?" Ana looked around at her colleagues. There were no other forthcoming suggestions.

Without further discussion, someone placed a call to a packing company in Chelyabinsk. The dry ice would be there forthwith. Simultaneously, a runner was sent to the parking lot to obtain the aid of several pipe fitters. By the time he returned with a couple of machinists and a pipe fitter, two shut-off valves and a length of pipe were lying on Ana's workstation. If they were to fail, it wouldn't be for lack of effort.

The three workmen studied Ana's diagram for a moment or two; then, ignoring Ana, discussed the project amongst themselves. Once they were in agreement, they picked up the pipe and the two valves and headed toward the machine shop. They never discussed the urgency nor did they discuss the risk involved. Such matters were irrelevant to professionals.

"We'll need to get the person who wrote the computer program working on a solution to the control rods," Ana told Tumanov.

"We can't. He's at a convention in Moscow."

Ana was about to say something, but then thought better of it. "Then get me a print-out of the computer code. There has to be a way to fix those control rods."

"It's over a thousand pages."

Ana glared at Tumanov who, after a moment of indecision, went off to find a copy of the code. Tumanov hadn't been exaggerating. When he returned, he was carrying no less than twelve hundred pages of computer gibberish on never-ending fanfold paper. He slapped them down on Ana's workstation with a sense of triumph, a smug smile on his face. He offered no comment, but his eyes said, "Let me see you make something out of this in two hours or less."

Ana had to admit the challenge was daunting, but she had nothing better to do until the dry ice arrived. The computer code would at least keep her busy. A brief perusal of the code revealed it was mostly written in the C++ computer language with small sections that needed to run exceptionally fast written in machine language. The software ran all phases of the power plant, which explained its bulk. Fortunately, it was well compartmentalized with frequent documentation notes explaining the sections.

Ana took a few minutes to scan the twelve hundred pages and commit the variables to memory. Like algebra, the variables were defined by letters or groups of letters. The C++ language allowed variables and related attributes to be grouped in packets called structs for bookkeeping purposes. She committed these to memory. It was a very intuitive language.

Ana mentally discarded any sections not related to the cadmium control rods, leaving a clear picture of the problem at hand. Each control rod was independently programmed. That gave the software more flexibility, but made the program more complex. She would have to separately reprogram each rod.

The machinists returned after twenty minutes. They had welded a shut-off valve to each end of the tube. In addition, they had machined a saddle to mate with the curved surface of the coolant pipe. The welds weren't pretty, but they were strong. This wasn't a beauty contest.

Ana set her computer program aside. The first priority was to infuse boron into the cooling system and buy additional time. If they didn't slow the reactor soon, there would be no control rods to reprogram.

"Anyone know when the dry ice will get here?" Ana looked at her coworkers.

"They left the warehouse ten minutes ago," someone said. "They have a police escort and aren't worried about speed limits. My guess is five minutes."

"We need to get started. The welder and I will suit-up first. No one spends more than thirty minutes in the containment building. Is that clear? If push comes to shove, we tag match it."

"Why do you have to go in?" It was Tumanov.

"I can't supervise this by video camera. If I'm not needed, I'll step outside. When I say no one spends more than thirty minutes inside the containment building, I include myself. No power plant is worth dying for."

No one offered any further argument, and the room was unusually quiet. There was no doubt in anyone's mind who was now in charge.

"We'll need two additional people to suit-up and help bring in the dry ice when it arrives. That and we'll need sheets of canvas as well as a roll of duct tape." Of all the inventions made by the West, duct tape had to be one of the most useful, at least in Ana's opinion.

The protective suits didn't offer complete protection, although they did provide a filter that prevented radioactive dust from lodging in the lungs. Barring some type of explosion, radioactive dust wouldn't be a problem. The fabric of the suit was similar to the lead aprons worn by X-ray techs. The thickness of the lead lining was proportionally greater over sensitive internal organs. The protection it provided came at a cost. The suits were heavy and mobility was reduced. Even with the lead suit, time inside the chamber had to be limited.

Ana entered the containment chamber first with a cartload of monitoring instruments in tow. Several monitors were hardened into the structure, but none specific to the area of operation. The portable monitors would gather on-site data and send them to the control room. A speakerphone would provide communication while a video camera on a tripod furnished visual information. The set-up should have taken no more than a minute or two; but in the bulky protective gear, the time stretched to five minutes—one-sixth of Ana's allotted time.

"We all set to go?" she asked over the speakerphone.

"The dry ice, canvas, and duct tape are outside your door. We have additional help suited up if you need them." Ana couldn't see the speaker but assumed it was one of the engineers.

"Let's get on with it. The sooner we get this done, the better."

The welder and two mechanists, all in protective gear, entered on cue. The two machinists carried a canvas stretcher piled high with dry ice. "We have more ice if you need it," one of them said.

Without further instructions, they packed the coolant pipe with dry ice and wrapped it in canvas. Duct tape held it all in place. Plumes of carbon dioxide vapor bellowed out from the canvas edges. They would have to replenish the dry ice several times before the project was completed.

"How much of the plastic explosive will we need?" the welder asked.

Ana broke off about a half kilo and molded it into a ball. "At this stage we're only guessing, but I think this will do."

The welder placed the explosive on a bare section of pipe between two dry ice wrappings. A blasting cap was inserted into the mass. The wire to the blasting cap extended through a small hole in the pipe they were about to attach. "Any chance of the heat from the welding torch setting this stuff off?" The question was academic, a matter of how best to proceed, not a concern for personal safety.

"If it gets too hot, it'll burn fiercely but not explode. The wild card is the blasting cap. If the fire from the burning explosive is too hot, the blasting cap will explode, and that will definitely set it off. My advice is head for the exit if it catches fire. You can shut the door on your way out since you'll be the only one left."

The welder placed the stainless steel tube over the plastic explosive. The arc of the saddle fit nicely over the coolant pipe. The technicians obviously knew their jobs. A close fit now meant a better weld later.

"Cut the power on the pump," Ana said into the speakerphone. A moment later the low-pitched hum that had been emanating from the coolant pipe was silenced. Ana touched the pipe. It was hot, but no further vibrations could be felt.

"Power is now off," someone from the control room confirmed.

Water had been flowing smoothly through the bundles of enriched uranium in the reactor core. The constant flow of water extracted heat and pumped it to the exchanger where it was transferred to the secondary system. Now, with the pump silent, the reactor core began to heat out of control. Bubbles of steam began to form along the ceramic-coated uranium pellets. Water was an integral part of the nuclear reaction. Working as a moderator, it slowed down the fast-moving neutrons, making them easier to be captured by the uranium nucleus. As the water changed to non-functional bubbles of steam, the reactor slowed. It slowed but not enough to save the reactor. The reactor continued in its relentless path toward meltdown.

"We have about fifteen minutes," Ana told the man. She felt a moment of shame. She and this humble man were placing their lives in danger to save the power plant, and she didn't even know his name. If the explosive were to blow prematurely, it would be nice to know with whom she was dying. But time was essential. The man was already placing a bead around the edge of the saddle. Introductions would have to wait.

"Give me a read on the core temperature every five minutes."

"Current temperature is 452 Celsius," came the reply over the speakerphone.

Normal core temperature for an active reactor was 350. The melting point for uranium was 1132, but long before the core reached that temperature, the water pressure would burst through the reactor shield. Superheated steam would fill the entire containment building. Protective suits would offer no protection, not against steam. One breath of the superheated steam and their lungs would fry in their own juices.

This wouldn't happen, of course, Ana convinced herself. Long before the temperatures reached critical stages, they would evacuate the containment building and turn on the pump. If that were to sufficiently lower the core temperature, they could return for a second try.

It took fifteen minutes before the man stepped back from his work. "That weld should be as strong as the pipe itself."

"Turn the pump back on," Ana yelled into the speakerphone, but it wasn't necessary. Someone from the control room had turned it on as soon as he heard the pipe fitter proclaim his work done.

"The core temperature is dropping."

"Let me know when it levels off," Ana replied. She had expected the drop in temperature when the pump forced the dry ice chilled water into the reactor vessel. This would be a temporary benefit. The core would eventually return to its steady temperature rise.

"It leveled off at 520 Celsius and is beginning to rise again."

"Bring in the boric acid solution," Ana said. "Let's find out if this is going to work."

Two men in protective gear brought in large containers filled with the solution and started filling the newly welded appendage. The tube had to be totally filled with non-compressible liquid before the charge was blown. Any gas within the chamber would act as a shock absorber, severely reducing the effectiveness of the blast. Once it was filled, the top valve was closed.

"Everyone out." Ana centered the video camera on the welded joint before she left the containment building. The door was lightly shut around the detonator wire. They would ignite the plastic explosives from the control room.

Ana removed her hood, but remained in her protective suit in case she needed to return in a hurry. The video feed had been diverted to the large screen at the back of the control room, and Ana found everyone standing around mute as they stared at the screen. There was nothing more any of them could do. It either worked, or it didn't. If it didn't, they would join the rest of the employees in the parking lot and wait for fate to take its toll, whatever that might be.

"Is everyone accounted for?" Ana asked.

"We're all here," Tumanov replied.

"Let's run some current through the detonator and see what happens."

There were too many imponderables. Was the charge too large or too small? What was the tensile strength of the vessel wall at that temperature? Right now Ana didn't even know what "that temperature" was. She preferred tidy problems where all the variables were understood and a discreet solution inevitable.

Someone did a slow countdown from ten. Ana found that a little too melodramatic. They weren't rocket scientists. At zero they heard a small muffled "puff" over the speakerphone, and the pipe vibrated, nothing more. There were no leaks along the weld. No leaks anywhere. The pipe just sat there. Other than the soft puff and vibration of the pipe, there had been nothing to indicate the charge had exploded.

"Hey, guys, it may be my imagination, but I think the rate of temperature climb has moderated." One of the engineers pointed to a graph on his monitor. It was barely perceptible, only a slight change in the slope, but it was there.

"Give it five minutes to drain," Ana said, "then shut off the lower valve and pump the fluid out of the reservoir. Check the fluid with a hydrometer. If it's anything close to one, we've hit pay dirt. Then refill it with more boric acid solution. I want fresh boric acid infused every five minutes. And alternate who goes into the chamber. No one spends more than fifteen minutes inside the containment building."

Ana removed her protective gear. They had bought extra time. It wouldn't shut down the reactor, but it would prevent a meltdown. To shut down the reactor, the cadmium control rods had to be reinserted. That would require a new computer program.

Ana sat down at her computer and began typing in code. She would use C. It wasn't as elegant a computer language as C++, but it was simple and straightforward. She didn't expect to win any awards for innovative coding. Each control rod had to be individually programmed. Fortunately the code would be similar, only a change in variables. She would program the thirteen center-most control rods. Because of their central location, they would produce the most dramatic results. That should be enough to shut down the reactor. The other control rods could be reinserted at their leisure, by hand if necessary.

It took Ana twenty minutes to finish her code, much sooner than she had expected. There still could be bugs in her program that would have to be fixed. That would consume additional time. It took another five minutes to run her program through a compiler to produce the finished software. She then uploaded the software to the mainframe. Ana typed in "run" and pressed return. The thirteen center-most control rods reinserted as if they had waited all day for the command.

"Very well done, Ana." Tumanov seemed genuinely pleased. "That should help some. Now see if you can get the rest of the rods back in."

"Thirteen is all we need. In six hours, you can push the rest in by hand."

"We need all of them." Tumanov was adamant. Now that the urgency had resolved, his normal personality had returned.

"The reactor just went sub-critical." An engineer to her left let out a war whoop. Handshakes and hugs were exchanged by some of the normally staid engineers. Others collapsed in their chairs, their energy expended.

"I'll be in my office if you need me." Ana had to get out of the control room. She needed someplace quiet. Due to incompetence, Chernobyl almost repeated itself. She had little patience for incompetence. But whose incompetence was it? Was it a design flaw? Or was it careless construction? Either way, they shouldn't have been in such a hurry to come on-line.

Ana collapsed into her office chair. She hadn't been aware of how tense she had become until now. Had it been like this for her mother in Chernobyl? she wondered. Unlike her mother, luck had been on Ana's side. Without that, the accident could have been as big as Chernobyl. But was it really an accident? Tumanov thought someone had tampered with the valve. He was talking sabotage. It wasn't unlike him to cast blame in some other corner. But what were the odds of two separate systems faltering simultaneously? The Americans had their Murphy's Law to explain such phenomena. Ana found such laws amusing, but they held no real validity.

Ana was momentarily startled when her computer monitor came to life. She must have jiggled her desk causing her mouse to move. Surprise changed to alarm when she saw her cursor move across her screen, scanning her files. It settled on a file labeled "personal." The file opened. Ana tried moving her mouse, but it had no influence over the cursor, which was now hovering over the sub-file "poetry." The file opened by command of some unseen intelligence. It finally opened the poem *Dorek, Forever My Darling*.

Ana turned off her computer, and the screen went dark. She rebooted and sent out an instant message.

Pegasus: *Dorek, I know you're out there. How dare you hack into my computer and read my poem. I wanted to read that to you personally.*

Apollo: *Sorry, I never was good at delayed gratification. It is a very lovely and romantic poem. I should have guessed it would be in French, the language of romance.*

Pegasus: *You can be so childish at times.*

Apollo: *But I am a child at heart.*

Ana knew he was right. He was a child at heart. But it was that childish mischievousness that she found so attractive. She should have known the temptation would be too great.

Pegasus: *How did you get past my firewall and virus checker? They are the best on the market.*

Apollo: *Your virus checker is turned off.*

Ana clicked on her virus program. He was right; it was turned off. She always left it on. Had someone been in her office and turned it off? There was no way Dorek could have orchestrated that, not all the way from Warsaw.

Pegasus: *How did you turn off the virus checker?*

Apollo: *You have to be more careful about the attachments you download. Remember the two pictures I sent you? The first picture contained a small virus. The code was so small it slipped under the radar so to speak. Its only function was to turn off your virus checker. The second picture contained the Trojan horse that allowed me to scan your files.*

Someday he would be caught. Dorek viewed a secure database or firewall as a challenge, not a warning to keep out. Hacking into computers was his hobby. She had to admit, when it came to computers, he was one of the best.

Apollo: *Why are you in your office? You were to bring the reactor on-line about now.*

Pegasus: *It's too complex to explain over the Internet. Let's just say we had a computer glitch, and the cadmium control rods froze in the up position. I was able to reprogram half of them to reinsert.*

Apollo: *That would be all you would need if they were the center-most control rods.*

Why couldn't it be that obvious to Tumanov? She needed a vacation. She needed to spend a week in Dorek's arms.

Pegasus: *Tomorrow I will be poked and probed by the Beckford Corporation. After that I plan to ask for a week's vacation. I think the power plant will be shut down for at least a week. Can we meet somewhere?*

Apollo: *My previous offer stands. Name the time and place, and I will be there. I do have to get back to work. My lunch break is over. I love you.*

Pegasus: *I love you too.*

Ana made sure her virus scanner was on and clicked off her computer. Then she slumped back into her chair.

3

It was forty minutes past one when Anastasia Petrova entered the lobby of the Kaminsky building, making her ten minutes late for her appointment. The office building was located in a seedier section of town, not an area Ana would have cared to visit after dark. Several neighboring buildings had been boarded up and were now inhabited only by flocks of pigeons that traversed freely through their choice of broken windows. During her two months in Chelyabinsk, this had been the first time she had ventured downtown. Now she knew why.

A bank of mailboxes with small glass windows lined the west wall near the lobby entrance. Few of them contained letters; most didn't have names. The lobby stank from the smell of stale cigarettes. In the corner, a broken beer bottle testified to the quality of the previous night's entertainment. Few people were in the lobby. Of those who were, most appeared to be vagrants seeking refuge from the afternoon sun. Over by the elevator Ana found a directory listing the room numbers of the tenants in the forty-two-story office building. All of the tenants were listed in bold type except for the Beckford Corporation, which someone had penciled in. They were located on the eighth floor, room 823.

Ana pushed the up button on the panel beside the elevator and waited for her car to arrive. It hadn't been a good day, and she was in a foul mood. She had spent the entire morning at the hospital while people in white coats poked, probed, violated, and analyzed her body. Her extensive physical exam had included a pelvic exam and sigmoidoscopy. In addition to the physical exam, she had endured an MRI of the brain and a CT scan of her chest and abdomen. They drew enough blood to start a blood bank. Being ten minutes late for the psychiatric evaluation only aggravated her already sullen disposition.

The door to the elevator opened, and Ana stepped inside. Cigarette butts littered the floor. Many of them were ground into the floor by a multitude of feet, giving the impression they had been there several days, perhaps weeks. Cleaning didn't appear to be high on the landlord's priorities. An assortment of graffiti describing various sexual exploits and political views covered the walls—obviously written by cretins. She was tempted to correct the spelling and grammar, but that would only provide further encouragement. She pushed button number eight, and the elevator lifted off with a groan. At least the worst was over. The psychological exam would be paper and pencil. She excelled at that.

The elevator stopped with a disturbing jolt, and the door opened into a small lobby. Dimly lit corridors extended out in both directions. Cheap blue-and-green striped wallpaper covered the walls; some of the wallpaper was beginning to separate from its backboard.

There was no directory on the wall, only a sign with an arrow indicating that rooms 801-825 were to the right. She turned to the right and headed down the hallway. Midway down the hall, she found a door with a half pane of frosted glass. At the top of the glass in gilded numbers was 823; below stenciled on wide masking tape was Beckford Corporation. Classical music filtered through the door.

Ana debated whether she should knock, decided against it, and then opened the door and stepped inside. A man in his late fifties or early sixties was sitting at a desk covered with papers and talking on the phone in English. An American calendar with a picture of a scantily clothed woman hung on the wall behind him. Somewhere behind the desk, a hidden portable CD player played soft background music. The man had a slender, muscular frame, his eyes dark. His hair was black except for a small lock on the left side that was silvery white. She recognized him as the American businessman from the tour, the Spaniard. He hung up the phone when she entered the room.

"Ms. Anastasia Petrova, it is so good to see you. Allow me to formally introduce myself. My name is Pueblo Riviera. I work for the Beckford Corporation." He offered his hand, which she shook, noting a firm handshake. She returned it in kind. "I hope you don't mind speaking in English. I'm afraid my Russian would be embarrassing, or we could use Spanish. I understand your Spanish is superb."

"English is good."

"Excellent. We are an American Company; therefore, all the testing will be in English. I hope that will be acceptable."

"I have no problems with English."

"Good. It'll give us a better assessment of your verbal skills." The Spaniard picked up a manila folder from his desk. In the left upper corner was a white label on which a computer had printed Anastasia Petrova in large letters. "Can I pour you some coffee?"

Ana shook her head no and followed it with a polite "No thank you."

"In that case, we might as well get started. If you will kindly follow me…"

The Spaniard opened a door at the rear of the outer office revealing a small conference room. In the center was a large oak table surrounded by four matching chairs. At one time the table had been the pride of office furnishings, but it had long since lost its luster and now had multiple dents and chips along its edges. The walls of the room were bare except for a few protruding nails from which pictures had previously hung.

"Please be seated." The Spaniard pulled out a chair for Ana. Knowing both cultures, she assumed the courtesy was more Spanish than American. "I trust your medical exam went well this morning?"

"I'm afraid no woman enjoys a pelvic exam, but otherwise it went O.K. It was more extensive than I had expected." Ana smiled, her first smile of the day. The Spaniard had a way of making her feel at ease.

"My employer is very thorough." The Spaniard sat down on the other side of the conference table and opened the manila folder. "I did arrange for a female examiner."

"I appreciate that."

"Let me explain what we'll be doing this afternoon, and then I'll answer any questions you might have. First of all, I'm not a psychologist or a psychiatrist. I'll merely be administering the tests. We will fax your answers to a psychological testing corporation in America for evaluation. You'll be given four tests: the Minnesota Multiphasic Personality Inventory, often referred to as the MMPI; the Stanford-Binet Intelligence Test, form V; the Thematic Apperception Test, or TAT; and the Rorschach Psychodiagnostic Inkblot Test. Since the latter two are projective tests, your answers will be recorded and sent by satellite to our evaluation team in the U.S."

"I'm familiar with the tests."

"If you have no questions, why don't we begin? The first test will be the MMPI. It consists of 566 questions. All answers are to be true or false. Be careful to fully blackout the circles on the answer sheet. Take all the time you need."

Ana didn't expect to need much time. She had taken all four tests many times in the past. "I do have one question. When will I get the results? When will I be hearing from you?"

"A special courier is flying your blood work to Bonn, Germany as we speak. We'll have the lab results by tomorrow morning. The results of this afternoon's tests will be sent out by satellite. They'll be evaluated this evening. My employer doesn't waste time. You should have your test results perhaps as soon as tomorrow afternoon. We could have you working for us in America in two weeks, assuming you pass all the tests to my employer's satisfaction."

"That would be nice. Someday I would like to immigrate to the west. My lover lives in Poland. We want to marry and have a family. I would name my first son, Alek."

"Alek is your father's name."

"Yes."

"I was sorry to hear of his recent passing."

"Thank you for your sympathy."

Ana was right about not needing much time. She completed all four tests in less than two hours and left the building with a feeling of elation. She could be in America in two weeks.

Ana's euphoria extended into the following day despite the gloomy dispositions of her co-workers. A disaster had been averted, but there would still be a heavy price to pay. Employees, aware that careers could be ruined, went into the defensive mode, establishing alibis and attacking co-workers. Committees were created to identify the scapegoats and prepare the sacrificial lambs.

The initial evaluation confirmed Tumanov's assessment: It had been sabotage. The computer glitch of the previous day couldn't be reproduced, but the valve controlling the flow of boric acid into the primary coolant system was totally dysfunctional and had to be replaced. Someone had opened the valve, placed a chemical on the threads of the screw mechanism, and then closed the valve. As the chemical hardened, the valve became frozen in the closed position. That couldn't have been an accident. Tumanov sent the valve to an outside lab for further analysis.

Although no one came forth to claim responsibility, Chechen rebels were, by default, the prime suspects. There was no rational motive or benefit from destroying the power plant. Only a political group that thrived on chaos for the sake of chaos would benefit from such an act.

Ana spent the morning writing a twenty-page summary of her involvement and actions, most of which was now public knowledge within the facility. She had no doubt it would be reviewed in Moscow. But the outcome of the investigation was of little concern to her. In two weeks she would be half a world away. She would have unlimited time with Dorek, maybe even get married. She wasn't about to let any investigation hamper her spirits.

The Spaniard inferred they might inform her by the end of the day. She was, therefore, disappointed when she received no word, and on the second day with no word, disappointment evolved into concern. When a computer search failed to find a trace of the Beckford Corporation, concern changed to alarm. Ana found it incredible that a large, high-tech corporation that consulted all over the world wouldn't have a corporate web page. A search of the phone book found no evidence of the Beckford Corporation at the Kaminsky building or any other building in Chelyabinsk. That, she rationalized, was understandable since they were new to the area.

On the third day she could wait no longer. Ana took the bus into downtown Chelyabinsk and walked the two blocks to the Kaminsky building. As on her previous visit, there were few people in the lobby. Being an older building, it didn't offer the amenities or the prestige of the city's newer buildings. It had nothing to attract prestigious companies. That was none of her concern. What did concern her was the most recent change in occupancy: The Beckford Corporation, which had been penciled in, was no longer listed in the directory.

There had to be a logical explanation, yet none came to mind. Ana rode the elevator up to the eighth floor, oblivious to the groans and strains of the elevator. Only when the elevator door opened to the eighth floor did her mind return to reality. Ana turned right and headed down the corridor.

One of the hallway lights had burned out since her last visit, but even in the dim light Ana could make out the gilded number 823 on the door's frosted glass. Conspicuously missing was the Beckford name stenciled on wide masking tape. No music escaped from behind the door.

Finding the door unlocked, Ana walked in. The desk where the Spaniard had been sitting was now bare of papers. The American calendar no longer hung on the wall. Ana lifted up the phone: There was no dial tone. Checking the drawers to the desk produced nothing to mitigate her discomfiture. There was no evidence that the Beckford Corporation had ever been there. She had allowed people to poke and probe her body, tinker with her mind; and now she didn't know who they were or how to contact them. Her only contact had been Pueblo Riviera—if that was his real name—and now he was gone.

Ana pushed aside her emotions and returned to logical thought. Someone spent a lot of money on her medical and psychological testing. Americans took pride in their capitalism. They wouldn't spend that kind of money without receiving something in return. She could think of no purpose except for what they had told her. Most people underestimate the time required to complete a project. She would have to be patient. At this point there was no other alternative.

At ten minutes past eleven Ana stepped off the bus in the power plant parking lot. Coming in this late wouldn't please

Tumanov. But he had been unhappy many times in the past. She was sure he would get over it.

"Good morning, Nicola," Ana said to the uniformed guard at the guardhouse. "I'm a little bit late this morning, but I see the facility's still standing."

"If you'd arrived late a few days ago it wouldn't be." The guard checked off Ana on his clipboard and handed her a film badge. "That was quite an accomplishment."

"The rumors are over rated. A lot of people worked to fix the problem."

The guard nodded, assuming it was all modesty. Everyone knew she was gifted, but she wasn't one to brag. "Dimitri Tumanov left a message for you. He wants to see you in his office as soon as you arrive. Maybe he'll give you a medal or something."

"Thank you for the kind words, but I doubt if that's what Tumanov has in mind."

Ana pinned the film badge on her shirt and headed for the control room. She wasn't surprised that Tumanov wanted to see her, but it wouldn't be to give her any medals. Ana greeted several of the engineers in the control room. Their natural levity had returned. Perhaps the inquisition was over.

"Tumanov is looking for you," one of them said.

"Is he in a good mood?" Ana asked.

"Is he ever in a good mood?"

The reply brought laughter throughout the control room. The inquisition had to be over.

Ana found Tumanov in his office shuffling papers. If there was anything he excelled at, it was shuffling papers.

"Ana, I've been looking for you. Please come in. Have a seat." Tumanov placed his papers in his "in" box, which always seemed more congested than his "out" box.

Ana took a seat in the chair opposite his desk, while Tumanov shut the office door—not a good sign.

"I have a letter for you." Tumanov passed a white envelope to her. The Beckford Corporation was printed in the upper left corner without address. This was the notification she had been waiting for. Life was indeed sweet. Ana opened the letter and scanned its contents.

Dear Ms. Anastasia Petrova:

The Beckford Corporation is a multinational consulting firm that specializes in scientific research and analysis. Due to the nature of our business, we often handle sensitive and confidential material. It is imperative that we hire only the most intelligent and emotionally stable individuals. You scored extremely high on the Stanford-Binet Intelligence Test; however, the results of the MMPI test indicated that you have a tendency toward anxiety and depression. We, therefore, must regretfully withdraw our offer of employment. You have unusual skills and aptitudes and should do well in life. Unfortunately you are not a good fit for our company. We wish you the best in your future endeavors.

Since you expressed familiarity with the MMPI test, I have enclosed a copy of the results.

Respectfully yours,

Pueblo Riviera

"I'm sorry," Tumanov said. He appeared truly sincere.

"You knew about this? You read my mail?"

"No, I didn't read the letter. Pueblo Riviera from the Beckford Corporation told me about its contents. He was worried about you. He was afraid that you might…might want to hurt yourself."

"He told you I might be suicidal?"

"Ana, it's been a difficult week. Maybe you should take some time off."

Ana looked down at the printout of her MMPI scores. The three validity scales were normal, as she would have expected. She hadn't tried to fake good or fake bad. What caught her eye were scales two and seven. Both had T-scores in the nineties. Scale two measured tendencies toward depression. Scale seven measured obsessive-compulsive neurosis. She had to admit she did have tendencies toward obsessive-compulsiveness, but not pathologically. Combined high T-scores on scales two and seven was the most commonly seen pattern in suicidal patients.

43

"I never did properly thank you for what you did during the malfunction. You saved the power plant. Without you, we would've had a meltdown for sure. And that's what I'm putting in my report to Moscow. The next week will be mostly clean up and repair, little for you to do. I want you to take a week off. I have access to a small dacha on the outskirts of Khosta along the coast of the Black Sea. It's warm there this time of year. You can use it for a week. Maybe your boyfriend can meet you there. It's peaceful and quiet. If you like the water, there's a small sailboat you can use. And Sochi's not far to the north. It's a great resort city with theaters and art museums."

"I'm familiar with Sochi." She didn't feel suicidal, but a week's vacation did sound inviting. Dorek said he would meet her any place, any time. They needed to reassess their lives. So much hope had been placed on the Beckford Corporation, and now that was gone.

4

"A card counter?" Riviera asked.

"If you check her pockets, I'm sure you'll find a clicking device. Six clicks for a six, eleven clicks for a Jack. It'll be wired to a small programmable device like a palm pilot that calculates the odds. If it's a go, she's notified by a vibration or some other silent mechanism."

"We got enough on tape to convict?" Riviera already knew the answer.

"Yes sir, enough to hold up in any court of law."

"Round them up and place them in separate interrogation rooms. Secure their chips. If they're not on the list of previous offenders and are willing to forfeit their initial stake, let 'em go— after you put the fear of God into them. If they're on the international list of dubious moral characters, turn them over to the Las Vegas police."

"Consider it done."

"And another thing, see that the dealer in the wheel chair gets a bonus in his next paycheck. He needs to know we reward both good and bad behavior."

It was a minor problem. The security man could've handled it himself and would have if the Spaniard hadn't been in the casino. There were always people who thought they had the unbeatable system, a method of cheating without getting caught. Very few succeeded, and those that did became greedy, returning to the scene of the crime to press their luck again, always trying to beat the odds. They could never understand that the odds were in the casino's favor. Success breeds arrogance, and arrogance leads to carelessness. Eventually, they are caught. The Spaniard had trained his security force well, and the surveillance equipment was the best in the business. Losses were negligible.

Riviera left the casino in his Jeep Grand Cherokee and headed west on US 95, allowing the bright lights to fade away in his rearview mirror. It was just past eight, but darkness comes early in the shadow of the mountains. He merged into the West Summerlin Freeway when US 95 turned north. About twenty miles west of Las Vegas, the freeway ended. The Spaniard turned onto a paved, but narrow, road heading into the hills. Bent by the topography of the terrain, the road twisted and turned like a contorted serpent. It was a private road, and he encountered little oncoming traffic. Tall pines mixed with patches of stunted scrub brush lined the sides of the road producing grotesque shadows in the wash of the Grand Cherokee's headlights. It wasn't the most hospitable land. If it weren't for the hordes of tourists willing to trade large sums of money for a fleeting glimmer of hope, this segment of Nevada would have nothing to offer.

The dry, parched land was nothing like the Spain of Riviera's childhood. He still had fond memories of warm summers along the Mediterranean coast where he collected seashells and played in the surf and fished with his father. But they weren't always the best of times. His father, the consummate idealist, had sided with Republicans and Communists during the Spanish civil war. It was an act the followers of General Francisco Franco would never forget. Riviera could still remember that overcast day in the fall of 1951 when his father came home and informed his family that he had been relieved from his teaching position at the University of Barcelona where he had been an associate professor of Grecian history. Riviera's mother wept openly. His father showed no emotion, but he was a changed man. Never again would he offer loyalty to a social cause or political view. He now reserved his loyalty for himself and his family. Times were tough and food scarce. The family lived on the sporadic income provided by whatever part-time jobs his father could find. Being an expert in Grecian studies did not make an impressive resume for most jobs. Riviera did not learn until years later that one of those part-time jobs was working for the American Central Intelligence Agency. Riviera and his family hastily immigrated to America in the middle of the night during the summer of 1952 when his father's cover with the CIA had been blown. Riviera was just shy of his seventh birthday. He graduated summa cum laude from the streets of Spanish Harlem ten years later—majoring in survival.

The Spaniard slowed when a wrought iron gate came into view. The gate was a portal in a ten-foot-tall fence, also made of black wrought iron. Spearheads at the top of the fence discouraged door-to-door salesmen and religious fanatics.

The Spaniard stopped in front of the gate and punched a numerical code into a transmitter box about the size of a garage door opener. The gate, mounted on rollers set in a track, groaned as the two halves began to separate. The gate closed spontaneously without further input once the Grand Cherokee had passed.

The transition beyond the gate was nothing less than spectacular. The dry scrub brush, home to horned toads and sidewinders, gave way to manicured lawns and flowerbeds, all courtesy of an extravagant irrigation system. Overhead lights tastefully hidden in the tall blue spruce illuminated the drive, which formed a circle in front of the house—if you could call it a house. It was more mansion than house. A series of white gothic columns provided support to an immense portico at the front of the structure, where steps made of red granite polished to a high luster led up to the large double doors of burnished oak. The white sides and black shutters gave the sprawling two-story mansion a regal appearance. A narrow breezeway attached the smaller, servants' quarters to the right side of the mansion.

The Spaniard walked up to the door and rapped on the brass knocker. The door opened momentarily, revealing a slender man in a black, heavily starched uniform. "Mr. Riviera," the man said. "Mr. Kaufmann is expecting you. He's waiting in the library." The man walked away, assuming the Spaniard would follow. The doors to the library were also double. Opening both doors, the man in the dark uniform stepped aside, allowing the Spaniard to enter, and then closed the doors behind him. Lamar Kaufmann was sitting in an easy chair reading the evening paper, his feet propped upon a stool of brown calf's skin. He stood up when the Spaniard entered the room, meeting him halfway with a firm handshake.

"Pueblo, it is good to see you again. I trust you had a pleasant flight—hopefully not too much jet lag. Please, have a seat." Kaufmann ushered Riviera to a plush chair facing the chair Kaufmann had just vacated.

"I readjusted my sleep cycle before I left Chelyabinsk to avoid any jet lag." Riviera sat down in the proffered chair. Conspicuously absent was his briefcase. He carried no written documentation. This report he would give from memory. "I would have been here sooner, but I had to stop at one of your casinos to check on an employee. He broke both legs in a recent accident, giving him a new perspective on life. I believe he'll now make a very loyal and honest employee."

The tall man in the dark uniform returned with a stainless steel tray balanced on his right palm. On the tray were two wine glasses and a stainless steel bowl containing a bottle of wine embedded in crushed ice. A towel of starched, white linen wrapped around the bottle. He placed the tray on the coffee table beside the two gentlemen.

"Thank you, Geoffrey. We can pour our own."

"As you wish, sir."

Kaufmann filled both glasses and passed one to Riviera. He took a sip while he waited for the man in the dark uniform to leave. The wine was lightly chilled, the way he liked it. "And what have you learned of our Anastasia Petrova?" he asked once the doors were closed.

Riviera sipped his wine and then placed the glass down on the tray. "She's everything we hoped she would be—and then some."

"And the tests?"

"She passed all parts of the physical exam, maxed out on the cardiovascular treadmill test. She could run a marathon if she put her mind to it. No genetic flaws found on DNA testing."

"How about the psychological testing? Any problems there?"

"We gave her four different tests: the MMPI, the Stanford-Binet, the TAT, and the Rorschach. We probed every inch of her mind. Most I.Q. tests don't perform well for I.Q.'s over 140. The one we gave her—the Stanford-Binet, form V—was specifically designed to evaluate the truly gifted individuals. She was still off the charts. We have no clue what her true I.Q. is. It's somewhere above 170-180. She's one in three or four million."

Kaufmann quietly nursed his glass of wine, allowing the Spaniard to continue.

"The MMPI is a personality inventory. It has three validity scales that pick up individuals who fake their answers to make themselves look good or bad. Her answers showed no signs of duplicity. The other ten scales identify individuals with a tendency toward depression, anxiety, schizophrenia, paranoia, and other personality disorders. She was in the normal range on all ten scales."

"Anything else I should know about her?" Lamar Kaufmann took another sip of wine, well pleased with the report he was receiving.

"There is one more item."

"And what is that?"

"Solving problems has always come easy. I wanted to see how she would react to a serious problem she couldn't resolve."

"Go on. You have my attention."

"At the nuclear plant where she works, I was able to place super glue on the threads of the boron regulator, freezing it solid so no boric acid could be introduced into the primary coolant."

"Pardon my ignorance, but what's the significance of this boric acid stuff?"

"Boron absorbs neutrons, slowing down the reaction. That's how they control the reaction. With the valve frozen, there'd be no way to control the reactor and they'd have to shut it down by reinserting the cadmium control rods. I bribed a computer programmer to insert a virus into their software that would prevent the rods from reinserting. Our subject would be faced with a run-away reactor heading toward meltdown, and there'd be nothing she could do to stop it. It would be just like the one that killed her mother."

"You put hundreds, perhaps thousands of lives in jeopardy—not that I care—just to test our girl?"

"The virus was programmed to erase itself once the reactor reached a specified temperature. There was no way it would meltdown."

"So, how does our girl react to insurmountable problems?"

"We may never know: She surmounted it."

"And you can't find any flaws in her?"

"None, you won't find anyone better for your needs."

"Is she still in Chelyabinsk?"

"For the moment, but I expect she'll soon take a week's vacation along the Black Sea coast. It's a major Russian resort area. We have her under constant surveillance. We'll know within hours, if she makes a move. Former KGB agents are quite helpful in such situations. For a little money, they'll do just about anything. I think they've discovered capitalism."

"When can we initiate phase II?"

"We need to begin setting up the logistics immediately. We'll need the *Chimera* stationed near the Balkans with a trusted chopper pilot on standby."

"Consider it done. You already have a plan then I assume?"

"A small villa along the coast of the Black Sea just south of Sochi has been discreetly rented in the name of the Beckford Corporation. I gave Petrova's boss the impression she's emotionally unstable and might be suicidal. He'll offer her the villa and a week's vacation in his name. He thinks the Beckford Corporation is providing the villa out of guilt. He's doing our bidding, and we didn't even need to bribe him.

"In the next forty-eight hours, we'll know if she's gone to the coast. That'd be preferable. I have more contacts there, and it's closer to the Mediterranean. If she stays in Chelyabinsk, we'll make other arrangements."

"And after she arrives on the coast?" Kaufmann, warmed by the wine, loosened his collar, and then took another sip.

"That we'll play by ear. The rooms of the villa will have listening devices installed by the end of the day." Riviera looked at his watch. It was just past six a.m. Sochi time. Their day was over and a new day starting. "It should be completed by now. The listening devices will provide us with the necessary information. Opportunity will knock sometime during the week, and we'll be there to take full advantage of it."

Lamar Kaufmann had known Riviera since Kaufmann was a child. Riviera had been working for Kaufmann's father then. He had never known Riviera to fail on a mission.

"I have to stop at your Atlantic City casino to resolve some security issues. Then I'll fly in to Sochi and personally oversee the operation."

Kaufmann poured himself another glass of wine. He offered more to Riviera who declined the hospitality. "Despite your adjustments for jet lag, you must be exhausted from your travel. The servants have prepared the master guest room and changed the water in the Jacuzzi this morning. I trust the water has warmed to your satisfaction."

"Your hospitality is always impeccable."

"Breakfast will be at nine. If you prefer, you can take it in your room. Del's on a shopping spree in Paris. We're less formal in her absence."

"Then I'll take my leave," Riviera said as he stood up. "I still have some final details of the operation I need to address."

Kaufmann didn't bother to get up but remained with his half-empty bottle of wine. His plan was finally taking shape. This was a time to celebrate.

5

Ana lay on the beach towel watching the hair on Dorek's chest rise and fall with each breath. Dorek could sleep anywhere. He could fall into a deep sleep in a matter of minutes, his mind oblivious to surrounding activities. Ana found that particularly irritating today. She had dragged him out of bed for a quick swim in the Black Sea. For her, it had been a refreshing experience; for him, it had been a rude awakening. The shock was short lived as he had fallen asleep before his head hit the beach towel. True, it was still five in the morning in Warsaw, but her biological clock was in Chelyabinsk, and there it was nine o'clock. Between the two of them, they had some serious jet lag.

Only a few cirrus clouds marred an otherwise cloudless sky, and the temperature felt comfortable even in her wet bathing suit. Behind her, to the east, the sun was rising over the Caucasus Mountains suffusing the foothills with color. The light haze of earlier had burned off, revealing green meadows and forests of oak and beech. In front of her was the Black Sea with its beaches of fine quartz sand. To her side, snoozing on the beach towel, was her paramour, Dorek Dolinski. Life was approaching utopia.

She should be happy. She should be grateful. Seven days on a seashore paradise with Dorek, and all of it free. But she had wanted more. She deserved more. With the two-year sabbatical in America, she would have been out of the limelight. People would have forgotten her. She could have quietly applied for citizenship in America or Poland and married Dorek. They could have had children. Instead of seven days together, they could have had a lifetime together.

Perhaps she was a spoiled. Life had come easy for her. What she couldn't earn by her own gifted talents the state freely provided. She had special privileges others could only dream about. She should be happy with her lot in life. Instead she had a feeling of dread. She couldn't push from her mind the premonition that something wasn't right, something more than rejection by the Beckford Corporation.

After twenty minutes of watching Dorek's chest rise and fall, Ana poked at Dorek's left ear with a feather some seagull had carelessly discarded. It may have been selfish, and it may have been unkind, but she wasn't about to let him sleep away their first day in paradise. Still groggy with sleep, Dorek batted at the "fly" and rolled onto his side. But the fly was persistent, this time attacking the right ear. It had no intention of leaving him alone. Finally, he opened his eyes to find his tormentor with the inculpating feather still in hand.

"You will pay for this," he said in fake rage. He grabbed her in a tight embrace and rolled her across the beach towel until he came up on top, then kissed her on the lips. He met no resistance.

"I think I'll keep this feather in case I need it again."

"Do you intend to spend your entire vacation violating my ear with that filthy feather?"

"If I have to."

Dorek rolled onto his back and stared mindlessly at the sky. He could now feel the pangs of hunger that had previously been sedated by sleep. It was a gastronomic injustice that he needed to address.

"They've provided you with a nice dacha; but if you haven't noticed, the cupboards are bare. As long as you won't let me sleep, I say we hike into Khosta and get some breakfast. I saw some nice sidewalk cafes when I arrived."

"That sounds good, although by the time we change clothes, it'll be closer to lunch."

"It may be lunch time in Chelyabinsk; but in Warsaw, they're eating breakfast. I'm eating breakfast."

Ana knew better that to argue the point. Dorek might be smart. His I.Q. might even be higher than hers, but the I.Q. of his stomach wasn't much higher than ambient temperature and wouldn't respond to logic.

The brisk walk into Khosta took no more than ten minutes. Khosta wasn't large by any standards, but it did straddle the highway between the Adler-Sochi International Airport and the city of Sochi. The old real estate adage is the same in any language: location, location, location. The town appeared to be prospering, mostly from the tourist trade, and the shopkeepers were happy to see fresh blood in town.

The proprietors officiously prowled the sidewalks in front of their cafes urging passers-by to sample their wares. Tantalizing menus posted on A-frame bulletin boards provided further encouragement. All were in Russian although many provided French and English translations, attesting to the worldliness of their clientele.

"How about this one?" Ana asked after studying the menu. It offered an eclectic selection of entrées to please a variety of palates. An American-style cheeseburger and fries were even available if so desired.

"As long as they serve breakfast."

The café had been constructed of fieldstone gathered from the surrounding foothills. Originally built as a livery stable, it had been used as a warehouse after the arrival of the automobile, and finally converted to the present café in the 1980's when urban sprawl incorporated it into the commercial zone. It appeared to have been remodeled in stages, each time with a different décor. Patio tables along the sidewalk supplemented the inside seating. With the warm weather and radiant sun, Ana insisted on outdoor seating. The menu expounded upon the excellence of their sausages, satisfying Dorek who ordered sausage and eggs. Ana went for a Reuben sandwich. Both settled on coffee to drink.

"You going to tell me about the Beckford Corporation?" Dorek asked after the coffee was served.

"What's there to tell? They didn't want me. I'm too emotionally unstable, possible even suicidal."

"Based on what?"

Ana pulled out the copy of the MMPI test scores Riviera had given her and handed it to Dorek. "Based on this."

Dorek studied the printout noting the high T-scores on scales two and seven and the mild elevation of scale six. "I have to agree. This looks like the profile of someone with paranoia and depression, even a suicide potential, but it doesn't match your personality. There has to be some mistake."

"*They* thought it was accurate. If they had checked my medical history, they would've found no evidence of mental illness. The physical and psychological exams were so thorough, yet they had no interest in my past medical history. Why would they spend that much money on testing and not corroborate the MMPI?"

"That's Americans for you. A couple of months ago, I was consulting for an American firm that was using radioactive tracers. They said my film badge came back exposed and gave me the same kind of exam. They checked everything. I think Americans are too obsessed with lawsuits."

The waitress brought their meals, and they ate in silence, each absorbed in their own thoughts as they watched the citizens of Khosta ply the roads and sidewalks. Most were probably on their way to work. Some may have been late for a doctor's or dentist's appointment. But they all appeared in a hurry to go somewhere, all except for the man across the street sitting at a bus-stop bench reading a newspaper. Two buses stopped for passengers, yet he didn't board either bus. The reason became clear when he lowered the paper far enough for Ana to see the red, bulbous nose and the scar on the right cheek.

"Dorek, see that man sitting on the bench." Ana made a subtle gesture toward the man without obviously pointing. "I saw him in Chelyabinsk. He was walking his dog outside my apartment. I think he's watching me."

"So? I've been watching you too. It just proves he has good taste."

"I'm serious. He was in Chelyabinsk. I never forget a face."

Dorek stuffed a piece of sausage into his mouth and looked over at the man. "He has dark skin, more Mediterranean, not what you would expect from a native of Chelyabinsk."

"Don't talk with your mouthful."

"You started the conversation," Dorek replied in his defense.

Ana ignored the comment. "His skin's darker, but the face is the same. A few hours in a tanning booth can change skin color. And it's not just him. There've been others."

"Maybe there's a shade of truth in your MMPI score. You seem a bit paranoid at the moment."

Ana glared at Dorek, not dignifying the comment with a reply.

"Sorry," Dorek said. He had obviously pushed her too far. It was time to back off. "If you feel that strongly, we can walk over, introduce ourselves, and see what he has to say."

"No, we can't do that. Maybe the KGB thinks I was involved in the power plant sabotage."

"In that case, let them watch you. You had nothing to do with the sabotage. Watching you all day will reveal nothing more than a well-proportioned sex goddess in a bikini."

Ana wished she had a dinner roll to throw at him. Instead, she threw her linen napkin, hitting Dorek in the face. "I think you look better with the napkin over your head," she said with a laugh, ignoring the stares of other patrons. During the distraction, no one noted when a bus stopped and the man with the paper climbed aboard.

Ana pushed the Dog Walker from her mind. Her seven days with Dorek were too precious to squander worrying about things over which she had no control. If it were the KGB watching her, they would find nothing of interest. She was here to relax and spend time with Dorek. If they wanted to watch that, that was their business.

The following morning Ana awoke early, her mind still on Chelyabinsk time. There was no quick cure for jet lag. She lay in bed wide-awake watching Dorek sleep, wishing she still had her feather. That would be selfish, she decided, although she knew she would have used the feather had it been available. Unable to sleep, Ana crawled out of bed. The sun was on local time and had yet to peek over the ridge of the Caucasus Mountains. Ana dressed in her bathing suit, covering it with a pair of shorts and a sweatshirt. She wrapped a beach towel around her neck as she headed out the door, although she seriously doubted that she would go for a swim. She could at least go for a walk along the shore while she waited for Dorek to awaken.

She shivered in the cool, matudinal air. It would have been better if she had worn her jacket, she decided in retrospect. In the east, a reddish glow behind the mountains hinted of dawn. The sun's rays were already reflecting off the scattered cumulus clouds above her. It would soon warm up.

Kicking off her sandals, Ana began walking briskly along the shoreline. That seemed to appease the chill. Several seagulls, apparently on Chelyabinsk time, circled overhead in anticipation of a handout. "I'll bring you some bread later," Ana promised the seagulls. They seemed to understand and, after a minute or two, drifted off. The meager wind generated little surf, and only infrequently, did a four or five centimeters wave lap at her ankles. Ana preferred the wet sand at the water's edge, finding it firm and easier to walk on. The dry sand farther from the sea was soft and gave way under her feet.

Fifteen minutes of walking brought Ana to a section of beach narrowed by large granite outcrops. The granite, sculptured by years of erosion, formed a formidable wall ten meters in height. Its irregular contour and massive size precluded any commercial or residential use, and the beach was for the most part deserted. Two hundred meters ahead of her, the rocky wall receded from the water line forming a wider beach where pilings, remnants of an old wooden quay, extended out into the water. At one time it had been part of a busy marina. Now, all that remained was a graveyard of rusty hulls that littered the shore, some piled high upon others. They appeared to butt up against the granite wall. Ana wondered if she would be able to walk around the barricade. Perhaps it was time to return to the dacha. Dorek should be awake. If not, with the sun up, she would no longer feel guilty about waking him.

Ana turned around and headed back toward her dacha. But she was no longer alone on the beach. A man was walking along the shore heading in her direction no more than two hundred meters in front of her. He was wearing cutoff jeans and a wide-brimmed straw hat. His head hung low as if he were searching for seashells. It was a popular stretch of beach; finding a beachcomber wasn't surprising. The sun, now well above the mountains, cast a shadow over his face, obscuring facial details. Ana walked toward the man, closing the distance between them. If he were a beachcomber, he was highly selective; he didn't bother picking up any stones or shells. He just kept walking toward her at a steady pace with his head down, his face hidden by shadows. He could be just out for the exercise, but it was a slow walk, not much of a workout. When he was within a hundred meters of Ana, he looked up. It was ever so slightly, but the sun momentarily caught his face, a face Ana had seen several times before. It was the Dog Walker!

Ana turned back toward the graveyard of small ships. Running would be submitting to panic. That, she refused to do. In the past, he had only watched her, never threatened her. If he wanted to harm her, he had missed excellent opportunities. He could be following her, nothing more. A backward glance revealed the Dog Walker had increased his speed. Sandwiched between the granite wall and the water, Ana could only go forward. With a bit of luck, she could climb over the obstacles or find a way around them. Maybe the granite wall would slope; then she could scale the wall. It was now less than five meters in height. Ana mentally considered her options; none appeared feasible.

Ana again paused to look back. The Dog Walker, now less than seventy-five meters behind her, was gaining on her. The gap was closing. Ana began running, but the soft sand slipped beneath her feet slowing her progress.

Running in panic was hardly a solution to her problem, she assured herself. She needed a plan. Somehow she had to escape the box created by the Black Sea to the west and the rocky ledge to the east. The wild card was the junkyard of rusty hulls and scrap metal in front of her. If she couldn't run around or climb over the obstacles, the Dog Walker would have her trapped.

A twenty-meter-long structure with a flat top blocked her path. Ana assumed it had once been a barge transporting grain or perhaps coal. It was now deeply embedded in the sand, and the iron hull had rusted through in spots. Some of the holes were large enough to allow passage. She rejected that option as impractical. It could lead to confinement.

The rear of the barge extended into the water, but the front fell short of the rock ledge leaving a two-meter gap. Ana headed for the opening, not knowing what lay beyond. She rounded the front of the barge and disappeared from the Dog Walker's view. It would only take a minute or two for the Dog Walker to reach the gap, but it was a minute or two of lost visual contact that she would have to use wisely.

She had hoped the obstacles would now be behind her, but on the far side of the barge was the carcass of an old fishing trawler lying on its side at a forty-five degree angle. With the addition of old rusty boilers, loading cranes, and power hoists, the ensemble extended up to the rock wall. She would have to climb over the ship. A quick survey revealed plenty of handholds and footrests. Climbing over the debris would be difficult, but not impossible. That would be the logical choice. But would the Dog Walker consider it the logical choice?

The area between the barge and fishing trawler had a floor of dry beach sand littered with discarded paint cans, cast iron pipes— some of which were half a meter in diameter—and larger items, the utility of which had long been lost to the world. A three-meter tall navigational buoy rested up against the side of the ship. Beside it lay a sheet of corrugated metal. Being of aluminum, it hadn't rusted and corroded like its neighbors.

Ana formulated her plan on the run and headed for a section of the hull where "U" shaped metal rods had been welded to the ship's side to form a ladder. This would be the easiest spot to climb. She dropped her towel at the base of the ladder and then ran over to the navigational buoy. The dry sand freely flowed into the depressions left by her footsteps and obliterated any footprints. Hopefully her pursuer would assume she had climbed over the ship.

Pulling the sheet of corrugated metal over her head, she leaned it against the ship's side creating a makeshift lean-to with the navigational buoy forming the side. It was barely large enough to conceal her small frame, but unless it was given close scrutiny, it should suffice. She was running short of options.

If the ploy of discarding her towel at the base of the ladder wasn't too obvious, it might mislead her pursuer. It was logical that a fugitive in a hurry would discard unnecessary items prior to making the climb. If her pursuer stopped to search the area and she had climbed over the top, he would lose. If he took the bait and climbed the ladder, she would win. With a head start, she could make it back to the safety of Dorek's arms. The choice would be up to the Dog Walker. No matter how Ana calculated the math, the odds came out fifty-fifty.

Ana leaned back against the ship's hull in the dim light of her hastily made cave. If she were so smart, why hadn't she picked up a weapon? Fragments of pipe and iron had been all around her. The Dog Walker was physically stronger than she was, but a good rapping across his kneecap with a pipe would even the odds. She hadn't had time, she decided in her own defense. He had been right behind her. Ana sank her fingers into the soft sugar sand and allowed the sand to slip between her fingers. Sand was a weapon. She wasn't totally defenseless.

Ana listened for any sounds from her pursuer, hearing only silence. Walking in dry sand left no footprints to her hideout, but it also left no sound. He could be walking past her hideout, and she would be non the wiser.

She waited for what seemed like three or four minutes. If he had climbed the ladder and she waited too long, he would have time to return. But if she left her cover too soon, she would be spotted. She was about to exit her hideout when the sheet of corrugated metal was ripped away, leaving her face to face with her adversary. His head was attached to his shoulders with thick muscles she hadn't noticed previously. Perhaps the tenseness of his muscles made them more obvious. His dark eyes were fixated on her causing her to freeze up like a terrified rabbit. The analogy wasn't far from the truth.

The Dog Walker was the first to respond. With his feet separated for good support, he leaned over and grabbed Ana's sweatshirt with both hands to pull her up. At arm's length, the Dog Walker's red, turgid nose was even more disgusting than Ana had anticipated. A drop of sweat from his brow dripped down hitting Ana in the face.

Ana felt the hands tighten on her sweatshirt. The end was at hand, and the dénouement of the melodrama was about to begin. She hoped it wouldn't evolve into a tragedy. Perhaps it was time to rewrite the script. With her right hand, she grabbed some beach sand and hurled it into his face. It was too quick and the range too short. Caught by surprise, the Dog Walker never had time to blink. He immediately released his grip on the sweatshirt and grabbed for his face. He let out a cry of pain. But his pain was minuscule compared to what he felt when Ana's bare foot struck upward between his thighs. Fortunately for Ana, the Dog Walker was short and she felt the bottom of her foot hit stiff resistance, almost lifting the Dog Walker off his feet. She heard a slightly audible gasp as the Dog Walker sucked in air before he folded like an accordion and fell to the ground in the fetal position clutching the family real estate. It would be a long time before he would be creating any little Dog Walkers.

In reality, Ana didn't know how long he would be incapacitated. She just knew she had to put distance between them. It was also unlikely that he was KGB. They would have come after her with a half dozen men, and they would have done it openly. Was he Russian Mafia? But she had no money, no drugs. What value would she be to them?

Those questions were best left for later when she could confer with Dorek. Ana jumped to her feet and began to run. She only stopped long enough to pick up her towel at the base of the ladder. It hadn't performed as she had hoped, but it still had value. As she bent over to pick up the towel, she heard a voice behind her—in English.

"Hello, Ana." Pueblo Riviera stepped out of the shadows. "We need to talk."

Ana turned toward the Spaniard. He was the last person she expected to see, at least not in Khosta. "Who are you? Are you KGB?"

"No, not the KGB, although my friend here is a former agent." The Spaniard nodded toward the Dog Walker who moved up to block any retreat. He walked cautiously as if in pain. "My employer is in the American private sector. This has nothing to do with politics. It's about money and power, but then I repeat myself. Money is power. My employer has need of your services. It'll take about a year, maybe less."

"And if I refuse?"

"My dear Ana, we aren't asking. We were hoping you will come willingly; if not, we are prepared to use force." The two men began to move toward Ana.

There was no way she would go willingly. She was in good shape; they were much older. The advantage was hers. She was sure she could out-climb and out-run them if she had to. Ana grabbed a rung on the ladder and pulled herself up. If the Spaniard did represent American interests, she needed to get to a populated area. There would be strength in numbers. They would be unable to use force in a crowd of Russians.

The Spaniard pulled out a strange looking gun from under his jacket, pointed it at Ana's back, and fired. Compressed air propelled two small metallic darts toward Ana, hitting her in the back, each dart attached to a thin wire. The Spaniard pulled the trigger again, and one hundred thousand volts surged through her body. Her muscles initially contracted, and then she lost all control of her muscles. Her mind became confused. Unable to hold onto the ladder any longer, Ana fell to the ground.

"Is that going to cause her any harm?" the Dog Walker asked.

"It just stunned her. It has high voltage, but very low amperage. It totally messes up the nervous system for a few minutes."

Ana could hear them talking, but the words made no sense in her confused mind. She felt someone tie a constricting band around her right upper arm. A needle was jabbed into her antecubital fossa, piercing the cephalic vein. She felt a warm sensation work its way up her arm and throughout her body. Then her mind went blank. She never felt the second needle that injected 3 cc of fluid into her right buttock.

6

Ana awoke in a daze. Her head throbbed, her entire body ached, and her thoughts, if you could call them thoughts, were a jumble of disjointed phrases. Nothing made sense. She tried to remember where she was, but her mind slipped in and out of consciousness. Some primordial force deep within her urged her to stay awake. She needed to be alert, although the reason for vigilance eluded her. Finally, as her eyes began to focus, it became clear that she was riding in the back seat of a car. It was a large car, and they were riding through the countryside. The land outside her window was hilly with flocks of sheep and goats grazing on green grass. There was a tall, snow-covered mountain range to her south, not to her west where she expected the Urals to be—and they wouldn't have snow this time of year. This wasn't Chelyabinsk. Sitting beside her, a man dressed in camouflaged fatigues and a military style cap was staring at her. He was talking to her, but his words seemed garbled. She strained to identify his facial features. His face was gaunt and well-tanned. His dark eyes were framed by age-induced wrinkles. His hair was black except for a small tuft of silver protruding from under his military cap. It wasn't Dorek.

"Good, you're awake," the Spaniard said. "You were more sensitive to the medicine than I expected. We had to bag you for a while."

It took a moment or two for the significance of the statement to fully register. On the window ledge behind the back seat was a bag-valve-mask device. Even in her foggy state of mind, she knew it was used for people who couldn't breathe on their own. Why had she been incapable of breathing on her own? she wondered. Her clothes were gone. She was now wearing camouflaged fatigues and heavy boots. Where were her clothes?

"Where are you taking me?" Ana's mind cleared further, and curiosity gradually turned to anxiety when she recognized the man sitting beside her, the episode on the beach now refreshed in her memory.

"That information is on a need-to-know basis. Right now all you need to know is that we are heading south into Georgia."

"You won't get away with this. When Dorek finds I'm gone, he'll notify the authorities. They'll be looking for me."

"I'm sure that's already happened, but they won't be looking for you here. When Dolinski finds your clothes on the shore along with your suicide note, they'll send out divers. After two or three days of fruitless searching, they'll presume the sea has no intention of giving up its dead. As far as the authorities are concerned, you no longer exist."

"They'll know the note's a forgery."

"Perhaps, but it's a good forgery, and they have no reason to suspect that. They have little of your writing to compare it with. All your writings, even your love notes to your boyfriend, have been written on a word processor—all except for the thousand-word essay we asked you to hand-write about your childhood. Remember, we wanted to see a sample of your penmanship? Obviously, there will be an investigation. Dimitri Tumanov will testify as to how disappointed you were at being rejected by the Beckford Corporation and how you were mentally unstable."

"Is Tumanov part of this?" Anxiety was turning to anger.

"Heavens no, he's just an inept administrator who is very suggestible. Once we showed him your MMPI results and the interpretation from our independent psychological testing facility, he was more than willing to fall in line. I might add that the copy of your test results will be found in your pants pocket. I'm sure the authorities will agree it's a profile of an unstable, possibly suicidal, person. It's all very tidy."

The car slowed for a corner. Ana reached for the door handle and gave the door a shove, but the door didn't give.

"Sorry, I should have warned you. The back seat has child locks. The doors can only be opened from the outside." The Spaniard pulled a black box-like object from his coat pocket. It was the size of two cigarette packs end-to-end. A leather wrist thong was attached at one end. He placed the other end, which had two prongs, against Ana's shoulder. As he pressed the prongs firmly into her flesh, a searing pain burned deeply into her shoulder muscle. It felt like a hot poker, like her arm was on fire. He held it against her for two seconds, although it seemed like an eternity. She screamed and tried to back away, but Spaniard had her pinned against the car door. She couldn't remember ever experiencing such pain.

"I regret having to do that, but we'll be working on the honor system—reward and punishment. If you try to escape, you'll be punished; if not, you'll be rewarded. The system wouldn't work if you were unaware of the punishment." The Spaniard held out the device for Ana's inspection, keeping the leather thong strapped around his wrist. "The taser device we used back at the beach worked on very high voltage—one hundred thousand to be precise. It penetrates deeply, messing up the nervous system. Since the amperage is low, it doesn't cause severe pain. This little baby," the Spaniard looked at it with admiration, "only generates forty-five hundred volts, but has high amperage. Runs on two nine-volt batteries and a compactor. It works quite nicely for prodding one-thousand-pound cattle. I've been told the pain can be quite excruciating, but I'm sure you now know that." The Spaniard returned the device to his pocket.

The two men in the front seat—the Dog Walker driving— ignored the conversation in the back, as if discussion of stun guns and cattle prods were idle chatter. They maintained a conversation of their own, discussing fishing, sports, and other casual men's topics. The road, originally paved, turned to gravel, then to dirt. Only the Land Rover's four-wheel-drive and high road clearance kept them going as they drove higher and higher into the mountains.

"This road isn't going anywhere," Ana said in half question, half statement. "It's not going to get us to Georgia."

"The road follows the Kuban River, which drains most of the northern side of the Caucasus and then empties into the Black Sea.

I suspect the road will eventually peter out in another five miles," the Spaniard replied. "The western end of the Caucasus Mountains is quite rugged. Some of the mountains are taller than the Swiss Alps. I've seen them both, and the Alps are, by far, much prettier. See that tall peak on your left?" The Spaniard pointed to one of the taller peaks. It was covered with snow, as were most of the taller peaks. "That's Mt. Elbrus, the tallest mountain in the range, 18,510 feet in elevation, that's over 5,000 meters."

"I'm well aware of the conversion factors between your antiquated English system and metric."

The Spaniard ignored Ana's sarcasm. "Because the mountains are so rugged, there are no roads or passes. We need to get to the other side, to Georgia. We could have taken the road along the Black Sea, going through customs at the Georgian border. Customs would present its own set of issues. Providing you with a fake passport would've been easy, but I suspect your behavior might not be appropriate for the situation, so we'll walk to Georgia."

The river in the ravine they were following divided and subdivided, constantly getting smaller until it was nothing more than a small stream. The road likewise deteriorated until it consisted of two parallel ruts heading further up the mountain. They were now well above the tree line, and the only vegetation was a few tufts of grass and the lichens clinging to the granite boulders. In the distance, far behind them, was a blue haze representing the Black Sea. Under different circumstances, it would have been an enjoyable scene, something to store as a pleasant memory.

"I don't think we can go much farther," the Dog Walker said from his vantage at the wheel.

"Pull over," the Spaniard replied. "It's a good day for a walk. We'll begin here."

With nowhere to pull over, the Dog Walker brought the Land Rover to a stop. On-coming traffic wasn't a concern.

The Dog Walker unlocked the doors from up front, and the Spaniard got out of the car. Ana remained in her seat until her door was opened and she was pulled out. She might not be in control, but she had no intention of assisting them.

Opening the back of the Land Rover, the Spaniard extracted a backpack. "This one's yours." He handed it to Ana who placed it on the ground.

"What if I don't carry it?" she asked.

"That's up to you. The backpack has your sleeping bag, not mine. It has your water and MRE's, not mine."

"MRE's?"

"Meals, ready to eat."

"That's the stuff they feed the American military?"

"Tastes pretty good if you're really hungry, which I'm sure you'll soon be. I doubt if you'll die from hypothermia without your sleeping bag, but I can guarantee a miserable night. And if you decide to go on a hunger strike, that's O.K. too. You have enough fat on you to last several weeks. That's longer than we need. Your backpack also has toilet paper, I might add."

Ana felt anger welling up inside her. She wasn't sure which was more irritating, being called fat or the logic of his argument. If she planned to escape, she would need a good night's sleep and the strength food and water would provide. Punishing herself wouldn't help her cause.

Ana picked up the backpack, put her arms through the shoulder harnesses, and lifted it to her back. It wasn't as heavy as it looked. That would mean a short hike, two or three days at the most, she guessed.

"Give me your hands." Ana ignored the request. The Spaniard, taking her passive aggressive behavior in stride, grabbed her wrists and cuffed them with a pair of handcuffs he produced from the cargo pockets of his fatigues. "You won't be able to remove the backpack without taking off the cuffs. If you try to escape, you will find it difficult to run in this terrain with your hands cuffed in front of you and a pack on your back. We'll easily outrun you. We also have the maps, GPS, and cellular phone. Without these, you'll quickly die in these mountains. We only need your services for a year or less; after that, you'll be free to go and do as you please. You have my word; if you follow directions, no harm will come to you."

Ana offered no reply. His word was meaningless.

The three of them began the hike up the mountain. Pueblo Riviera took the lead with Ana in the middle, and the man she had named Dog Walker bringing up the rear. The third man returned with the car. Ana assumed he would meet them on the other side of the border.

The trail, if there ever had been one, soon ended, and they climbed over or walked around whatever obstacles lay in their path, always heading upward and southward. Riviera frequently consulted his map and GPS, giving Ana the impression this wasn't the first time he had commanded such an operation.

"How high are we?" Ana felt her heart racing, and she was breathing heavily, too heavily for the amount of activity. "The air must be thin."

"A little over twelve thousand feet. I'm not sure what that is in meters."

"That's three thousand six hundred and fifty-seven point six meters," Ana replied.

Riviera wondered if she were bluffing. He also knew the conversion factor between feet and meters, but the math was too complex to do in his head. If it were a bluff, it was a good one. Her number was in the correct ballpark.

Any delusions Ana had about the two men being old and out of shape were quickly dispelled. For the next five hours, they pushed forward and upward, stopping only occasionally to drink water and consult the map. It was all Ana could do to keep up. Her legs were aching, and the backpack that she thought was light was now pressing deeply into her shoulders, cutting circulation to her arms. Her hands were tingling and starting to swell. On top of it all, she had a throbbing headache.

"What's the hurry? Can't we slow down, even take a break?"

The Spaniard looked at his watch, then back at Ana. It was almost a compassionate look. "I suppose we can take a ten minute break."

Ana sat down on a rock and leaned back against a rocky ledge, taking the weight of her pack off her back. "From the rush, I assume you guys don't get paid by the hour."

"The rush isn't for our benefit; it's for yours."

"Your concern is touching." Ana hoped there was a healthy dose of sarcasm in her voice.

"Your fingers and hands are beginning to swell. You probably have a throbbing headache, maybe some nausea."

Ana was nonplused. His concern appeared genuine. Even more disconcerting, his description fit her symptoms perfectly. "You think I have Acute Mountain Sickness?"

"Anyone can get it. Being young and female are additional risk factors. We ascended pretty fast. I don't think it's serious, but I'd rather not take chances. At these altitudes there's the additional threat of sudden snowstorms. The top of the ridge is still another five hundred feet up. I would like to get over the top before nightfall and camp at a lower altitude in the valley on the other side. That's our rush." Riviera took a medicine bottle from his pack and tapped out a pill. "Here, take this."

Ana skeptically looked at the pill. "What is it, a cyanide capsule?"

"Look, if we wanted to kill you, we would've done it by now. You're of no value to us dead. It's a four mg. tablet of dexamethasone, if you really need to know."

"A steroid?"

"It'll help with your mountain sickness."

The Spaniard began removing the water bottles and MRE's from her bag and transferred them to his pack.

"Why are you taking all my food and water? Did you forget your own?"

"Just trying to lighten your load. Like I said, you're of no value to us dead. Now get up. We need to get going. Hold out your hands." Riviera removed the handcuffs. There was no way she could outrun them in her current condition.

They continued toward the top of the ridge. The reduced weight in her pack was easier on her shoulders and arms, but did nothing for her throbbing headache. It was at least nice to know they needed her alive. She could be bolder in her actions knowing they wouldn't harm her—except for the cattle prod. He seemed to have no reservations about using that. It was a painful experience she didn't wish to relive. The reason for the kidnapping remained unclear. The most common motive was ransom. If that were the case, the suicide note made no sense. Nothing made sense with her current headache.

But there was another possible motive. That was the one she feared most. She was young, female, and physically attractive. Was she destined to become a sex toy for some rich pervert or misogynistic warlord? She would have felt better if her abduction had been a random act, but it wasn't. Young, attractive women were everywhere. Any number of them could have been abducted, if it were only for sex, but they had selected *her*. Whoever was behind her abduction knew her or had heard of her. She had risen to the top of a field normally reserved for men, an achievement many men would resent. Sexual exploitation could be secondary to some cretin's perverse desire to put her in her place. Rape is seldom a simple sex act or a desire for sexual pleasure. It's an act of domination in which the victim is purposefully and relentlessly subjected to physical and mental intimidation. She could expect torture and humiliation at the hands of such an individual. That she vowed would never happen. If she were unable to escape, she would take her life. She wouldn't need lethal weapons. Running at full speed and spearing her head into a stone or brick wall would crack her skull and produce instant brain death. It would cause blowout fractures of C-1 and C-2, the top two bones in the neck. Total body death would soon follow.

It took Ana another hour of hard walking to reach the top of the ridge. Below were far more mountains than she ever wished to see. It was a depressing sight, although they didn't look as formidable as the ones they had just climbed. Directly below them was a narrow valley running north and south. This had to be the valley the Spaniard had referred to. If it were true, the end of their trail would be on the other side of the far ridge just beyond the end of the valley. There would be people there and towns. Crowds of people would be her salvation. It would dramatically increase her chances of escape.

Going down the mountain was easier. Breathing required less effort, and her headache dissipated. Except for the hostage situation, life was again livable. They reached the valley floor as the sun was setting. A full moon rose in the east providing extra light to set up camp. The Spaniard picked a flat grassy area free of stones and protruding roots. If she had to sleep on the ground, this was as good a place as any. The way her muscles ached, Ana felt she could sleep anywhere.

They ate their MRE's in silence and then spread out their sleeping bags. Without any discussion, the two men placed their sleeping bags on either side of Ana's, allowing three or four feet between sleeping bags for privacy.

"Sorry I have to do this, but you aren't extremely trustworthy." The Spaniard replaced the handcuffs on Ana's wrists. He then took a hank of cord from his pack and ran the cord through the loop formed by Ana's arms and cuffs. The two loose ends, he tied to his left wrist. "This is parachute cord. It's only three-sixteenths of an inch in diameter, but it's five hundred and fifty pound test. You can't break it, chewing only makes the nylon soggy, and if you are looking for stones to abrade it, forget it. I removed all the stones from your area. The cord's long enough so we can both roll around in our sleep."

Ana, giving the cord a tug, agreed that it wasn't about to be broken. A cigarette lighter or other form of heat would quickly melt the nylon. Unfortunately, she didn't smoke, and she didn't think they would respond favorably to a request for a match. Totally exhausted and with nothing better to do, Ana crawled into her sleeping bag fully clothed and fell asleep.

The full moon was high in the sky when Ana awoke. Initially confused, it took a moment to remember where she was, but an adrenaline rush brought clarity to her thoughts. She guessed it was two or three in the morning based on the position of the moon. With minimal movement, she looked around to further assess her situation. Both men were breathing heavily, and she assumed they were asleep. At least they hadn't taken turns standing watch. It was either pure arrogance or overconfidence. Neither fit the psychological profile she had been developing on the Spaniard. Either way, it provided an opportunity for escape if only she weren't tied to the Spaniard. She tried chewing the cord, but like she had been told, it only got soggy and swelled. The Spaniard had also been correct about the stones—none was within reach. The cord was so small and flimsy, yet so strong. She needed to approach the problem in a logical, systematic manner, a scientific approach.

Every insuperable opponent or problem had its Achilles heel; she just needed to find it. In her mind, Ana reviewed the properties of nylon. It had extremely high tensile strength, doesn't rot, and maintains its integrity with age. Those are its strengths, she reminded herself. She needed to know its weaknesses. It melts easily. That was a major weakness, but she had no matches or sources of heat. She had explored that possibility previously, finding it unproductive. Acid would destroy nylon, and there was acid in flashlight batteries. She had seen a flashlight in the Spaniard's backpack, although that was out of reach, and even if she could get the batteries, she had no means of opening the metal cases. Nylon can be easily cut. Should she boldly ask the Spaniard for a knife? Frustration was starting to make her giddy. She needed to return to serious thought. It didn't have to be a knife. It could be anything sharp: a pair of scissors, toenail clippers. Now she was getting into wishful thinking. She didn't have access to either of those…but she did have access to a *chain saw*!

Ana unzipped the fly of her camouflaged fatigues. The zipper was made of heavy-duty brass, not the cheap plastic often found in high quality fashion pants. Ana ran her fingers across the zipper, feeling the texture of the metal. The zipper's individual teeth were precision machined with crisp, sharp corners. Ana wrapped several loops of the nylon cord around her thumb and likewise to her index finger of her right hand. Separating the two digits pulled the cord taunt. Then, while holding the top of the zipper with her left hand, she stroked the nylon cord across her simulated chain saw. She could feel the cord vibrate as each tooth of the zipper bit into the nylon. She continued for one hundred strokes before holding the cord up to the moonlight—the cord was definitely frayed. Nine hundred and twenty-three strokes later, by precise count, the cord separated—she was free, at least free from her tether.

Ana lay in her sleeping bag listening to the men breathe while she formulated a plan. This wasn't the time to panic and bolt for freedom. They could be light sleepers. After she was sure they were still sleeping, Ana slowly slipped out of her sleeping bag. She was tempted to steal a backpack with its food and water, but they were stacked together. Moving them risked making noise. She decided not to press her luck. Escape was the primary consideration. She would worry about food and water later.

This section of the valley was carpeted with grass, which had been well trimmed by mountain goats. It would be quieter to walk on than loose gravel. One overturned stone could easily awaken her captors. She slowly rose to her feet and started walking out of the camp. She gently lowered each foot to the ground. No weight was applied until the firmness of the footing was established. She didn't look back until she was ten meters away. No one was following.

Now she needed to put distance between them. If they slept until daylight, she would have a three or four hour lead. By then, she might be able to cover five kilometers if she forced herself and the terrain wasn't too difficult. There would be no tracks to follow in the dark. In the grass and gravel, her trail would be difficult to follow even in daylight. They would have to search in all directions, giving her a distinct advantage. It was unlike the Spaniard to carelessly give her such an advantage.

If she were really lucky, they would assume she headed back the way they came. That had been her first thought. Instead she had decided to continue south. It would be easier walking in the valley, and she could cover distance more quickly. The mountain ridge at the end of the valley, she had been told, wasn't as high. And beyond the ridge of mountains was civilization.

The full moon provided sufficient light for walking, but not for distance vision. They would never see her in the dark. When daylight came she would have to be more careful.

The terrain was uneven and strewn with rocks. With her hands in cuffs, balance was difficult. Even with the moonlight, she had fallen several times, her hands now bruised and abraded. She would have to tolerate minor injuries for the sake of speed. Cuts and bruises would heal with time. If she were to make good her escape, she would need all the distance between them she could get before they discovered her missing.

At first she thought her sleep deprivation and physical exhaustion were playing mind games with her. The shadowy outline of a bush thirty meters to her right appeared to be changing. It was subtle to be sure, easily explained by stress and a vivid imagination. Ana was about to dismiss it as a harmless aberration when she heard a rock being overturned. The sound came from the direction of the shadow. Whatever it was, it stayed close to the cover of the underbrush. Had the Spaniard found her in the dark? Her heart began to pound with such intensity within her chest that she feared the sound alone would give her away. But the shadow was too low to the ground for the Spaniard unless he was crawling, and that was unlikely. He would boldly walk up to claim his prize. It had to be a wild animal.

Ana squinted into the darkness, finding another moving shadow. There were at least four, maybe more. In the beginning, they kept their distance, following thirty meters to her right. Sometimes they would be on her left. They would disappear only to reappear at a different position. Gradually they came closer. She could now clearly see their outlines—it was a pack of dogs. No, not out here. It was too far from any civilized area. They had to be gray wolves. Like a shark, they had zeroed in on the blood scent from her bleeding hands.

Ana found a dead tree that had fallen the previous winter. One of the branches was partially broken when the tree had hit the ground. With considerable effort she was able to break it loose. It would have been easier if not for the handcuffs. It didn't make the best of clubs, but it might encourage the wolves to keep their distance. Wolves aren't fearless hunters. They hunt in the safety of a pack and select only the easiest prey. A woman stumbling in the dark with blood on her hands apparently fit their criteria.

The wolves would key their actions with the leader of the pack—the alpha male. Ana identified him after five minutes of observation. He was bigger than the rest and appeared darker in color, although that was difficult to judge in the moonlight. He was also bolder. Alpha males of any species have to maintain that image of invincibility. Ana thought she could fight off a lone wolf, but not a pack of four or five. They would surround her and nip at her heals. Her peripheral vision only extended so far. Four or five wolves against one club. Eventually, they would be victorious. Her best bet was to make sure her first blow was to the alpha male. Perhaps that would give the others second thoughts.

It took over an hour for the wolves to work up their courage. They were no different than a mob of humans. Courage is fortified by the interaction of large numbers over a period of time. They caught her in an open area where they were free to circle around her and still have open areas behind them for a fast retreat. Ana was tempted to run, but there was nowhere to go. It would only give the wolves more courage. They already had more courage than Ana.

As they circled around her, Ana circled with them, always keeping the alpha male in front of her. Her club was a little over a meter in length. If she stretched, her arms might extend her reach by another half meter. Ana was right handed. Her best and strongest swing would be to her left. She turned until the alpha male was on her left side. She held the club on her right side, away from her body. To a wolf that is unfamiliar with the mechanics of a club, it would appear less threatening.

The alpha male feigned several attacks, but stopped short only to quickly retreat. Ana waited passively like the defenseless prey she hoped to portray. A pack of wolves has more brute strength than a human, but the human has the superior brain. The alpha male's last attack brought him within striking distance of Ana's club. The next time he would come even closer. Ana waited until the wolf made its next lunge, timing it so his forward momentum was maximum. Force equals mass times acceleration. The wolf would need maximum effort to negate his forward momentum and change course. Leaning into the swing, Ana swung the club with all her might. She aimed for the head, but the wolf flinched at the last minute and the blow glanced off his shoulder. Just the same, it produced the desired results. The wolf gave out a large yip and made a hasty retreat. The others quickly followed. The wolf pack still followed her, but with a new respect for its prey, maintained a discrete distance.

Dawn came none too quickly. It was a mixed blessing. Another hour or two of darkness would have been nice. Except for the wolves, darkness had been her friend. Now she was no longer invisible. A good set of binoculars could pick her up from several miles away. Although the valley had some brush, it wasn't enough to provide cover. It did provide cover for the wolf pack, which vanished as dawn approached. They were nowhere to be seen. Ana was now below the timberline, but the climate was still harsh and what trees there were measured no more than three meters in height and clung tenaciously to the rocky soil. Many of the less fortunate trees lay rotting in a horizontal position where the wind had fallen them. She could only hope she had traveled too far to be seen.

Along with dawn came hunger and thirst. It would have been wiser if she had taken some water bottles and MRE's, she decided in retrospect, even if it had increased her danger. That was the wonderful world of 20/20 hindsight. She had come across several small creeks where she could have obtained water. She even cupped her hands to drink at one stream, but then deferred in fear of Giardia and other parasites. The streams were used by mountain sheep and other wild animals. Their scat littered the edge of the streams. She had to assume they had also defecated in the stream, and she had no purification tablets. She was sure there would have been some in her backpack, if she had elected to bring it. Diarrhea and abdominal cramping would be debilitating, not what she needed at the moment. Eventually, she would have to drink. The water in the mountains at the end of the valley would be cleaner, she rationalize. She could hold off until then.

By late afternoon, she had reached the end of the valley. On the other side of the mountain ridge was freedom. But she could go no further. Freedom would have to wait another day. She was tired, thirsty, and hungry. She had gone 24 hours without sleep, and it was beginning to affect her judgment. If she were to survive, she needed a sound mind. She found a small stream, and stopped to soak her feet. She was again tempted to drink the water and again deferred. She was probably overly cautious, but diarrhea from tainted water was too big of a risk. In the wilderness, diarrhea could kill. Tomorrow she would drink her fill from a stream near the top of the mountain where the water from melting snow would be cool and fresh. Just thinking about it was an enjoyable fantasy, which she had to force from her mind lest she succumb to the temptation.

In the water by her feet were several large, brown snails. She scooped two of them up for closer examination. In France they were a delicacy. But those were cooked. Any bacteria would be killed. She threw the snails back into the water. That too must be postponed. Much as she hated to admit it, the Spaniard had been right about one thing: Food wasn't an immediate concern. She had enough fat to last several days, although the lack of caloric intake would seriously reduce her energy. Water was the more serious problem. Twenty-four hours without water would cause significant dehydration. But so would diarrhea, her mind countered. She was starting to get confused. She needed sleep.

It was too late to start up the mountain. The sun was low in the sky, and climbing the mountain by moonlight was more danger than she cared to risk. Having been up half the night, sleep was her first priority. She selected a small patch of bushes beside the stream for cover. Unless viewed from above by a low-flying plane, she wouldn't be seen. Even without the cover, the odds of the Spaniard finding her now were slim. They were no longer the problem. Now she had to fight the elements. She hadn't seen the wolves since sunrise. Apparently, they had moved on in search of less aggressive prey. She no longer needed her club, but it gave her peace of mind. She laid it down beside her.

Despite her exhaustion, it was a fitful sleep. Several times during the night she awoke cold and shivering because the ground had sucked away her body heat. There were no flat surfaces on which to sleep, and protruding rocks probed deep into her body. Half way through the night, she was awakened by a severe pain in her right leg down near her ankle. It was a crushing pain as if a large rock had fallen on her ankle. With eyes still closed in half slumber, Ana instinctively retracted her leg. She felt resistance at first and then a heavy tug on her ankle. She opened her eyes. A gray wolf, the alpha male, had a death grip on her right ankle and was now violently shaking it to inflict maximum damage. Several other wolves were moving in to share in the kill. Wolves seldom go for the jugular like a large cat. They go for a leg or a hamstring. They incapacitate their victim by degrees, a system that had served wolves well over the millenniums.

Ana kicked at the wolf with her free leg. The wolf was on her far side. What kicks struck home had expended their energy before contact, rendering them ineffective. The wolf hung on tenaciously. This time he was unwilling to consider defeat. He began dragging Ana across the ground away from her shelter in the brush. In the open area she could expect wolves to come at her at all angles. She reached out in the darkness for a rock or anything she could throw at the beast. She found instead her club. With both hands she swung the stick at the wolf's head. He didn't let go until the third blow. The wolf backed off a safe distance and stared at Ana. He let out a deep growl and disappeared into the darkness. There would be no further sleeping. Ana watched the circling shadows for ten minutes. Then she heard a high-pitched yelp that reminded her of a friend's dog that got its paw caught in a door. Perhaps it was some internecine bickering. The alpha male had come up short twice. In the human pecking order, that would be grounds for a change in leadership. The yelp must have had some significance. She saw no more moving shadows. She decided to stand watch for the rest of the night.

Ana awoke at dawn. She didn't know when she had fallen asleep, but it felt like she hadn't slept at all. A cursory exam of her right leg revealed no puncture wounds. With no concept of combat boots, the wolf had grabbed at her ankle. Removal of her boot revealed only bruises. The wolf's teeth had failed to penetrate the leather.

Hungry and dehydrated, Ana started up the mountain, promising herself that she would stop at the first creek to replace her lost fluids. The climb wasn't as steep or as high as the previous range, but dehydration sapped her energy, forcing her to stop frequently to rest. Her right ankle was beginning to throb. She had no doubt that the ankle was also swollen.

She arrived at the summit around noon, not having found any water. Her mouth was dry. She was no longer producing adequate saliva, a sure sign of severe dehydration. If the ridge top had been as high as the first ridge, she never would have made it. Now before her was Georgia. It might be her imagination, but she thought she could make out a farmhouse in the distance.

Ana didn't stop to admire the view. Instead, she headed down the mountain. Eventually she would find a stream, perhaps even a trail or road. She followed a gully down the slope for no particular reason other than it was easy walking. The gully widened, giving the impression that someone had trod the ground before her. Her optimism increased. One kilometer further down the slope Ana found parallel erosions that only a truck could have made. It was old, to be sure, but still a sign of civilization. If she followed it, it would lead her to a road and then civilization.

The discovery rekindled her enthusiasm, and she pushed on with a fresh vigor she thought she no longer possessed. The farther she progressed, the more pronounced the trail became. She became ecstatic. Her eyes watered with tears of joy. She had it made.

Then she rounded a bend in the trail. Ana came to a stop and stared ahead in disbelief, wondering if dehydration and exhaustion were playing tricks with her mind. Sitting in front of her on a rock, eating an MRE was the Spaniard! Ana turned to run, but the Dog Walker—materializing out of nowhere—blocked her path.

"We were wondering how long it would take you to catch up with us." The Spaniard threw the empty MRE wrapper on the ground and took a bottle of water from his pack. He drank it slowly, savoring every swallow. Then he poured the rest of the water on the ground.

"That sure is good water," he said. "You should be pretty thirsty by now. Yep, you should have drunk the water back in the valley when you had the chance. And by the way, the snails aren't very tasty, but they are edible."

"How did you find me? You couldn't have followed me in the dark."

"No, we needed our sleep. We waited until morning." The Spaniard took out another bottle of water. He played with the container for a moment or two before taking a small sip. "I suppose we can tell you now. We have a transmitter in the heel of your right boot. Works like a wolf collar. The big question is how you cut the parachute cord without abrasive rocks or sharp objects."

Ana ignored the question, staring instead at the bottle of water.

"Thirsty?" he asked. "You should have taken your backpack with you. Then you would have both water and food."

"You put all my water and food in your pack."

"So I did. I suppose then some of this must be yours." The Spaniard tossed a water bottle to Ana. Ana caught the water bottle and fumbled with the bottle cap until it came off. She couldn't remember when water tasted so good. "Don't drink so fast." Ana ignored the suggestion. "You also need to take another pill." The Spaniard passed Ana another pill, which she swallowed without question. "My employer expects you to be healthy."

"Your precious employer almost got a dead hostage. A wolf pack thought I would make a good buffet."

"I must apologize for the first night. There's strength in numbers. The wolves would've never taken on the three of us. You didn't tell me you were taking off on your own."

"And the second night?"

"I gave the leader of the pack an attitude adjustment with the taser, the same one I used at the beach. The wolves now have a healthy respect for humans."

"Did you kill him?"

"No. We dragged him off a ways by the tail. Let the rest of the pack watch. Puts the fear of God in them. He'll be in a daze for twelve hours or so, but he'll recover. No sense killing him. He was only doing what wolves do."

"You spared him out of professional courtesy?"

"In a matter of speaking." The Spaniard threw Ana an MRE.

"Thanks."

"Don't think me. It's your MRE."

"No, I mean for sparing the wolf."

"Ana, you're a very complex woman. Now eat. Our Land Rover is waiting for us two miles down the road. You'll need your strength. And when you're done eating, we have some unfinished business to attend to." The Spaniard pulled out his black box, the one with two prongs on the end.

Ana emptied the water bottle and then opened her MRE, all while watching the black box. "If you knew where I was, why did you wait until now to stop me?"

"You were heading in the right direction and making better time than if you were with us. It was an easy decision."

Ana finished her MRE but made no effort to get up from the rock on which she was sitting. Her full attention was on the black box that the Spaniard continued to play with.

"It's time to go." The Spaniard stood up and walked toward Ana with the black box in his hand. Ana stood up and turned to run, but the Dog Walker caught her by the shoulders. She felt a searing pain in her back that seemed to reach all the way to her kidneys. It felt worse than before. She would have collapsed had not each man grabbed her by an elbow. She only vaguely remembered the walk to the car.

The Spaniard removed the handcuffs once he had Ana securely locked in the back seat of the car. "The rest of the trip should be much easier—it's all by car. We'll cross into Turkey during the night. They are capitalists, so there'll be no problem at the border. For a respectable remuneration, the border guards are willing to look the other way."

Ana heard little of what the Spaniard was saying. Sleep deprivation was taking its toll, and she quickly slipped into a deep sleep. She didn't wake when the Turkish border guard flashed his light on her face at the border crossing. She didn't wake during the long drive across Turkey on bumpy side roads. She finally awoke after the car had come to a stop and the engine turned off. It was the sudden quietness and the lack of motion that aroused her from sleep.

Ana looked out the window into the blackness, obviously nighttime. There were no lights from towns or houses. "Where are we?" She didn't expect an answer. It would be a need-to-know answer, and they would assume she didn't need to know.

"We are southwest of Gaziantep, Turkey near the Syrian border."

"Why the sudden honesty?"

"Because you asked, and I have no need to keep it secret."

"In that case, can you tell me why we are parked here in the field during the middle of the night?"

"First of all, it isn't the middle of the night. You slept through most of that. In another hour, the sun will be up. See that light in the sky?" The Spaniard rolled down his window and pointed to a bright light to the south. "That light is a Bell 430 helicopter. It'll provide transportation the rest of the way."

"I assume the helicopter isn't courtesy of the Turkish government?"

"That's the advantage of helicopters; they fly low. All radar systems have seams. In this area radar can't pick up anything under one hundred feet. Our pilot is flying at fifty feet, totally undetectable."

"Are you going to tell me where the helicopter is taking us?"

"Today, you get to meet my employer. We'll be flying out to his yacht, the *Chimera*."

"I can't wait," Ana said sarcastically.

The Spaniard, ignoring Ana's comment, got out of the car. Ana crawled out after him. She considered making a run for it, but decided it would be futile. She was still wearing the shoe with the transponder, she had been placed back into handcuffs, and the Dog Walker was always at her side.

The light in the distance gradually grew brighter until the helicopter itself could be seen. It landed in the field illuminated by the Land Rover's headlights. The pilot didn't cut the engines. He didn't intend to stay long.

"Come on, that's our ride." The Spaniard pushed Ana toward the aircraft. He opened the side door and helped Ana strap herself into the rear seat. "These doors don't lock. I hope you don't do anything foolish like opening the door to jump out." The Spaniard climbed into the co-pilot's seat.

"*Signor*, we meet again." It was the Italian. "You were right. Your employer does reward handsomely."

"Let's head out to the *Chimera*."

Fifteen minutes later, they were over international water, and the pilot climbed to eight hundred meters. Waiting for them six kilometers to the south was the *Chimera*.

The pilot picked up his mike. "Bell 430 to *Chimera*."

"This is *Chimera*, go ahead Bell 430."

"We are preparing to land." The pilot swung around and approached from the rear. It was a textbook landing.

7

"This will be your room for the next year or so." The Spaniard opened the door and stepped back, allowing Ana to enter. "It has a refrigerator, microwave, and sink. In the cupboard, you'll find microwave popcorn, tea, coffee, and other routine amenities. You even have satellite TV. It wouldn't surprise me if a Russian station were available. You'll also have your own computer—sorry, there's no modem."

Ana surveyed her new abode. It was plush. "And what do I owe for all this luxury...besides my soul?"

"I'll explain that when the time comes. In the meantime, you're free to wander around the ship. There's a two-lane bowling alley, a swimming pool, an exercise room with hot tub, and you might find the library enjoyable."

"I have freedom to wander around, but I have to wear handcuffs." Ana held up her cuffed hands.

"We have a replacement." The Spaniard removed the cuffs and strapped a black box to her right ankle. It locked with a key. "There's a wire in the cuff. It'll be hard to cut without a hacksaw. It's waterproof. You can wear it in the shower."

"I can see it's a fashion statement. I bet all the girls in America are wearing them."

"It'll let us know where you are on the yacht. If there's anything else you need, let me know."

Ana looked around the room. They obviously wanted her to be comfortable. They even had an entertainment center with CD player. "Any chance I can get some CD's to play?"

"I only have access to American artists."

"How about some classical music. That's the same in any language. And maybe some American folk music, like John Denver or Sally Rogers."

"I'll see what I can do. It might take a week to have them flown in. Anything else?"

"A key to the door?"

"That won't be necessary. We only hire honest employees."

"I never would have guessed."

"We have a cafeteria open twenty-four hours a day, but tonight you'll be dining with my employer, Lamar Kaufmann. I'll pick you up at seven, and do try to be civil. He doesn't have the same wonderful sense of humor I have. Attire will be semi-formal. I'll be wearing a coat and tie."

"I hope these three-day-old fatigues are considered semi-formal, since that's all I have."

"I'm sure you'll find something." Pueblo Riviera stepped out of the room, shutting the door behind him.

Ana looked around her suite of rooms. The opulence was unbelievable. She had never had or even seen anything so plush. There was a walk-in shower and a full-size Jacuzzi in the bathroom. She opened one of the closets: Someone had filled it with expensive clothes—all her size. Whoever was behind her abduction had planned well in advance and had the wherewithal to pull it off.

Ana spent the afternoon exploring the ship. The ship's staff, of which there were many, treated her as a guest, as if her appearance had been expected. Only the doors to the bridge, radio room, and a third room labeled "Laboratory" were locked. It was the laboratory that intrigued her the most. Why would there be a laboratory on a luxury yacht? At seven o'clock she was to have dinner with the man behind it all. Hopefully, he would provide some insight into this madness. It was no longer a matter of need-to-know. She had been physically and emotionally traumatized, perhaps irreversibly. She should have a right to know why.

The Spaniard showed up precisely at seven wearing a light green sport coat and a red tie. In any other situation, he could have passed as a businessman, although few businessmen carry cattle prods in their pockets.

"I hope you're prepared for an evening of culinary enchantment. Lamar Kaufmann's chefs prepare only the best." The Spaniard waited at the door. Ana wasn't sure if it were true manners or if he had no desire to inspect her premises. She assumed he had seen it many times. Either way, she had no intention of voluntarily inviting him in.

"Do I have a choice in the matter? I'm normally more selective in my dining companions."

"Let's not be surly. You're the guest of honor. A lot of effort was expended to get you to this dinner party."

"You could have sent out an invitation...RSVP."

"We were afraid you might have declined."

Ana had chosen a brown pantsuit for the occasion, feeling that the semi-formal dresses didn't go well with an ankle tether. She wasn't sure if anything went well with a tether. The pants at least kept it covered. It wasn't her choice attire, but then she wasn't out to impress anyone.

"Let's go meet the boss. If I'm lucky, maybe he'll fire me."

Three guests were present when the Spaniard ushered Ana into the private dining room. They were standing in a small circle, each with a glass of red wine in hand. A waiter in a black tuxedo obsequiously refilled the glasses as needed. If this was semi-formal, Ana wondered what formal would be. The lone woman wore an ankle-length, pink dress with half sleeves. The neckline plunged tantalizingly low and was augmented with a string of pearls. Ana assumed they were real. The woman gave the impression of someone who didn't settle for less than the best. The two men were also elegantly dressed in silk shirts and well-tailored sport coats. The conversation in which they had been so thoroughly engrossed came to a sudden stop when Ana entered the room. She felt like a church pastor intruding into the middle of a parishioner's dirty joke.

"And you must be Anastasia Petrova. It's so nice to finally meet you." The man shook Ana's hand. She guessed he was in his late thirties or early forties. "My name is Lamar Kaufmann. I'll be your host while you are onboard my ship. I do hope you'll have a pleasant stay. If there is ever anything you need, please let me know." Kaufmann put his arm around the other woman, pulling her into the conversation. "This is my wife, Cordelia. Everyone calls her Del." The woman nodded and smiled, but didn't offer her hand.

"Last, but not least, we have Dr. Carl Mason. I'm sure you'll be seeing a lot of him over the coming months. He took his residency in gynecology at Johns Hopkins and also holds a Ph.D. in embryology form the University of Wisconsin at Madison. He's doing research in stem-cell technology. Unfortunately, this is difficult in the United States due to the political climate; but in international waters, matters are less restrictive."

Ana found the introductions almost surreal. They had violently abducted her, dragged her across two borders, tortured her with a cattle prod, and now they treated her like a débutante at a coming out ball. There was no logic to the string of events. No common thread. Her world had always been structured. She could define it with a set of equations. Even though she couldn't always control them, she knew all the variables and how they affected her life. Her last week had been nothing short of randomized chaos. The suicide note eliminated ransom as a motive for her abduction, and Kaufmann didn't act like the sadistic misogynist she had envisioned. With the blond bimbo clinging to his side, he apparently already had his sex toy. The obsequious waiter offered her a drink, which she gladly accepted. She needed a drink.

"I understand you had some Acute Mountain Sickness." It was Dr. Mason. Of all the people in the room, he appeared to be the least pretentious. Men of science tended to be that way. The more they learn about the universe, the humbler they become.

"I had a touch of it. Pueblo Riviera, if that's his real name, gave me some dexamethasone. I'm feeling better now."

"In addition to research, I also provide healthcare services for everyone on the ship. Why don't you come down to the infirmary tomorrow, and we'll check you over."

"If I can break loose from my busy schedule, I will." Ana's sarcasm was returning now that the initial shock of the evening was wearing off. She was also feeling bolder, time to be assertive.

Breaking away from Dr. Mason, Ana edged over toward Lamar Kaufmann. "Mr. Kaufmann?"

"Please, the name is Lamar. There's no need to be formal."

"Lamar, why am I being held hostage on this ship, and how long do you plan to keep me locked up here?"

"You aren't to be locked up." Kaufmann feigned the airs of someone insulted. "I have given specific orders for you to have free access to almost all areas of the ship. But let's not ruin a good dinner with business talk. We'll discuss those details after our appetites have been sated."

"Ansel, may we begin the meal?" Kaufmann nodded to the chef who disappeared into the kitchen. "Let's take our seats."

The table in the middle of the dining room had five place settings. A bouquet of fresh-cut flowers graced the center. The napkins were of starched and hand-pressed linen. Solid silver tableware surrounded the ornate china. It was a glimpse of a social life Ana had never before experienced.

The meal consisted of five courses, each of which was artistically presented. One of the courses was escargot. They didn't look any different than the snails she had rejected two days earlier. These, however, had been sautéed in a garlic-butter sauce. She forced a bite—it wasn't bad. Some people probably found Russian caviar repulsive. Everyone to his or her own tastes. For dessert, they had orange sherbet presented in a stainless-steel dish balanced on a five-centimeter pedestal.

Kaufmann finished his sherbet and wiped his mouth with his napkin. "Now, Ana, you had some questions?"

"Yes, I do. What is going on here? What do you want from me?"

"First of all, we wish you no harm. Dr. Mason is doing some very important stem cell research, research that couldn't be done in the United States. Sometimes, we Americans lack imagination. You're a very unique person. You have an extraordinary I.Q. We just want to sample some of your blood periodically to analyze its genetic composition. It's all for the benefit of science. As a scientist, that should be understandable. We'll be done with you in less than a year, and then we'll return you to Russia unharmed. That I guarantee."

"What gives you the right to do that?"

"It's not about rights, my dear; it's about power. You probably think knowledge creates power, but it's money that creates power. I happen to have the money to purchase all the power I want. You don't have money; therefore, you don't have power. You can cooperate, or you can resist; in which case, we'll need to use force.

Either way, our power will prevail. Do you have any other questions?"

Ana offered no comment. With the anger and frustration welling up inside her, she feared what she might say. Kaufmann was right about one thing. He currently had the power. But if he thought there was no power in knowledge, he was seriously mistaken.

"Well, then, do you have any questions about the facilities on the *Chimera*? I do hope they're adequate. Has anyone given you a tour?"

"I've walked around a bit."

"We have a beauty salon on the lower deck," Del said.

"Del, why don't you give Ana a quick tour of the ship? It'll give you a chance to talk woman to woman." Kaufmann offered it as a suggestion, although everyone at the table assumed it was a command. Kaufmann was obviously used to giving orders.

"Excellent idea. Ana, let's go check out the salon." Dell cheerfully rose to her feet. "They have a masseuse. A back rub will do you good."

Ana felt as if she were being dismissed. That was fine with her. She didn't care for the present company. She doubted she had much in common with Del, but she at least appeared sincere. That alone would be a major improvement. As if on cue, Del began an inane prattle about the pros and cons of various facials, leading Ana to wonder if Del's company would be any better than the company she was leaving. Having little choice, Ana followed Del out the door.

Lamar Kaufmann waited until the door closed before turning to Pueblo Riviera. "Do you think she has any idea what's going on?" he asked.

"Right now, she's confused. The recent events make no logical sense to her, given the limited information we have provided. She knows we have no intention of physically harming her. That'll make her bolder. She'll push the limits, but I don't think she'll do anything foolish. She's extraordinarily intelligent. Let's not forget that. Given an opportunity, she'll take full advantage of it."

"But she did take the progesterone?" Dr. Mason asked.

"I got her to take two tablets, and that was only because she thought it was dexamethasone for Acute Mountain Sickness."

"How about that cocktail of medicine I gave you? You gave that to her also?"

"We did that on the day she was abducted. We knocked her out with I.V. Versed. Then we injected 3 cc of your medicine into her buttocks as you had instructed. I don't think she even knew about the second shot."

"What's with this 'cocktail stuff'?" Kaufmann asked. "I didn't pay you guys for cocktail parties."

"It's a mixture of leuprolide acetate, follicle stimulating hormone, and human chorionic gonadotropin," Dr. Mason replied. "We can't proceed without those medications onboard. Normally, they have to be injected daily. Since we didn't have that luxury, I mixed them with another substance that slows the absorption. We should find out tomorrow if it worked."

It was all beyond Kaufmann's understanding, and he let it go. That's why he hired the best. He knew his objective. As long as his employees produced results, he wasn't concerned with methods.

Del's quick tour of the *Chimera* turned into a two-hour marathon accompanied by endless prattle about cosmetics, body toning, and the virtues of the cabbage diet. By the end of the tour, Ana had endured the unabridged version of Del's entire life history with heavy emphasis on her Hollywood starlet years. It was well past nine o'clock when Del terminated the tour at the door to Ana's new luxurious domicile—or was it a prison? In Ana's current state of confusion, it was hard to tell. She would have to give her situation some serious thought in the morning. Maybe her mind would be clearer then.

Despite her exhaustion, Ana spent a restless night on her queen-size bed, her mind perseverating over the many inconsistencies of her abduction. She awoke the following morning with a severe headache. She had been awakened by persistent knocking at her door. There was no sense ignoring it. The door wasn't locked. Whoever was there was capable of walking in on his or her own.

Ana was wearing pink pajamas. The person who made the purchase had the right size, but was unaware of her dislike for pink. She wrapped a bathrobe around her and walked to the door.

"Who's there?" she asked from behind the door.

"Room service. I have your breakfast."

She hadn't ordered breakfast. She wasn't even aware room service was an option on the boat, although it didn't surprise her. She opened the door, and a man in a servant's uniform entered carrying a circular tray the size of a pizza pan on his right palm. A silver dome covered the tray. It appeared to be real silver polished to a high luster. In his left hand was a foldable tray holder. He opened it up, placed the tray on tray holder, and removed the cover revealing scrambled eggs, sausage, and an assortment of fresh fruit.

"If the eggs aren't to your liking, we can have them cooked differently." The waiter appeared sincere. He was most likely just a man working for a living. Ana decided to forbear any sarcasm.

"No, this looks excellent." Ana waited until the man left before she began to eat. On the tray was a menu for the next twenty-four hours with a checkbox next to each item. She didn't understand the purpose of her being here, but they did feed her well.

Ana ate everything on the tray except the grapes. She placed those in her small refrigerator for future use. She checked off the menu card and returned it to the tray. Living like the rich had its perquisites. She never would have lived like this at home.

After dressing in jeans and a sweatshirt, Ana sat down in the recliner and punched on the TV with her remote. Most of the channels were in English, since American programs dominated satellite TV. Ana flipped through the channels looking for a news program, finally settling on CNN. It was mostly American news, but it was still news. She had been without any news for almost a week. After thirty minutes, when the news began to repeat, she switched to the History Channel.

The current program described how the Americans, while fighting a war on two fronts, single-handedly won World War II. They didn't paint a flattering picture of Stalin. On that point, she and the Americans were in agreement. Stalin had been a brutal and heartless dictator.

Ana heard someone knocking on her door. Whatever it was they were selling, she didn't wish to buy any. She decided to ignore it. The knocking continued. Finally, the door opened and Pueblo Riviera walked into her room.

"When someone knocks on your door, you need to answer it."

"I was busy."

The Spaniard walked over to the TV and turned it off. Using her remote control, Ana turned it back on.

"Give me the remote."

The Spaniard came toward Ana, holding out his left hand. Pretending to ignore him, she tightened her grip on the remote and continued watching the History Channel. She expected a mild skirmish as the Spaniard pried the remote from her hand. She expected to lose, but she would still have a moral victory from her defiance.

She should have seen it coming. The searing pain in her left shoulder was all too familiar. Her entire arm went numb, and she dropped the remote. The Spaniard held the black box against her shoulder for two seconds before backing off—message delivered. It took a moment or two before Ana could regain her breath. It seemed each time she was shocked, the pain was more excruciating. It must be the psychological component, she decided.

"You seemed to have forgotten our system of reward and punishment," the Spaniard said. "Don't let all this opulence go to your head."

Ana drew her legs up to her chest and crossed her arms while closely watching the black box. She was almost in a fetal position. The pain was only now starting to subside.

"The reason I'm here isn't entirely social. Dr. Mason wants to see you in his laboratory. I just recharged the batteries. I'm sure there are a couple more shocks left in it if needed."

The Spaniard reached for Ana, who withdrew further into a fetal position. He returned the black box to his pocket and gently took Ana's elbow. There was a gentleness, which bordered on compassion. The Spaniard was a complex individual, Ana decided.

Pueblo Riviera led Ana down two flights of stairs. They followed a corridor toward the bow and stopped at a door labeled Laboratory. It was the one Ana had wondered about the day before. This time the door was unlocked. Riviera opened the door, and they walked in.

The room was quite capacious and would be the envy of any serious scientist in Russia. Along the wall were several workstations, some with vacuum hoods, and others with isolation chambers accessible only through gloved access ports. Large cabinets were filled with assorted chemicals. On the far wall were box-like structures with white, enamel-covered doors. They appeared to be either refrigerators or incubators. Ana assumed there were some of each.

Riviera led Ana into a smaller room, smaller only in comparison to the first room, where Dr. Mason was busily entering data into his computer. This room appeared more medical. Anatomical charts hung from the walls, and an I.V. stand stood on standby in the corner. Three attached exam rooms with overhead lights and EKG monitoring equipment appeared ready for any emergency. One had a heart monitor with defibrillator paddles.

"Ah, Ana, it is so good of you to visit," Dr. Mason said as he looked up from his work. Ana wondered if he was aware of the circumstances of her visit.

"Mr. Riviera, here, said you wished to talk to me." Ana placed an appropriate amount of sarcastic tone on the "Mr."

Dr. Mason placed his pen in his lab-coat pocket and stood up, showing some semblance of manners. "Lamar tells me you will be staying with us a few months. I thought I would give you a tour of the lab, and if you have any free time, I would be honored to have you assist me in some of the work. I know your background is in the physical sciences, but what we do here can be quite exciting."

"I haven't decided how long I'll be staying yet, but I'll keep your offer in mind."

"I'm also concerned with your bout of Acute Mountain Sickness. That can be quite serious, even deadly. It can cause edema of the brain and fluid buildup in the lungs. You aren't having any breathing problems, are you?"

"No, I'm feeling fine. I did have a burning sensation in my shoulder earlier, but that has resolved." Ana gave the Spaniard a glaring look.

"Just the same, I'd like to check you over. I'm responsible for the health of everyone onboard the ship, even the guests."

Ana hadn't realized she fell into the guest category. The English translation of guest must be different than the Russian version.

Dr. Mason led Ana into one of the larger exam rooms. The Spaniard followed at a discrete distance. The exam room had far more electronic monitoring devices than the others. One appeared to be ultrasound. They used a similar instrument at the hospital when she had her exam for the Beckford Corporation.

"Would you mind sitting on the exam table?"

Since it was worded as a request, not a demand, she decided to comply. Dr. Mason checked her ears, eyes, nose, and throat. He listened to her lungs and heart and palpated her abdomen. She was about to draw the line at the pelvic and rectal exam, but he didn't express interest.

"I'd like to do some blood work to make sure your electrolytes aren't messed up. As Lamar Kaufmann explained yesterday, we will also be analyzing your genetic code. This might be easier if you lie down."

Dr. Mason tied a rubber tourniquet around her upper arm and palpated for a vein. She had excellent veins. "It would be best if you looked away. We only need 25 cc of blood, so it shouldn't take long." Dr. Mason retrieved a syringe from a drawer, wiped her arm with alcohol, and inserted the needle into her vein. Ana didn't watch. It wouldn't have mattered if she had. Dr. Mason's hand covered the barrel of the syringe, and she wouldn't have seen the 2 cc of Versed in the otherwise empty 25 cc syringe. He pulled back the plunger to ensure he was in a vein and was rewarded with venous blood. "Having a little trouble finding the vein," he said as he slowly injected the two milligrams of Versed over two minutes. Any further subterfuge was unnecessary as Ana's eyes became glazed. Dr. Mason removed the needle and replaced it with a saline lock to provide easy access to the vein should more Versed be needed.

"Pueblo, help me get her into a gown."

"What's happening?" Ana slowly asked in a slurred voice.

"Doc., you didn't give her enough. She's still conscious."

"That's to be expected. It's what we call conscious sedation. She'll be a space cadet throughout the procedure and hopefully will be able to breathe on her own. Versed is three to four times more powerful than Valium. It causes amnesia as a side effect. She won't remember any of this."

Ana was stripped of her clothing and placed in a hospital gown. Mason attached a three-lead heart monitor to her chest, and gave her supplemental oxygen at two liters per minute by nasal cannula. He placed an automated pressure cuff on her right arm. To monitor her breathing, Mason placed a pulse oximeter device on her finger. That would give a real-time readout of the oxygen saturation in her blood. Lastly, he inserted a Foley catheter into the bladder and filled the retaining balloon with sterile water to secure the catheter tip inside the bladder.

"Why the catheter?" The Spaniard cringed. He was thankful he wasn't the one being catheterized.

"Ultrasound bounces off surface interfaces." Using the catheter, Mason filled the bladder with 500 milliliters of normal saline. "A full bladder creates a window, so to speak, for us to look through."

Mason pulled back Ana's gown exposing her abdomen. He squirted a clear gel on the abdomen from a squeeze bottle, and applied an ultrasound probe to the skin through the gel. A black and white, cone-shaped picture immediately presented on the video monitor. He twisted and angled the probe to view the different organs, first the kidneys, then the uterus, and finally the ovaries.

"Bingo! See those follicles on that ovary?"

"I don't see anything," Riviera confessed.

With his free hand, Mason pointed to several small circles on the ovary. "There must be four or five of them. And they all look ripe. The other ovary is just as good. The fertility drugs you gave her worked like a charm."

"So when do we harvest them?" Harvest was a crude term for surgically removing a woman's eggs, Riviera thought. But, then, they didn't pay him to be judgmental.

"We do that right now while they're ripe. If we wait too long the follicles would rupture, and we would never find the ova. Can you pass me that vaginal speculum?"

Riviera looked at the surgical tray loaded with instruments, not sure what he should be looking for.

"It's the one that looks like a duck's bill."

Riviera passed the speculum to the doctor. "Don't you have to cut her open?" he asked.

"We could. A lot of physicians do it laparoscopically through small incisions in the abdomen. I prefer to do it through the vaginal wall guided by ultrasound. It's less dangerous and leaves no noticeable surgical wounds. When I'm done, there'll be no evidence that we took her ova."

Dr. Mason lubricated the speculum with KY Jelly and inserted it into the vagina. The lubricant wasn't really necessary, since Ana was in deep sedation and wouldn't feel pain. It was more a matter of habit. He then inserted a long, large-bore needle through the vaginal wall. A stylet filled the lumen of the needle to prevent the needle from coring any tissue and fouling the lumen. With the aid of the ultrasound, he guided the needle toward the left ovary. He pierced a follicle with the needle and removed the stylet. Mild suction from a syringe aspirated the ovum and surrounding fluid from the follicle. He repeated the procedure eight times before he withdrew the needle and speculum. Mason placed the ova in separate test tubes and transferred them to incubators for temporary storage.

Dr. Mason removed the heart monitor leads from Ana's chest. "Pueblo, help me get her clothes back on." The surgical gown was removed and the patient redressed in her normal clothes. All surgical and monitoring equipment were returned to their normal locations, only the saline lock remained. Dr. Mason injected 0.2 mg of Romazicon into the saline lock before he removed the venous access port.

"What does that medicine do?" Riviera asked.

"Romazicon is the antidote for Versed. She'll quickly come out of sedation."

Within two to three minutes, Ana began to stir. The glassiness of the eyes had resolved, and her mind began to clear. "What happened?"

Dr. Mason placed a caring hand on Ana's shoulder. "I was taking some of your blood, and you passed out for a few seconds. It happens to a lot of people."

"It's never happened to me before."

"I want you to lie here for a while. When you get your sea legs back, Pueblo will take you back to your room. I want you to rest for the remainder of the day. The tour of the facilities can wait a day or so."

Dr. Mason checked Ana's heart and blood pressure one more time and pronounced her healthy. He waited until Ana and the Spaniard left the room and then retrieved the ova from the incubator. Mason added a small quantity of semen to each of the eight ovum-containing test tubes, before he returned them to the incubator. He would check on them daily.

8

Dr. Carl Mason placed the slide containing follicular fluid from test tube number eight under the dissecting microscope. A thin film of oil covered the fluid to prevent evaporation. The ovum hopefully contained within the fluid would be highly susceptible to changes in temperature and osmolarity, both of which would be affected by evaporation. A microscopic image immediately appeared on the large video display he used for scanning the slide. A small human ovum can be easily lost in that vast sea of follicular fluid and finding it can be challenging. Sometimes a follicle doesn't contain an ovum. Mason had wasted many hours in the past searching for ova that didn't exist. This wasn't the case today. Luck was on his side. The ovum quickly came into view. But it was no longer an ovum. It had divided into eight cells. Fertilization had occurred. It was now an embryo. That was six out of the eight, excellent results.

Mason centered the embryo and switched to the binocular viewer. The large screen was nice for scanning, but for what he had to do next, he would need binocular vision. The embryo was in the center of the field as he expected. He brought it into focus for closer examination: It appeared normal, no obvious defects. Slowly, he adjusted the micromanipulator. It was controlled by three screw knobs that moved the micropipette in each of the three dimensions. This was the part he hated and enjoyed the most. One small mistake, one miscalculation, and the glass micropipette would break or the embryo would be destroyed. That didn't happen often. He had perfected the skill over the years. It was mostly about patience. It was the impatient technician who courted failure.

The glass tip of the micropipette came into view. This was when he needed to slow down, take his time. He envisioned himself as an astronaut docking two vehicles in space—a critical maneuver at best. The distance between the eight-celled embryo and the micropipette began to close. *Everything looks good, Mission Control.* Commander Mason picked out his docking port. It would be the cell nearest to his microscopic spacecraft. All systems were go. The distance continued to close. The space probe was almost touching the embryo. This part had to be taken very slowly. He didn't want to ram the space station. The micropipette gently punctured the cell membrane's outermost cell and came to a halt. *Mission Control, the Eagle has landed.* He applied a small amount of suction to the pipette, and the cell's contents, including the nucleus, filled the tip of the pipette. A slight twist to a control knob and the pipette backed out of the embryo, mission accomplished.

Dr. Carl Mason, returning to his role as research embryologist, placed the embryo back into test tube number eight. To achieve optimum results, they needed five more days of incubation before implantation. He now had nuclei from all six of the fertilized eggs. The next step would be karyotyping. He would look at the individual chromosomes. And discard any embryo with a double X chromosome. Kaufmann had requested a male offspring. Even odds would suggest three usable embryos; he only needed one.

***

Two days of self-confinement watching *I love Lucy* reruns on satellite TV was more than Ana could handle. Her mind craved stimulation, more stimulation than TV could provide. On the third day, Ana willfully presented herself at Dr. Mason's laboratory. It was only idle curiosity, she told herself. But she never was much of a spectator when it came to research. She was soon deeply involved in Dr. Mason's research activities. She began by mixing the chemical broth in which the stem cells were incubated, a critical step in their growth, and then moved up to more complicated tasks. More recently she had been perfecting her skills on the micromanipulator, removing genetic material from some cells and adding it to others.

Dr. Mason assumed Ana was only knowledgeable in the physical sciences, but he soon discovered she hadn't ignored the medical and biological sciences on her way to her degrees in nuclear physics. What she didn't know, she quickly learned from Mason's textbooks. She proved to be a great asset to his research and, except for Mason's computer and an incubator kept under lock and key, she was given full laboratory access.

On the fifth day of her captivity, Dr. Mason approached Ana on a personal matter. "Ana, I've finally received the results of your blood test. My blood chemistry analyzer broke down, so I sent your blood to an outside lab." He handed her a copy of the report. "This explains why you passed out when I took your blood. Your sodium level was low. Acute Mountain Sickness can cause loss of sodium and water, but this is surprising for the amount of time you were on the mountain."

"I feel fine now." Ana had all but forgotten the blood tests, except for the ignominy of passing out. That had been embarrassing.

"It should have self-corrected by now. We could repeat the test to see if it's back to normal. Although, I don't want you passing out again," Mason said as an afterthought, but it was a calculated afterthought.

"If you want to repeat the blood test, I don't care. I don't think I'll pass out again." But she did care. Passing out during a blood draw had been a social embarrassment, a blow to her ego. Now more than anything, she needed to redeem herself. She needed to prove to Dr. Mason, as well as herself, that she was capable of handling a minor needle stick. It couldn't be any worse than a poke with a cattle prod. She had survived three of those.

Dr. Mason returned a moment later with a rubber tourniquet and a syringe. "Why don't you lie done on one of the exam tables? This should be quick."

Ana lay down on the exam table and extended her right arm over the attached arm board as she had done in the past. This time she wouldn't pass out. She would even watch the needle go into her arm.

Mason placed the tourniquet around her upper arm and palpated for a vein. When he found a good one, he wiped it with alcohol. "A little poke," he said.

Ana watched as the needle pierced her skin, the barrel of the syringe concealed within the doctor's hand.

"I'm having trouble hitting the vein. Can you pump your fist?"

Ana began pumping her fist. With her eyes focused on her pumping fist, she didn't notice when the Mason pushed in on the plunger instead of pulling to aspirate blood. The pumping action of Ana's fist began to diminish, and then it quit altogether. Her breathing slowed and her eyes became glazed.

Mason withdrew the needle and removed the tourniquet. He checked her pupils to see if she was focusing—she was not. He removed her clothes from the waist down. This time he didn't bother with lubricant. Ana wouldn't know the difference, and he was in a hurry. Once the speculum was in place and the cervix located, he inserted a semi-rigid catheter through the cervix and about five centimeters into the uterus. Then he injected a five-day-old embryo along with 2 cc of fluid through the catheter and into the upper uterine cavity. Mason withdrew the catheter and gave the cervix one last inspection to ensure no fluid was leaking out before removing the speculum; mission accomplished. For the next seven days, he would have food service add progesterone to her meals. That would create a better environment for implantation.

Mason redressed his patient and smoothed out her clothing. He applied a tourniquet to her arm and reinserted the needle into her vein. This time he injected Romazicon into the vein to counteract the Versed he had given earlier. He left the needle in the vein while he waited for Ana to respond to the antidote. She gradually began to stir.

"How you feeling," he said as he began to aspirate blood from the vein.

Ana was feeling light-headed, but wasn't about to admit it. "I'm feeling fine." She had watched him stick the needle into her vein, and now he was withdrawing the blood. At least she hadn't passed out.

9

It was five weeks later when she first noticed the illness. It started with occasional bouts of nausea. That was tolerable. She could live with that. And it wasn't every day. Some days she felt fine. But the nausea gradually progressed to full-blown vomiting. There were times when nothing stayed down. She assumed it was a viral gastroenteritis that, given time, would run its course. She switched to a clear liquid diet to give her bowels a rest as suggested in one of Dr. Mason's medical books. That didn't help either. Even her dinner of soup broth and Jell-O came back up. Ana wasn't one to run to the doctor for every minor ailment, but after ten days of on and off retching, it was time to discuss the matter with Dr. Mason.

Ana headed for the laboratory hoping to catch Dr. Mason in his office. He often used his evenings to catch up with delinquent paperwork. By personal choice, he shunned the ship's evening social life preferring the companionship of his microscope. It wasn't as if he were antisocial—he always had a smile or friendly word, even for custodial staff. He just lived for his research.

Ana found the door to the laboratory unlocked, confirming the physician's presence. The laboratory was dark except for light emanating from Mason's office. Ana walked over to the doorway and waited a moment or two to be recognized. Dr. Mason was engrossed in a computer printout, his back to the door, totally oblivious to Ana standing in the doorway.

"Dr. Mason?"

Mason set the computer printout on his desk and turned to face Ana. "Ana, this is a surprise. Surely there must be more exciting activities on board ship to occupy your evening?"

"This isn't exactly a social call. I think I'm sick."

Dr. Mason appeared sincerely concerned. He would have done well as a family physician. After listening to Ana's complaints, he asked a few pertinent questions, and then gave her a complete physical exam. He took a sample of blood (she experienced no dizziness) and ran it through the Coulter hematology analyzer. Her white cell count was normal—nothing to suggest a bacterial infection—but her hemoglobin was slightly low.

"Ana, it looks like you got a bit of a viral bug," Dr. Mason concluded after he completed the exam and reviewed her lab results. "It'll resolve in a few days."

"What if it doesn't?"

"Sometimes nerves can cause stomach upset. I know your situation here is stressful. I'll give you something for the nausea, and I want you to take a daily vitamin pill with iron. You need more iron."

The nausea resolved with Dr. Mason's medicine, but she still didn't feel right. She attributed missing her first period to the illness. She hadn't always been regular in the past. When she missed her second period, she became concerned. She and Dorek had used protection in the past. They had been careful, but no system is foolproof. An unwanted pregnancy could explain her nausea. A pregnancy would definitely fall under one of the Murphy's laws Americans always talked about. She stewed about that possibility for three days before she decided to take action.

She found Dr. Mason at his desk, about to enter data into his computer. Notes from various experiments cluttered his desk.

"Dr. Mason, can you give me a pregnancy test?"

"Let me enter these data into the computer first. If I don't do it now, I'll forget."

Ana had to agree. Dr. Mason was an excellent scientist, but his organizational skills were lacking. Mason moved his mouse, and the computer came out of hibernation. A blue log-on screen filled his monitor screen. He typed *CarlMason*, no spaces, in the I.D. box. If Ana had been watching, she would have seen five asterisks fill the password box. But Ana was watching Mason's fingers instead, noting the sequence of movement, and whether a finger moved up or down, to the right or to the left. It was *nosam*, Mason spelled backwards. Not very creative—or secure. Ana didn't know why she needed the password. It was like climbing a mountain; it was there, and she was capable of doing it.

Mason finished entering the data and looked up at Ana. "So, we think we're pregnant, do we?"

"I've never had unprotected sex, but I guess it's a possibility."

"I can give you the test, or you can do it yourself." Mason handed Ana a specimen cup. "First we need some urine. We don't need much."

Ana returned moments later with her container half full of yellow fluid. Dr. Mason took the container and walked over to a counter. He retrieved three small bottles with medicine droppers for tops. One was labeled *Negative Control*, one was labeled *Positive Control*, and the last was labeled *Reagent*.

"What we're looking for," he said, "is Human Chorionic Gonadotropin or HCG for short. It's produced by the developing placenta. Some people call it the pregnancy hormone."

Mason found a porcelain slab in one of the drawers. It was about the size of a cigarette pack and a half-inch thick. It had three dime-size depressions on one side. He washed it clean and dried it with paper toweling. Taking a medicine dropper, he added two drops of urine to the middle depression. "That's your urine, which we want to test for HCG." From the negative control bottle, he added two drops to the depression on the left. "This liquid has no HCG and should test negative." He added two drops from the positive control bottle to the depression on the right. "And this one has HCG in it and should test positive."

Mason handed the third bottle to Ana. "This is the reagent. Add two drops of this to each of the three samples, and if everything goes right, it will bind with the HCG and turn blue."

"How accurate is this? Does it ever go wrong?"

"I've never seen it happen. I suppose the reagent could go bad. That's why we have the controls. Most of the newer tests have the reagent impregnated into dipsticks. I guess I'm a bit old fashioned."

Ana added two drops to each of the three samples, but nothing happened.

"You have to wait five minutes," Mason said.

After one minute, the positive control began turning blue. After five minutes, the positive control was very blue; the other two remained clear and colorless.

"Well, Ana, you're not pregnant."

Ana felt a wave of relief. She had no desire for a pregnancy in this stage of her life, but it would have been nice to have a reason for the nausea and her missed periods. She still had nothing to explain the way she felt. Maybe it was nerves. She had been forcibly abducted, her friends thought she was dead, and she still didn't know why she was here. They had yet to begin any physical or psychological experiments on her. She had plenty of objective reasons for having a good old-fashioned nervous breakdown.

During the next three months, Ana fell into a routine with most of her time spent in Dr. Mason's laboratory. She still had no periods, but otherwise she felt fine, except for occasional gas. She could feel her bowels fluttering now and then. With a little imagination, she thought her belly might be swelling from the gas. She ran the pregnancy test three more times just to make sure: They were all normal.

It was an early Monday morning when she found it, an unopened pregnancy test kit. She had been searching a cupboard for acetone. It had the three medicine-dropper bottles, the porcelain slab; and, more importantly, it had the package insert with the manufacturer's directions. Maybe the insert would provide further insight. Without giving it additional thought, Ana slipped it into the pocket of the white lab coat Dr. Mason had loaned her. She would look at it later. She found the acetone hidden behind a gallon can of denatured alcohol. The bottle was only half full, but it was enough to finish her experiment. She would have to tell Dr. Mason to order more.

Ana returned to her apartment—as she now liked to call it— late in the afternoon. Her dinner was sitting on the counter of her kitchenette. It must have just arrived. Steam was still leaking out from under the silver, bowl-shaped cover. That was good since she was famished. She had definitely overcome her nausea and anorexia. Now she was constantly hungry.

Ana was about to take off her lab coat when she felt the pregnancy test kit in her pocket. She had forgotten about that. She opened the package and scanned the directions and other pertinent information. *Ninety-nine percent accurate when used according to the directions. Most false negatives were when the test was performed very early in the pregnancy. Early morning urine specimens are best.* There was nothing new.

Ana crossed her legs. Like Pavlov's dogs; just thinking about urine gave her the urge to go. Grabbing a small container, Ana headed toward the bathroom. If she had the new kit, she might as well give it a try. She went through the routine motions as she had done so many times before, placing drops in all the appropriate places. Then she stared at the porcelain slab in disbelief. The mixture in the center depression was turning blue faster than the control. She washed the porcelain slab and repeated the test with similar results. There was no denying it. She was pregnant!

Why hadn't it turned blue before? She mused over the possibilities. How could it pick up the HCG in the control but not in her urine? The depression on the right turned blue because reagent came in contact with HCG. The one in the center didn't turn blue because reagent didn't come in contact with HCG. But her urine had HCG; therefore, what she added to her urine couldn't have been reagent.

Ana washed the porcelain slab and repeated the test, placing the negative control in the depression on the left, her urine in the center, and instead of the positive control, she placed reagent in the depression on the right. Then she placed two drops of the positive control in each of the three depressions. Only the liquid in the depression on the right turned blue. Someone had to have switched the reagent label with the positive control.

That brought an even more depressing thought. If it had been a failure of birth control and Dorek were the father, why the cover-up? A cover-up only has value if there is something to hide. Dorek couldn't be the father. With all the stem cell and embryology research going on, she wasn't even sure she was the biological mother. A lot of money and expertise had gone into her abduction. It would be inconceivable that she hadn't been used, or abused, in some way over the last four months. Apparently, she was being used without her knowledge. Whatever was going on, Ana was confident she could discover on Dr. Carl Mason's computer.

The following morning, Ana found it difficult to concentrate on her work while wondering if she was working on the same experiment that had violated her body. It was difficult being cordial with Dr. Carl Mason, a person she had previously considered a friend and trusted colleague. The advancement of science was an inalienable right of all mankind, but it had to be performed in an ethical and moral manner. Dr. Mason had stepped beyond those boundaries.

All she needed was ten or fifteen minutes of computer time. That was all she wanted. Dr. Mason had made it clear from the beginning that the computer as well as the locked incubator were off limits. Otherwise she had free reign of the lab. Mason even left her alone in the lab for brief periods in the past. It wasn't as if Dr. Mason was lax with security, he was working under the assumption that the incubator was safely protected under lock and key and that the computer was safely password protected. He was unaware that his assumption was only half correct.

Mason's brief and unpredictable absences wouldn't suffice. She needed a block of time she could count on. If they caught her, there would be no second chance. She would strive for lunch break.

Most employees ate lunch in the small onboard cafeteria that offered a salad bar and whatever they could obtain at the grill. Ana could have had all her meals delivered to her room if she preferred; but being an extrovert, she found the social life in the cafeteria rewarding and usually joined Dr. Mason in a half-hour lunch break. It was also a welcome hiatus from the laboratory routine. Most of the time, they left together. A few times Mason had left before her, leaving instructions to shut the door when she left. The door would self-lock.

Ana's morning assignment was collecting nuclear material from stem cells for karyotyping. Over the months, she had become quite proficient with the micromanipulator, but today, she took her time. When looking through the binocular eyepieces of the dissecting microscope, it is difficult for an outsider to judge the effort expended. Slacking off was easy, and by late morning, she had accomplished only two-thirds of her task.

"You going to lunch?" Dr. Mason asked. It was well past noon.

"I still have a bit more to do." Ana didn't look up from her microscope. "I'll be up in a few minutes."

"Well, I'm not as dedicated as you. I'm hungry. I'll meet you upstairs. Be sure to pull the door closed when you leave." Dr. Mason removed his white coat and headed out the door, grossly underestimating how dedicated Ana now was.

Ana waited a minute, allowing time for Mason to climb the stairs and leave the hallway. Finding no one lurking in the hallway, Ana shut and locked the door. She didn't need any passers-by looking in.

Ana turned on Mason's computer and brought up the log-on screen. For user ID she typed in *CarlMason* with no spaces. For the password, she typed in *nosam*. The computer immediately allowed her access. The number of files was excessive. She wouldn't have time to search them all. Ana clicked on *Start* from the tool bar at the bottom of the screen, then chose *search*. She typed Petrova in the search box and hit return. After a two-minute search, it located a sub-file entitled *Anastasia Petrova—accepted*. It was part of a larger file entitled *Female Candidates.* She scanned the names on the files. They were all names of people she knew. All of them were members of the Supererogatory Society. As far as she knew, they had never made that list public. After each name on the file was the word *rejected*. Her file was the only one with *accepted* beside the name. She had apparently won the lottery.

Ana opened another file labeled *Male Candidates*. There she found the male members of her elite group of thirty-four. They, too, had *rejected* next to their names—except for Dorek Dolinski. Ana opened his file. It contained a complete social history, much of which Ana already knew. She scrolled down to the medical information. It was mostly normal. What caught her eye was the sperm count: 146 million. That was on the high side of normal. How many girls knew the sperm count of their boyfriends? Ana wondered. An additional footnote stated they were highly motile. Not only were there a lot of sperm, the suckers were armed and dangerous! Ana returned to her folder and found a complete biography of her life. Someone must have worked on it for months, perhaps years. She checked her MMPI scores: The T-scores on all the scales fell in the normal range.

Ana closed the folders and signed off the computer. Any further time spent on the computer was pressing her luck. She shut the door to the lab and headed toward the cafeteria. She had some thinking to do.

10

The information obtained from the computer files introduced as many questions as it produced answers. It now appeared to be Dorek's baby she was carrying. But why spend all that time and money just to get her pregnant? Was it a normal baby she was carrying or had it been genetically altered to fit some sinister and diabolical scientific experiment? And how did they accomplish it without her knowledge? Ana had no doubt the Beckford Corporation orchestrated Dorek's physical exam after his alleged over-exposure to radiation. It had been a thorough exam, he had said; although, he had failed to mention the semen examination.

Ana ran her fingers across the swelling of her abdomen. There was no way they could keep the pregnancy quiet much longer. She was already in that awkward stage where people wondered whether she was pregnant or just putting on weight. She could confront Dr. Mason, but he would likely prevaricate, providing little, if any, new information. For the last three weeks, Lamar Kaufmann had been at his mansion outside Las Vegas. He was the one she should confront. He had arrived by helicopter earlier in the day with a Venezuelan client he was wining and dining. Now was a good time for a confrontation. Ana fully expected to make a scene and didn't care one iota if Kaufmann's client found it embarrassing.

***

Ana opened the door to Kaufmann's office without knocking—she wasn't in the mood for etiquette—and found him sitting at his desk. Kaufmann, appearing surprised, looked up from his computer where he had been typing numbers into a spreadsheet. "Ana, it is so good to see you." His demeanor exuded insincerity.

"We need to talk."

"I believe you're right." The phone on Kaufmann's desk rang. He picked it up on the second ring, listened for a moment, and then said, "She's with me." He hung up the phone. "They were just checking up on you. This room's considered off limits unless, of course, you're with me. Let me enter a few more numbers, and then we'll have a long chat."

The computer, printer, and monitor were plugged into a power-strip/surge-protector lying on the floor beside Kaufmann's desk. A red glowing toggle switch indicated the "on" position. More out of spite than a clear-cut plan, Ana switched it off with her foot, causing the computer to crash. She found satisfaction in Kaufmann's momentary displeasure. After Kaufmann finished his expletives, she turned it back on. She was in the mood to repeat that all day if Kaufmann continued to ignore her.

"Damn computer." The comment was more for the computer's ears than Ana's. "I got about six more figures to put into the computer, and I'll be with you."

Kaufmann booted his computer and waited for the log-on screen to appear. When it did, he typed *LKaufmann* into the user ID box. He typed six asterisks into the password box, while Ana watched the movement of his fingers.

Topdog. She should have known his password would be some arrogant epithet. Ana, now satisfied with her minor victory, allowed Kaufmann to enter the last of his numbers without intervention. There would be no telling what information she might find on his hard drive. Getting access to it would be more difficult than breaking into Mason's computer—maybe impossible.

"Now, Ana, what can I do for you today?" Kaufmann said after he entered the numbers. "Please, have a seat." He motioned to the chair in front of his desk.

"I'm pregnant."

"So you are." Kaufmann leaned back in his chair.

"I want to know how, and I want to know why." Ana glared at Kaufmann. "If I appear surly, it's because I'm feeling a bit raped."

"First of all, you weren't raped. Dr. Mason artificially inseminated you with donor sperm. If you were a virgin before this, which I doubt, you are still a virgin now."

"Who's the father of my child?" Ana would have enjoyed telling him she already knew.

"That is best left confidential. No sense dragging another individual into the equation. He doesn't know he's a donor. Let's not complicate his life."

"You still haven't answered the why."

"That, Ana, is a bit embarrassing. I wasn't always as cautious as I am today. In my youth, I came down with a disease, gonorrhea to be precise. I didn't seek immediate treatment, and it developed into epididymitis. It caused me to become sterile. Unlike you, I can't have children, not biological children at least. My wealth you see on the *Chimera* is only the tip of the iceberg, so to speak. I own four large casinos and have billions in offshore accounts. Some of it I inherited from my father, but most of it I've accumulated on my own. I need someone who can one day take over my empire. I need a son."

"I could've referred you to some adoption agencies, but they would want good references."

"Adoption agencies are for common folk. When you have money, you only buy the best. Not to augment your ego, but we selected you from a large pool of candidates to be the mother of my child. You have no medical or genetic defects, you are mentally stable, and you have incredible intelligence. We used the same criteria to select the father. Fortunately, it was possible to obtain his sperm without his knowledge, if you can believe that. He shall remain anonymous."

Finally, she was hearing the truth. Despite the arrogance of the plan, it made sense; at least it would make sense to Lamar Kaufmann who was accustomed to having anything he wanted. In his world, everything could be bought and sold. Everything had a price tag, and if you had the money, everything could be yours.

"What gives you the right to depredate the lives of others?"

"My dear Ana, I thought we already discussed that. Money gives me that right. It buys power. With power you can do anything."

Ana had heard all she wanted to hear and stood up to leave.

"Please sit down. There's more you should know. I'm not by nature an evil person."

"You had me fooled." Ana sat back down, although she didn't know why.

Kaufman ignored the sarcasm. "After my baby is born, you'll be returned to Russia. You will find a large sum of money in an account with your name. I reward handsomely those who serve me well."

"My baby isn't for sale at any price."

"But Ana, this isn't your baby. What did you do to make it? You were using birth control to prevent having a baby."

"What's to prevent me from coming back to claim my baby? Genetic testing will prove it's mine."

"It'll never come to genetic testing. My son and I will be living in the United States, and you will be in Russia. You will be the deranged girl who faked a suicide. You are very bitter because the Beckman Corporation, which really does exist, refused to hire you due to your mental instability. No, Ana, it has all been worked out. There's no way you'll get the baby back. I have money and you don't. It's as simple as that. Now if there is anything you need, any additional creature comforts, please let me know. You did get the John Denver and Sally Rogers CD's, didn't you?"

Ana walked out of the office and headed back to her room. She couldn't listen to any more mendacious arguments without becoming physically assaultive. Kaufmann was right about one thing; it would be difficult getting her baby back through legal channels. There would be little, if any, physical evidence that any of this actually happened. He paid his staff well, and money bought loyalty. She was also powerless aboard his yacht. If she wanted to get her baby back, she would have to do it on her own after she was off the yacht.

Powerless or not, she needed to do something proactive, even if it was only token harassment. What she needed was to get inside Kaufmann's computer. There had to be documents on the hard drive he didn't want to see the light of day. She had his password, but it was meaningless without access to his office. Her tether had given her away after only minutes in his office.

. Since it hadn't interfered with activities, she had given her tether little thought. She had almost forgotten about it. Ana pulled up her pant leg to inspect the tether. It was fastened around her right ankle by a thick nylon band. She assumed cutting the wires running through the band would set off an alarm. That was only logical. It couldn't work off a GPS system since the signals wouldn't penetrate the layers of metal in the ship's structure. In fact, no radio signal could get past the metal in the walls and ceiling. There had to be a sensing device in each room.

Ana looked about her room. The walls were solid. The only logical place to hide a receiver would be in the drop-down ceiling. Standing on a chair, Ana began lifting the acoustical ceiling tiles. It didn't take long to find a small black box with a short antenna. Attached to the box were two doorbell-size wires. Ana used a table knife to remove the two screws holding the cover in place. Inside were a nine-volt battery and a small integrated circuit board. It would be impossible to understand the electronics without extensive documentation. At this point, she could only guess. One wire was attached to the negative pole of the battery. The other wire was connected to the circuit board, which was attached in turn to the positive battery pole. Logic suggested the tether's signal triggered the receiver, completing the circuit, which would then notify whoever was monitoring her that she was in that particular room. If that were true, connecting both wires directly to the battery would send a constant signal with or without the tether in the room.

Using a paper clip, Ana made a connection directly to the battery bypassing the circuit board. That should send out a constant signal. She replaced the ceiling tile. Next she needed to turn off the tether. She found some aluminum foil in the top drawer of the kitchenette and slid a small piece between the tether and her ankle. A second sheet wrapped around the outside of the tether totally enclosed the tether in foil and rendered it inoperative; no radio signal could transmit through the foil—at least in theory.

Ana sat back in a chair to wait. If her plan failed, she would know within the next few minutes. Thirty minutes passed with no commandos knocking down her door. She pronounced that portion of her plan a success. She removed the foil and repaired the receiver. There would be no telling when someone might come by to check the battery.

The following morning appeared normal. If Kaufmann told Dr. Mason about the previous evening's conversation, Mason didn't let on. He didn't mention the pregnancy, and Ana didn't bring it up, feeling it best to avoid confrontations, at least until the logistics to her plan were firmed up. She still needed to be on Mason's good side, although she now wondered if he had one.

Ana spent most of the morning looking through the dissecting microscope while trying to act casual. It was like telling someone to breathe normally: It can't be done. She hoped her anxiety wasn't obvious; cloak and dagger activity hadn't been part of her academic training. By noon she was an emotional invalid. Small tremors in her hands made working with the micromanipulator impossible, and there was a palpable quiver in her voice when she spoke. It was as if *guilty* were tattooed to her forehead. If it was, Dr. Mason didn't appear to notice. At least he didn't comment on it. All of this stress and she had yet to implement any part of her plan. The opportunity had yet to present itself. It would, she knew. Eventually it would, if not today then tomorrow or the next day. Time was on her side. She had a nine-month commitment.

Opportunity came late in the afternoon when they ran out of the broth used to incubate the stem cells. Mixing up the solution was a tedious task, which she normally would have postponed until the following morning, but she needed access to the chemical cabinet.

"Want me to mix up some more broth?" she asked.

Mason was on the computer adding notes to his daily log. He didn't bother to look up. "It's up to you. We won't need it until tomorrow."

Ana walked over to the chemical cabinet. It was normally locked, but Mason had drifted into the habit of locking it only at the end of the day. Ana opened the glass doors and sorted through the chemicals until she found a bottle of black crystals. The label identified it as iodine. She looked over at Mason, who was still on the computer, before slipping the bottle into the pocket of her white lab coat. She could feel her heart beating in her chest. With all her feelings of guilt, she wouldn't have made a good criminal.

Further searching found a bottle of ammonia. She wrapped the bottle in paper toweling and placed it inside a beaker. She added this to her other pocket. She found a glass filter and filter paper on the counter.

"Dr. Mason, I'm going to the bathroom. I'll be back in a few minutes." Ana hoped her voice sounded normal; it didn't feel normal. He gave a wave of approval. It wasn't an unusual request. All the guest rooms had bathroom facilities; therefore, few public facilities were provided on the ship. It was assumed guests would return to their rooms for such activities.

Heading down the hallway, Ana expected to be accosted at any moment by men dressed in black wearing ski masks and brandishing Uzi submachine guns. After noting the guilty sign tattooed to her forehead, they would take appropriate action. Her mental image of that action wasn't a pleasant sight. Her only human encounter was two kitchen workers dressed in white on their way to work. They greeted her by name, hardly a threat. Otherwise the corridor was empty. If she had that much anxiety walking to her room, she couldn't envision how she could execute the rest of her plan. She arrived at her room with nothing more adverse than sweaty palms and a sudden urge to pee. The contraband she hid in her refrigerator's crisper for later use. It was an unlikely place for someone to routinely search. Then, still feeling an urge to pee, she drained her bladder. It would be awkward asking to again use the bathroom. She returned to the lab in high spirits. She was finally on the offensive.

Evenings on the *Chimera* were normally quiet. It was a pleasure yacht by design, but for most of the *Chimera's* inhabitants, it was a place of work. After the sun had set and meals had been served, most employees returned to their rooms to read, watch TV or otherwise entertain themselves. Only the men working on the bridge or the engine room labored through the night.

Lamar Kaufmann was an exception to the rule. He split his time between his mansion northwest of Las Vegas and his yacht. Both were places of business, one more legal than the other. When he was aboard the *Chimera,* he took advantage of the quiet evenings to work in his office, sometimes until the wee hours of the morning.

The fact that the Spaniard wasn't currently onboard the *Chimera* was to her advantage, Ana thought as she headed toward Kaufmann's office with a wad of wet toilet paper in her left hand. He would have been harder to fool. Kaufmann's office was at the stern of the ship, two decks above Ana's residence. After dark the hallways were illuminated, at the Spaniard's insistence, with red light, which wouldn't ruin an employee's night vision, should he have to go on-deck during an emergency. It provided a surreal experience as she walked down the halls. As she had expected, the hallways of the *Chimera* were deserted, its employees having found better things to do with their free time.

Ana found a stream of white light leaking from under Kaufmann's door—he was at work. Deciding this was a good time to display manners, Ana knocked on the door instead of barging in. Kaufmann came to the door momentarily.

"Ana, what can I do for you this time of night?" Kaufmann studied Ana trying to deduce her mood. "Please come in."

"That's O.K. I just have a quick question."

The phone rang, and Kaufmann walked back to his desk to answer it. "She's with me," he said into the phone and hung up.

Ana remained in the doorway, leaning against the frame while she stuffed wet toilet paper into the door-latch hole with her left hand.

"You said you had a question?" Kaufmann asked.

"Yesterday, you said you needed a son. What happens if it's a girl?"

"It's a boy. Dr. Mason did genetic testing. If it had been a girl, we wouldn't have allowed the pregnancy to proceed."

"Thank you. That's all I wanted to know. I'll shut the door for you."

Ana shut the door, slowly releasing the doorknob. The door stayed shut.

Ana returned to her room. So far, everything was working as she had planned, but that had been the easy part, the part with minimal risk. The rest was fraught with possible complications. Ana made a mental list of all the possible complications and then added some that weren't. The only thing that pushed her forward was her deep-seated anger.

Standing on a chair, Ana lifted the ceiling tile, exposing the tether's receiver. She short-circuited it with a paper clip as she had before. She again wrapped aluminum foil around the tether making her electronically invisible. Whoever was monitoring her whereabouts would now assume she was in her room no matter where she happened to be on the ship. At least that was how it worked in theory.

Ana placed Sally Rogers' *Unclaimed Pint* CD in the CD player and sat back in a chair. It had worked before; it would work again. She had more confidence in the aluminum foil rendering the tether inoperative; that was simple physics. Her alteration of the receiver was more problematic. It was based on a lot of assumptions and guesswork. After fifteen minutes with no commandos bursting through her door, she declared her system still functional. It was time to go to work.

Since it would draw attention if she were to walk around the ship with a chemistry set, she decided to "brown bag" it. She placed the ammonia, iodine, beaker, and funnel in an old brown bag along with some extra brown paper towels. If she were to meet someone in the corridor, she would be on her way to the cafeteria or the library or perhaps she was on her way to the swimming pool with her swimsuit in the brown paper bag. Unless they compared her whereabouts with the input from the tether, no one would pay much mind. She restarted the CD and turned up the volume.

Ana found no one present when she stepped into the hallway. Even with her door closed, she could hear Sally singing *I Wish I Had Someone to Love*. It was very apropos. Ana walked to the stairwell and took the stairs up two flights. An emergency exit led her to the outside deck where she waited a minute while her eyes adjusted to the moonless night. It was also a night without clouds, not an uncommon finding at sea. Without any streetlights or industrial smog, the brilliance of the stars was spectacular. She had come out on deck many nights in the past, not only to see their beauty, but to enjoy the solitude. The solitude had been a relaxing and fortuitous pleasure. Now it was a necessity.

With her night vision intact, Ana walked along the outer deck toward the ship's bow. The only external lights were at the doors leading inside the ship. As long as she stayed in the shadows, she remained invisible. Ten meters from the bow, near one of the lifeboats, Ana found a utility closet filled with mops and cleaning supplies. A forty-watt bulb illuminated the windowless room, perfect for her needs. She stepped inside and shut the door.

Ana sat on a five-gallon drum of cleaning solution and opened her brown bag. She placed the iodine crystals and the bottle of ammonia on a carton of paper towels. She had never made nitrogen triiodide, only read about its properties in textbooks, but the synthesis was simple—if the textbooks were accurate. She filled the glass beaker half full with ammonium. The noxious ammonia fumes burned her eyes and sinuses, one of the drawbacks of the enclosed space. She had considered leaving the door open, but rejected the option. Not only would the toxic fumes diffuse out, so would the light. For her unborn child, she could endure the misery.

She added the iodine crystals to the ammonia while stirring the mixture with a pencil. The iodine chunks disintegrated into a fine black powder, almost a mud. It was hardly the most exciting chemical reaction she had ever witnessed.

Ana folded the filter paper twice, forming a cone, and placed it in her funnel. The ammonia fumes were almost unbearable. Fortunately, she was about done. She poured the ammonia and black mud into the filter, allowing the filtrate to fall into a mop bucket. About twenty grams of wet nitrogen triiodide now covered her filter paper.

Ana divided the chemical in half and spread it thinly across two sheets of paper toweling, forming thick black smears. She threw the beaker, funnel and chemical bottles overboard; she had no further need for them. She was about to empty the mop bucket over the side then, assuming Kaufmann could afford it, threw the bucket overboard. The only remaining evidence of her clandestine operation was two pieces of paper toweling covered with wet nitrogen triiodide. Ana had special plans for their disposal—one would go into the port side forward ventilation duct and the other into the starboard duct. These were tuba-shaped stainless steel tubes arched at the top like a walking cane to keep out rainwater. The rainwater it did keep out, but it did nothing to prevent Ana from inserting the nitrogen triiodide over the arch where it fell into the depths of the ventilation system.

Ana walked slowly toward the stern. She was in no hurry. It would take twenty or thirty minutes for the powder to dry. The compound was stable while wet. As it dried, it would become highly explosive and extremely unstable. The touch of a feather or a gust of wind could detonate the explosive; at least that's what the textbooks said. Ana assumed there would be enough vibration in the boat to detonate the powder as it dried. If it would gradually detonate as it dried, it would give off a series of small firecracker-size bangs instead of one large explosion. That was how a friend of hers had described the drying process. The noise would resonate throughout the ventilation system. The fact that it gave off a noxious purple vapor of iodine wouldn't hinder the expected hysteria.

***

Lamar Kaufmann was still in his office when he heard the noise. It was distant and indistinct, to be sure, but a definite popping sound. He was prepared to ignore it when his phone rang.

Kaufmann picked up the phone. "Kaufman here."

Kaufmann's muscles tensed as he listened to the phone. There were reports of gunfire in the forward compartments. They had yet to localize it. It could be nothing more than a TV western with the volume turned up. Just the same, he didn't take such reports lightly.

"Where's Ana?" he asked. "Let me know if she leaves her room."

Kaufmann hung up the phone, turned off his computer, and headed out the door. He pulled the door shut behind him—it would self-lock.

Ana waited a full minute after she heard the door close before she stepped out of the broom closet just down the hall from Kaufmann's office. The chemical reaction started sooner than she had anticipated. For the next few minutes, attention would be focused on the forward sections of the ship. That was all the time she needed. Ana pushed on Kaufmann's door. It opened without further encouragement. She removed the toilet paper from the door latch hole and shut the door behind her.

The computer was top of the line Dell, but several years old. Ana turned it on and entered *LKaufmann* in the user ID box. She typed in *Topdog* for the password, and a list of files immediately presented as expected. Searching through Kaufmann's desk drawers, Ana found a blank recordable CD and slipped it into the CD drive. There were too many files to copy all of them. She would have to be selective. She opened a file labeled *personal finance* containing quarterly reports from offshore bank accounts. Kaufmann had been right. His worth was in the billions. Ana downloaded the file to the CD. Other files listed weapon sales to emerging nations and prominent terrorists. He was selling arms to both sides of many conflicts. He didn't let political considerations interfere with making a fast buck. There were dealings with some of the drug cartels, but this was a small fraction of his business. Separate files listed spreadsheets for each of his four gambling casinos. Ana wasn't much of an accountant, but it appeared Kaufmann was laundering a lot of the dirty money through his casinos. She assumed these records wouldn't match the records proudly displayed for the Internal Revenue Service. Ana hit the download button.

Ana scanned the rest of the files while she waited for the selected documents to download. There wasn't room on the CD for more files. She opened a filed labeled personal health. It had a report of a physical exam from Mayo Clinic. Unfortunately, Kaufmann was in perfect health. She pulled up a lab report, a CBC. That was also disgustingly normal. The file was a JPEG file scanned from the original report. With nothing better to do while she waited for her files to download, Ana opened the Microsoft Paint program that came with Windows XP and loaded the CBC file. She erased the 8,500 white blood cell count and replaced it with 52,000. She decreased the percent neutrophils from 65 to 25 and increased the percent lymphocytes from 30 to 70. She saved the altered lab report to its original file. She felt better now that Kaufmann had a severe case of Chronic Lymphocytic Leukemia.

Ana returned to the main screen where a horizontal thermometer was marking off the percent of the downloaded files. Like the watched pot, it didn't seem eager to reach its goal. Ana looked at her watch. She had spent fifteen minutes in Kaufmann's office. Time was a precious commodity. It was a matter of time before Kaufmann checked her room. A CD playing in the background wouldn't fool them for long. They would find her missing and the hunt would be on. Kaufmann's office would be one of the first places they would look. When they found her, they would destroy all the data she had collected. Even worse, they might decide she knew too much. She was already dead as far as the rest of the world was concerned. There was no additional penalty for killing her twice. She looked at the computer screen: It was seventy-five percent complete.

***

When Kaufmann arrived at the bow of the ship, the gunfire was obvious. It wasn't a full-blown shoot-out, only one shot every one or two minutes, but it was unmistakably gunfire. Several of his security men were standing around with pistols drawn.

"Break out the M-16s," Kaufmann said. "I want every man armed with a rifle."

Kaufmann listened to the latest gunshot, trying to determine which direction it was coming from. It was difficult to tell, as the sound appeared to be coming from the ventilation system that connected all the rooms. The intruders could be anywhere.

Kaufmann turned to one of the security men. He had a two-way radio and appeared to be the man in charge in Riviera's absence. "We have any idea how many we're up against?" Kaufmann asked.

"I haven't heard of any visual contact yet, but I haven't had a chance to talk to all of my men. They're obviously shooting at someone. When everyone is armed with M-16's, we'll do a room-to-room search. The ventilation system is distorting the sound, but we'll still get them."

"Is Ana in her room?" Kaufmann asked.

The security officer spoke into his two-way radio before he replied. "She's still in her room, sir."

"Good, let me know if she so much as puts a foot outside her room."

"Yes, sir."

"Are the bridge and engine room secure?"

"Yes, sir. That was our first priority."

As the men with M-16s began to accumulate, Kaufmann sent them off in various directions for a room-to-room search. Over the years, Kaufmann had made his share of enemies. Any number of them were capable of a commando raid on his ship.

"What's going on?" Dr. Mason asked. He was wearing a green terry cloth bathrobe over his striped pajamas. Slippers covered his feet. He had already turned in for the night.

"Gunfire," Kaufmann explained. "We may have commandos onboard."

More popping noises echoed from the ventilation system. A fine purple mist flowed from one of the vents.

"Have you seen any commandos?"

"Not yet," Kaufmann replied.

"Any smell of ammonia?"

"No, not as far as I know."

"Excuse me, sir," the security officer said. "Several of the men did report smelling ammonia."

Kaufmann turned to Dr. Mason. "What are you thinking?"

"I'm thinking tomorrow when I take inventory of my chemical stock, I'll find a jar of my iodine crystals is missing. I'm going back to bed."

"Ana? You saying Ana's behind this?"

"Nitrogen triiodide…it's an old chem. 101 prank. I think she's just getting back at you. For the most part, it's quite harmless. Talk to you in the morning." Mason headed back to his room.

Kaufmann pointed to two of the men standing around with M-16s. "You two, follow me."

Kaufmann led the two men down the corridor toward Ana's room, stopping just outside Ana's door. Sally was singing *Lady Margaret*. Kaufmann knocked on the door. There was no response. He again beat on the door. When there was still no response, the two security men positioned themselves on either side of Ana's door. On a signal from Kaufmann, they opened the door and barged in, each armed guard covering half of the room. Ana was seated in a recliner reading from a book of Ralph Waldo Emerson's poems and munching on a bag of microwave popcorn. In the background, Sally Rogers was now singing *Where the Coho Flash Silver*. On Ana's small range, a teakettle was whistling.

"Don't you guys ever knock?" Ana asked, pretending she hadn't heard them knocking.

"You been in your room all evening?"

Ana lifted up her pant leg to show Kaufmann her tether. "You should know the answer to that as well as I would. Would you guys care for some tea? I have some water boiling. If you don't have anything better to do tonight, the four of us could play a bit of bridge."

There was no doubt in Kaufmann's mind that Ana was responsible for the evening's entertainment. He didn't know how, but she had to have done it. He would have the Spaniard deal with her in the morning.

After Kaufmann and his entourage departed, Ana held Sally Rogers' CD over the teakettle until the label peeled off. She placed the label on the CD of the Kaufmann files and added it to her CD collection. Tomorrow, Sally Rogers' *Unclaimed Pint* would get a sea burial, with full honors of course.

Ana was eating breakfast the following morning when the Spaniard burst through the door. He hadn't bothered to knock.

"Let me see your ankle."

Ana purposefully lifted the left pant leg.

"The other ankle."

The Spaniard checked the tether and strap, finding no evidence of tampering. He held a receiver beside the tether. The tether was transmitting perfectly. Then Ana felt a slight jab in the small of her back. She tightened her muscles, knowing what was to follow. Her back arched as forty-five hundred volts of electricity pulsed through her back. Her diaphragm went into spasm, momentarily preventing inspiration as if someone had hit her in the stomach.

"Can't I leave for a few days without you getting into trouble? You'll find people aboard this ship don't have a sense of humor for your practical jokes. In the future, we will no longer need your services in the laboratory. Consider it off limits. Furthermore, there will be a guard outside your door at all times. If you leave your room, you better have a good reason. When you do, the guard will be at your side. Any questions?"

"Does this mean I'm no longer on your Christmas list?"

11

Ana spent the following months confined to her room, venturing out only to the ship's library or occasionally to the outside deck for a view of the ocean, always in the accompaniment of a guard. The ocean view never changed, and the trips to the library provided minimal reprieve from her boredom. For someone addicted to cerebral stimulation, the daily routine became unbearable.

The library, large for the size of the ship, lacked even the most rudimentary books on nuclear physics and the physical sciences; but under Dr. Mason's guidance, it was well stocked in medical textbooks and journals, giving Ana something of substance to pique her interest. The ineluctable changes occurring within her belly now dominated her thoughts and had redirected her interests from the physical sciences to the biological. Ana began her study with *Guyton's Medical Physiology*. Finding *Gray's Anatomy* too detailed even for her, she committed to memory only the basics. Her knowledge in biochemistry was already substantial. Pharmacology she found informative, but she reserved her real interest for obstetrics and pediatrics. Those texts she read cover-to-cover. Knowledge was power and when the inevitable confrontation took place, she had no intention of being powerless.

Her belly had begun to swell, and the fluttering gas sensation she now recognized as forceful kicks from her unborn son. Previously, her desire to keep the child had been strictly academic, a matter of ownership. Now, a maternal attachment was developing, a biological bond. This was her baby, hers and Dorek's. Her resolve to keep the child only strengthened with each passing month.

Despite considerable thought on the subject, Ana could find no way to escape from the *Chimera*. She was stranded in a castle surrounded by a thousand-mile-wide moat. She did have her Prince Charming, but he thought she was dead. Everyone thought she was dead. There would be no outside intervention. No Russian commandos storming the ship in the dead of night to set her free. Her fate was out of her control.

Several months earlier, during a moonless night, the *Chimera* had slipped through the Straits of Gibraltar. The only knowledge Ana had of this event came from the ever-changing clocks. She had awakened more than once to find the ship's clocks set back an hour. From the best Ana could figure, they were now in what Americans called the Eastern Time Zone. They were somewhere off the coast of America. She tried to estimate her latitude with a homemade sextant constructed from a plastic protractor, but the error was too great. It placed her anywhere from New Jersey to Virginia, not that it seemed to matter. The *Chimera* had no real destination. It cruised up and down the American coast, always staying beyond the twelve-mile territorial jurisdiction. With no particular destination, the *Chimera* only made speed sufficient for steerage.

During the eight months Kaufmann had confined Ana on the *Chimera*, the ship had yet to make port. Every two or three weeks, a tanker would pull alongside and transfer fuel. Other ships provided pallets of food and other perishables. The staff, which wasn't insignificant in number, worked thirty-day shifts, another reason for traveling close to the coast where ferryboats could sail out to rotate workers. Kaufmann, Riviera, and others in the privileged class transferred to shore and back by helicopter. The *Chimera* was a city unto itself and totally self-sufficient.

It would soon become a hospital as well. Ana didn't think she could get much bigger. She rubbed her swollen belly, which she now viewed with pride. Her best estimate was less than a month. The ship's infirmary was equipped for emergencies and the occasional illness, but not for obstetrics. That was another source of concern. As far as she knew, there was no nursing staff, no incubators for a newborn. And what if she were to require a C-section? She had brought those concerns to Dr. Mason's attention on several occasions and had been informed those concerns would be addressed at the appropriate time.

It was two weeks from her due date when she heard the knock on the door. She rolled over in bed to view her alarm clock. It was two in the morning, not the time of the day for entertaining guests. Ana placed the spare pillow over her head to drown out the noise, although she could still hear the insouciant interloper knock twice more. Whoever was looking for a party had obviously come to the wrong apartment. Then the door opened, and the lights came on. Her uninvited guests were making themselves at home. If they were burglars, she hoped they didn't find the summer sausage in the fridge. That was the only item she had of value. Her bedroom light came on next.

"Wake up, sleepy head. It's morning, time to rise and shine." It was the Spaniard, and he was in a disgustingly cheerful mood.

"It's two o'clock in the morning!"

"That's what I said, it's morning. We're going for a boat ride."

"We're already riding on a boat."

"This is a ship. We're going on a boat. Give me your right foot."

Ana placed both pillows over her head. She was tempted to give him the foot, but he might not like where she would put it.

The Spaniard grabbed her right foot and inserted a key into the black box of her tether. The strap fell free. "Someday, when this is all over, you'll have to explain how you did it."

"Did what?"

"Got the tether off."

"It wouldn't do you any good. I don't think you'll qualify for a tether program. I think you'll get maximum security."

Ana was now fully awake. They obviously had serious plans for her today. She would have jumped out of bed, except she was feeling like a bloated walrus.

"Pack some underwear and a few clothes. Nothing fancy." The Spaniard threw a duffel bag at her. It was hardly the type of luggage a lady uses to pack fine clothing.

"If we're going on a trip, shouldn't I at least see the travel brochure?"

"If you're not ready in twenty minutes, you'll be traveling in your pajamas. Pack some maternity clothes and some regular clothes. I'll be back in fifteen minutes."

Ana dressed and began packing clothes. Whatever they had in mind they preferred to do during the darkness of night. Obviously, it wasn't an activity approved of the Better Business Bureau. It also did not appear she would be delivering on the *Chimera*. She filled the duffel bag and was sitting in her recliner when the Spaniard returned.

"Let's go." The Spaniard picked up the duffel bag and headed toward the door.

"Wait. I need my CD's."

"Leave them. You'll be coming back. Where we're going, there'll be no place to play them."

Ana tried to think of a reason for bringing them, but couldn't negate the Spaniard's logic. Why hadn't she placed them in the duffel bag?

The helicopter was revving up its engine when Ana and the Spaniard arrived at the *Chimera's* stern. It wasn't using running lights. Apparently, they didn't wish to advertise the nature of their mission.

"In Russia, we call those helicopters, not boats."

"Did I ever mention you sometimes appear sarcastic?" Riviera set Ana's duffel bag on the deck, and a deck hand immediately loaded it on the helicopter. "For your information, the chopper is our transportation to the boat. It beats swimming in shark infested waters."

"I don't know. Sharks have better personalities. At least they're sincere."

The Spaniard strapped Ana into the back seat before taking his place in the co-pilot's seat. "We're waiting for one more passenger," he told the pilot. A moment later, Dr. Mason, with black bag in hand, took his place beside Ana. The helicopter lifted off the deck and headed west, skimming over the waves, well below any radar.

After twenty minutes, the lights of a small vessel materialized on the horizon. The blinking red light at the bow and steady white light at the stern signified a moving vessel, not shore-based lights. The helicopter pilot headed directly toward it.

"That's the *Diamond Stud*," the Spaniard announced over the headphones.

The eighty-foot yacht slowly came into view. Light radiated from many of the round portholes in the hull as well as the rectangular windows of the superstructure. They obviously had nothing to hide. It was a classy yacht by any standards when not compared with the *Chimera*. The superstructure, newly painted in white, reflected the ambient light. Several masts displayed the latest in radar and other navigational equipment. At the stern, a floodlight proudly illuminated the Stars and Stripes, which fluttered in the gentle breeze. The posterior third of the craft had been reconfigured into a small helipad.

The pilot didn't turn on his landing lights as he approached the boat from the rear. The helipad was flooded with light making additional lighting superfluous. With little chop to the sea, he gently set the helicopter on the center of the pad. Conspicuously absent were the obsequious deck hands rushing to help the passengers disembark, suggesting limited staffing on the *Diamond Stud*.

Ana unbuckled her seat belt and tried to extract herself from the cramped helicopter cabin. In her present state of pregnancy, her high center of gravity precluded a graceful exit. Her feet reached the deck only with Riviera's assistance. Pregnancy wasn't as glamorous as portrayed by women's magazines.

"Follow me." The Spaniard picked up Ana's duffel bag and headed down a flight of stairs into the bowels of the ship. With nothing better to do at three in the morning, Ana followed closely behind. The corridors on the *Diamond Stud* weren't as wide as the *Chimera's*. She was now more sensitive to such inconveniences than she had been in the past.

The Spaniard opened a cabin door and tossed in her duffel bag. "This is your room. Unlike the *Chimera*, it comes with a lock on the door."

Ana noted it locked from the outside. The room was small: only a bed and a small desk with a gooseneck lamp. It did have a window, a round porthole that was too small to crawl though even in her non-pregnancy state.

"If you need anything, Dr. Mason's cabin is next door and I'm across the hall."

"How about a bathroom? My bladder's not as big as it once was."

"We share the bathroom. It's at the end of the corridor. I suggest you use it now. There's a bedpan in your room for use during the night when your door is locked."

Ana used the facilities and tumbled into bed, her youthful stamina replaced by the watermelon in her belly.

She awoke the following morning with a backache, another reminder of her pregnancy. It took a moment or two to assimilate her new surroundings into her consciousness, the events of the night still hazy in her memory. The sun was streaming through her porthole. She actually had a window to the outside world, something that had been lacking on the *Chimera*. Looking out the window Ana saw land with green trees and brightly painted houses. Freighters and ore boats were steaming past on a regular basis. Ana tried to open her window for an unobstructed view but found it had been welded shut. The weld was new, no doubt in her honor.

Still dressed in the clothes from the night before, Ana surveyed her surroundings. With no shower or bathroom, it was rather Spartan compared to the *Chimera*. She did have a plastic bedpan. She had been hoping that had been part of a fiendish nightmare. There was no TV or kitchenette, only a bed and desk, but she was sure there would be a Gideon Bible in the desk drawer. It was a place to sleep, nothing more.

Ana tried the door, finding it locked. The sight of the bedpan stimulated her basic biological urge, which she would soon have to address. It didn't take much with her diminished bladder. Hearing noise in the corridor outside her room, she knocked on the door, hoping for an alternative to the bedpan.

"Good, you're up," the Spaniard said as he opened the door. He was wearing a black sweatshirt and camouflaged fatigue pants with cargo pockets. "It's time for breakfast."

"No, it's time for the bathroom."

"You remember where it is?"

"Pregnant women don't forget such things. It's at the end of the corridor."

"I'll be waiting outside the door."

"Wow, what a gentleman."

Ana, not having paid much attention to the bathroom the previous night, now examined it in detail. The room was immaculate. Someone had spent considerable time keeping it clean. There was a sink with large mirror and a walk-in shower. A round window provided a view out the other side of the ship and actually opened. Even more surprising was the view. There was also land on this side of the ship. They had to be in a channel or river. Ana wondered if anyone would take seriously a note in a bottle. If it would help, she could write it in six languages. She decided they wouldn't, although she wasn't above giving it a try if she had pencil and paper along with a watertight bottle.

"You about done? A whole platoon of men could have peed in the pot in this amount of time."

"Women take longer." Ana decided to finish her business before her guardian angel decided to bust through the door.

"It's about time," Riviera said when Ana opened the door. "You ready for breakfast?"

"Where are we?"

"Let's discuss that over eggs and hash browns. I'm hungry."

Ana followed the Spaniard into a small dining room with two tables—definitely not the cafeteria on the *Chimera*. Riviera grabbed a tray at the front of the serving line. Ana did likewise.

"You going to tell me where we are?"

Riviera grabbed a plate with eggs-over-easy and hash browns. Ana did the same, and they headed toward a table.

"Ana, I haven't even started to eat, and you've already given me heartburn."

"I believe you need a heart for that. Now are you going to tell me where we are, or do I have to break out the chemistry set?"

"In the future, your chemistry set will be limited to hair shampoo and body soap. Hopefully, you won't be able to make that explode. And as to where we are... During the night, we entered the St. Lawrence Seaway. The land you see on both sides of the boat is Canada. By evening you'll have Canada on your starboard side and the United States on your port side."

"I assume there is a logical reason for what's going on?"

"It's spring. We thought you might enjoy a scenic tour of the Great Lakes."

"That'll give me something to write home about. Can you point me toward the post office?"

"We do have a few rules aboard the *Diamond Stud*."

"Party pooper."

"I'll be your escort any time you're outside your cabin. When you're in your cabin, the door will be locked. Most of the time you'll be allowed to move around the boat, but when we're close to land or when other boats are passing close by, you'll be confined to your cabin. The *Diamond Stud* left from an American port, and we are returning to an American port. We, therefore, don't expect to go through customs. If the Coast Guard wishes to board, you'll be heavily sedated—with or without your cooperation. In your current condition and with your personal doctor at your side, I don't think they'll question it."

"It'll be all over if the Coast Guard asks for identification. I wasn't expecting to travel. I'm afraid I left my passport back at the dacha on the Black Sea."

"You worry too much, Ana. We found your passport." Riviera pulled a passport out of the cargo pocket of his fatigue pants and opened it up.

Ana looked at the passport. The name on the passport was Cordelia Kaufmann, but the picture was hers. It was the picture the Beckford Corporation had taken at her interview. They thought of everything.

Riviera flipped through some of the pages showing stamps from various countries. "See, you're a world-class traveler."

"Can I see that?" Ana reached for the passport, but the Spaniard pulled it back.

"You can see it from a distance. It takes over a month to make a good forgery like this. I don't want you tearing it up."

True to his word, the Spaniard was Ana's constant companion over the following four days. Ana spent most of her time sunning herself on a deck lounge chair with the Spaniard at her side. Unlike the *Chimera*, there wasn't much to do on the *Diamond Stud*. Del Kaufmann had left a box of paperback novels, but Ana had no interest in the sexploits of nurses at Doctor's Hospital. As Riviera had suggested, the Canadian scenery was magnificent. She would have enjoyed traversing the locks. Unfortunately, these events were viewed from the porthole of her cabin. Traveling through the

St. Lawrence Seaway on the *Diamond Stud* provided a plethora of escape possibilities for the motivated hostage, but they all required a limited amount of freedom and privacy, both of which were lacking. On the second day, even the window in the lavatory was welded shut. If she had had access to a flight manual, she might have considered absconding with the helicopter lashed to the stern of the boat—assuming she could fit in the pilot's seat.

On the fifth day they passed through the locks at Sault Ste. Marie, Michigan and entered Lake Superior, the largest freshwater lake in the world. Up until that point there appeared to be a plan with a well-defined goal, like whoever was in charge had a purpose for their actions. Once they had entered Lake Superior, the *Diamond Stud* slowed to a crawl to conserve fuel. They wandered in small circles just offshore from Whitefish Point. They even slowed to trolling speed so Dr. Mason could try his hand at fishing. He caught two fair-sized lake trout, which supplemented their evening meal.

On the sixth day, the Italian helicopter pilot took off for the mainland. He didn't return until six hours later. On board was Lamar Kaufmann. Whatever was happening appeared to be coming to a climax. Ana assumed she was central to the plot. Her due date was only a week off. She could go into labor any time, and she had yet to see any plan for that event. They had spent too much time and effort to let their plan fall apart in the endgame.

Later that evening she was prematurely confined to her cabin, having been given the impression that a council of scoundrels was about to convene in one of the wardrooms with Kaufmann, Riviera, and Mason in attendance. She had no doubt she was somewhere on the agenda. Various scenarios came to mind. Up to this point, she had been of value. She was the surrogate mother. They needed her. This would cease at the moment of birth. What was to prevent them from tying her to cement block and feeding her to the fish? That would be the expedient solution to her existence. It would be convenient logistically, no need to transport her back to Russia. No questions would be asked. After all, she was already dead.

No verdict was handed down by eleven o'clock. Either the jury was still out or they didn't have the courage to notify the condemned. For the first time, Ana felt depressed. It wasn't for her, but for her son. What kind of a life would he have? True, he would never be wanting for creature comforts, but with a blond bimbo for a mother and a world-class narcissist for a father, there would be no nurturing. No one would be there to read him bedtime stories or kiss his skinned knee.

The following morning, Ana awoke with her customary back pain and full bladder. The clock on her desk said 8:30. She had slept longer than normal, a testimony to her increasing fatigue. Ana crawled out of bed and squeezed into some maternity clothes. Just to augment her misery, her baby gave her a swift kick. He had the potential of a good soccer player.

Ana rapped on the door to ring up the warden. There was no answer. Apparently, he wasn't in the cellblock. Ana crossed her legs to see if that would help—it didn't. She wasn't desperate enough to consider the bedpan, but it was getting close. Out of idle curiosity, she tried the door, finding it unlocked. It wasn't a major oversight. There was no place to go on a small boat, and she could see no land in any direction. If there were a way to take advantage of the situation, it would have to wait. Right now she needed to take advantage of the bathroom. The Spaniard was waiting for her when she exited the bathroom.

"Dr. Mason needs you."

"Tell him to take a cold shower."

"Must you always be so contrary?"

"Yes, I must. Junior's hungry, and I'm feeding him breakfast."

Riviera followed Ana into the mess hall. It might be a while before she ate again. Giving her time for a light breakfast wouldn't hurt their schedule. Ana ate two eggs, two slices of toast, hash browns, and two pancakes. She washed this down with a large glass of orange juice. She would have eaten more, had Riviera given her more time.

"Now can we go see the good doctor?" the Spaniard asked.

"Did we get a new doctor?"

Riviera, ignoring Ana's customary sarcasm, led her into a large wardroom. The chairs had all been pushed to the side. In the center of the room was a gurney covered with a sheet and pillow. Dr. Mason was checking the medical supplies scattered across the room. If they had wanted an onboard delivery, they would have fared better on the *Chimera*. The facilities were more suitable. Riviera led Ana past the gurney to a chair at the edge of the room.

"It's time we discuss our final plans."

"Then you do have a plan?"

"Are you familiar with Pitocin?"

"It's the trade name for oxytocin. Doctors use it to induce labor. Is that what Dr. Jekyll has in mind?"

"Dr. Mason is going to induce labor. When your contractions are significant, we will fly you to the Cade County airport by helicopter. It's just south of here and a few minutes from Tamarack Memorial Hospital. A private ambulance will take you to the hospital. Tamarack Memorial doesn't have an O.B. department per se, but they do have excellent physicians who are capable of delivering a baby in their ER. They also have a surgeon experienced in performing C-sections should that become necessary. We checked them out in advance. We will schedule the delivery for a day when Dr. Gillespie is on call. She's the best physician at the hospital for O.B."

"You're going to trust me in a civilian hospital?"

"That's a weak point in our plan, I have to admit, but you'll be well supervised. Now we need to have you lie on the table so Dr. Mason can start the Pitocin. I just recharged my cattle prod in case you should need encouragement."

Having no choice, Ana lay down on the gurney. If they were being honest, which was still in doubt, and they were transferring her to a civilian hospital, it might provide her best opportunity for escape. Establishing her identity while she and the baby were still in the hospital would force genetic testing. The burden of proof would be on Kaufmann and crew. Hospitals had large staffs. One good yell would bring any number of them to her bedside.

"Good morning, Ana. Pueblo explained Pitocin to you, did he?" Mason tied a rubber tourniquet around Ana's left upper arm. "We need to start an I.V. first. Then we add the medication."

Ana felt the needle enter her vein. Once the needle was well inside the vein, Dr. Mason slid a plastic catheter in place. This was hooked up to a liter of normal saline. An I.V. pump forced it in at precisely 100 cc per hour.

"Now I'm going to add the Pitocin." Mason injected the medicine into the I.V. tubing just above the portal to the vein.

"Isn't Pitocin supposed to be given as an I.V. drip instead of a bolus?"

Dr. Mason didn't need to answer. Ana's eyes were losing focus, and her speech was beginning to slur. Within two minutes, she was in conscious sedation and unaware of surrounding activities.

"We'll need Lamar's help on this," Mason said. "It'll take all three of us."

Mason attached the pulse oximeter and heart monitor while Riviera made the call. Kaufman avoided menial labor when possible, but the fewer people involved in the conspiracy the better. Kaufmann arrived moments later.

"Before we do anything else, we need to intubate her," Mason informed his co-conspirators.

Medicine was Mason's entire life. That was what he lived for. There were few areas in life in which he excelled. Medicine was one of them. Treating others as subservient students pampered his ego.

"Now I'm going to give her succinylcholine. That will paralyze her muscles and make her easier to intubate. The dose is point six milligrams per kilogram. I'm giving her forty milligrams."

Ana took a few deep breaths, and then her breathing became labored. Within a minute, she was no longer breathing.

"It paralyses the diaphragm. She can no longer breathe on her own. We'll have to breathe for her."

Mason took an Ambu Bag with facemask and pressed the mask against Ana's face. Her chest rose and fell as he pumped air into her lungs. The reading on the pulse oximeter, which had dropped into the eighties, now climbed back into the nineties.

Mason hyperventilated his patient for a minute in anticipation of intubation. When the pulse oximeter reached ninety-six percent, he inserted the blade of a laryngoscope into Ana's mouth with his left hand, pushing her tongue to the left with the MacIntosh blade. He found himself holding his breath. It was an old habit. If he were running out of air, so was his patient. But he quickly visualized the vocal cords. With his right hand, he inserted the endotracheal tube between the vocal cords and into the trachea. He removed the laryngoscope and withdrew the stylet from the lumen of the endotracheal tube. A few milliliters of air filled the cuff around the end of the tube, firmly sealing it in the trachea. Mason attached the Ambu Bag to the endotracheal tube and pumped air into Ana's lungs at the same time he resumed his breathing. The entire procedure took less than fifteen seconds.

Mason passed the Ambu Bag to Pueblo Riviera. "Here, hold the tube near her mouth. We don't want the tube to slip out. With your other hand squeeze the bag twelve times a minute."

Mason reinserted the laryngoscope into the oral pharynx. He could take his time now that Ana was intubated. Once he visualized the vocal cords, Mason passed the handle of the laryngoscope to Lamar Kaufmann.

"Pull up on this. Don't crank it back or you'll chip her teeth."

Kaufmann did as he was told, not that he cared about the teeth.

Mason attached a large syringe filled with Botox to the end of a short piece of I.V. tubing. At the other end was a 25-gauge needle. He flushed the tubing until he saw liquid squirt from the end of the needle. Using McGill forceps, Mason guided the needle through the oral pharynx. He injected a small amount of into the cricoarytenoid muscles bilaterally as well as some of the accessory muscles.

"What does that do?" Kaufmann asked.

"It's a neurotoxin produced by bacteria. It's used in weak doses to prevent muscle spasms in localized muscle tissue. More recently, physicians have used it to cosmetically relax facial muscles and remove wrinkles. In high doses, it can totally paralyze a muscle. That's what we're striving for. Ana won't be able to use her vocal cords for the next two or three days. After that, she'll be able to use them with extreme effort."

Mason withdrew the needle and removed the laryngoscope. "Now she won't be able to talk, but she'll still be able to whisper. You don't need vocal cords for that."

Kaufmann assumed there was more to the lecture, but his patience was wearing thin. "How do we prevent whispering?"

"We insert this thin plastic tube into the right cheek near the facial nerve." Mason held up the small tube for inspection. It wasn't much bigger than a needle "It's filled with medication that will slowly leak out and paralyze the facial nerve. She won't have any control of the right side of her face. Any whisper will be unintelligible. They once used a similar device for birth control. It was good for five years. This one's smaller. It's only good for a week or two."

Mason made a small nick on Ana's cheek with a number eleven scalpel blade and inserted the tube like a sliver. "It has a small metallic stripe so we can remove it under fluoroscopy."

"Now are we done?" Kaufmann asked. "I'm not good at this blood and guts stuff. Makes my stomach queasy."

"That's it. Now we start the Pitocin drip and wait for the baby to come out." Mason removed the endotracheal tube and hung the bag of premixed Pitocin. "She should wake up in ten or fifteen minutes."

"Call me when she comes around."

12

Ana awoke to a tempest of confused thoughts that made little sense in her partially sedated mind. Despite her fuzzy vision, she could see men moving about her in apparent random fashion. Her brain accepted their movements with apathy. The visual input was excess mental stimuli nudging her already overloaded neurons into regression. Garbled voices only added to her confusion. She didn't care. She wanted to sleep.

If it hadn't been for the throbbing head pain, she would have returned to sleep. As her mind cleared, she became aware of the pain in her throat. Through sheer willpower, she forced fragmented thoughts into complete sentences. She tried to remember where she was. Was this the *Chimera*? Above her, she could see an I.V. bag filled with fluid. A plastic tube connected it to her arm. The image, fuzzy at first, cleared and came into focus. She was on the *Diamond Stud*, and they were inducing labor. She felt a squeezing sensation on her right arm as Dr. Mason checked her blood pressure. A sarcastic comment came to mind, but when she tried to verbalize it, she produced a mildly audible wheeze. She tried again: not even a wheeze this time.

"Good, you're awake." Mason removed the pressure cuff from Ana's arm and the stethoscope from his ears. "You'll find you won't be able to talk. That's temporary and should resolve in a week or two. I injected Botox into the muscles around your vocal cords. The right side of your face may also feel strange. It appears you have developed Bell's palsy. I'm hoping that will be temporary, but I expect you will have to live the next week or two as a mute."

Ana again tried to mouth some words. She produced a breathy noise that bore no resemblance to words of any language. She tried to whistle, but the right side of her lip drooped, and she was unable to force her lips into an oval. Even swallowing was difficult and painful. As her mind further cleared, apathy turned to terror as the significance of her situation became more apparent. They had paralyzed her vocal cords. They had preempted any thoughts she had about calling for help in a civilian hospital. That had been her means of escape. They had thought of everything. She was always one step behind them, always following their game plan, always on the defensive.

"Well, Ana." It was Lamar Kaufmann. "You ready to deliver my baby? Dr. Mason informs me everything is working as planned. You should be going into labor anytime now. I have the helicopter on stand-by. We're just waiting for Dr. Mason to give us the word. Then you, I, and Father Ginatti will fly in to Tamarack Memorial Hospital."

Ana gave Kaufmann an inquisitive look, as much as she could with her paralyzed face.

"You haven't met Father Ginatti? He's our priest and close personal friend of the family."

A slender, but agile looking, man dressed in black with a clerical collar stepped forward. He had a dark tan and black hair— all except for a tuft of silvery hair on the left side. This has to be some sort of hallucination, Ana thought. There was no way reality could be this bizarre. It was like one of those stories by that American author. What was his name…Stephen King?

"We have been fortunate that Father Ginatti has been able to provide spiritual guidance following the car accident. You don't remember the car accident? It was the shoulder harness riding high on your neck that caused your vocal cord paralysis and possibly your Bell's palsy. That's how you broke your right wrist."

Anna lifted up her right hand for inspection—it was in a short arm cast. She couldn't even write.

"Having a baby can be stressful. We want you to know that either Father Ginatti or I—as your husband— will be at your side twenty-hour hours a day. I'm sure we can answer any questions that might arise. Father Ginatti has fabricated this most wonderful device in case we do run into any problems."

Kaufmann pulled a clear plastic blade from his shirtsleeve. Two wires ran the length of the material, ending in metal prongs that protruded out like a viper's fangs. The entire device was small and easily rested in the palm of his hand, hardly noticeable to the casual observer.

"I don't suppose I have to tell you what the wires are connected to. Both Father Ginatti and I will have these inspirational devices, but I'm hoping we won't need them. You won't be staying more than twenty-four hours. All you'll need is a small satchel of clothing. That's already packed. You will have your purse, of course, with all your identification."

Kaufmann opened a black purse. The metal trim was plated with real gold. It was unlike anything Ana could ever afford.

"I believe Father Ginatti has shown you your passport. In addition you have your Nevada driver's license." Kaufmann held out the license for her inspection. It likewise had her picture above the name of Cordelia Kaufmann. "You have two credit cards: a Visa and a MasterCard. They're both platinum, good for one hundred thousand, so try not to lose them. There is a thousand dollars in fifties and hundreds. Del likes the green stuff. You have some perfume—imported from France—and other female necessities. We'll help you keep an eye on the purse."

Kaufmann returned the items to the purse. "Ana, I know we've stretched the truth on occasions, but you have my word. When this is all over, and it will be in a day or two, you will be transferred back to Russia, and you will be financially rewarded beyond your greatest dreams. I can afford it."

Ana was no longer listening. Instead she doubled up as a cramp dug into her abdomen. It was as if her abdominal muscles were being twisted up and sucked down a shower drain.

"Are you having a contraction?" Dr. Mason asked. Ana nodded in the affirmative, but it wasn't necessary. Dr. Mason had delivered his share of babies before going into research and had seen that look before. He checked his watch. "Tell me when the pain stops."

Ana nodded again when the pain began to ease. If that was a sample, childbirth wouldn't be much fun. There was no way she was going to go through that level of pain only to give up the baby to the likes of Lamar and Cordelia Kaufmann. It might take time, but she would get her baby back through legal channels or whatever channels it required.

"I think we better fire up the helicopter," Mason said after the fifth contraction. "They're starting to come pretty close together. We can continue the Pitocin drip on the chopper and pull the I.V. at the airport just before the ambulance arrives."

Ana hadn't realized how late in the day it had become. When she stepped out on the open deck, the sun was setting in the west. She had lost a good portion of the day. It had taken Kaufmann and crew considerable time to do the devil's work. The blades of the helicopter were rotating in anticipation, but Ana had to stop as another contraction doubled her over. The Italian priest with a Spanish accent found a chair for her. He could be quite thoughtful on rare occasions. The thought of providing a chair would never have occurred to Kaufmann or Mason.

Once the contraction had subsided, Ana proceeded toward the aircraft. With no desire to deliver onboard the helicopter, she didn't wish to dawdle. Having qualified personnel attending to her would be emotionally reassuring even if she were unable to communicate her thoughts. The Spaniard strapped Ana into the helicopter, making sure the strap wasn't too tight around her waist. Maybe the priesthood was rubbing off on him.

Ana had assumed the Cade County Airport would be small, but she had expected it to be paved. It was nothing more than a field of well-mowed grass. Blue lights at its edge formally defined the runway. They had been turned on even though it was only dusk. At the far end of the runway, near a group of small hangers and maintenance buildings, were five single-engine Cessnas of varying vintages. This airport didn't have problems with aircraft congestion. Next to the airplanes was the flashing red light of an ambulance awaiting their arrival.

Dr. Mason removed the I.V. from Ana's arm as the helicopter approached the waiting ambulance. He placed the I.V. and tubing in a brown paper bag—out of sight, out of mind. The fact that Mason had induced the pregnancy was need-to-know information, and Dr. Gillespie and the staff at Tamarack Memorial Hospital didn't need to know. Such knowledge would only stimulate awkward questions that would be best left unanswered. This was to be a fast delivery with an even faster discharge from the hospital. All they needed from the hospital was the formal birth documentation of Lamar and Cordelia's son. An endowment fund for the hospital would be forthcoming, in the Kaufman name of course. What hospital administrator would tolerate inquiries concerning a hospital benefactor?

***

Dr. Carrie Gillespie was in the doctor's lounge signing charts when she heard the call.

"Tamarack Memorial, this is Cade County 202."

Gillespie looked at her watch: It was too early for a radio check. A Cade County ambulance had to be bringing in a patient. Being a small rural hospital, Tamarack Memorial didn't have dedicated emergency room personnel. Instead, appropriate personnel were pulled from the inpatient unit as the need arose. The inpatient ward clerk would be monitoring the radio and would answer by default. In this case, she wouldn't be given that opportunity. Dr. Carrie Gillespie was a hands-on physician who was never reluctant to take charge. They had a radio terminal in the doctor's lounge. She picked up the mike. The ward clerk would be listening in at the nurses' station.

"Cade County 202, this is Tamarack Memorial, go ahead."

"We are bringing in a twenty-three-year-old white female with a full-term pregnancy. She appears to be in the advanced stages of labor. Contractions are about three minutes apart. Membranes have ruptured. Vital signs are…"

Gillespie listened to the vital signs. The patient was stable. Since Tamarack Memorial didn't have an OB. department, most pregnant patients were evaluated and then transferred to a larger hospital for delivery. But if the paramedics on the ambulance were correct and the membranes had ruptured, this baby was coming fast. It wouldn't be the first baby Dr. Gillespie delivered in the ER.

"What is your ETA?" Gillespie asked.

"We should be there in fifteen minutes."

"We'll be ready, Cade County 202. Let us know if there are any changes in vital signs."

"Roger, out."

The ambulance was fifteen minutes away. When the patient arrived, the nurses and staff would admit her to the ER, place her in a hospital gown, and obtain her vital signs. That would take another ten or fifteen minutes. If they needed her sooner, the ER nurse would page her. Dr. Gillespie returned to her paperwork.

***

Ana didn't think the pain could get any worse. This had to be full-blown labor. The contractions were almost continuous. It felt like her guts were ready to rip open like a piñata; except in this case, the child with the baseball bat was swinging from inside. And the ambulance gurney wasn't the most comfortable bed. The attendant had placed her on her side to remove the baby's weight from her vena cava. That helped somewhat, but the gurney was too narrow for a woman in full-term pregnancy. To augment her misery, the sheet she was lying on was sopping wet. It was as if she had emptied her entire, pre-pregnancy bladder. That had to be her bag-of-waters. It was impossible for her bladder to hold that much fluid.

"Sorry we can't change the sheets," the attendant said, as if reading her mind. "It would only slow us down. The hospital's not far. We'll be there in a few minutes."

The Spaniard, a priestly wolf in sheep's clothing, rode shotgun in the front while Kaufmann played the role of doting husband in the back.

"You're going be all right, dear." Kaufmann took Ana's hand in his, but she pushed it away. She might not be able to talk, but at least she could reject his phony affection.

"The pain of childbirth can place a lot of emotional strain on a woman," the attendant explained to Kaufmann. "Any disaffection will be temporary."

A plethora of sarcastic rebuttals immediately came to mind. Forgetting her handicap, Ana tried to vocalize some of the more descriptive repartees, but produced only a few breathy exhalations.

It was a fifteen-minute ride to the hospital, but it seemed longer. Since she didn't hear a screaming kid, she assumed they made it in time. The paramedics opened the back of the ambulance and unloaded the stretcher in the presence of several dozen curious bystanders. Multiple comments were made, all in low, respectful whispers. Apparently, it was a slow day in the town of Tamarack. Excitement was savored wherever it could be found, and with the copious number of emergency scanners in town, it hadn't taken long for a respectable crowd to materialize.

The ambulance attendants pushed the stretcher into the ER waiting room and paused in front of the door labeled *Emergency Room*. It was locked. Since the hospital was small, the ER was opened only as needed. They had no full-time emergency staff. One of the attendants punched five, three, and one on the lock's five vertical buttons to unlock the door. Hardly the most secure lock. A nurse from the inpatient unit arrived as Ana was wheeled into the ER.

"You'll have to wait outside until we get her settled," the nurse told the priest and anxious husband.

"You don't understand," Kaufmann said, pleading his case. "She injured her neck in a car accident and can't talk. With her broken wrist, she can't even write. She has to be scared. She didn't get pregnant by herself, and she shouldn't have to go through the delivery by herself. I'm not leaving her side."

"O.K., but just the husband. Sorry, Father."

"That's O.K. I'll wait out here and pray for a healthy mother and child."

The nurse turned her attention to her new patient. "My name's Cindy. I'll be your nurse, at least until midnight." Ana judged her to be in her mid-forties. Her superficial friendliness belied her wealth of experience accumulated over years of nursing. She was dressed in navy blue scrubs. A stethoscope protruded from one of her pockets. Her nametag identified her as Cindy, RN, no last name. "I understand you're going to have a baby." Ana offered no reply.

Cindy helped the paramedics transfer her patient to the birthing table. Then she looked over at Kaufmann. "You say she can't speak at all?"

"The shoulder strap rode up too high and injured her neck. The specialists think it's only bruised and will resolve with time. Right now they want her to rest her voice. She shouldn't be encouraged to talk."

"Any other problems?"

144

"She broke her right wrist, a Collie's fracture I believe they called it. And she has a facial palsy. Otherwise, she is in excellent health. No chronic medical problems."

"We need to get you into a gown." Cindy covered Ana with a sheet and expertly removed Ana's clothing without undue exposure. When she removed Ana's panties, she lost her composure, but only for a moment.

"The baby's crowning. Page Dr. Gillespie. Tell her we need her in the ER stat." The command was devoid of emotion, a people skill Cindy had perfected over the years to avoid unduly alarming the patient. Her intent was still crystal clear.

The clerk, who had been filling out forms, dialed Dr. Gillespie's page number and left the oral message. Dr. Gillespie burst through the ER doors two minutes later.

"What's up?" Dr. Gillespie didn't need to wait for an answer. One look at the business end of her pregnant patient summed it up. She immediately put on latex gloves while the nurse and clerk helped her slide into a secretion-proof gown.

"Her name's Cordelia, but she prefers Del," the nurse said. "She can't talk."

The baby's head, already partially exposed, was in an occipital-transverse position, the most common presentation. It didn't appear unduly large. Hopefully, it would be an easy delivery. Some babies delivered themselves. The baby's head turned face down as it rotated through birth canal. Dr. Gillespie applied gentle pressure to the head. If the baby came too quickly, the vaginal wall would rip. It was a common occurrence and easily repaired; still, it was best to prevent ripping tissue if possible. Once Dr. Gillespie delivered the head, she suctioned the mouth and nose to remove secretions.

Dr. Gillespie placed slight downward traction on the head forcing the anterior shoulder out from under the pubic arch. After the shoulder was delivered, the rest of the baby squirted out. A technician drew a sample of cord blood before Gillespie tied and clipped the cord. With its source of oxygen now cut off, the baby made a few labored gasps, and then progressed into a forceful cry.

"It's a boy." Dr. Gillespie held the baby up for Ana to see. "Let the nurse clean him up, and then you can hold him."

She passed the baby to Cindy who placed him under a radiant heater and began drying him off. The mouth and nose were again suctioned. Once he was dry, Cindy placed the baby in Ana's arms. The baby's bluish extremities turned pink as its lungs increased in efficiency.

"It's a beautiful baby," Cindy said. "What are you going to name it?"

"Lamar Kaufmann Jr.," Kaufmann replied.

"It's not over yet," Dr. Gillespie told her patient. "We still have to deliver the placenta."

As far as Ana was concerned, it was over. She had her baby in her arms. Anything else would be anticlimactic. The baby's eyes were closed, and he was no longer crying, but his lips were working in a sucking motion. Ana placed her index finger in the baby's mouth and it latched on tightly, his tongue massaging her finger. Somehow she would have to keep this baby.

Dr. Gillespie kneaded the upper pole of the uterus with her hands as she placed mild traction on the umbilical cord. Within five minutes, the placenta separated from the uterus and fell into a waiting basin. It was far easier to pass the soft placenta than her baby, Ana decided.

A fair amount of bleeding persisted despite the passage of the placenta.

"You have some bleeding," Dr. Gillespie informed her patient. "I'm going to examine the vaginal wall for tears. This shouldn't be too painful."

Dr. Gillespie examined the vaginal wall for tears and found none large enough to require repair, nothing to explain the excessive bleeding.

"Your bleeding appears to be coming from the uterus. Not a major problem. I'm going to give you a shot of Pitocin. That'll help the uterus contract and shut down the bleeders." Dr. Gillespie walked over to a keyboard with attached flat computer screen. She was a fast typist, far more challenging than Kaufmann and Mason had been. Her password was accepted and a screen prompt asked for name of the drug and the dosage. She filled in the information, and a small drawer opened in a large cabinet of small drawers. None of the drawers was labeled and none had handles. Without the proper password, the medicines were secure. None could be removed without leaving a computer trail.

Gillespie gave the shot of Pitocin into Ana's left shoulder. "We're going to get a quick ultrasound to make sure you passed all of the placenta. That can cause bleeding."

"Before you go to ultrasound, we need your thumbprint for the hospital birth record." Cindy held up a formal-looking card. It had her baby's length, weight, and time of birth. There was also a footprint. It was so small. It was the first record of her baby's existence. "We need your right thumbprint next to the footprint. Cindy pointed to a thumb-sized box on the document. "It's a security precaution."

They finally screwed up, Ana thought. It didn't matter whose name was on the birth certificate. The thumbprint would be that of the biological mother. The thumbprint would be as good as DNA testing. Their elaborate plan had a flaw, a detail they had overlooked.

"Let me help with that," Kaufmann said. "I've done this before."

Probably once when he was arrested, Ana thought. He now plans to smear the print, but she would demand they repeat it until done properly.

Kaufmann took the inkpad and expertly rolled Ana's right thumb across the pad. Then, just as expertly, he rolled Ana's thumb across the birth certificate.

What is he doing? Ana wondered. Surely he must know it will be incriminating evidence. He can't be that stupid.

"You make such a lovely thumbprint." Kaufmann held the print up for everyone to see. There were no smears. It was a perfect print.

"Here are some alcohol wipes. It'll remove the ink from Del's thumb." Cindy passed several individual packets of alcohol swabs to Kaufmann.

Ana couldn't believe her eyes. As Kaufmann rubbed the alcohol swab across her thumb, he carefully peeled off a thin layer of latex. They had covered her thumb with latex, and she hadn't even known it. They had concealed the edges under her cast. They must have glued on the finger print the same time they casted her arm. There was no doubt in Ana's mind whose thumbprint was now on the certificate. That was why they picked this hospital. It was small, and they placed thumbprints on their certificates. It would hold up in any court. Any chance of getting her baby though legal channels was virtually nonexistent. A new wave of depression descended upon Ana. She had never felt so helpless and so alone.

The sonographer, a young lady in her mid-twenties, arrived to take Ana to the radiology department for her ultrasound. She must have been on-call as she was wearing jeans and a sweatshirt, not normal hospital attire. "Just stay right where you are. We can wheel you over on the gurney." She grabbed the foot of Ana's gurney and began pushing Ana through the double doors leading to the Radiology Department.

"Let me come with you," Kaufmann said. "She gets scared easily."

"You can help push the gurney."

The radiology department was located across the hall from the emergency room. It also had a combination lock with five vertical buttons. The technician pushed five, three, and one, the same as for the emergency room. Obviously, security at the hospital wasn't a major issue.

The sonographer wheeled Ana past two rooms used for general X-rays before turning into the ultrasound exam room. Except for the present company, the radiology department was deserted. Only the on-call staff worked this late in the evening. The sonographer slid Ana over to the exam table, sending a chill against the exposed skin at the back of Ana's peek-a-boo gown. All of this technology and they can't design a decent gown. Under Kaufmann's supervision, the sonographer placed gel on Ana's abdomen and probed with her transducer. The pressure of the probe against her abdomen was painful, but nothing compared to childbirth. Five minutes of poking and probing revealed nothing of interest. They returned Ana to the ER with a clean bill of health— at least as far as the ultrasound was concerned.

"I see you've survived the ultrasound," Dr. Gillespie said. "They aren't as much fun when there is no baby to see." Dr. Gillespie gave Ana another quick exam and found no new bleeding. "Looks like the Pitocin worked; the bleeding's stopped." She scribbled a few notes on Ana's chart that only a pharmacist could decipher and passed them to Cindy. "You can take them down to the floor. I'll stop by in an hour or two to check on them."

Cindy placed the baby in Ana's arms and pushed the gurney down the hall toward the inpatient unit. Lamar Kaufmann and Father Ginatti followed alongside the gurney. True to their word, they weren't about to allow Ana out of their sight.

"How many patients do you have in the hospital," Father Ginatti asked. It sounded like an innocent question, although Ana was sure the question was motivated by some ulterior need.

"We have twelve at the moment. The census is down."

"Any chance Del could have a room by herself? She's been through a lot in the last week or two. We would prefer to keep stress to a minimum."

"I think we can arrange that. No one's currently in room 124. If it gets busy, we might have to bring in another patient, but that's unlikely."

The room was no different than any other hospital room. It had two hospital beds separated by a curtain, providing privacy in name only. At the head of the beds were ports for oxygen, suction, and the call light. A small three-drawer dresser was at the left of each bed. A cheap visitor's chair completed the ensemble. Cindy did her best to explain the obvious.

"When do you think they'll be discharged?" Father Ginatti asked.

"If everything goes well, probably tomorrow morning when Dr. Gillespie makes her rounds."

Ana pointed toward the bathroom.

"You need to use the bathroom?" Ana nodded in the affirmative. "If you have to go, we can try now. You haven't been on your feet since the delivery. Some people can become light headed."

Ana sat up on the edge of her bed, but felt no dizziness. Then she walked over to the bathroom without problems.

"There's a call light in the bathroom if you need help."

Ana stepped into the bathroom and shut the door. It was the first time she had been alone since she had awoken in the morning. She might spend a lot of time in the bathroom, she decided. With no real need for the bathroom, Ana sat down on the toilet lid to assess her situation. Any way she looked at it, the situation was bleak. Tomorrow after discharge, her baby would be flying to Nevada while she would return to the *Diamond Stud* and eventually to the *Chimera*. The farther she and her baby were separated, the harder it would be to get him back. It was time to go on the offensive, although no immediate plan came to mind.

The bathroom had a sink, toilet, and walk-in shower with stool for the unsteady. The hospital had installed a smoke detector and sprinkler system to discourage smokers, not that Ana had any desire to smoke.

"You OK?" Cindy asked.

So much for privacy. Ana flushed the toilet to maintain her charade. She washed her hands, dried them on paper toweling, and threw the toweling into the metal waste can.

"You're doing well for someone who just delivered a baby," Cindy said as Ana walked back to her bed. "That's the benefit of youth."

Ana pointed to the hallway and made a walking gesture with her left index and middle fingers. Knowing the layout of the hospital might be of value; although, at this point she didn't know what that might be.

"If you want to walk in the hall, that's fine, but you should have someone with you."

"One of us will be with her," the priest said.

"We do have visiting hours, but that doesn't apply to spouses or clergy. You may come and go as you please. If you have any questions, feel free to use the call light or come to the nurses' station."

Ana lay back in bed and turned on the TV with her remote. She found a channel she thought Kaufmann or Riviera might enjoy and then waited five minutes for them to get interested before turning the channel to a new program. At this point she savored small victories. After an hour even that was no longer any fun.

Ana got up and headed for the hallway.

"I'll go with her," Kaufmann said. They weren't looking for confrontations. She would have to press that to the limits.

It was approaching midnight and the hallway was deserted. The nurses had chased out all visitors at nine o'clock and most patients were asleep. The lights in the hallway had been dimmed. Ana walked past the nurses' station. The night shift had arrived, and two nurses and a clerk now manned the nurses' station. It was a skeleton crew, but not much happened during the night. If they were to get busy, others could be called in. The only evidence of activity was a cleaning cart farther down the hallway. The cleaning lady was in one of the rooms or on break, leaving the cart unattended.

The cart was laden with cleaning chemicals, brushes, and other assorted housekeeping tools. Ana checked them one by one as she walked past to see if any of them had potential. Except for one, they appeared useless. What caught her eye was the fine steel wool that the cleaning lady used to scrape up old wax and other undesired materials.

Ana walked ten feet past the cleaning cart and turned to head back to her room. As she passed the cart again, she pulled off a piece of steel wool with her left hand, rolled it into a ball, and placed it in the pocket of her hospital pajamas. Kaufmann was none the wiser.

Ana stopped when she came to the bassinet at the foot of her bed. Her son was sleeping soundly, unaware of the duplicity that had ordained his conception. She might have had no input into his conception, but she would provide for his future. She wouldn't abandon him to the likes of Lamar and Cordelia Kaufmann. She would have to leave him. In her heart she knew there was no other alternative. But she would come back for him. She wished she could tell him that. Ana pulled her son's blanket up closer to his chin. It wasn't cold in the room. It just seemed like a motherly thing to do. Ana turned so Kaufmann and Riviera couldn't see the tears in her eyes, and then she climbed into bed.

Ana lay quietly in bed. There was no way she could sleep. Patience is a potent weapon, but the most difficult component of any plan. Kaufmann and her friendly priest were taking turns standing guard. One of them was always awake when the other was grabbing some sleep. One o'clock passed, then two o'clock. There was no noise coming from the hallway. The hospital had shut down for the night.

Ana sat up in bed, which attracted Kaufmann's attention. It was good he was the one on watch. The Spaniard wouldn't be as easily fooled. Anna pointed to the bathroom. Kaufmann nodded his approval. Ana wrapped her bathrobe around her pajamas.

Kaufmann's became concerned when Anna picked up the hospital bag with her clothes and personal belongings. She pulled out her purse and extracted some feminine hygiene products that Mason had thoughtfully added to the purse's contents. It wasn't unusual to have vaginal bleeding following a delivery, Kaufmann decided. He offered no further protest when Ana dropped the purse back into the bag and headed to the bathroom. Assuming there was little she could do in the bathroom, Kaufmann settled back in his chair.

Ana removed her bathrobe and changed into her street clothes. If her plan were to work, she would have to work fast. She removed the stool from the shower and placed it under the sprinkler head. The chemical-filled bead that prevented activation of the sprinkler had to remain below 165-175 degrees Fahrenheit. The bathroom would soon be hotter than that. Ana wrapped toilet paper around the sprinkler head forming a large loose ball. It should provide adequate insulation from the heat. She could have totally inactivated the sprinkler, but she wanted it functional in case her plan got out of hand.

While still standing on the stool, Ana removed the cover to the smoke detector. A functional smoke detector was counter to her plan. She removed the nine-volt battery. With the bulky cast still on her right arm, she was amazed she could remove the battery without at least a small bleep from the alarm.

The wastebasket was metal, not plastic. That was good; she didn't need any toxic fumes. All she needed was smoke. Ana filled the bottom of the wastebasket with toilet paper and paper toweling. She retrieved the steel wool from her pocket, stretched out the fine threads of steel, and placed them across the terminals of the nine-volt battery. The fine wire immediately began to glow red like the filament in a light bulb. She held the steel wool in place with wraps of toilet paper. The paper began to smoke. She watched it smoke for a moment before gently placing the battery in the wastebasket and covering it with additional paper.

Ana stashed her pajamas in her bag, keeping the purse separate, and placed her bathrobe over her street clothes. Now was the crucial point in her plan. She turned off the bathroom light and opened the door. One small night-light illuminated her hospital room. Hopefully, Kaufmann wouldn't notice her shoes. He didn't appear too concerned. Just staying awake for the duration of his shift was enough of a challenge. Ana shut the door behind her and crawled into bed. Kaufman didn't notice that she climbed into bed still wearing her bathrobe.

More waiting. Ana waited five minutes, then ten. She mentally listed all the things that could have gone wrong. Maybe the steel wool lost contact with the battery terminals. Perhaps there wasn't enough heat to create combustion. She would wait five more minutes, and then check it out.

Three minutes later, Kaufmann began to stir. Ana wasn't sure if he had smelled smoke or was just trying to stay awake. A minute later he got up and walked over to the bathroom door. He opened it and was pushed back by a mild explosion. The fire had used up all oxygen, and the inward rush of fresh oxygen ignited the gaseous fuel sequestered in the bathroom. Smoke bellowed out activating the smoke detector over Ana's hospital bed. It not only activated the fire alarms in the hospital, it also sent an alarm to the local fire department. Other patients—at least those who were ambulatory—stepped into the hallway.

The fire alarms, at painful intensity, reverberated throughout the hospital. Patients in the hallway began coughing as smoke filled their lungs. The clerk and the two nurses pointed the ambulatory patients toward the far end of the hospital, away from the inpatient unit. With the meager hospital staff engaged in evacuating the bedridden patients, they would have to be on their own.

The confusion was just what Ana had hoped for. She grabbed her purse and ran for her baby, but the Spaniard had already scooped him up. That part of her plan had been a long shot. She would come back for him. Ana stepped into the confusion in the hallway. Patients, at the staff's directions, were migrating down the hall away from the fire and smoke. Some were pushing I.V. poles; some wheeling portable oxygen tanks; all were moving slowly. Ana squeezed past a patient on a gurney being pushed by the ward clerk. When she got to the head of the group, she broke into a run. It wasn't a fast run. The pregnancy and childbirth had weakened her too much for that, but it was still a run. She didn't look back until she reached the corner at the end of the corridor. A nurse coerced Kaufmann into pushing a gurney—it was hard to refuse such a request in a state of emergency. The Spaniard had his hands full with her baby. Neither of them had any chance of catching her now. She turned the corner and looked for a place to hide. An emergency exit would have taken her out of the building, but that wasn't her immediate goal.

Ana checked several doors, finding them locked. The fifth door was an unlocked dirty utility room. It contained three canvas carts on wheels, each one filled with dirty sheets and towels. She climbed into the cart farthest from the door and covered herself with sheets.

Ana lay in the canvas cart for two hours according to her watch. Twice someone opened the door and looked in. It had only been cursory searches. They hadn't bothered to check the laundry carts. She heard people talking in the corridor outside the utility room. From their conversations she assumed they were firemen. That ended an hour ago. It was now four in the morning. If she was to proceed with her plan, she had to complete it before the morning shift came to work.

Ana climbed out of the cart. At the back of the utility room was a large sink for dumping dirty mop water and washing out mop heads. Ana turned on the water and saturated her cast. Plaster doesn't hold up well in water, and the cast became soft and soggy. It easily slid off giving her full use of her right hand.

Ana opened the door and peered down the hallway. It was only partially lighted to save money during times of minimal use. It was also empty. She walked to the emergency room and listened at the door—silence. Punching in five, three, and one on the lock, she opened the door and walked in. The ER was minimally lighted, but that was plenty of light for Ana's needs. She began checking the drawers of which there were many. In one of the drawers she found what she needed, a two-inch-long needle and a large syringe. Another drawer contained alcohol swabs. Now was the real test of her memory. Dr. Gillespie was a fast typist. Ana still thought she had the password right. She went over to the drug cabinet and typed Carrie Gillespie into the user ID box. She typed in what she thought was the password. Seconds later a screen appeared asking for the name of the patient. Ana typed in Anastasia Petrova and hit return. The next screen asked for the name of the drug and dosage. Ana typed in acetylcholine chloride, 20 mg. One of the drawers in the cabinet opened revealing vials of acetylcholine chloride. Ana took several of the vials and signed off on the computer. The drawer closed.

Next, Ana crossed the hall to the radiology department. The same five-three-one code got her past the door. She needed a fluoroscopy unit. It worked like regular X-rays, but it displayed the image on a TV monitor. She lucked out. In the first X-ray room was a video screen. It had to be a fluoroscopy unit. The controls were labeled and self-explanatory for those familiar with electronics and radiation. It turned on and off with a foot pedal.

Ana lay on the exam table and pulled a lead apron up over her chest, exposing only her neck. Fluoroscopy was still radiation and should be kept to a minimum. She placed the foot pedal under her left calf. It would turn on when she pressed down with her leg. She filled the syringe with acetylcholine and cleaned her neck with the alcohol. Ana turned her head to face the video display. It showed the profile of her neck, but that was the view she needed. Her trachea, filled with air, appeared as a black tube under fluoroscopy. With the tip of the needle, Ana puncture the membrane between the cricoid and thyroid cartilages and felt a give as it enter her windpipe. Assisted by the fluoroscopic image, she guided it up and laterally where the thyroarytenoid muscle should be. When she felt the slight resistance as the needle penetrated into the muscle, she gently squeezed the plunger of the syringe. She backed the needle out and hit the muscle from a different angle. Using the same technique, she infiltrated the thyroarytenoid muscle on the other side with acetylcholine.

Ana withdrew the syringe completely and tried out her vocal cords. It was phenomenal. It was low pitched and breathy, but her vocal cords made noise. The facial paralysis made her speech garbled but it was speech just the same. She was about to get off the table when the fluoroscopy unit focused on her face. It was small, but unmistakable. She had a metallic foreign body in the right side of her face, just a thin stripe. As far as she knew, she never had an injury in that area to explain a foreign body. She viewed it from different angles; it was just under the skin. With the needle, Ana made a superficial scratch at both ends of the foreign body. It was located right over the facial nerve. It had to have some connection with her facial paralysis. The only way to know for sure would be to remove the foreign body.

Ana returned to the ER. Finding a set of needle-nose tweezers was more difficult than she had expected. It took ten minutes of searching through all the drawers before she found one. Finding a number eleven scalpel blade was much easier. The whole project was taking longer than she had planned and invited exposure. It had to be getting close to the morning shift. Someone could come through the door at any minute.

Ana slipped out of the ER in search of a mirror. She found one in the uni-sexed bathroom just outside the emergency room. At least now she was no longer out of bounds. With the door locked, she could take her time. The foreign body in her cheek was an unexpected finding. She looked in the mirror at the spot she had scratched. As she had expected, there was already a small puncture wound. They had to have inserted the foreign body that morning while she was unconscious.

With the point of the number eleven scalpel blade, Ana made a small stab wound, enlarging the previous wound. It was amazing how much blood a small facial wound can produce. She dabbed it dry with tissue paper and inserted the tip of the tweezers. She could feel the object, but found it difficult to grasp. On the eighth try she was able to capture it between the tips of the tweezers and extracted a one-centimeter long plastic tube. The tube wasn't much bigger than a hypodermic needle. Along the side of the tube was a fine metal wire, allowing visualization on fluoroscopy. It had to be a medical device. She wrapped it in tissue paper and placed it in her pocket. Three minutes later, she was walking away from the hospital.

13

Dr. Carrie Gillespie finished her dictation and hung up the phone. It had been a long night. Fortunately, the fire had been confined to the metal wastebasket, and no structural damage had occurred. Nevertheless, it had placed patients in harm's way. Only by the grace of God was no one injured. Since the battery in the smoke detector had been removed and the sprinkler head wrapped in toilet paper, it was clearly arson.

But it would never go to trial. Cordelia's husband had apprehended her not far from the hospital and, at the advice of his attorneys, was flying her back to Nevada. The expense of extraditing her from Nevada would be more than the county would be willing to pay. With Kaufmann agreeing to make good on damages and assuring Cordelia would receive psychiatric help, there would be nothing gained from a trial.

The real victim was Lamar Kaufmann Jr. He was the one Carrie felt sorry for. In her present condition, there was no way Cordelia Kaufmann could be an effective mother. Perhaps after therapy and with a lot of family support, she might develop into a caring mother. That was still iffy. And Lamar Kaufmann was a cold, calculating businessman. Maybe she was reading him wrong, but she couldn't picture him as a nurturing father.

Dr. Gillespie was reaching for another chart in need of a discharge summary when her office door opened and Cordelia Kaufmann stepped inside. She shut the door behind her. If Dr.

Gillespie was taken aback by Cordelia's appearance, she didn't let on.

"Good morning, Del. Won't you have a seat?" Gillespie motioned toward an office chair. "I thought you were flying back to Nevada."

"Who told you that?"

"Your husband."

"He lied...and he's not my husband. My name's Anastasia Petrova. My friends call me Ana. I'm a Russian citizen kidnapped by Lamar Kaufmann."

"You want to tell me about it?"

Dr. Gillespie listened like a seasoned psychiatrist as Ana recounted the events of the preceding months. The story was filled with delusions of grandeur and feelings of persecution. Cordelia was in need of extensive psychiatric help, perhaps even as an inpatient at a psychiatric center. A transfer to the psychiatric unit in one of the larger hospitals might be in order.

Ana finished her account and looked at Dr. Gillespie for any kind of reaction. "You don't believe me, do you? You think I'm lying."

"Lying is such a harsh word. I believe you believe your story. I think you may be somewhat confused."

"I'm not the one who's confused. I'm not the one who has been doing the lying. Kaufmann said I broke my wrist two weeks ago." Ana held up her castless arm. "Take an X-ray if you want. You won't find any evidence of a fracture. They said I had Bell's palsy. Have you ever seen Bell's palsy resolve so quickly? It disappeared two hours after I removed this from my cheek." Ana opened up the tissue paper revealing the small plastic tube. She placed it on Dr. Gillespie's desk.

"They injected Botox into my thyroarytenoid muscles so I couldn't talk."

"You seem to be talking quite well now."

"I counteracted the Botox with acetylcholine."

"What made you decide on acetylcholine?"

"Botox is the trade name for botulism toxin A, which is a neurotoxin. It interferes with the SNAP-25 protein and inhibits the release of acetylcholine in the nerve cells. It was just a guess that adding additional acetylcholine would counteract the Botox."

Her confabulation was impressive as well as sophisticated, Gillespie noted. Not only was her patient confused, but she was remarkably intelligent.

"Where did you get the acetylcholine? That's a prescription drug."

"I got it from your medication dispenser in the ER."

"If you had broken into that, an alarm would've gone off. The only way to get drugs from the med cabinet is with a password."

"I used your name and password. I watched your fingers when you typed the password."

"That's hard to believe." Gillespie chose her words with care. She needed to bring Del back to reality; but if done too quickly, it could invoke violent behavior. "I type seventy words per minute. No one can follow fingers moving that fast."

"I can. Give me a pair of double-digit numbers."

"What for?"

"Just give me a pair of double-digit numbers."

" O.K., twenty-three and forty-two."

"The product is nine hundred sixty-six."

Gillespie checked with her calculator—the answer was nine hundred sixty-six.

"Sixty-four and fifty-seven."

"Three thousand six hundred and forty-eight."

The calculator again confirmed the answer.

"One hundred thirty-three and five hundred twenty-one."

Ana paused for a moment. "Sixty-nine thousand two hundred and ninety-three. I sometimes have problems with triple digits."

"Not according to my calculator." Gillespie had never known anyone capable of performing calculations at that level in his or her head. She had to be a savant.

"I'm not an idiot savant in case you're considering that. An idiot savant is retarded in other areas. I speak five languages. I routinely do equations in quantum mechanics. I can program computers in three different languages. I play concert-quality violin. Is your computer connected to the Internet?"

"Yes."

"Do a Google search on Anastasia Petrova."

Gillespie typed it into the search box and hit return. The search returned several articles on nuclear genetics, all in Russian with English and French translations available. An Anastasia Petrova with expertise in nuclear genetics did exist. Whether or not the person in front of her was that person remained to be seen. The psychiatric diagnosis wasn't as clear-cut as she had earlier presumed.

"I could read the articles, but I doubt if I would understand them. I never did well in physics."

"Have you heard of Dr. Marsilius Rousseau?"

"Isn't he the Canadian neurosurgeon who was awarded the Nobel Prize in medicine a few years back? I think he's from Quebec."

"He works at the Montreal Neurological Institute. Give him a call. He'll vouch for me. I play computer chess with him. His number is 1-514-555-4873 extension 304. You might catch him before he starts his surgeries."

Dr. Gillespie reluctantly dialed the number and asked for extension 304. She wasn't sure what to say even if she reached Dr. Rousseau. A female voice answered: Dr. Rousseau was scrubbing for surgery. Could she take a message?

"Tell him the message is from Pegasus," Ana said.

Dr. Gillespie felt a bit foolish but relayed the message and left her phone number. She wasn't optimistic about Dr. Rousseau calling back. He was an internationally known Nobel laureate and an active neurosurgeon. It was unlikely he would find time to talk to flying white horses; but less than a minute later, the phone rang. Gillespie picked up the receiver.

Dr. Gillespie: *Hello.*

Man on phone: *Hello, Ana?*

Dr. Gillespie: *No sir, this is Dr. Carrie Gillespie, her physician.*

Man on phone: *Is Ana all right? I heard she committed suicide.*

Dr. Gillespie: *She's alive and well.*

Man on phone: *I found suicide hard to believe. She was always so upbeat.*

Dr. Gillespie: *Dr. Rousseau, the reason I called…Ms. Petrova put you down as a reference. Can you…*

Man on phone: *I would recommend Ana for anything she wants to do. You'll have a hard time finding anyone more*

*knowledgeable in any field. Don't tell her I said so, but she is also
a pretty decent chess player. Listen, I really can't talk now. I'm
late for my date with a meningioma I promised to take out. Can
you have her give me a call tonight? She knows my home phone
number.*

Dr. Gillespie: *I'll do that.*

"Tell him knight to queen bishop three," Ana said.

Dr. Gillespie relayed the message and hung up. Dr. Rousseau
seemed to think Anastasia Petrova was real. Ana, or whoever she
was, did present a strong argument with evidence to back it up.
Either this was one very sinister hoax or the woman in front of her
was the victim of an elaborate transgression in Machiavellian
proportions.

"Is that my baby's birth certificate?" Ana pointed to a pile of
medical papers on Dr. Gillespie's desk.

"Yes, I have his entire chart here. I have to do a discharge
summary on it."

"If you need further proof, give me an ink pad."

Gillespie pulled a black inkpad from her desk drawer and
passed it to Ana. Ana rolled her right thumb across the pad and
then placed her thumbprint on her son's birth certificate next to
the previous thumbprint.

"You saw me place both thumbprints on the certificate. Do
they match?"

Gillespie looked at the two prints. One was a swirl and the
other an arch, definitely not the same prints. If there was any
lingering doubt, it was now gone.

"Let me run this by Levi Stone. He's our county sheriff. Can
I keep whatever that is you pulled out of your cheek to show
him?"

"That's fine."

"Maybe I can arrange a meeting for the three of us. He needs
to hear all of this from you...are you going to be all right? You
have a place to stay, food to eat?"

"I have some money. I'll be O.K."

"How can I reach you?"

"You can't. I'll get back to you in a day or two."

Ana thanked Dr. Gillespie for her time and left the office.
She had little doubt the Spaniard would be looking for her. It was

time to disappear. For the next twenty-four hours the advantage would be hers; she would have to make the most of it. Kaufmann had returned to Nevada with her baby, and there hadn't been time to bring in additional help. Only the Spaniard remained, and he couldn't be everywhere. It was time for the fox to establish real or imaginary distance from the hounds. If she were to work with Dr. Gillespie, she needed to remain in Michigan's Upper Peninsula, but there was no reason she couldn't have the hounds looking elsewhere.

Being a small town, Tamarack had no formal Greyhound bus terminal. Tickets were sold at the local drugstore and passengers loaded curbside. Riding the bus would be risky, but so was hitchhiking. At least the bus offered the anonymity of a crowd. The Spaniard would find it difficult to exert force while others watched. She was young and attractive. He was old and had an accent. Yelling "rape" would quickly bring assistance.

Ana watched the drugstore from the gas station across the street. Once she was assured the Spaniard wasn't observing the drugstore, she purchased a one-way ticket to Chicago, paying with a credit card. She could have paid cash, but she needed to know if the credit card had been reported lost and the account canceled. She wasn't surprised when the clerk accepted her card. Kaufmann wasn't worried about losing money. The credit card provided a paper trail that was far more valuable than money. The paper trail now pointed to Chicago. She, however, would be getting off the bus during its stop in Marquette, one hundred miles west of Tamarack.

Ana waited in the shadows until the bus was about to leave. At one time she thought she saw the Spaniard drive by in a rental car. Tamarack wasn't a big town; still, there were many places one could hide. If the Spaniard were trying to cover them all, as she knew he would, he would be spread thin. As long as she wasn't too obvious, she would make it out of town. It would take an hour or more before the Spaniard had access to her credit card purchase. By then it would be too late for him or any of his hired hands to apprehend her in Marquette. She had no doubt there would be people waiting to welcome the bus when it arrived in Chicago.

The number on the side of the bus just above the door identified the bus as 1313—double thirteens. Americans find such numbers unlucky. Ana couldn't believe civilized people would skip an entire hotel floor to avoid using the number thirteen. Superstition was a sign of ignorance. She had little patience for such drivel. Ana showed her ticket to the bus driver and stepped onboard.

With only twelve people on the bus, Ana secured an entire bench seat for herself. She would have preferred more people, but the extra space had its advantages. Using her purse as a pillow, she curled up on the seat. Her body was weak, not only from the recent childbirth, but also from lack of sleep. Sleep came quickly. She didn't wake until the bus slowed for a traffic light on the outskirts of Marquette. Ana checked her watch: she had slept two hours.

There had been safety while the bus was in motion. The Spaniard had no authority to stop a moving bus. It was the bus stations she feared most. She assumed there would be a short layover in Marquette before the bus continued to Chicago. It was unlikely the Spaniard had time to react, but there was no need to take chances. She had underestimated the Spaniard too many times in the past. With access to a helicopter, it was possible he would be waiting for her at the Marquette bus station. Ana grabbed her purse and walked to the front of the bus.

"Excuse me, sir. How much farther to the bus station?"

The bus driver, a young man in his mid twenties, looked up at the woman asking the question. She was standing beyond the white line, but rules were made to be broken. Driving a bus for long stretches can be boring. A little conversation with a good-looking lady couldn't hurt. "It's about six more blocks."

"Any chance you can let me off at the next red light?" Ana smiled and looked him in the eyes, hoping American males responded to flirtation similar to Russian males.

"It's against rules, but for you I think we can make an exception."

"Thank you. I appreciate that." Ana exited the bus at a red light five blocks from the bus stop. If someone were waiting for her at the bus stop, he would be disappointed.

Ana's first stop was the U.S. Post Office. A bystander graciously provided directions. It was in the center of town, well within walking distance. Ana secured a post office box paying with cash. Since identification was needed, she registered under Cordelia Kaufmann, but mail would be delivered to her post office box with or without a name, giving her a degree of anonymity.

Her second stop was a bank. As luck would have it, a branch of the Wells Fargo Bank was no more than a block away. Not wishing to be seen in the open, Ana walked briskly, keeping close to the shop doors. If a motor vehicle were to act suspiciously, she could dart into one or the shops and possibly out a back door before her stalker found a place to park. Ana entered the bank uneventfully.

"Can I help you?" the bank teller asked when Ana approached his window. The name plaque by his window identified him as John Simmons.

"Yes, I would like to open a checking account and apply for a credit card."

Ana filled out the appropriate forms in the name of Cordelia Kaufmann, using her new post office box for a mailing address. Nothing would trace back to the real Cordelia Kaufmann. Ana returned the forms along with one hundred dollars from her dwindling cash supply to start her account.

"John, I don't suppose I could trouble you to call a cab for me?" Ana gave him her best smile augmented with her helpless female demeanor. She despised herself for dissembling, but desperation knows now boundaries. He made the call without hesitation. It would fall under routine bank courtesy.

The taxi dropped Ana off at the General Motors dealership near the edge of town. The lot was filled with an assortment of new and used cars. Placards on the windshields extolled the virtues of the individual vehicles. In the capacious showroom were a dozen more cars, all shinny and highly polished, each one the top of its line, but only one caught Ana's interest: the red Corvette convertible.

It didn't take long for a young salesman to take notice of his "mark." Although a pretty car, he had little doubt the Corvette was beyond the young lady's financial reach. He would steer her toward a more affordable car and still cop a fair commission. Single women were easy prey. They knew nothing about cars.

"Can I help you?" he asked.

"I'm looking for a car. This one is a pretty color. I always liked red."

"Five hundred and five horsepower is a lot of car for a little lady." The salesman gave his most charming smile. Typical of a female, she was turned on by the color. It was time to ease her over to something more practical, something in her price range. Red Corvettes were attractive, but too much car for a woman to handle.

"I believe you're mistaken. If you check the invoice you'll find this car has four hundred horsepower." Ana hated patronizing salesmen. He was arrogantly assuming only men knew anything about cars. It was time for an attitude adjustment. "You are aware the LS7 V8 engine only comes in the ZO6 model? Too bad they can't put it in a convertible. Convertibles, by the way, only come with the LS2 6.0 V8 engine, but it'll still produce 400 lb.-ft. of torque at 4400 rpm." Ana walked over to the driver's door. "Do you mind if I sit behind the wheel?"

"Sure, go ahead. I don't know if you noticed, but it has a price tag of sixty-five thousand."

"At that price does it come with a standard suspension or the Magnetic Selective Ride Control?"

"I'll have to check the invoice." To be truthful, he had no idea what the lady was talking about. "I have the documentation in the office."

Feeling chastised, the salesman headed toward his office to lick his wounds while Ana checked out the interior. Ana sat down in the driver's seat. The bucket seats were covered with cashmere high-wear nuance leather. They were quite comfortable, although she wondered if they would trap moisture on a hot day. She preferred fabric that *breathed*. On the dashboard was a GPS with a 6.5-inch LCD color display. The vehicle had a stereo CD player and MP3 playback with Bose premium seven-speaker sound. It was the car of her dreams.

"It has the Magnetic Selective Ride Control," the salesman proudly said upon his return, his manhood now restored.

"I'll take it. I assume you can have the plates and paperwork done in two hours?"

"I think we can have it processed by then."

"I'll also need insurance. I'm sure you're aware that sixty-five thousand is a premium price for this vehicle, and you'll be making a hefty commission. For that price I expect you to make arrangements for insurance. Have the papers ready, and I'll be back in two hours to sign them. Any questions?"

"What about financing? You'll need credit approval for a loan."

"I don't plan on financing it." Ana handed the salesman her platinum Visa card. "The card's good for one hundred thousand. I'm sure you can verify that in the two hours. Here's some identification." Ana gave the salesman her driver's license and passport. The salesman seemed impressed with the variety of stamps on her passport, although he remained skeptical about the limit on the credit card.

"If everything is as you say, we can have it ready to drive off the lot in two hours."

"How long does it take to get the title from the state?"

"Ten days. If you need it sooner, we could expedite it. The state charges extra for that. You could have it in two days."

"Do it. I assume you can cover the extra charge." Ana gave him her post office box number. "I'm walking over to the mall to buy some clothes. I have a MasterCard I can use for that. I'll be back in two hours."

She did need clothes. All she had was what she wore on her back. But new clothes would have to wait. Right now she was more interested in the Radio Shack she had seen advertised outside the mall. The mall wasn't large, but was conveniently located across the street. Ana found the Radio Shack in the center of the mail. It was a small store. Hopefully, it would have what she needed.

"Can I help you?" The sales clerk was in his early twenties. He was slender in build, short hair, and had dark rimmed glasses—a classic geek. That was good. She could communicate with geeks. They would know what she was talking about.

"I need a lap-top computer with built-in Wi-Fi card and an external antenna port."

"We have several that fit that billing."

The clerk led Ana toward the rear of the shop where several computers were on display. She would pay cash for this purchase. This time she didn't wish to leave a paper trail. The less they knew about her activities the better. Just the same, it would make a big dent in the thousand dollars she had in cash.

"I'll take this one," she said after reviewing the selection. "I'll also need a soldering iron, some solder, an N type female chassis-mount connector, wire cutters, duct tape, and a screw driver. And I'll need a pigtail connector with an N type male connector on one end and a connector at the other end that is compatible with the Wi-Fi card on the computer."

The clerk collected the requested hardware and tools without comment. To a true geek, the requests made perfectly good sense. Ana paid with cash and left with a sack of hardware and a laptop computer still in the box. She killed additional time eating lunch at a nearby Taco Bell restaurant. Americans had a nice variety of fast-food restaurants. She only wished she had more time to explore the vagaries of American life. On the way back to the dealership she passed a Holiday Gas Station with convenience store and picked up a can of Pringles Potato Crisps. She would need them later.

It wasn't quite two hours when Ana returned to the dealership. The salesman was accommodating and solicitous—her credit card had passed muster. The paperwork was in order, and after fifteen minutes of filling out forms and signing Cordelia Kaufmann in the appropriate places, Ana drove off the lot in her new Victory-Red Corvette. She was assured the title to the car would be in her post office box in two days.

Now she needed a place to stay. For security purposes she would have preferred a small motel on the outskirts of town, but she needed something tall. After driving around town and comparing hotels, she settled on the Landmark Inn. It was in the center of town, tall, and overlooked Lake Superior. It should fit her needs. She signed in under an alias using cash as a down payment. No one asked for identification. Cash has its advantages. The rest of the fee wouldn't be due until she checked out. By then she expected to have unlimited financial resources.

Ana unloaded the car and then parked in the city parking lot two blocks away. She didn't need any red flags parked in the hotel lot. The Greyhound bus would soon be arriving in Chicago. When she wasn't found on the bus, attention would revert back to Marquette.

The Landmark Inn was an old building recently refurbished to provide a unique combination of old world charm and modern-day convenience. It overlooked Marquette's lower harbor. The view of Lake Superior from the upper floors was magnificent, she was told, but she settled for a room on the top floor facing the city instead. Esthetics had to take the back seat to practicality.

Her room was plush by Russian standards, although it couldn't compare with her room on the *Chimera*. It had a queen-size bed, small desk, large dresser, and a TV. Overall, it was a charming room. At the moment, the bed offered the most charm. She looked at the bed almost with lust. The two-hours sleep on the bus was hardly enough to rejuvenate her mind and body. But sleep would have to wait.

Ana opened the Pringles can and dumped the chips on the dresser—she would eat those later. She washed the metallic coated inside of the can to remove any grease. The can was eight centimeters in diameter. According to her calculations, that would make the one-quarter-guide wavelength approximately nine and a half centimeters. Ana measured that distance from the closed end of the Pringles container and poked a hole through the side of the can. She now needed three centimeters of twelve-gauge copper wire. It was time for the Landmark Inn to donate to a worthy cause. Using her screwdriver, Ana removed the plate from an electrical outlet. American building codes required six inches of wire inside outlet boxes. Americans did everything to excess. This was more wire than needed. Avoiding the "hot" wires, Ana disconnected the bare ground wire and snipped off three centimeters before reconnecting the ground wire to the outlet. It would work as well as before. She replaced the outlet cover.

Ana soldered the twelve-gauge copper wire to the brass stub on the N-connector. Then she trimmed the brass stub and copper wire to three centimeters in total length. The length of the wire was critical. She inserted the copper wire end of the N-connector into the hole in the Pringles can and secured it on the other side with a nut. Finally she attached the Pringles can to the laptop computer with the pigtail connector. Her directional antenna was now complete.

All she needed was a Wi-Fi system with an open channel to the Internet. Ana opened the window overlooking the city of Marquette. There had to be Wi-Fi systems out there somewhere. She pointed the directional "cantenna" at the city below, slowly moving it back and forth. She found a couple of Wi-Fi systems, but the signals were too weak for her use. Finally, at the southern edge of town, she found a signal strong enough to be of value. She slowly rotated the can on its longitudinal axis. Since the antenna had linear polarization, the signal strength was dependent on the degree of angular rotation. When she had obtained maximum signal strength, Ana strapped the can to the windowsill with duct tape.

Ana could have used the complimentary broadband Internet access that came with her room, but there was a finite chance someone might backtrack her messages to the hotel. That possibility was remote, but it is never wise to underestimate your adversary. If they were to backtrack her messages, it would lead them to some unfortunate soul on the southern edge of town who would be clueless during an interrogation.

Ana typed in Dorek's Internet address and sent an instant message.

Pegasus: *Dorek, are you out there?*

Dorek, please be on-line. Ana waited for what felt like an eternity. Until now, she hadn't realized how lonely she was. She needed his response. She needed him to know she was still alive. If he wasn't on-line, she could try later. He spent a lot of time on-line. Sooner or later she would contact him, but she needed him now. If he couldn't hold her in his arms, they could at least communicate over the Internet. She could call him by phone, but she didn't trust phones. They were too easy to tap.

Apollo: *Who is this?*

Could this really be Dorek from thousands of miles away in Warsaw? She saw it on the screen, but it was still difficult to believe after all those months.

Pegasus: *It's Ana. I need your help.*

There was a long pause…He didn't believe her. He thought she was dead. Why wouldn't he think she was dead?

Pegasus: *It's the person who torments you with feathers.*

Apollo: *Ana, is it really you? You're alive?*

Pegasus: *No, I'm e-mailing you from heaven.*

Apollo*: Only the real Anastasia Petrova can be that sarcastic.*

Pegasus: *I need your help. Can you send me that computer program you used to hack into my computer…remember when you wanted to read my poem?*

Apollo: *I'm sending it to you in the background. Now tell me; where are you. What's going on?*

Ana could see a file being transferred to her computer.

Pegasus: *I'm in America. Can you fly to America? I need you here as soon as possible. I need your help getting our baby back.*

Apollo: *Our baby?*

Pegasus: *You have a baby boy, but it wasn't conceived in the normal manner.*

Apollo: *I'm not big on biology. I thought there was only one way to make babies.*

Pegasus: *Americans have a new variation on making babies. I wouldn't recommend it for the faint of heart. I can't be on the Internet too long. Please come to America. I can't say where I am, but if you register at the Landmark Inn in Marquette, Michigan, I'll find you.*

Apollo: *I'm packing my bags now. It still might take a day or two to get the flights. I love you.*

Pegasus: *XXXOOO*

Ana disconnected. She wasn't sure if she felt better or not. It only increased her desire for Dorek. One or two days seemed like a long time. Until then, she would be on her own.

It was now time to send Lamar Kaufmann an e-mail message. She had found his home e-mail address when she broke into his computer on the *Chimera*. She knew it would come in handy.

She sent two e-mails, labeled part one and part two. She explained in her first e-mail message that the bill for hospital expenses was attached. She didn't explain that a small virus, too small to be detected, was also attached and would turn off any virus scanner and firewall that might be protecting his computer.

The second message had an attached bill from the fire department along with a more complex virus. That was the virus that would allow her to sort through Kaufmann's computer files as Dorek had done with hers. She signed Carrie Gillespie, MD at the bottom of both messages.

With her work done for the day, Anastasia Petrova set her alarm clock for three in the morning and collapsed on her bed. It would give her ten hours of sleep. It was sleep she desperately needed. She could push her body no further.

Lamar Kaufmann was standing at the Chimera's stern, shotgun in hand, while the Spaniard propelled clay pigeons high over the wash of the ship's propellers. Each one was efficiently shattered by the blast from the shotgun. Beside Kaufmann, lying in a basket, was a newborn baby. Kaufmann nodded at the Spaniard and another clay pigeon winged its way into the sky only to shatter like the rest. Kaufmann nodded again at the Spaniard. The Spaniard didn't say anything, but gestured to the box of clay pigeons, turning the box upside down. It was empty. Kaufmann nodded at the baby. The Spaniard offered a protest, but Kaufmann again nodded at the baby. The Spaniard picked up the baby and prepared to toss it into the air. The baby cried out in fear. It was only a newborn, still, it cried out. "Mommy, help me." The words were in Russian. Ana tried to run to him, but her legs wouldn't respond. "What gives you the right to do this?" she said. "Money," he said. The Spaniard threw the baby into the air, and Kaufmann raised his shotgun. "Please help me, Mommy!" The shotgun's blast reverberated throughout the bedroom.

Ana awoke drenched in sweat, the room now dark. She looked over at her alarm clock: it was twenty minutes past two. She lay quietly in bed until she ceased hyperventilating; then she turned off the alarm. There was no way she would get back to sleep. She took a shower and dressed in the same clothes she had worn the last two days. When the sun came up, she would have to buy new clothes.

The shower cleared her mind, but it did nothing to resolve her anxiety. That would be alleviated only by action. It was approaching one in the morning Nevada time. Hopefully, Kaufmann would be in bed or at least not near his computer. Ana turned on her computer and was pleased to find the Wi-Fi system still functional. She typed in Kaufmann's e-mail address. An additional hard drive immediately appeared on her computer. She opened it: It contained all of Kaufmann's files, both social and business.

"Dorek, you're a genius," Ana said aloud. Ana went to the e-mail. Both incoming and outgoing mail was stored in an electronic file cabinet. Most of the mail was of no interest, junk mail at best. What she was interested in were the e-mails from the Spaniard. A welcoming party had been arranged for her in Chicago. They also knew about her Corvette. They had made a cursory check of local motels, finding no red Corvettes. This came as no surprise. They assumed the Corvette was for traveling, and they expected Ana to be hundreds of miles from Marquette. The Spaniard had urged Kaufmann not to cancel the credit cards, feeling that Ana's cash was limited and eventually she would use the credit card again. They assumed the credit card would be her downfall. They should give her more credit than that, Ana thought. They were seriously underestimating her.

What really disturbed her was the Spaniard's last e-mail. He recommended Kaufmann transfer her son to the *Chimera*, outside the United States jurisdiction; and Kaufmann had followed that suggestion. Her son was now on the *Chimera* heading for the South Pacific with the assumption that Asian countries would be less likely to extradite a baby back to the States. Kaufmann hired a professional nanny to care for the child. They weren't even planning to raise the child themselves.

Ana couldn't read any more of the e-mails. They only depressed her and added little of substance, nothing she could use to get her son back. Ana closed the e-mail filing cabinet and searched through the remaining files. This also proved to be a disappointment. There were files on Kaufmann's four casinos, but they provided no specific data. That kind of data must have been stored at the casinos themselves. All four casinos were heavily leveraged, financed at five percent through large commercial banks. As long as the casinos returned more than five percent on capital, Kaufman would have a tidy return on his investment. If he made less than that, his losses would be magnified. Kaufmann might find a future slump in the gaming business. Ana copied the files to her computer in case she was unable to return to

Kaufmann's computer. A fifth filed labeled B.C. Corp. had a few JPEG photocopies of documents from the Bear Cat Corporation. She had seen references to the Bear Cat Corporation on the *Chimera's* computer. The letterhead gave its address as Nevis, a small island in the Caribbean. Those documents were mostly administrative in nature and then only few in number. Ana copied the B.C. Corp. file to computer anyway. She signed off and went back to bed, still unclear of her next move.

Ana awoke just past eight in the morning. It was time for the fox to exercise the hounds. Over the Internet, she secured a room in a five-star, Philadelphia hotel with a six o'clock arrival, paying for it with Cordelia's Visa Card. The credit card wouldn't be debited until she checked out. The hounds would need a fresher scent than that. A little more searching on the Internet found a progressive pizzeria that allowed consumers to build their own pizzas over the Internet with a guaranteed four-hour delivery. She hoped the hotel desk clerk liked pepperoni and mushrooms. Within an hour or two, the hounds should be converging on Philadelphia.

That being done, Ana headed back to the mall in her Corvette. She needed new clothes and underwear, all paid for out of her dwindling cash. The purchase of a small suitcase provided storage for her clothes. On her way back to the Landmark Inn, she stopped at a McDonald's. She had always wanted to taste one of those Big Macs. She ordered the meal with fries and washed it down with a Coke. Dorek wouldn't show up for another day or two, and the title to the Corvette wouldn't arrive until the following day. With little else to do, Ana spent the rest of the day across the street from the Landmark at the Peter White Library.

Late that night she checked her e-mail—courtesy of Lamar Kaufmann. The Spaniard had taken the bait, but was, by the tone of his e-mail to Kaufmann, angered when the fox didn't arrive at the Philadelphia hotel at six o'clock as scheduled. The hounds spent the rest of the evening checking local motel parking lots looking for a red Corvette.

During the afternoon of the following day, Ana stopped by the post office to check her mail. Her post office box contained a letter from Wells Fargo thanking her for opening her checking account. Formal checks would arrive in seven to ten days. Until then she could use the starter checks. There were two letters addressed to occupant—it hadn't taken long for people to find her post office box. And then there was a letter from the Michigan Secretary of State. It was the title to Corvette and had come in two days as promised. Ana drove back to the car dealership, finding the same salesman on duty.

"How do you like your new Corvette?" he asked when Ana walked into the show room.

"I decided I don't like the color. I want to buy that used blue Impala you have for sale at ten thousand."

"What are you going to do with two cars?"

"I don't want two cars. I want to trade the Corvette in for the Impala."

That wasn't what the salesman wanted to hear. Trade-ins were supposed to generate money, not expend it. "You realize the Corvette is used. We can't sell it as a new car. The value has decreased considerably."

"The Corvette has seventeen miles on it. I'm sure you will still sell it as new—or at least allow the buyer to assume it's new. I purposely left the invoice sticker on the window."

"I'll have to discuss this with my manager," the salesman said.

"You do that. Tell your manager I want fifty thousand for the Corvette and I'm willing to pay ten thousand for the Impala, which is more than it's worth. You and I both know I can do better at another dealership if I'm willing to haggle. Fortunately for you, I don't like to haggle."

Ana checked out the Impala while the salesman discussed the situation with his manager. It was no Corvette, but it had cruise control, CD player, and antilock brakes. It also was less conspicuous than a red Corvette. The salesman returned five minutes later with a check for forty thousand dollars. Ana now had unlimited cash and an untraceable car. As far as the Spaniard was concerned, she had disappeared.

14

Ana pushed her tray down to the Bonanza Restaurant's cashier who rang up her shrimp dinner. She didn't normally eat much for lunch, but she was hungry. She paid with a twenty-dollar bill and waited for her change. The aroma from the steaks sizzling on the grill further whetted her appetite. She received her change and asked the cashier for directions to the back room. The cashier, a young girl in her late teens, led Ana down a back corridor to a dimly lit conference room. Dr. Gillespie and two men were chatting at one of the tables. The room was otherwise empty; one of the reasons the Bonanza Restaurant had been chosen. It was just past one o'clock, not normally a busy time of day. Both men stood up as Ana walked toward the table.

"Ana, I would like you to meet Levi Stone," Dr. Gillespie gestured to a man wearing a gray sport coat and light blue shirt. "He's the Sheriff of Cade County."

Ana estimated the sheriff to be in his mid-sixties. He was a big man, at least six-foot-two and about two hundred twenty pounds. Hopefully, he would be on her side; he gave the appearance of a formidable opponent—except for his eyes. He had grandfatherly eyes that generated warmth and compassion. Ana shook his hand.

"And this is Marshall Peterson," Stone said. "He's with the FBI. From what Carrie tells me, this is bigger than Cade County. I figured we should get Marshall onboard from the start."

Ana shook hands with Peterson. Like Stone, he was wearing a sport coat and tie, but his coat had a bulge just below the left shoulder. He had to be in his forties and appeared to be all business.

"Shall we sit down and attack the food while it's still hot." Stone was obviously in charge of the meeting. "We can talk between bites." Stone took a bite from his steak. His wife had him on a strict diet, making lunch meetings all the more enjoyable. "The story, at least as Dr. Gillespie tells it, is hard to believe on face value. I did take the liberty of running both thumbprints through the Nevada police records. One—apparently the first print—matches a print taken of Cordelia Kaufmann several years ago when she was picked up for DWI. There was no match for the other. That supports your story of a fake fingerprint. Dr. Gillespie will attest that you were the mother of the child and not Cordelia Kaufmann. The Nevada police send a picture of Mrs. Kaufmann. It was several years old, but Carrie will swear Cordelia is not the mother of the child. That's when I contacted the FBI." Stone looked over at Marshall Peterson. It was a subtle gesture that the floor was now his.

"I sent that small plastic tube to our lab in New York. They found traces of succinylcholine. It's used to paralyze muscles."

"We use it in medicine to paralyze patients during surgery," Dr. Gillespie said.

Assuming he still had the floor, Peterson continued. "It won't be any value in court since you took it out yourself. We have no proof it was removed from your face."

"Does that mean you won't help me? What about that wonderful justice system Americans brag about? Surely something can be done."

"You could take him to court, and you'd probably win. But Kaufmann's attorneys would file so many affidavits and request so many injunctions it would be tied up in the courts for years. By the time you win, your son will be old enough to vote."

"What gives him the right to do that?"

"Money."

"Where have I heard that before?"

"He currently has your baby. His wife's fingerprint is on the birth certificate in the appropriate box. Your fingerprint looks like it was added later—which is what happened."

"You make it seem hopeless."

"Look, Ms. Petrova, we would like to help, but I'm not sure what we can do. The central office has a three-inch thick file on Kaufmann. There is nothing we would rather do than sear his anal sphincter muscles over hot bear grease. We know he's into gunrunning—and not just small arms, and we think he's involved in the drug trade. If it's illegal and there's money to be made, he's involved. He launders the money through his casinos. Unfortunately, he's currently the CIA's Honey. That hasn't helped. He's also squeaky clean in the U.S. All the illegal records are onboard the *Chimera*, which flies under the Panamanian flag. Unless the ship comes within our legal boundaries, we have no jurisdiction. Some of the nation's best legal minds have worked on the case, but he's outsmarted us every time."

"If I deliver Kaufmann along with incriminating evidence, will you help me get my son back? Maybe he won't be able to outsmart me."

"If you could do that, our nation will be eternally grateful. We'll keep his lawyers so busy they won't have time to think of paternity suits."

"Ana." Dr. Gillespie said. "When I delivered your baby, I noticed a birthmark on his right buttock. If we can get the baby, I can testify that he's your son."

"The problem is getting the baby," Peterson said. "As long as the baby is in international waters, we can't touch him. If we could get possession of the baby and Dr. Gillespie identifies him, the burden of proof would be on Kaufmann," Peterson added. "We'll make sure his attorneys have plenty to do."

"What about the CIA?" Ana asked. "They won't interfere?"

"They'll get over it. They tend to be fair-weather friends. Panama's Manuel Noriega and Iraq's Saddam Hussein were also Honeys of the CIA. When the going gets tough, they'll turn on Kaufmann just like they did Manuel Noriega and Saddam Hussein."

"Mr. Peterson, how can I contact you once I have him gift-wrapped?"

"Here's my card. Like I said, if you can help us put him away, this nation will be grateful."

Ana left the restaurant with mixed feelings. It was nice to know others shared her antipathy toward Lamar Kaufmann. She was no longer alone. Unfortunately, her newfound friends were impotent, totally helpless to right the wrong. The American justice system, along with all their legal statutes, was powerless in face of Kaufmann's wealth.

Ana parked her blue Impala in the Landmark Inn's parking lot. With the Spaniard et al. combing the East Coast looking for a red Corvette, she could relax her defense. She registered under an alias. There was nothing to identify her as Cordelia Kaufmann or Anastasia Petrova.

Only a few guests were wandering the hotel lobby. Those who were leaving had already left, and those who were coming wouldn't arrive until later in the day. Several cleaning ladies were running hither and yon trying to look busy. A big burly man in a blue blazer smiled and tried to look friendly, but instead gave the impression he could hold his own as a bouncer in a singles bar. He had to be a house detective. Ana picked up a copy of the Marquette Mining Journal at the reception desk, paying the clerk with a dollar bill and telling him to keep the change.

She stepped into the elevator and punched the number of her floor. The elevator responded with a slight jerk before smoothly lifting upward. While waiting for the elevator to come to a stop, she scanned the front page, looking for any references to her disappearance. The lead picture depicted a burned-out bus. The rear of the blackened bus was twisted and knurled as if hit from behind by a bulldozer. The center of the bus had been blown away. But what drew Ana's attention was the number 1313 above the door. Ana scanned the accompanying article. *Bystanders state the bus bound for Chicago was rocked by two explosions before it burst into flames and careened off the road. ...cause of the accident is still under investigated.* This was no accident. Two antitank rockets could have caused the damage shown in the photograph, and she knew who had access to such weapons. They not only wanted her—they wanted her dead. By now they would know she wasn't on the bus, and Kaufmann would direct all available resources toward her demise.

The door opened and she stepped into the hallway. Except for a cleaning cart parked at the far end, the hallway was empty. They had cleaned her room earlier in the morning and were now about finished with her floor. The cleaning staff took pride in their work; the hotel was spotless. Ana headed toward her room.

"Excuse me, Miss," the cleaning lady said as she stepped out of a room. "I let your husband into your room. I hope that's all right. He said you had the key."

"That's fine, thank you."

No, that wasn't fine. How had they found her? Had she been outsmarted again? At least she was on neutral turf. As long as she didn't get trapped in a room, there was little they could do. It would be hard to drag a screaming woman through the lobby, money or no money. She could run. She had money. She could replace the clothes and computer. On the other hand, whoever was in her room—if he was still there—was breaking and entering. She could press charges. If he tried to run, she could phone the front desk before the elevator reached the lobby. She was sure the ape in the blue blazer was capable of handling the situation. That would give her the satisfaction of pressing charges against someone. The maid would be a witness to the crime. The person inside wouldn't be the Spaniard. He would have picked the lock, not asked help from the maid. She was sure he had picked his share of locks during his career of crime.

Ana cautiously opened the door. A suitcase lay open on her bed. She could hear water running in the bathroom—whoever broke in was still here. She retrieved her car keys from her pocket. She only had two keys, one for the ignition and the other for the trunk, but when they protruded between the fingers of her clenched fist, it was better than brass knuckles. She could do some serious face scratching, perhaps gouge an eye.

"Who's there?" Ana stepped into the room, leaving the door open to provide an avenue for escape.

A man stepped out of the bathroom. He had a hotel towel draped around his shoulders and remnants of shaving cream on his face. He was wearing nothing but boxer shorts.

"I hope you don't mind me using your shower."

"Dorek!" Ana kicked the door shut with her foot and ran to her lover, collapsing in his arms. She drenched the towel around his shoulders with nine and a half months of pent-up tears. When her tears were exhausted, Ana pushed Dorek back far enough to see his eyes. "I didn't expect you for another day or two"

"I can go back to the airport and wait."

"How did you know this was my room? I registered under an alias."

"The Pringles can taped to the windowsill was the giveaway. How many people can make a directional antenna out of a Pringles can? I also have to 'fess' up. I got hungry and ate the last of the Pringles. They don't serve meals on planes anymore."

"Did you bring your flak jacket?"

"Flak jacket?"

"You'll need it. We're going to war." Ana pushed Dorek toward the bathroom. "Get dressed. I'll explain it on the way to the airport. We're picking up Jacinta Rios in forty-five minutes. She's flying in from Brazil."

Dorek listened in silence on the way to the airport as Ana briefed him on the kidnapping, insemination, and birth of their son. If anyone else were telling him, he wouldn't have believed it. It did explain her disappearance and the questionable MMPI results. And the free week on the Black Sea had seemed too good to be true. It also explained why they had given him the extensive physical and psychological exam including the sperm sample. The entire exam had seemed excessive for a radiation exposure of questionable veracity.

Dorek Dolinski was normally passive, allowing life's little irritations to roll off his back like raindrops on a duck's feathers. He wasn't quick to anger, a trait that endeared him to his friends. He preferred diplomacy to confrontation. Now he felt anger he was unable to control, that he did not wish to control. He hadn't yet had the pleasure of meeting Lamar Kaufmann, but already despised him. What he had done to Ana was despicable, beyond the boundaries of human decency. Dorek was feeling that he too had been raped. They had wanted to marry. They had wanted to have children. But they wanted it on their schedule. They had wanted the child to be a product of natural love. Now they had a first-born son, a composite of their genetic make-up, created by a wicked and nefarious scheme. That child had been abducted, not to love and raise in a caring family, but to fill a void in the hierarchy of a criminal dynasty.

"I assume you have a plan to get our son back?" Dorek asked when Ana finished her narration.

"His name's Alek. I named him after my father. I hope you don't mind."

"I can live with that. Your father was a good man."

"As for the plan, it's somewhat nebulous at the moment. It's more a set of goals than a concrete plan of attack."

"I'm listening."

"Lamar Kaufmann is filthy rich, all of his money obtained illegally I might add. That's where his power is. He can afford to buy anything he desires, independent of the morality of his desires. The American legal system wants him but is powerless due to the vast number of attorneys at his disposal. If we want to get to him, we have to get to his money first. We strip him of his money, and he'll have less power than a cocktail waitress at a temperance meeting."

"I love your similes. Do you have thoughts on how to separate Scrooge from his money?"

"That's the problem; I know how to separate U-235 from U-238. When it comes to finances, I have difficulty balancing my checkbook."

"And you expect me to help? My specialty is quantum mechanics."

"I figured we'd need more help. That's why I called Jacinta. Her Nobel Prize in economics must be good for something. Dr. Rousseau is flying in from Quebec. Professor Hansen from Harvard Law School arrives tomorrow. I contacted everyone in our group. Over half of them are coming. No one's turned me down yet. In a couple of days the Landmark Inn will be hosting more Nobel Laureates than has ever congregated in one place outside of Oslo."

"Jacinta should be arriving on a puddle-jumper from Detroit," Ana said when they arrive at the airport lobby. At one time K. I. Sawyer Air Force Base had played host to B-52s of the Strategic Air Command. Now it was only a feeder link for the major airlines, usually twin engine turboprops. Ana checked the arrival board looking for Jacinta's flight; there weren't many on the board. Only one plane was coming from Detroit, and that would be ten minutes late due to a thunderstorm—at least according to the board.

The plane, having caught a tailwind, still arrived on schedule. Ana and Dorek watched through the lobby window as the pilot taxied the plane to a preordained spot on the tarmac before shutting down its engines. Jacinta was the third person to disembark. She was wearing a light blue pantsuit with a red ascot. That was the difference between business people and scientists. Ana and Dorek both wore jeans. They had no public to impress. Hugs were shared all around.

"What's this all about? You sounded pretty distraught over the phone," Jacinta asked when the hugs, handshakes, and formal rituals of greeting were completed.

"Distraught is an understatement. But we can't talk here. I'll explain it to you on the way to the hotel. I booked you in a room at Lamar Kaufmann's expense."

"Who's Lamar Kaufmann?"

"That'll also have to wait until we get in the car."

"He's a scumbag," Dorek said. "But then I've never met him. Maybe my opinion will deteriorate once I get to know him better."

Ana filled Jacinta in on the essentials as they drove back to the hotel with Dorek adding deprecating comments whenever he felt it justified, which was quite frequently.

"From what you tell me, I think calling him a scumbag is an insult to the microscopic denizens that make up pond scum," Jacinta concluded at the end of the briefing.

Ana drove into the hotel parking lot. Having good friends at her side instilled her with courage she hadn't felt since the kidnapping. She was beginning to believe getting Alek back was a possibility.

"Any chance of getting something to eat? I'm famished. I haven't eaten all day." Jacinta checked her belt to see if it was still holding up her pants: It seemed a bit loose.

"I wouldn't be too optimistic," Dorek said. "All she fed me was some Pringles, and I had to steal those."

"You two can stop wallowing in self-pity. I made reservations for three at the Sky Room Restaurant. I understand they have excellent food and a beautiful view of the Lake Superior coastline. We need to get Jacinta checked in first."

"If we don't eat soon, I'll be checking out—permanently."

"She does appear to have the early stages of pellagra. I think we need to feed her fast." Dorek checked the condition of his skin. "I do believe I'm also exhibiting symptoms."

Ana helped Jacinta through the hotel registration and then guided her to her room. It was two doors down from Ana's room. Dorek, who had been designated the project's pack animal, set Jacinta's luggage on the bed. Jacinta could unpack after they had eaten. Even though Ana had eaten a large lunch, she was also feeling the pangs of hunger. Her metabolism had yet to revert to a non-pregnancy state.

The Sky Room, located on the top floor, was as awe inspiring as advertised. A large panel of windows provided a panoramic view of Marquette and the Lake Superior coastline. The décor was European in style with a hand-painted ceiling. The white clouds and angelic cherubs painted on the ceiling appeared to be lazily floating by. A waitress met them at the door.

"Can I help you?"

"We have reservations for three."

"This way please." The waitress led the threesome to a corner table with a view of both the lake and south Marquette and handed them menus.

Dorek perused the menu including the hefty price tags. All of the entrées were top of the line. "Ana, you have developed expensive tastes since you've been in America. In Poland I could eat an entire week for the price of one of these meals."

"Neither of you have to worry. Lamar Kaufmann provided me with a forty thousand dollar expense account. I'm sure it'll cover the meal."

"This Lamar Kaufmann," Jacinta said, "I think maybe I do know him. Does he work from a large yacht that never comes to shore?"

"That's the one. Jacinta, you really need to be more selective in choosing your friends."

"I only know him by reputation, and his reputation isn't good. He's supplied guns to rebels in many South American counties, not out of political support, but for greed. He'll do anything for money."

"That's my Kaufmann."

"And he has your baby?"

"I'm hoping that's temporary. That's why we need your help."

The conversation paused when the waitress returned to the table for their orders. Jacinta ordered the seared Black Island

Swordfish. Since Kaufmann was paying for it, Dorek went with the Breast of Chicken stuffed with blue crab and spinach. After considerable thought—these decisions couldn't be made lightly—Ana went with the Prosciutto Wrapped Salmon finished with Caper Sauce on a bed of sautéed spinach.

"Jacinta, we need your economic expertise," Ana said after the waitress left. "We need to separate Kaufmann from his money. As long as he's filthy rich, he can buy all the power he needs. He can manipulate the legal system with his army of attorneys, making him untouchable. There's no way we can get our baby without breaking through that financial shield."

"I'm sure that can be done. Can I assume we aren't concerned with ethics?"

"Kaufmann hasn't let ethics get in his way. I don't know why we should. I'll do anything to get my baby back."

"O.K., tell me what you know about his finances." Jacinta took a pen out of her purse and prepared to take notes on the napkin.

"I know he has four casino hotels. Two are in Las Vegas, one in Atlantic City, and one in Monte Carlo."

"Probably for laundering money. Go on."

"According to the American FBI, his dealings on land are squeaky clean. They can't pin anything on him. He uses the *Chimera* for his illegal activities."

"The *Chimera*?"

"It's his yacht, actually a ship. It has Panamanian registry, but it never goes to port. It's refueled and re-provisioned at sea. That's where he keeps the records of his illegal activities. I had a brief look at the files on his computer. He's worth billions, all in an off-shore account in Bermuda."

"Do you remember the account number," Dorek asked. Ana gave him the look she reserved for males asking dumb questions.

"Most transactions in off-shore accounts are done over the Internet," Jacinta said. "But it's going take more than an account number. We'll need the proper password. I'm sure he uses a dynamic password generator."

"What's a dynamic password generator?" Ana asked.

"It's a small, hand-held device that's programmed to generate apparently random numbers that vary with the time of day. The offshore bank will have a similarly programmed device. The numbers are used for the password. Knowing what the password was is of little help since it is constantly changing."

"That sounds like a dead end. I thought knowing the account number would be of some value."

"Piece of cake," Dorek said. "If you have the account number, I'll get the password."

"I don't know if this is significant, but when I was going through Kaufmann's *Chimera* files, I found references to a Bear Cat Corporation on an island called Nevis. I've never heard of Nevis."

"It's not likely that you would have heard of it. It's not in your neck of the woods. Nevis is an island country with a population of ten thousand. The island is only seven miles long and five miles wide, hardly worth mentioning in a geography class. It was British at one time but became independent in 1983. Despite the small size, it has considerable financial significance. Ownership of a Limited Liability Company isn't a public record and is therefore confidential. Any deposits or wire transfers to the offshore corporation would be off the radar of any agency trying to track cash flow. The most private method is to use cash to purchase money orders from one of the larger grocery stores and send them to the dummy corporation. That leaves no paper trail in the country of origin. The dummy corporation can then invest the money in Bermuda or Switzerland. For less than two thousand dollars, anyone can obtain an offshore corporation with an offshore bank account. It's not just used for the black market. People do it to hide money from ex-spouses or from malpractice attorneys."

"Assuming Dorek can hack into the system, where do we go from here?"

"This swordfish is good," Jacinta said before returning to the subject at hand. "Tomorrow I'll fly to Nevis and set up two dummy corporations in my name. I'll call one the BearCat Corporation. To the computers that do all the work, BearCat and Bear Cat will be seen as two separate corporations, but to any human interface, it will look like the same company. I'll then open an account in the same Bermuda bank. They won't question a shift of money between what appears to be two accounts of the same corporation. When you get access to Kaufmann's account, you will transfer the money to the new account—I'll e-mail the account number to you. You won't need a password to add money to the account, only the account number. Once the money is in the BearCat Corporation, I'll switch it to the second corporation, which I'll call the Supererogatory Foundation. By then the money will be untraceable. Do you have any plans for the money?"

"Expenses only, the rest goes to charity."

"Can some of it go to the Fragile X Foundation?"

"For your brother? By all means. Make sure they get a good share of the money."

"In that case, as soon as the money hits the new account, I'll start sending it to charitable organizations. If he has as much as you say, it might take several days. It'll draw attention if I remove too much at once."

"You said the American CIA is involved in this?" Dorek asked.

"Not in Alek's kidnapping, but the FBI thinks the CIA uses Kaufmann to run guns to groups politically friendly to the United States. He thinks the CIA may have protected him in the past or at least looked the other way. According to Peterson, it's a fair weather relationship. He feels the CIA will turn on Kaufmann once he is no longer useful or becomes politically too hot."

"Have you heard from Shahzad Ahmed?" Dorek asked.

"He said he would be here in a couple of days. He was having trouble getting a flight out of Islamabad."

"He might be more useful if he stayed in Pakistan. Maybe he can send me some digital pictures of crowd scenes in rural village markets. Is this FBI friend of yours willing to help?"

"Marshall Peterson? I guess so. He gave me his card."

"Call him and see if he'll send some pictures of Lamar Kaufmann. If he's been a thorn in their sides, they must have a file on him with pictures. Digital pictures would be preferred, but I'll take anything he has."

"What do you have in mind?" Ana asked.

"I'm going to ensure that Lamar Kaufmann is no longer useful to the CIA."

"He shouldn't be useful to anyone," Ana said. "At least he has Chronic Lymphocytic Leukemia."

"He has leukemia?" Jacinta asked.

"Not really. When I had access to his computer, I doctored some of his medical records. It just looks like he has leukemia. He'll probably never notice, but it felt good when I did it."

"Maybe we'll have to make sure he notices," Dorek said.

The rest of the dinner was accompanied with small talk typical of individuals with normal I.Q.'s. Despite the urgency of their reunion, they were still friends who hadn't seen each other for a considerable length of time. Tomorrow would be a new day. Jacinta would be flying to Nevis; others would replace her. Formal plans had to be drawn and time tables set. Equipment needed to be purchased or constructed from available parts. For now, it was a time of friendship. They talked until exhausted and then went to bed, but not before Ana called Marshall Peterson and Dorek sent his e-mail request to Shahzad Ahmed. Tomorrow they would begin in earnest.

15

The following morning, Ana pulled her blue Impala out of the hotel parking lot and headed toward K. I. Sawyer Airport. She turned south on US 41. Traffic was light. What traffic she did encounter was coming into the city, leaving her lane clear of vehicles. She was in no hurry. The twenty-five-minute drive provided opportunity to converse with her long-time friend. Jacinta's visit had been short—too short. There had been little time to share those frivolous activities in their daily lives that made such friendships meaningful. Ana could count on her fingers the number of women her age she could relate to at her level. Jacinta was one of those precious few. She was someone Ana could rely on. At Ana's request, Jacinta had vacated her busy schedule and had flown in from Brazil to offer assistance. Jacinta could do serious jail time for what Ana was now asking her to do. How does one repay a friend like Jacinta? Ana shed a few silent tears as Jacinta boarded the plane for Nevis.

Two hours later, Ana returned from the airport with three other members of the Supererogatory Society who were making similar sacrifices. They too were busy people who were dropping everything to come to her aid. This went beyond simple friendship. Another six members would arrive later by car. Unbeknownst to Lamar Kaufmann, a small army of overachievers was assembling at the Landmark Inn to do him battle. They were people unaccustomed to failure and unwilling to accept defeat. They would be matching their collective genius against Kaufmann's vast financial empire, a formidable battle to which most Americans would not be privy. It would unlikely make the six o'clock news.

With much to be done and limited time, Dorek Dolinski had remained at the hotel to organize logistics. A conference room needed to be secured. Additional Internet access ports had to be obtained and extra phone lines installed. Every participant would expect and would receive a computer with Internet access. It was beyond the understanding of hotel staff who initially grumbled, but once cash was provided along with generous tips for the acquiescent, the hotel staff became accommodating. Room service even agreed to provide an endless supply of pizzas and soft drinks—the universal energy source of high technology.

Ana returned to find a conference room with rows of workstations lining the walls. On each desk was a computer in an unopened box waiting to be assembled. Several hotel staff members were adding additional outlets to accommodate the multitude of electronic devices thirsty for electrical power. The computers would eventually hook up to the hotel's complementary Internet access.

"Dorek, you're a genius. How did you get this done so quickly?"

"You'd be surprised what can do in America if you have money."

"Tell me about it. I just hope forty thousand dollars will buy us enough power to accomplish our goals."

"Your guy from the FBI came through." Dorek held up several pictures of Lamar Kaufman, all of which appeared to have been taken from a distance with a telephoto lens. "They aren't the best quality, but that can be an advantage for what I have in mind."

"That was quick."

"We received them by e-mail two hours after I sent the request. The FBI also wants to nail that worthless miscreant to the barn door, but they're nervous about our methods. He specifically asked us not to provide any details."

"Let them be nervous. No one outside our group needs to know our methods. Some of what we're about to do won't pass muster in the American courts."

"Some of it?" Dorek asked.

"O.K., most of it. But it's for a good cause." Ana slumped into a chair. Post-partum fatigue was taking its toll. She had to be mildly anemic. That was an expected complication. Combine that with sleep deprivation as well as constant emotional stress and she was ready to collapse.

"Ana, you need to slow down...get some rest. There's nothing going on that we can't take care of. You're not alone in this. In a day or two we'll need you at full strength."

As tired as she was, it was still painful being a non-participant. It wasn't in Ana's personality, but she had to acknowledge the wisdom of Dorek's argument. Her son's future would depend on her health. The next several days would be more stressful. She would need all the strength she could muster. Ana headed for her room.

Dorek booted up his computer. He was still waiting for Shahzad Ahmed's pictures. It was still early, less than twenty-four hours since he sent the request, but when he checked his e-mail, thirty digital pictures of people in a rural Pakistani marketplace were waiting for him. "Thank you, Shahzad." With the ten candid snapshots of Lamar Kaufman Special Agent Marshall Peterson provided, Dorek could begin removing the CIA from the equation.

Finding pictures of Osama bin Laden had been easy. There was a wide choice of pictures available over the Internet through the various news agencies—more than he needed. Dorek loaded the pictures into his computer and painstakingly created several composite photographs one pixel at a time. Clarity was intentionally less than perfect. It was best not to be too obvious. Even with a fuzzy picture, a computer mapping of the face measuring distance between eyes, length of nose, width of mouth, and height of cheekbones was as accurate as fingerprints. It would be time consuming, but if there were a strong desire, identification could be obtained. Dorek copied the pictures with a non-digital camera, obscuring individual pixels and removing all evidence of digital manipulation.

Dorek took the film to a nearby one-hour photo center and made several sets of eight-by-ten glossies. He dropped off one set at the Shipping Shop with instructions to FedExed it to Shahzad Ahmed by overnight mail. For Pakistan, overnight mail would still take two days.

By evening, nine members of the Supererogatory Society had arrived: Makalo Shukuma from Kenya, Clifford Hansen from Harvard Law School, Dr. Marsilius Rousseau from Quebec, Chaiprasit Mongkut from Thailand, Fred Carson from NIST (National Institute of Standards and Technology) in Boulder, Colorado and several others.

As promised, Fred Carson brought a Chip-Scale Atomic Clock, which he "borrowed" from NIST. It was one hundred times smaller than any other atomic clock and consumed less than seventy-five thousandths of a watt—it could run on batteries. The smallness of the device was crucial to their plan. The atomic clock would have to be married to a hand-held GPS, a laptop computer, and a directional antenna. For this task, a Pringles can wouldn't be adequate. Dorek ordered a sophisticated directional antenna from an electronics specialty store with overnight delivery. He delegated the task of designing the computer program needed to make the apparatus functional to four society members.

From a local sporting goods store, they purchase several "Space Blankets." These were thin, metal-foil lined sheets designed to trap infrared radiation thus keeping a person warm. That was the manufacturer's rational for their use. Dorek had other plans. He cut the Space Blankets and reassembled them into ponchos using duct tape. Remnants were reconfigured into Ku Klux Klan style hoods, albeit silver in color instead of white. The blankets had to cover the entire body.

Dr. Marsilius Rousseau drafted eighteen medical letters from fictional physicians and addressed them to the Centers for Disease Control. Each one notified the CDC of a suspected case of Legionnaire's Disease. They were accompanied by a complete history and physical of the patient in question. Rousseau would have done well as a fiction writer. They would mail the letters from a variety of locations around the United States over a five-day period. One letter—the one with a Mayo Clinic return address—they would mail last. Rousseau stamped that envelope "Confidential" in red ink and addressed it to Lamar Kaufmann.

On Tuesday evening, Ana received an e-mail from Nevis: Jacinta was staying in a Charlestown hotel. The corporations and bank accounts were functional and ready to go. She would be awaiting further instructions. The number for the new bank account was attached. With everything intact, Ana sent an e-mail to Shahzad Ahmed. It said nothing more than "Begin operation."

***

It was Wednesday, just past noon Pakistani time, when Jason Carter left the American embassy in Islamabad and headed for the park a little more than a block away. It had become a daily habit. Eating his sack lunch in the park provided a respite from the fast-paced embassy. Officially an advisor to the Pakistani Office of Agricultural Affairs, he knew next to nothing about agriculture. His undergraduate degree was in political science, and his masters was in mid-eastern studies. His true qualification for his job came from three years as an army intelligence officer, not from any natural ability to grow corn.

Carter found an empty bench and sat down to eat. He had come to work earlier than usual providing an hour for lunch if he so desired. Carter opened his bag and retrieved the ham-on-rye sandwich he had thrown together earlier in the morning. Looking around, he found the park full of people, both children and adults. That was what he enjoyed about his lunch break—watching the people. He was a people person. He enjoyed speculating on the mental mechanics that shaped their behavior. Today several school-age children were playing football or, as he had always known it, soccer. No one was keeping score. They were playing for the fun of it. American children would have kept score, part of their competitive nature.

Carter finished his lunch and reached for the newspaper he brought with him. His job required keeping current with the local news. He read most of the front page; but finding little of interest, he folded the paper and tucked it under his arm; he would read the rest later. It was time to return to work.

As Carter stood up to leave, a local man, perhaps in his late twenties, bumped into him, knocking his newspaper to the ground. He was wearing the traditional turban and robe of the lower class Pakistani. The man had been in a hurry, but paused to pick up the paper Carter had dropped.

"Excuse me, sir," the man said in broken English. He appeared genuinely apologetic. "You dropped your paper." He handed the folded newspaper to Carter.

Carter looked down at the newspaper. Inside the fold was a large white envelope. "This isn't mine," he said. But the man was gone.

Carter looked at the envelope with the cautiousness generated by years of training. His name was on the envelope. Whoever gave it to him hadn't done so by mistake. It was too thin for a bomb. That didn't rule out anthrax. If he were to open it, it would be best done outside where there was plenty of fresh air. He didn't need to bring anthrax back to the embassy.

Carter opened the envelope while holding it downwind. No white powder fell from the package. Instead, the package contained four eight-by-ten glossy photographs. The quality wasn't the best, giving the impression the pictures had been taken through a telephoto lens.

All the pictures were taken in the same small marketplace. He didn't recognize the background; it was not from the local area. Several men were in the picture. The one that caught his attention was the man in the center. Even with the poor quality, it was easy to recognize Osama bin Laden. He was in all four pictures. One other man appeared in every picture. He was European, not Pakistani. Carter flipped the pictures over. On the back of one picture was scribbled, "You have a traitor in your midst."

Carter was a field agent. It wasn't up to him to interpret the significance of the photos. He would pass them up the chain of command. Within an hour they would be digitalized and sent by satellite to Langley, Virginia. The original photographs, he would send by overnight courier.

It didn't take long for CIA analysts at Langley to match the second face to Lamar Kaufmann. The fact that the real Osama bin Laden was six inches taller than Kaufmann but the same height in the picture wouldn't be noticed for several weeks.

Eight hours later, one of the pictures surfaced on a website sympathetic to Al Qaeda. The accompanying story explained that Osama bin Laden was alive and well and had recently purchased twenty stinger missiles. It didn't mention the role of the European in the picture, but the insinuation was obvious. The Al Jazeera News Network picked up the story and broadcast it across the Mid-East. The American news media also broadcast it, but with the disclaimer that the CIA had yet to verify the picture's authenticity.

A confidential source close to Capitol Hill who wished to remain anonymous said the CIA had identified the arms dealer as none other than Lamar Kaufmann. The Washington Post printed the statement with the warning it was also unconfirmed. They ran pictures of Lamar Kaufmann next to the unknown man in the marketplace, allowing the viewer to decide on his or her own. The decision wasn't difficult.

***

On Friday morning, members of the Supererogatory Society vacated the Landmark Inn. Some left for Monte Carlo, some for Atlantic City, while others headed for Las Vegas. At various locations along the way, they would mail the letters to the Centers for Disease Control. The battle was about to begin in earnest.

Although most society members left by plane, Ana and Dorek departed for Las Vegas in Ana's blue Impala. They filled the car with an arsenal of electronic gear as well as the suits fabricated from the Space Blankets, items that would be difficult to explain to inquisitive airport security personnel. They drove through the night, arriving in Vegas Saturday afternoon. The city was recovering from the previous night's festivities, and traffic was light. At the edge of town, they found a cheap motel—by Las Vegas standards—and unpacked their bags, leaving the electronic equipment in the vehicle. A Chicken Shack provided a quick lunch before they headed west on US 95. At a gas station, Dorek filled the car with gas, while Ana purchased two bags worth of canned food, chips, and an assortment of junk food not commonly available in Russia. She had found the American plethora of gastronomic opportunities intoxicating. Americans obviously loved their food. They were both chewing on candy bars when they returned to the highway. Except for the billboards in English, the landscape looked no different than parts of Russia. It was hard to believe her homeland was half a world away. She was finally getting to see America as she had dreamed. She only wished it had been under more favorable circumstances.

"We need to merge into the West Summerlin Freeway when US 95 turns north. That's right up ahead." Ana had a Nevada map on her lap and was comparing it to the directions provided by

Marshall Peterson of the FBI. Also on her lap was a large bag of chips. Dorek merged into the freeway as directed.

"How far do we follow the freeway?" Dorek asked.

"The West Summerlin Freeway ends twenty miles west of Las Vegas."

Dorek checked his odometer. "That shouldn't be much farther."

"Then we turn left on a paved road."

"What's the name of the road?"

"According to the directions from the FBI, it has no name," Ana said. "It has a big sign that says 'Private, Keep Out.' There can't be too many like that."

Dorek turned the vehicle onto a paved road matching the description and headed into the hills. Hopefully, the directions were accurate. They drove another six miles into the foothills.

"That must be the place," Ana said when an ornate wrought iron gate came into view. Beyond the fence was a large house with pillared portico.

"Now we need to find a place to hide the car." Dorek turned the car around and drove back down the road. For the most part, the sides of the road were covered with sagebrush and small shrubs, nothing taller than the car. A quarter mile from the gate, they found a clump of trees on the right. Dorek turned off the road and headed toward the trees. He would have preferred four-wheel drive, but the ground was hard. As long as he took his time and avoided large rocks that could puncture the gas tank or oil pan, he would be all right. He found a spot behind some trees that partially concealed the car. They covered the side of the car facing the road with camouflaged ponchos. A few added spruce boughs rendered the car invisible. It was far enough off the road that few people would have seen the car even without camouflage. The vehicle, which would be their headquarters for the next several days, was still accessible from the lee side. Ana reached into the car and grabbed a bag of chips.

"Hey, go easy on the junk food or you'll be looking like a sumo wrestler. That stuff is addicting." Dorek reached into Ana's bag of chips and withdrew a handful. "See."

"Last week I felt like a sumo wrestler. I don't think my body has transitioned back to the non-pregnant state. It still thinks I need to eat for two."

"Maybe you can work some of it off." Dorek secured a small backpack to his back and placed a pair of binoculars around his neck. "It's time to go for a walk."

Ana stuffed several Hershey bars into her pockets and followed him through the woods. A quarter mile is a lot farther when walking through brush. It took all Ana's energy to put one foot in front of the other. Ana was panting heavily when the wrought iron fence came into view. She glanced over at Dorek who looked like he had just strolled across a lawn. Fathers apparently recovered faster after childbirth.

The shrubbery had been cut back thirty feet from the fence providing a moat of sorts around the fence. Dorek raised the binoculars to his eyes. He could see no one beyond the fence, no one working the grounds. Then he focused on the fence. At the top was a lone strand of wire held in place with insulators.

"The top of the fence is either electrified or they have a proximity detector. My guess would be the latter. Anything getting close to the wire will alter the electromagnetic field and ring an alarm inside the house."

"I should think you'd have to be within a meter or two to activate it," Ana said. "We're still going through the front gate aren't we? I wouldn't want to mess up my hair climbing over a fence."

"The front gate sounds good to me. But we'll need the electronic code to open the gate." Dorek opened his backpack and took out a small metal box held together with machine screws, obviously a piece of homemade equipment. Dorek opened the lid to make sure the batteries were in place—they were. Two black wires connected the batteries to a small circuit board and a hand-held tape recorder, the kind used for dictation.

"Now we'll find out if this contraption works. If it doesn't work, we'll both have a bad hair day."

"Don't even say that in jest."

Dorek hide the device in the shrubbery near the front gate. "Time for us to head back to the car and see if you left anything to snack on," Dorek said. His grumbling stomach was beginning to share Ana's predilection for food.

They returned to their car, found some summer sausage and crackers to eat, and settled down for some relaxation. There was nothing more they could do until after dark. This was the first free time they had since Ana had been abducted from the shore of the Black Sea. That seemed so long ago. So much had happened. Neither of them would ever be the same. Dorek held Ana in his arms, and they talked long into the night. They explored the what-if's and the what-could-have-been's, and how their lives had been altered. Left unanswered was the future. What were their alternatives if they did recover their son? Their son was American by birth, Dorek was a Polish national, and Anastasia Petrova no longer existed.

As they had expected, several cars left the Kaufmann estate while they talked. They would be the non-live-in staff heading home after a long day's work. It was well past two in the morning, when Ana looked at her watch. They had talked longer than she had thought. "You ready to go?" she asked.

Dorek nodded in the affirmative, and then stood up to stretch. He had spent too much time sitting in the car over the last twenty-four hours. He repacked his backpack with the tools and equipment he would need: a six-inch-diameter, heavy-duty, pizza cutting wheel; wire cutters; pliers; and a rectangular metal box containing the Intelligent Optical Switch. He hefted it into position on his back and then hung a hundred yard coil of fiber-optic cable over his shoulder before helping Ana with her pack. Her pack contained more tools, a heavy-duty battery pack, plus the Space Blanket ponchos. Dorek had made it the lighter of the two packs.

The quarter-mile hike back to the gate was more difficult in the dark. They did have a flashlight with a red lens to light their way. In theory, the red light would be absorbed by green foliage and wouldn't scatter as readily as white light. Just the same they used it sparingly. After a discussion of the pros and cons, they elected to walk along the road. At this time of night, it would be unlikely to meet anyone on foot, and if a late-night car were to approach, they could disappear into the woods long before they would be illuminated by the wash of the headlights.

The gate appeared more formidable in the dark. The wrought iron was thick and heavy, and the gate appeared taller than Ana had remembered. She began to wonder if their plan would work. It looked good on paper when they conceived it. But it was too complex with too many opportunities for something to go wrong, too many variables.

"Ana, I think we have a problem."

That wasn't what she wanted to hear. She didn't need problems. This part of her plan was crucial. If they couldn't get past the gait, all else would be in vain.

Dorek pointed to a small plastic box next to the motor that operated the gate. "I'm not sure, but I think this is a transmitter that sends a radio signal to the house every time the gate is opened, sort of like a doorbell. It has a call button for visitors without an electronic door opener. That may be all it does. It wouldn't take much more to signal the house when the gate is opened and closed by staff."

"I say we don't take the chance. Let's make it inoperative just to be on the safe side," Ana said.

"I assume you have something in mind?"

"Wrap it in foil. The radio waves can't penetrate foil. It works real well on ankle tethers."

Dorek decided it best not to ask. "I have no doubt that would work. It's just that I happened to leave my roll of aluminum foil at home." There was a bit too much sarcasm in his voice to suit Ana.

"Men can be so helpless at times," Ana replied with matching sarcasm. She pulled out two Hershey bars from her pocket and handed one to Dorek. "Here, eat up. And don't worry about the calories. It's for a good cause." Ana removed the brown outer wrapper revealing a foil-covered inner wrapper. Between the two candy bars they would have enough foil to cover the transmitter.

"I knew there was a reason I brought you along," Dorek said.

Dorek retrieved the monitoring device hidden in the bushes. The hand-held recorder was equipped with voice activation, but in this case they had redesigned it to record electrical impulses coming from the attached scanner. Hopefully, it picked up the radio code of the automatic gate opener when the staff left for the night. Dorek rewound the tape and turned it to play. Ten seconds later, the gate began to open. "Don't you love technology," he said.

Dorek pushed the button again after they entered the compound, and the gate closed. He hoped it would work as smoothly on their way out. Large halogen lights periodically spaced along the drive illuminated driveway up to the house. They stepped into the shadows of some well-manicured shrubs. It wasn't as if they expected to be seen. At this time in the morning, there would be no reason for anyone to be awake. There would be security once they got near the house. The Hollywood image of men walking snarling dogs was just that—a Hollywood image. Electronic security was more reliable and less costly. It was also more predictable. Motion sensors were of little value outside the mansion. There were too many birds, raccoons, and tree boughs blowing in the wind to be of any value. Infrared would be the method of choice for outside monitoring. It would ignore all but the warm-blooded creatures prowling around the yard. Any non-stationary thermal images would set off the alarm. The sensitivity would be set to pick up large moving thermal images, avoiding birds and small animals. The grounds were quiet. That would change if the alarm were to sound.

Ana and Dorek slipped into their Space-Blanket ponchos. They wrapped their legs in the same material and taped it in place with duct tape. The foil lining of the Space Blankets would trap most of the infrared signature inside their suits. They covered their heads with hoods.

"If anyone comes along, we'll fake it," Dorek said. "We'll ask them to take us to their leader."

Not wanting to combine the effects of any infrared leakage, Dorek and Ana maintained a space of five meters between them as they approached the house—if you could call it a house. It was more of a mansion. The area in front of the house was park-like in appearance with closely clipped grass. Islands of green shrubs embedded in shredded redwood bark added spice to the design. Low-level landscape lighting illuminated the shrubs. They produced enough light to illuminate any intruders if someone were to look out over the front lawn. Fortunately, the windows of the house were still dark.

They were right about the infrared sensors. They found several thermal imaging devices on the way to the house. No lights were coming on in the house; their Space Blanket suits had to be working. Any infrared radiation that escaped from their suits decreased with the inverse square of the distance from the sensors. They, therefore, gave the infrared sensors a wide birth. So much of what they were doing wasn't pure science, but probability assessment. The odds were in their favor. Unfortunately, probability has a way of sneaking up and biting people in embarrassing places. They needed to be quick as well as cautious.

It didn't take long to find what they were looking for. On the south side of the house, three wires exited the house's stone frame. One was labeled AT&T—obviously the phone. The other two had to be for TV and computer access. The three wires followed the house frame into the ground. Dorek took his pocketknife and nicked the insulation in one of the lines revealing minute copper strands—a coaxial cable. That would be for Kaufmann's TV. Someone with his money would have a fiber-optic line for broadband computer input. That would be the third line.

"This one has to be it," Dorek said. He began digging a hole at the base of the wire then cut the fiber-optic line below ground level. "Hand me the optical switch."

Ana reached into one of the packs and retrieved a rectangular metal box with multiple connection terminals on one side. "Any idea how this handles moisture," she asked.

"Hopefully, we'll never find out. The ground is dry, and it doesn't often rain in Nevada. It only has to last a day or two."

Dorek connected the two cut ends of the fiber-optic cable to the optical switch. "Now I need the coil." Ana passed one end of one hundred-yard-long fiber-optic coil to Dorek. Walking backwards towards the fence, Ana began unwinding the coil as Dorek connected his end to the optical switch box. If the system worked as planned, the microcomputer inside the Intelligent Optical Switch unit would, upon command, switch input between the three cables using silicon micromirrors. Normally, the optical switch would operate from hard-wired power. It would have to be content with the battery pack Dorek cobbled together. If should last forty-eight hours. If they needed for a longer period, they would have to replace the battery. Dorek covered the unit with dirt.

"How far did the cable go? Did it reach the fence?" Dorek asked when Ana returned.

"And then some. I suppose now we have to stoop to manual labor. Do you want to cut or bury?"

"I'll start cutting. We'll switch when one of us gets tired."

Dorek removed the pizza cutter from the pack and began cutting the sod alongside the cable. Ana followed behind, lifting up the edge of the sod with her fingers and burying the cable. They had to reach the fence before the sun came up. Cutting the sod with the pizza cutter proved easy. Lifting the sod was difficult and painful work. After forty minutes, they had gone less than twenty feet. At that rate they wouldn't finish before sunup.

"This isn't going to work." Ana looked down at her fingernails: They were bleeding. The possibility of failing momentarily dominated her thoughts, and she had to forcefully suppress her tears. Getting emotional wouldn't help. It was a problem. She was good at solving problems. "We need some sort of tool to separate the sod after it's cut." There had to be a better way. Ana looked around for ideas. There wasn't much to offer in way of tools. It was all grass and shrubs, but at the base of the shrubs were the low-intensity landscape lights. They were attached to quarter-inch-diameter metal rods embedded in the ground. Ana pulled one up from the ground and unscrewed the rod from the light. She placed the end of the rod in the cut Dorek made in the sod and gave it a pull. It took some work, but it made a quarter-inch groove in the sod. Dorek pushed the cable in behind her.

"Ya know, Ana, for a *girl*, you're pretty smart."

"If you were smart, for a *boy*, you would have brought such a tool with you. You packed everything else. This was your part of the project."

"I brought you instead. I knew I wouldn't need anything else. Does that get me back in your good graces?"

"Probably, I'll decide after you finish burying this cable."

They finished the cable an hour later, long before the sun was to rise. They covered the cable outside the fence with leaves. It was half past four in the morning when they returned to their car. They could do nothing more until Monday morning. The rest would be in the hands of the other Supererogatory Society members. Totally exhausted, they reclined the front seats of the Impala and fell asleep.

16

Jason Turner waited until all bets were placed before dealing two cards around the blackjack table. He was midway through his shift, and his legs were starting to cramp. The pain added insult to what had been a miserable day. Although his braces provided support, his leg muscles had atrophied over the months he had been confined to his wheelchair making prolonged standing difficult. At his age fractures didn't heal quickly. At his age nothing healed quickly. He took two pain pills and washed them down with a soft drink. He would have preferred something stronger if house rules would have permitted. In the past he would have considered bending the rules. Now that he was under constant surveillance, he needed to be more circumspect. He didn't need any new fractures.

Not only had it been a bad day, but the prospects for the remainder of his shift were less than promising. His table had been inexplicably and consistently losing chips, not from a single jackpot, but from a steady and relentless drain. Some losses were to be expected; that was the nature of gambling; the casino didn't always win. But there was that expectation from management that over time the house should win. It should have averaged out, but it hadn't. He should have sufficient chips in his box to offset his losses, but he didn't. The casino management would not be happy. He had experienced their displeasure before and had no desire to relive another "spontaneous accident."

The large black man to Jason's left signaled for a hit. He was dressed in a multicolored robe and spoke with an accent. Turner assumed he was a true African. It wasn't unusual in Las Vegas to have multinational visitors. The African had been one of the heavy winners. If it had been only the African, he would have considered unscrupulous behavior, perhaps another electronic cheater. The truth was—everyone was winning at his table. He had pushed the security button under his table several times to alert the people sitting behind the surveillance monitors. They hadn't responded— apparently they found nothing amiss. Turner dealt a nine from the card-dispensing shoe to the man's five and six giving him a twenty count. That would beat the house, and the African had bet the maximum. Money continued to flow out from Jason's table.

The African collected his chips without emotion and left the table. A young lady in her mid-thirties took his place. She gave the impression of a housewife on vacation, usually an easy mark. Experience at church bingo parlors didn't prepare one for serious casino gambling. She had also been lucky. And she had been wagering sums of money beyond the reach of the average housewife.

Then there was the man on the far right, the one with the turban on his head. He had to be a rich sheik or something. He was throwing money around like it had no value, but every time he threw his money on the table, Turner had to throw a larger sum back at him. Management wasn't going to be happy.

The men in the back room sitting behind the surveillance monitors weren't happy either. Dealers at all the tables were pushing their surveillance buttons. They couldn't watch every table. The dealers had identified over twenty-five individuals for closer scrutiny. It wasn't unusual for teams of individuals to assault the casinos in hopes of making a dishonest buck. The group from MIT had done it quite effectively. But twenty-five people aren't a team—that's a mob.

True card counters were easy to spot. They were all business. Counting cards is hard work; concentration is everything. These people were gabbing with their neighbors as if on a vacation where winning at the blackjack table was an expected bonus.

It wasn't illegal to count cards, and in most cases it was tolerated. The majority of the card counters were amateurs who lost as much as they won. Dealers would engage them in conversation since most people find it difficult to count cards while conversing. The few hard-core, expert counters were quickly identified and banned from the casinos. Every casino had its list of persona non grata and readily shared it with others. If a banned player returned, it would be considered trespassing, punishable by law.

"Whatcha got?" the Spaniard asked when he entered the room.

"We have a problem." The head of security was unsure how best to present the situation. The Spaniard's reputation had been well earned. He didn't accept failure graciously. "We're losing a lot of money."

"How much is a lot of money?"

"Best I can figure—two million plus." The chief of security braced himself for the feared reaction, but the Spaniard took it in stride as if he had expected this.

"That's a lot of money. Where's it going?"

"That's the problem. It's going everywhere. We must have twenty to thirty big winners out there. It's too big for a team, and they have nothing in common. They're of all ages and nationalities. If we put them in a line up, it would look like a party of U.N. delegates."

"Think they're counters?"

"No sir, counters use systems. They never count all the cards; no one has the mental capacity to do that. We plugged the play into our computer that does have that capacity. It matched what they're doing at the tables. Like I said, no one can count all the cards in several decks. No one has done that since Dustin Hoffman did it in the movie *Rainman*. They have to have electronic help."

"No radio signals?" It was a rhetorical question. The chief of security was well trained and would have eliminated the obvious.

"No sir, that was the first thing we looked for. No transmissions of any kind. The computer system has to be on their persons. No one has left with any earnings yet. If we can prove they're cheating, we can forfeit their earnings and break even. That shouldn't be hard."

The Spaniard wished it were that easy. He had expected something like this. Calls to Atlantic City and the other Las Vegas casino confirmed similar scenarios. They were all suffering losses at the blackjack tables. Kaufmann's casinos were losing millions of dollars, and he had yet to hear from Monte Carlo.

"So you think they have an electronic counting device?" The Spaniard asked. "If we haul them in and find nothing, the Nevada Board of Gaming will be all over us. It'll open us to lawsuits."

"If we don't, we stand to lose millions, and that's just one day. There's no telling how long they'll keep this up." The head of security held his ground. "I don't want to be the one to tell Mr. Kaufmann he's been cheated out of millions of dollars. Whatever we do, we need to do it fast. We're losing over a hundred grand an hour. We need to either pull them in or ban them from the casino."

The Spaniard gave it a moment of thought. Whatever the decision would be, he would be the one to make it. The head of security was right about one thing: Kaufmann wouldn't be happy about the loss. But if they could find incontrovertible evidence of cheating, the loss would be annulled.

The head of security waited for a decision. "No one can track cards like that without artificial intelligence," he said, trying to influence the Spaniard's decision.

"All right, pull in five of them. Put them in separate rooms; then shake them down, strip search if necessary. I'll talk to them after you finish. Don't let anyone cash in their chips until we get to the bottom of this." Riviera wished he were as confident as his chief of security. The apparent randomness of activities at the tables belied an underlying element of order and sophistication. They were taking the casino to the cleaners. The big question left unanswered was how.

***

Clifford Hansen sucked the last of his Coke through his straw and threw the empty container into the trash. He had been watching table four for the last fifteen minutes, counting the cards as they were being played. The mechanical shuffler had randomized the blackjack cards. But like all randomizations, anomalies occur. An unusual number of high cards had been played leaving the deck heavily weighted in smaller value cards. Hansen mentally calculated the odds. The dealer would stand on any combination of cards adding to seventeen or above. Hansen could go to eighteen or higher and still have an advantage over the dealer. Hansen pulled a chair up to the blackjack table.

Dressed in jeans and a Las Vegas tourist shirt, Hansen looked the part of a tourist in his mid-fifties on a pre-retirement fling. Most people would have pegged him as a blue-collar worker, perhaps from some assembly line in some inner city factory or maybe a construction worker. A closer look would reveal the midriff bulge, soft hands, and lack of tan consistent with a man who rode a desk for a living, not a jackhammer.

Hansen counted out his chips and bet the maximum, placing the chips in the circle on the felt table. Since the odds were in his favor, there was no sense betting low. His first two cards were a four and a jack to the dealer's eight and five. He scraped his cards across the felt in the signal for another hit, and the dealer rewarded him with another four. At eighteen, the odds were in Hansen's favor for another hit. He again scraped his cards across the felt. This time he was dealt a deuce. Hansen slipped the corners of the two cards in his hand under his chips to signify his "stand." The dealer had drawn a four and was forced to stand at seventeen.

"Twenty wins," the dealer said as he passed the winning chips in Hansen's direction.

Hansen scooped up the chips without comment or show of emotion. He won the next five out of seven hands, and the chips in front of him began to accumulate as they had all day. Two other players, the black man in the colorful robe and the man of Middle Eastern origin wearing the turban, were also raking in the chips. The dealer dealt another round of cards. Hansen was preparing to play his hand when two men wearing green blazers with the casino's logo over the breast pocket stepped up behind him.

"Excuse me, sir," one of them said, "will you please follow me."

"Sorry, I'm busy."

"Sir, please come with us. We'd like to talk to you for a few minutes."

"I'm all ears. Start talking." Hansen picked up an ace and a four, the beginning of a good hand. He signaled for another card.

"Sir, you *have* to come with us." This time the security man placed an ominous emphasis on the "have." It was no longer a request. It was a demand. The two agents grabbed Hansen's elbows to ease him out of his chair. It was only intended to provide subtle encouragement, polite yet forceful. Hansen grabbed their jackets as he fell backwards pulling the security men down on top of him. As his head gently hit the floor he let out a groan that would have won a Tony on any Broadway stage or maybe it should have been an Oscar, as it was all captured on overhead camera. He lay on the floor in his ersatz coma until picked up by the confused security agents. He was still holding his head when they led him away to the interrogation room. Four others were, likewise, ushered out of the casino lobby.

The interrogation room was Spartan in its design. No more than eight by ten feet in dimension, it had a backless metal stool as its only piece of furniture. This sat in the center of the room under a solitary floodlight recessed in the ceiling. The walls were painted white as was the ceiling giving the room the feeling of sterility. Mounted on the wall were a red phone and a half-length mirror. Hansen assumed a camera was rolling behind the mirror. He wasn't sure where the microphone was hidden.

"What's this all about?" Hansen rubbed his head for the benefit of the hidden camera.

"We caught you cheating. You didn't think you would get away with it did you?" The security men had been hand-picked for their intimidating factor. Both men were over six feet tall and towered over Clifford Hansen's meager five-foot-eight-inch frame. As per their custom, they began with the assumption of guilt. Given enough pressure, most people rapidly confessed, feeling that some irrefutable evidence had been caught on tape.

"What do you mean I was cheating? I won my money fairly."

"You can do serious jail time for fraud." One of the security agents ran a wand over Hansen's body checking for hidden metal objects and found none. "Will you please remove your clothes?" The wording was well chosen. On any court transcript, it would come across as a request even though the verbal reflection was that of a demand. Legally, they had no authority to demand a strip search.

"I'm not removing my clothes."

"They'll go easier on you if they feel you're cooperating."

Hansen removed his clothes and handed them to one of the security men who checked each article for wires or other electronic devices, finding none. The agent then gave back his underwear. Having the subject in question sit on the cold metal stool almost naked encouraged reluctant individuals to talk if nothing more than to terminate the ordeal. Hansen merely stared back.

Finding no incriminating electronics, the security guards took a new tact. One of them slipped out of the room. Moments later the phone rang. The other guard answered the phone. For the most part he listened, adding only an occasional vague comment. "We have your accomplice in the room next door," he said after he hung up the phone. "Your accomplice is telling everything. They'll go easy on your accomplice because of that." The security officer avoided any reference to the accomplice's gender, not wanting to tip his hand in the bluff.

Clifford Hansen sat on the cold metal stool for the better part of five minutes wearing nothing more than his underwear, maintaining his dignity the best he could under the circumstances. He stared at the security guard and the security guard stared back.

"We're just waiting for the full report from your accomplice," the security man said, breaking the awkward silence.

The staring contest continued with neither man willing to blink. It was interrupted only when an older man entered the room. He was tall with a well-toned muscular frame and carried the air of a man in charge. His hair was black with a small tuft of silver in the front. "My name is Pueblo Riviera," the man said with a Spanish accent.

Hansen stood up and offered his hand. "I'm Clifford Hansen. Am I correct in assuming you're the man in charge?"

The Spaniard made no effort to shake Hansen's hand. "I hope you realize the gravity of the situation. People do hard time for gambling fraud of this magnitude. We have a document that explains in detail the legal consequences in the State of Nevada." Riviera handed Hansen a twelve-page document printed in small font on legal-size paper.

Hansen flipped through the sheets of paper as if counting the pages and then handed the document back to Riviera.

"Don't you want to read it?" Riviera asked.

"I just did. If you were one of my students, I might have given you a 'B'. That would be charitable at best. The verbiage is constipated and wordy. The legal trend these days is to make documents concise, but readable, avoiding big words. If you insist on using big words, you should know how to spell them. Verisimilitudinous has one "m." Your document is ostentatious and pompous, but I assume that is for the intimidating effect."

"Who are you?"

"As I said, my name is Clifford Hansen. I'm a Professor of Corporate Law at Harvard Law School."

"You should be aware we are obligated to notify the Nevada State Gaming Control Board when we have gaming fraud of this magnitude. Even if you don't do hard time, you'll lose your professorship."

"It won't be necessary to notify the Gaming Control Board. One of my associates notified them as soon as I was forcefully abducted. One of their representatives is on the way over now. I'm sure he or she will want to look at your evidence, including the statement by my accomplice. Can you give me the spelling of your last name?"

"Why do you need that?" Riviera asked.

"I detest misspelling a defendant's name on a legal document. In addition to the criminal charges of assault and battery, unlawful detention, and conspiracy to defraud, there will be the usual civil suits concerning defamation of character, mental anguish, and punitive damages. My neck is starting to hurt. I bet I'd look good in a cervical collar. I'm sure we will find many documents where we can put the correct spelling of your name. I've been thinking of turning this over to my law students as a learning project. It'll give them something to sink their teeth into. I get a fresh batch of students every year. It'll be a good introduction to white-collar and corporate crime."

Riviera passed Hansen his clothes. "Here, put some clothes on. You look stupid sitting there half naked."

"Thank you. May I use that quote in my summation to the jury?"

The Spaniard ignored the sarcastic comment. Both men knew the casino had been bluffing. There would be no evidence to show to the Nevada State Gaming Control Board. If the other two American casinos were hit equally as hard, they could be out eight to ten million dollars in gambling losses, and that didn't include legal settlements. That could be another ten to twenty million. Kaufmann could afford it, but he wouldn't be happy.

"You should be aware that a federal judge is in the process of signing an injunction to prevent destruction of your surveillance tapes, and that includes the one behind the mirror. If there should be any gaps on the tape, it'll be considered obstruction of justice."

Riviera turned to his head of security. "See that their chips are cashed in. Have the cashier write checks to cover their winnings but date the checks for Wednesday. Mr. Kaufmann might have to move some funds around before the checks will clear."

He then turned to Hansen. "Mr. Hansen, you have our apologies. You and your friends will be paid the full amount of your winnings. Any legal questions will be worked out later. You and your friends are no longer welcome in any of our casinos. If you should chose to return, you will be charged with criminal trespass and prosecuted to the fullest extent of the law. Do I make myself clear?"

17

Dr. Adam Wainwright reshuffled the papers as if it would provide additional insight. He removed his glasses, rubbed his eyes, and then looked out the window of his Atlanta office. It was Sunday afternoon. Even from his desk chair he could see that the sun was shining. He should be playing golf, he told himself. He had gone into epidemiology after medical school to avoid long hours and weekend call. If he wanted to work weekends, he could have been a surgeon or a family practitioner.

For the most part, the Center for Disease Control was closed on weekends and holidays. Only a skeleton crew kept the doors open, and then it was mostly technicians and lower-waged employees. Wainwright tried to remember the last time he worked a Sunday. It had been over two years. He shouldn't complain.

Wainwright pushed his office chair away from his desk and stood up. He walked over to the window for a closer look at the Atlanta skyline. Although his eyes were focused on the city below, his mind was not. No matter what decision he made, there would be an onslaught of hostile criticism, and it would come from people of influence, people with money. It had the potential for adverse political fallout, not just for him, but for the entire CDC. As head of the pulmonary infection department, it was his call— and he had to make it today.

Wainwright returned to his chair and again shuffled the papers. Over the past four days he had received twelve reports of Legionnaire's disease. The patient's history and physical accompanied each report. The patients were scattered across the U.S. Their ages ranged from twenty-three to sixty-eight. There were blue collar-workers and white-collar workers. Some were highly educated, others were high school dropouts. It was a diverse group. They provided unique histories except for one common denominator—they had all recently returned from trips to gambling casinos in Atlantic City or Las Vegas and they had all stayed at one of three attached hotels.

Twelve people in a country as large as the United States wasn't a lot, but it could be the tip of an epidemic iceberg. How many reports would he get tomorrow? In July of '76 one hundred and eighty people attending an American Legion convention in Philadelphia came down with Legionnaire's disease. Twenty-nine died. That was seventeen percent—not good odds. It was little solace that the disease was named after them. The CDC had been instrumental in that investigation. It was determined inhaling contaminated water droplets produced by the air-conditioning system in Philadelphia's old Bellevue Stratford Hotel caused the pneumonias. It could happen again.

The prudent action would be to close down the three hotels until CDC staffers could take appropriate samples from the hotels' most likely sources. If they found any *Legionella* bacteria, the hotel could be treated and the source eliminated. If none were found, it could be written off as a coincidence. Either way, the people would be protected and any epidemic prevented. That would be the prudent course of action.

Unfortunately, these weren't simple hotels. These were enormous hotels with attached casinos and nightclubs. The twenty-four-hour cash flow generated from just one of those hotels boggled the mind. Closing them down for a week would create serious financial consequences for the owners. Their wrath would be directed at the CDC in general and Dr. Adam Wainwright in particular. He had no doubt local politicians would weigh in—none of the infected individuals were from their districts. They had nothing to lose.

Wainwright searched through his papers until he found the document profiling the three hotels. He had one of his clerks research the hotels the day before. The report provided little additional insight. Unlike the Bellevue Stratford, which had been seventy-two years old at the time of the epidemic, these hotels were fairly new, not that it makes any difference to bacteria. One advantage in Wainwright's favor: All three hotels were privately owned by the same individual—Lamar Kaufmann. At least there wouldn't be a slew of stockholders writing their congressmen.

A week ago he would have worried about Kaufmann. He would have been a powerful force that would have come down hard on the CDC if his hotels were closed or even linked to an outbreak of Legionnaire's disease. When money talks, people listen. According to *Forbes Magazine*, Kaufmann was one of the top four hundred richest men in the world. No one knew his exact worth. He was introverted and avoided publicity. Now Wainwright knew why—Kaufmann had been selling weapons to Al Qaeda. For the last two days the news media had discussed nothing else. The government had yet to confirm it and they had not lodged any charges. The government had offered only a firm "no comment." The pictures circulated over the Internet and eventually by the networks showed a man who presented a striking resemblance to Lamar Kaufmann. It was hard to respect a man like that. Given a choice of creating a financial hardship to a man like Kaufmann versus preventing a potential life-threatening epidemic, the choice was clear. Kaufmann would undoubtedly sell more guns to al Qaeda to cover any loss.

Wainwright picked up his phone and made the call. The quiet Sunday afternoon at the CDC would soon be ending. Someone would contact a federal judge who would issue a warrant closing the three hotels. Technicians would be given notice. While they were packing their bags, clerks would be contacting airlines to arrange transportation to Las Vegas or Atlantic City. On Monday morning, a squad of federal marshals would arrive at the hotels with warrants in hand. By noon the hotels would be empty. It wouldn't be a popular decision, but it was a decision that had to be made. Wainwright returned the medical reports to their folders and placed them in his desk. His work was now done. It was time to go home.

18

The sun was shining through the partly cloudy sky that hung over Bermuda like an abstract acrylic painting. The temperature was already in the 80's and gave every indication it would reach 90 before the day was over. It was a typical morning in Bermuda. Tourists dressed in suntan lotion and skimpy swimsuits were heading for the beaches to worship the sun god, while shopkeepers were unlocking their doors in hopes of relieving the tourists of their excess wealth. At nine o'clock sharp the Bermuda banks opened for business. They were on Atlantic Standard Time. In Nevada, just west of Las Vegas where it was Pacific Standard Time, Ana's watch registered five o'clock. Unlike Bermuda the sun had yet to make an appearance, but the east was glowing red. It wouldn't be long before the sun would be peeking over the horizon.

Ana readjusted her back against the aspen tree trunk in hopes of relieving a spasm. She had been there most of the night. She didn't expect anything to happen until later in the morning, but too much was at stake to cut corners. Dorek was asleep, his head resting in her lap. He could sleep anywhere. In a few minutes she would awaken him to spell her for an hour or two. She wasn't sure she could sleep, but she wasn't sure she could remain awake much longer either.

If the drama were unfolding as planned, Lamar Kaufmann should be strapped for cash. To cover his losses, he would have to transfer additional funds from his offshore account in Bermuda.

When this might happen was unknown. That was the wild card. They had battery packs to cover twelve hours. After that, one of them would have to find a battery charger for their laptop. That would divide their forces. She was confident she could manage without Dorek, but it felt good to have him at her side. Hopefully, Kaufmann would make his move before noon.

Ana again arched her back to relieve a spasm. The motion caused Dorek to stir. He sat up and rubbed his eyes to clear his vision. "Anything happening?" he asked. He looked at the computer screen: It was blank.

"Nothing worth writing home about. I'm sure Kaufmann is asleep on a nice, soft mattress, unlike two people I know. His breakfast in bed won't be served for another three or four hours. Which reminds me, we're low on candy bars. I'm hungry."

"Breakfast may be a little late today. My guess is closer to noon. If this works, I'll treat you to a steak dinner at the fanciest restaurant in Vegas."

"Why wouldn't it work?" Ana had known something could go wrong, but had forced that possibility from her mind. She didn't need to be reminded.

"Suppose he's not there. Suppose he's on that fancy yacht of his."

"Dorek, don't even think such thoughts." She hadn't considered that possibility. He could easily transfer funds from the computer on the *Chimera*. If he did, all their plans would be for naught. "He was here two days ago. We have nothing to suggest he left for his yacht."

Ana looked down at the blank computer screen as if she could will it into action. The fiber-optic line connected the computer to Kaufmann's Internet access port and would show nothing unless he connected to the Internet. If that were to happen, the silicon micro mirrors on the optical router would split the beam. They would be receiving the same input seen on Kaufmann's computer.

"I'll stand watch. Why don't you get some sleep? It'll be several hours before anything happens."

"I'm sleepy, but I don't think I can sleep."

Dorek pulled a deck of cards from the breast pocket of his shirt. "How about a game of Fish?"

"Too bad you didn't bring a chess board. I could humiliate you at chess."

Dorek dealt out the cards. "That's not what Dr. Rousseau tells me. He says he's been kicking your butt."

"What do you expect? He's a grand master. I still beat him one out of three."

"Tell me about my son. What does he look like?"

"He's beautiful. He has dark hair—lots of hair. And he has your eyes. Actually, he looks a lot like you."

"He must be cute then."

"Your modesty is overwhelming."

"You were the one who said my son was cute and looked like me. I'm just agreeing with you."

"Do you have a five?"

"Go fish."

One can play "Go Fish" only so long. After an hour it turned into a display of Dorek's card tricks of which only half worked. The sun was rising higher in the sky. Kaufmann should now be awake, making it difficult to maintain interest in cards. Both Ana and Dorek were drawn to the computer screen. It was like the 'watched pot' that never boiled. It remained blank. Maybe he was on the *Chimera*. Ana couldn't bear the thought that Kaufmann had won again. It wasn't fair.

It was ten minutes past nine when the screen came to life. It was what they had been waiting for; but when it came, it had taken them by surprise. They stared at the screen in disbelief. It was actually working. The home page of a Bermuda bank came into view. They watched as the cursor moved across the screen. It selected the login icon. The home page changed to another screen requesting a password.

When asterisks began to fill the password box, Dorek sprang into action. Six asterisks filled the box, and the cursor moved to the "Submit" button. Dorek typed in some commands as the screen again changed. A hundred yards away, buried under the ground, the Intelligent Optical Switch acknowledged the command. The silicon micro mirrors shifted ever so slightly, but it was enough to cut Kaufmann's computer from the loop. In the Kaufmann mansion a computer was displaying "Internet connection lost."

"We're in." The screen displayed a page with "Welcome, Bear Cat Corporation" displayed at the top. It was prompting for an account number. "You still remember the account number?" Dorek asked.

"I think it's 456F89TR2043."

"You think? I thought you knew."

"Excuse me, but I had a lot on my mind."

Dorek typed in the account number, and was rewarded with the account balance—there were ten digits to the left of the decimal place. He had never seen so much money in one account. If money was power, Lamar Kaufmann was a very powerful person. That was about to change. Dorek clicked on the transfer button. He entered the account number for the Bearcat Corporation and entered the full amount of Kaufmann's account in the amount box. He clicked on the submit button. The screen froze for a moment and then proclaimed "Transaction Complete."

"Did it work?" Ana asked.

"I don't know." Without logging out, Dorek sent an instant message to a computer in a Charlestown hotel on the island of Nevis.

Dorek: *Are you out there, Jacinta?*

Jacinta: *I'm here waiting for some action.*

Dorek: *The money should be coming your way.*

Jacinta: *Let me check.*

Jacinta logged in to the Bearcat Corporation account and selected "Account Balance."

Jacinta: *I don't see any new funds. Are you sure you properly transferred the account? Wait...it's coming in now. Holy wow— you didn't say it would be that much money. A lot of nations have annual budgets smaller than that. A girl can do some serious shopping with that kind of money.*

Ana took over the keyboard.

Ana: *Jacinta, it's not our money. Use it only for expenses. The money belongs to the people and we need to return it to the people.*

Jacinta: *That must be Ana talking. Dorek has more sense than that. O.K., expenses only, but I think I might be moving up to a classier hotel, and there will be a fancy dinner tonight with some champagne. I'm signing off now. I have a lot of work ahead of me if I'm going to switch the money over to the Supererogatory*

Foundation account. I'll have to move it in small chunks of ten or twenty million at a time to avoid suspicion.

Just to be on the safe side, Dorek recheck Kaufmann's account—it registered zero. "I think your Superman just run into Kryptonite. His empire is imploding in on him. He'll soon be powerless.

"Now we have to get our baby," Ana said.

Two hours later, the Fragile X Association in Brazil received a wire transfer of ten million dollars to be used in research. The money came from an unknown organization called the Supererogatory Foundation. Later in the day, a small nursing home just outside Rio de Janeiro would receive a check for one hundred thousand dollars to be used in capital improvements.

.

19

Pueblo Riviera turned his Grand Cherokee off the Summerlin Freeway and headed up the canyon road toward the Kaufmann mansion. Behind him was a van with a roof-mounted satellite dish. He couldn't see the logo on the panel door, but he assumed it was a TV network. Like flies on a carcass, it never takes long for the media to home in on someone's misfortune.

Riviera stepped on the gas. He never had been a patient man, and today he had a full schedule. He had to move Kaufmann to a secure location, schedule a press conference, and reply to the allegations bantered around by the press. Without properly scripted information, the press would use its imagination—never a good idea. He also needed to find that Russian girl before she caused more trouble.

Riviera pulled up to the wrought iron gate. A dozen media cars were scattered around the gate. A woman with microphone in hand was talking into a TV camera. Other TV cameras, with telephoto lenses protruding through the wrought iron bars, focused on the portico, bedroom windows, or anywhere else that luck might provide a story. Two of Kaufmann's uniformed guards held the mob at bay.

Recognizing Riviera, one of the guards pushed a button to open the gate. As Riviera waited for the gait to open, a newswoman knocked on his window and held up a microphone in the universal sign for "give me an interview." Riviera ignored her and drove through the gate. He would deal with the media later. At the moment he had greater priorities. Riviera pulled up in front of the portico and parked his car. It blocked the portico entrance, but any visitors who came today wouldn't be there to wish Kaufmann well. A little inconvenience wouldn't hurt them.

As he had expected, Kaufmann was in the library. The wine bottle smashed against the wall confirmed Kaufmann's foul mood. Kaufmann looked up with anger in his eyes. "It's about time you showed up. They cheated my casinos out of twelve million dollars."

"I know. I was there."

"And my picture is plastered across every TV news channel. They have pictures of what they say is me with Osama bin Laden. I've never met the guy. Someone like that you'd think I'd remember." Kaufmann took another swig of wine. He was drinking directly from a second bottle even though he had several clean wine glasses at his side. "The guy in the picture did look like me."

"It's a forgery, a fake. The CIA will arrive at the same conclusion in a week or two. They need more time to analyze the photo."

"Then what? I get a small retraction on the back page?"

"It's not a perfect world."

"Are you aware three of my hotels have been shut down? A slew of federal marshals descended on them this morning. They say it could take a week or more before I can reopen. I have the best attorneys money can buy, and they all tell me there's nothing I can do. I'm losing millions of dollars every day the hotels are down. I've got mortgage payments to make, payrolls to meet. Even after I reopen, who'll want to stay in a hotel where people are getting deadly diseases? The tabloids are suggesting I've been using my hotels to test biological weapons for Osama bin Laden. I don't even know that raghead. If I can't cover my loans, the banks could foreclose. I could lose my casinos."

"Pull in money from your offshore account. You have plenty."

"You don't think I've thought of that? The damn Internet is down." Kaufmann threw his wine bottle against the wall. The glass shattered, and the pieces fell to the floor with the other shards of glass. "Nothing is going right today. I still can't get on the Internet."

"When did this happen?"

"Early this morning. I had just logged on to transfer some money when the Internet crashed."

"Did you enter your password?"

"That's when it crashed. I had just entered my password when it disconnected. Does that make a difference?"

Riviera ignored the question.

"If I pull money out of my offshore account, I'll have to pay taxes like common people. Do you realize how much that would be?" Kaufmann filled one of the unbroken glasses with wine from his third and last bottle. He emptied the glass with a few quick swallows and added it to the pile of glass by the wall. "That Petrova girl is behind this, isn't she?"

"It appears so." Riviera removed the half-empty wine bottle. Kaufmann didn't need any more liquid courage. "You had the bus blown up. We had agreed she would be returned to Russia unharmed."

"Sometimes you can be too sentimental. She needed to be dead." Kaufmann reached for the bottle of wine that was no longer there. "You aren't the only one on my payroll who knows how to use a Stinger missile."

"She wasn't on the bus. A lot of innocent people were."

Kaufmann leaned back in his chair and relaxed. Riviera had seen it happen before. Kaufmann was as predictable as rain in Oregon. He attacked his problems with alcohol, temper tantrums, and broken wine bottles. In that state of mind, he wouldn't listen to reason or logic. Offering help was a useless gesture, a waste of time. Riviera could only wait patiently until Kaufmann's anger was spent. Sometimes it took five minutes; other times, an hour. Eventually, he would slip into despondency. Then he was pliable; then he would listen to suggestions. He could be helped. From the accumulation of broken glass, Riviera assumed Kaufmann had been venting his anger for a considerable period of time. Kaufmann now sat in his chair, mute. His eyes were glassy and bloodshot. The alcohol was having its effect.

"You have other problems."

Kaufmann looked up in disbelief. He had assumed it couldn't get worse.

"The CIA wants to talk to you about those pictures. The pictures are forgeries of course, but the CIA doesn't know that. I expect someone from the CIA will show up later today."

"What'll I tell them?" Kaufmann asked.

"You'll tell them nothing, because you won't be here. We need to get you out of here, away from the news media, someplace where the CIA has no authority." In reality there wasn't a place where the CIA had no authority. Riviera didn't mention that. But there was no advantage to making life easy for the CIA. "We're moving you to the *Chimera*. You can conduct your business from the *Chimera* as you can here—probably better."

"Let me call my chauffeur. A change of scenery will do me good." Kaufmann picked up his phone and began to dial.

"No chauffeur, no limo." Riviera gently removed the phone from Kaufmann's hand and placed it back on the cradle. "You have an army of reporters and TV cameramen bivouacked at your front gate. You wouldn't get ten feet before they surrounded your limousine and forced it to halt. The six o'clock news would have a field day. You'll look like a convicted felon trying to escape."

"What'll *we* do?" Kaufmann was normally egocentric except when in trouble, then he reverted to the plural.

"I have keys to your gardener's pickup. You'll ride to the airport in the back under a tarp. A private jet will fly you to San Diego. From there you'll fly by helicopter to the *Diamond Stud*, which is waiting just off the California coast. Four days sailing will get you to the *Chimera*. The South Pacific isn't bad this time of year. You can spend time with your son."

"I don't want to spend time with my son. That's why I hired the Filipino nanny. She's an RN. How many babies have registered nurses for nannies? That's more than that Russian peasant girl could have provided."

Twenty minutes later, a brown, rusted-out pickup passed through the front gates. The driver wore bib overalls. A dirty straw hat covered his black hair, although a small lock of silver hair dangled down over his forehead. The media people converged in unison upon the driver.

"Please, *amigos*," the driver said in a thick Spanish accent. "I have work to do."

The back of the pickup was loaded with bags of fertilizer, rakes, hoes, and other gardening tools. A coil of hose lay on top of a canvas-covered mound. The reporters checked out the back and, deciding the gardener wasn't worthy of time on the six o'clock news, allowed him to pass.

20

The Spaniard leaned against the railing on the *Chimera's* fantail and watched the ship's prop churn up the water. They were cruising in the Coral Sea just southeast of New Guinea where the air was hot and humid despite the breeze created by the ship's ten knots. Ten minutes of exposure outside the ship's air-conditioned interior had stained the Spaniard's armpits with sweat, but sweat cleansed the pores and purged the body of harmful toxins. Sweat, he could tolerate.

As usual, the ship had no destination, no place to go. It had been years since the ship had visited a port and then only for engine repairs not fixable on the open sea. Except for the gurgling sound of the water, the ship's stern was quiet; one of the reasons Riviera visited the fantail when he needed a place to think. He would have preferred a stroll in the woods, as he wasn't a seaman by nature, but that wasn't an option on the *Chimera*.

A passing sea gull turned to follow the ship, flying fifteen feet from the Spaniard. It flew in tandem with the ship and appeared motionless. The gull watched the Spaniard, hoping some small morsel of food might be thrown its way. The Spaniard ignored the bird. He had more important matters on his mind. The world as Kaufmann knew it was coming unglued just as the Spaniard had expected. Kaufmann had always lived to the fullest, blind to any risk it might generate. Now his luck had run out. It wouldn't be the first time. In the past, the Spaniard had always been there to pull Kaufmann to safety. This time the Spaniard's efforts would be futile. There was nothing more he could do. Kaufmann was on his own—in deep water of his own making.

"There you are." It was Dr. Mason. "I've been looking for you." He had a folder in his hand suggesting it wasn't a social visit. "Is it true Lamar's money is gone?"

"Bad news travels fast." Riviera studied Mason's face. He hadn't realized how much Mason had aged over the years. The wrinkles were deeper than he had remembered. Mason wasn't the only one who had aged with the years. Maybe they both should consider retirement.

"Any chance of getting the money back, finding who took it?" Mason had the look of a man grasping for straws, someone who needed hope.

"It's hard to report missing money you weren't supposed to have. He had paid no taxes. He could do serious time for tax evasion. No, the money's gone. The *Chimera* is worth several million. If he sold the *Chimera,* he might generate enough cash to salvage some of his casino business. He won't starve, but neither will he be able to continue his opulent lifestyle."

"If he sells the *Chimera*, I'll lose my research lab. I'll have to shut down." Mason looked pensive for a moment. "I suppose I could use the time to write up my research. I could publish a lot of papers, perhaps write a textbook on stem cell physiology."

"You'll survive."

"I'm sure I will, but that's not why I need to talk to you. I'm afraid Lamar has more problems, medical problems." Dr. Mason gestured toward a patio table just forward of the fantail. "Can we have a seat?"

The Spaniard didn't reply but walked over to the table. It was made of frosted glass and had an umbrella attached to a post protruding from the center of the table. It came in handy when the sun of the South Pacific was high in the sky. The Spaniard sat down in a lounge chair and waited for the doctor to elaborate. Mason wasn't prone to social conversation unless he had something to say. He sat in a chair opposite the Spaniard.

"Lamar has some serious problems."

"Tell me something I don't know," the Spaniard said.

"No, he's got problems beyond the money thing." Mason pulled a letter from his folder and passed it to Riviera. The letterhead identified Mayo Clinic as its origin. Riviera read the contents.

"Kaufmann has leukemia?"

"It appears so. He needs further testing to be sure. Mayo Clinic is suggesting a bone marrow biopsy."

"Any chance this letter is bogus?" Riviera had been conned too many times by that Russian girl. He wasn't about to let it happen again.

"Lamar let me look at his old medical files. When he had his physical last year at Mayo Clinic, they did some blood work including a CBC."

"Speak English."

"A Compete Blood Count. It's a blood test that looks at individual blood cells. According to the report, he had 52,000 white cells per cubic millimeter. Normal is 4,000 to 10,000. Seventy percent of them were lymphocytes."

"Meaning?"

"He probably has Chronic Lymphocytic Leukemia. I ordered the test a year ago, three or four months before Ana came on board ship. There's no way she could have been involved. I wish Lamar had shown me the lab results earlier, but it had no meaning to him."

"You say he needs a bone marrow biopsy?"

"That would confirm the diagnoses. It's still possible the test results were a fluke. He seems healthy enough."

"Can you do the test here?"

"No. He needs to have it done in a hospital, somewhere where they have a lab close by to handle the specimen. I wouldn't have it done in a foreign country. Too big of a chance of getting AIDS from a dirty needle. He needs an American hospital."

Riviera pondered the consequences. "If he goes back to the States, he'll be at the mercy of the press. The CIA will be all over him. I'd prefer waiting until the pictures are proven to be forgeries."

"That could be a while."

"Would any American hospital do?"

"I would assume so. The procedure isn't difficult."

Riviera sat back in his chair and took a deep breath. He slowly exhaled. "Last I checked, we were fifteen hundred miles west of

American Samoa. They have a hospital in Pago Pago. We could slip him in and out of there with minimal problems. If we smuggled him in by small boat, we could avoid customs. No one will be expecting him to show up in Pago Pago."

"That'll work for me."

"Where's he at now?" Riviera asked.

"He's in the conference room planning his revenge. He's overcome his depression. Now he's hyper, almost manic. He's obsessed with getting back at that Russian girl."

"We need to talk to him." The Spaniard stood up. Dr. Mason assumed he was to follow.

They found Kaufmann in the conference room as they had expected. He was seated at the large table surrounded by numerous sheets of yellow paper ripped from his legal pad. A half-empty wine bottle was within easy reach. In the background, hard rock music blared. Kaufmann wasn't normally a fan of rock music. The Spaniard turned off the music.

Kaufmann looked up from his work. "Good, I was about to go looking for you two." He refilled his wine glass in mid-thought. "I have a plan to get my money back. We need to abduct that Russian girl again. This time we'll use that baby for bait. She'll come for the baby. Women are like that." Kaufmann got up and staggered to a map he had tacked to the wall. He tapped his wine glass against the Pacific coast of Mexico, staining the map with spilt wine. "Here is Mazatlan. There's a small resort town fifty miles to the south. I found a bed and breakfast resort on the beach. It's small, but that's to our advantage. Del and I will be spending time lying on the beach with our newborn baby. It won't be the real baby of course. We'll have one of those baby carriers. I'll have this leaked to the social columns. You can count on them to spread the gossip. You guys will be hiding in the brush with binoculars. When that Russian girl comes for the baby, we abduct her just like we did at the Black Sea. We'll drug her and fly her back to the *Chimera*— which I'll have waiting for us just off shore." Pleased with himself, Kaufmann walked back to the table and sat down. "Once we get her onboard, we'll make her tell us where the money is. She may be smart, but she's also sentimental. That's her weakness. We'll put that cattle prod to her baby. When she hears that baby scream, she'll tell us everything we want to know."

Kaufmann reached for the wine bottle, but the Spaniard grabbed it and pried it from Kaufmann's hands. "We need to talk," the Spaniard said.

"What's there to discuss? It's a perfect plan."

"Dr. Mason tells me you may be sick. You may have leukemia."

"That's just a possibility. It's not for sure. I feel fine."

"We need to do further testing. Mayo Clinic is suggesting a bone marrow biopsy."

"I can have Mason do that." Kaufmann reached for the wine bottle, but Riviera pulled it farther away.

"Dr. Mason says it has to be done in a hospital setting. I don't want you going back to the States until that problem with Osama bin Laden is cleared up. I'm going to instruct the ship's captain to head for American Samoa. We can be there in a few days. I'll make arrangements for a small boat to pick us up during the night. The *Chimera* will have to stay outside the twelve-mile limit."

"Why don't we fly in by helicopter like we normally do?"

"If you land at the airport, you'll have to go through customs. It's best we don't flaunt your presence."

Kaufmann studied his map again. "American Samoa is on the way to Mexico. I don't see a problem. We do need to start working on this Mexican project. We'll make that Russian girl pay for what she did to us." Kaufmann reached for the wine bottle. This time the Spaniard offered no resistance.

Three days later, the green peaks of Tutuila presented on the *Chimera's* port side. From fifteen miles, the rainforest-covered mountains appeared no different than what Dutch sailors had seen three centuries earlier. The largest of seven islands comprising American Samoa, it measured only fifty-four square miles in area, hardly worth noting on a map. By most measures, it was no different than any of the other small islands that dotted the South Pacific—except for Pago Pago Harbor. That was what placed it on the map. It was one of the largest deep-water harbors in the South Pacific.

"Where to *signor?*" the Italian pilot asked when Riviera strapped himself into the copilot's seat.

"We're going to the Pago Pago International Airport. I have business on Tutuila. It'll take three or four hours at most. You'll have to wait for me at the airport."

Without further comment, the pilot eased the helicopter off the *Chimera's* deck and headed toward Tutuila. He enjoyed flying. One reason for flying was as good as the next. The island's lush foliage became more vivid as they approached the shoreline. Various shades of green covered the old volcanic mountains, and then abruptly changed to white coral sand at the water's edge. The surrounding water was emerald-green and crystal clear. It would be a diver's paradise.

The pilot wouldn't need his GPS to find the airport. Unlike urban airports, the air was clear and free of smog. Visibility was almost limitless. The Pago Pago International Airport immediately came into view. Built on a coral reef, it protruded out over the water forming the southern border of Pala Lagoon. The pilot approached from the east, heading along the east-west runway. He could approach from any direction, but it was customary and safer to approach, as would a fixed winged plane. He passed Coconut Point at the entrance to Pala Lagoon and headed down the runway, coming to a stop near the terminal. They would have to report to customs. With no luggage, it was a minor annoyance.

Riviera found it more convenient to secure a taxicab than rent a car. The taxi would come with a driver who could serve as a guide to the island. Riviera had no time to waste getting a feel for the island.

"Take me to Tafuna," he told the driver.

Although Samoans had their own language, most Samoans were bilingual. The cabby was no exception. The driver headed north along the shore of Pala Lagoon toward Tafuna. It was a two-mile drive. On Tafuna's main street, rustic boat docks jutted out into the sea as if they were the town's natural appendages. Tafuna was a fishing town. "Pull over to the curb," Riviera said when they approached the first dock.

It was early in the day, and the docks were quiet. Few people milled around. This would change when the fishing boats returned. Riviera told the driver to wait and exited the cab. What he had to do wouldn't take long.

Unlike Pago Pago Harbor, Pala Lagoon wasn't a deep-water port. The docks mainly catered to small fishing boats, most of which were currently out to sea. Riviera walked out on one of the docks where a few boats remained tied to rusty cleats. The dock was in need of repair, reflecting the sad state of the Samoan economy. Built out of weatherworn planks supported by wooden pilings, the dock was slowly succumbing to the power of the sea. The support pilings were no longer perpendicular to the water line, but uniformly leaned toward the west at an angle that would have redeemed the Leaning Tower of Pisa. Riviera passed two fishing boats that had returned early with full loads. Their crews were busy cleaning their catch in hopes of reaching the local fish markets before the afternoon shoppers selected the dinner meal. They tossed the fish heads and entrails into the lagoon. The water where the fish heads landed erupted violently. The water swirled for ten or twenty seconds before becoming calm. It reminded the Spaniard of piranha in the backwaters of the Amazon River.

Farther down the dock, a young Samoan was working on an outboard motor to a Zodiac CZ7. It was a twenty-three foot inflatable that sported twin 150 horsepower engines, obviously military surplus. In his younger days, when he had been working for the CIA, Riviera had logged many hours on similar inflatables. Under good conditions, they could make fifty knots.

"You Keoni Naikelekele?"

The young man nodded. He appeared to be in his early twenties and wore the universal uniform of youth: sandals, dirty jeans, and a tee shirt advertising his favorite beer. The only evidence suggesting he worked for a living was the bulging muscles under his shirt. Riviera would have preferred an older man. With age comes reliability. He would take what he could get.

"I'm Charles Walton." There was no advantage in using his real name. "We talked on the phone." The Samoan nodded again leading the Spaniard to wonder if he spoke English. "Is the motor working?" Riviera gestured toward the port engine. The cover was off, and the engine appeared under repair.

"It'll get you there," the Samoan said in perfect English.

"You have GPS?"

The Samoan nodded. He was a man of few words.

"Here are the coordinates." Riviera handed the Samoan a slip of paper with the proper coordinates. "I need you at this location at four o'clock tomorrow morning. My client has an early appointment at the LBJ Tropical Medical Center. He doesn't want to be late."

"If he doesn't make it, it won't be the fault of my boat."

"Riviera removed a hundred dollar bill from his wallet and passed it to the Samoan. " You get the other hundred when he gets ashore."

Another nod concluded the conversation, and Riviera headed back to his waiting cab. He lacked confidence in the Samoan. He would have preferred full payment only after the job was complete. Fortunately, the stakes were small. If he didn't show up, alternate arrangements could be made for the following day. "Now we need to go to the LBJ Tropical Medical Center," he told the cab driver.

As the taxi pulled away, Keoni Naikelekele picked up his cell phone and dialed the number for the Tradewinds Hotel in downtown Pago Pago. He asked for room 204. "Your man with the lock of silver hair has arrived," he said into the phone.

21

Dorek Dolinski replaced the phone on its cradle. "He's here."

It took a moment for the significance to register. She had chased Kaufmann half way around the world, and now he was coming to her...and he was bringing their baby. Disbelief gradually changed to elation. Ana had prepared herself for failure. Plans of this magnitude were fraught with uncertainty. They were filled with too many opportunities for fate to take an unpredictable turn. Now she allowed the excitement to grow within her. She could feel the adrenaline rush flowing through her veins and her hands began to tremble. Despite all of the obstacles, their plans were about to bear fruit. There really was a God.

Ana threw a hotel pillow at the ceiling and fell backwards onto the bed, allowing her body to bounce gently on the soft mattress. Grabbing the other pillow, she covered her eyes and tried to picture her newborn son. She had only known him for a short time, yet the picture was clear and vivid.

"When's it going to happen?" she asked.

"Tomorrow at four in the morning. We have the coordinates." Unlike his jubilant girlfriend, Dorek was not euphoric. He couldn't share her enthusiasm—not at this time. It was far from over; and worst of all, the denouement of this real-life theatrical performance was no longer under their control. It would now depend on the Americans.

"Are you sure the Americans will help?" he asked. Dorek wasn't one to delegate authority. Over the years he had relied on his own judgment. His judgment, he could count on. He found leaving such an important task to others unsettling. It might have been remnants of the cold war mentality, but he had doubts about the Americans' willingness and capability to pull it off.

"We have to trust the Americans," Ana said, sensing Dorek's doubts. Marshall Peterson of the American FBI had seemed sincere. She didn't know why, but she trusted him. He did provide Kaufmann's pictures.

Ana looked at her watch: It was almost noon. Her biological clock was lost somewhere between Michigan and Nevada. Four in the morning would be eight o'clock by her mental clock. She should be at her intellectual peak. Right now she was exhausted. They were both exhausted. With nothing more they could do, Ana set the alarm for 2 a.m. and collapsed on the bed.

It seemed like the alarm rang ten minutes later. Ana turned on the light beside the bed and checked her watch to confirm the time. "Dorek, it's morning. Time to get up."

Dorek crawled out of bed in a somber mood. Pitch black wasn't his definition of morning. Still half asleep, he slipped into jeans while Ana brushed her teeth and combed her hair. As the stupor of sleep dissipated, Dorek was overcome by the premonition that Ana would inform him there wouldn't be time for breakfast. That would make a long day. "I'll load the van." If he had to be up, he might as well be productive.

Ana gargled an unintelligible reply though a mouth filled with toothpaste. Dorek—assuming the reply was a cryptic form of acquiescence—picked up the Chip-Scale Atomic Clock and headed toward the van. Most of their equipment was rugged and could take abuse. Not so with the atomic clock. The clock needed the same care and respect one would give nitroglycerine. The mission depended on the accuracy of that small nuclear timepiece. If it were off by a nanosecond, their mission would fail. He gently set it down on the passenger seat of their rented van. He would have Ana hold it on the drive to the lagoon. He stashed the rest of the equipment in the back.

Ana emerged from the hotel dressed in jeans. "Here's breakfast." She handed Dorek a candy bar from her unending supply. Dorek would have preferred pancakes and sausage with a glass of orange juice. Apparently, Ana hadn't programmed that into their plan. He wondered what other flaws lie hidden in their plan.

Keoni Naikelekele was waiting for them when they arrived at the lagoon. He had stashed his personal equipment in the rear of the Zodiac. No longer dressed in jeans and sandals, he now wore combat boots and military fatigues. His face was painted black. On his right lapel was a subdued silver bar of a Lieutenant Junior Grade. On his left lapel was the insignia of a Navy SEAL. A true Samoan, he had joined the navy after college.

"Ma'am, can I help you with that?" A professional demeanor that evinced confidence replaced the Samoan's devil-may-care attitude of the previous day. He relieved Ana of the heavy battery before she had a chance to reply and placed it in the inflatable boat next to an M-16. Until now, Ana hadn't appreciated the seriousness of their mission. She hoped the M-16 wouldn't be needed.

Dorek loaded the atomic clock, placing it near the front where he would be sitting. He needed to assemble the equipment before they hit the high seas. Later they couldn't risk using flashlights. Despite previous practice, it took ten minutes to link the atomic clock, laptop computer, GPS, and directional antenna. To avoid exposing the atomic clock to stray voltage, he wouldn't connect the car battery until later.

"We ready?" Naikelekele asked.

"I guess so," Dorek replied. They had done what they could. The rest would be up to the U.S. Navy.

The navy lieutenant passed them each a life vest. "Navy regulations."

Lt. Keoni Naikelekele started the twin 150 horsepower engines and edged the Zodiac into the lagoon. With the sky overcast, there was no starlight and the lagoon became a large black hole into which the Zodiac was engulfed. Guided by the LCD display of the boat's GPS, Keoni pointed the boat toward Coconut Point and the exit from Pala Lagoon. Out of respect for the residents of Tafuna and his other countryman living around the lagoon, he didn't open the throttle until he passed Coconut Point and had headed into open water. He then pointed the inflatable toward the southwest and opened the throttles to both engines. The boat leaped out of the water. Forty miles per hour may seem slow by car, but racing across the waves in the absolute darkness can be exhilarating. Ana and Dorek held tightly to the rope anchored along the perimeter of the boat, wondering if that much speed was necessary. The lieutenant obviously enjoyed his work.

They were to rendezvous with the *Chimera* fifteen miles south of Steps Point at the southern tip of the island—at least that had been the Spaniard's plan. Lieutenant Naikelekele cut the engines nine miles south of Steps Point, well within the jurisdictional waters of the United States Government.

"We wait here," he said.

In the distance—far to the south—lights flickered near the horizon. "Is that the *Chimera*?" Ana asked. Naikelekele nodded in the affirmative. It looked so small on the horizon. It was hard to believe their son was on the ship, so close—yet so far away.

Dorek hooked the apparatus up to the car battery and typed some commands into the computer.

"How does that contraption work?" Unable to race his boat, Keoni turned his interest to the scientific aspect of the mission.

"GPS works on the principle of triangulation," Ana said. "There are twenty-four satellites in geosynchronous orbits, meaning they hover over the same spot on earth. They send out digital radio codes. These are picked up by the GPS receiver. Since we know the speed of the radio waves, all we need is the time it takes for the signal to travel from the satellite to the GPS monitor to calculate the distance from the satellite. The satellites have atomic clocks that measure time in nanoseconds. Using sophisticated algorithms, the GPS monitor calculates the transmission time and hence the distance to the satellite. We need the distance from four satellites to determine our position down to meters."

"Sounds like gibberish to me. I like my GPS better. I turn it on and it works." Keoni watched as Dorek typed in further commands.

Dorek completed the instructions and closed the lid to his laptop. Even the light from the computer display could give them away in the blackness of the sea. "O.K., point the antenna toward the *Chimera*. Let's see what happens."

Ana pointed the directional antenna toward the *Chimera*.

"How is this GPS stuff going to help us?" Keoni asked.

"We have an atomic clock connected to our computer. With our directional antenna, we can mimic one of the GPS satellites. Since we're closer, our signal will be stronger. If we can override their GPS, we can give them a false reading by slightly altering the timing of the signal. They think they're going to stop fifteen miles offshore. Instead, they will be coming to us, inside territorial waters. If we do it gradually, they'll assume they're fighting a heavy current."

"I hope it works as you say. If it doesn't, we just went for a joy ride."

22

"I don't know why we have to go so early." Kaufmann paced the walkway on the lower deck, chewing out any staff member who had the misfortune to cross his path. He wasn't a cheerful early riser, and he wasn't about to change his ways for a medical test of questionable necessity. He was feeling perfectly fine. That was sufficient for him. He didn't need a medical test to confirm his good health. Dr. Mason had him NPO in case fasting blood work was requested. That meant no breakfast. Mason was giving *him* orders. Kaufmann was accustomed to calling the shots. Taking orders from others, even those he respected, wasn't to his liking. This stop of dubious need was costing him an entire day. One more day before he could implement his plan. Delayed gratification was another of Kaufmann's limited virtues. He wanted that Russian girl abducted, and he wanted it now. He wanted to enjoy her pain when he touched the cattle prod to her baby. He wanted to see the torment in her face as the baby screamed in anguish. Her pain would increase each time the electrodes prodded the infant. She would talk. She would tell him where his money was. She would pay dearly for what she had done. The more he thought of his plan, the better he liked it. The plan was perfect. The Russian girl was a sentimentalist. That was her weakness. As smart as she was, she would still succumb to her primitive maternal emotions. She would follow him to the Mexican resort. Using the baby for bait would make her putty in his hands. Abducting her the second time would be no more difficult than the first time.

"You'll need a life vest." Riviera said, rescuing Kaufmann from his thoughts. "Riding a Zodiac can be risky. It's not your normal ferry boat."

The Spaniard threw a rope ladder over the side. Even from the lower portside deck, it was still thirty feet to the water line, making for a difficult descent to a bobbing Zodiac. Kaufmann wasn't in the best of shape, and the Samoan would be of little help. It was questionable if he would even show. The Samoan was the paradigm of the new generation's soft, impulsive youth who wore their jeans and sandals like the uniform of the irresponsible. The Samoan would never survive in the military or CIA.

The Spaniard looked out over the water with his binoculars, but saw only darkness. Either the Zodiac lacked running lights or it was nowhere in the area. Riviera checked his watch: It was twenty minutes past four. He would have to find a more reliable person and reschedule for the following day. The delay wouldn't improve Kaufmann's irritable mood.

"Excuse me, sir." It was one of the ship's crew. "The captain requests your presence on the bridge. We may have a problem." The crewman was addressing Kaufmann, but his furtive glances toward the Spaniard suggested Riviera's services would also be required.

"Tell him we'll be right there." Riviera replied. Riviera and Kaufmann removed their life vests. The Zodiac was a no show. If Riviera had more time, he would go ashore, retrieve his hundred dollars, and give the Samoan degenerate an attitude adjustment. Fortunately for the Samoan, time restraints precluded such activities.

"What's the problem?" Riviera asked when they reached the bridge. The captain didn't appear overly concerned. Perhaps the problem was trivial.

"I'm not sure it's a problem, but we have a ship heading toward us on the starboard side." The captain pointed to some lights on the horizon. "It's unusual for a ship to be heading into Pago Pago this time in the morning. They'd have poor visibility and little dockside help."

Riviera studied the radar screen. The ship was three miles south of them but closing fast. He walked to the window and looked out with his binoculars. All he could see were the ship's running lights. The rest of the ship was blacked out.

"Could be a tuna boat bringing their catch to one of the canneries. We're lit up like a Christmas tree. I'm sure we're a strange sight…probably coming by to look us over. Keep on the same course, but stay outside the twelve-mile limit." Riviera returned the binoculars to its case. "We'll give our wayward sailor another half hour before we declare him a no-show and move out to sea." Riviera checked the GPS: They were over fifteen miles from the nearest land and moving only fast enough for steerage.

As the distance between the two ships closed, the approaching ship turned to starboard. If it continued on course, it would pass within one hundred yards of the *Chimera*, well within safety parameters. The captain of the *Chimera* maintained his slow course, giving the approaching ship the right away.

Except for the running lights, the ship remained dark. The Spaniard looked at the stern with his binoculars in hopes of seeing a flag of registry—he saw nothing in the darkness. The ship reduced its speed when it came within one hundred yards, traveling parallel to the *Chimera*. They were wasting fuel. This had to be more than idle curiosity.

"What do you think they're up to?" Kaufmann asked.

"I don't know, but I don't like it," Riviera replied.

A bright beam of light interrupted further speculation, suffusing the *Chimera*'s bridge with its glare. The phantom ship had come to life, its decks now flooded with light from stem to stern. A diagonal red stripe on the bow identified the ship as a U.S. Coast Guard Cutter, its bow searchlights now focused on the *Chimera's* bridge.

"Officer in charge of *Chimera*, this is the U.S. Coast Guard Cutter *Hamilton*. Please stand by for boarding." It was coming from a speaker aboard the Coast Guard Cutter.

Pueblo Riviera checked the GPS—they were still fifteen miles from shore. He set the radio dial to the international distress frequency. "*Chimera* to the captain of Coast Guard Cutter *Hamilton*. Be advised we sail under Panamanian registry. We are in international waters. You have no authority to board this ship. Request denied."

"This is the Captain of the *Hamilton*. You are currently in jurisdictional waters of the United States Government. Boarding your ship is not a request. It is an informational statement."

The Spaniard looked at the LCD display on the GPS. The cursor representing the ship was fifteen miles from the southern shore of Tutuila, clearly in international waters. Then, as he watched, the cursor faded away and a new cursor emerged nine miles south of Steps Point. They had been tricked. They were inside the twelve-mile limit.

"Ninety-degree turn to starboard," Kaufmann said. He had also seen the change in the cursor and realized the significance. "Give it full steam. Take her into open water."

A geyser of water erupted twenty-five yards in front of the *Chimera*'s bow.

"Mr. Kaufmann, they're shooting at us." The *Chimera's* captain had turned the bow as ordered but wasn't confident about outrunning the 378 foot cutter—not when the cutter had a 76 mm deck gun.

"If they're shooting at us, they're poor shots," Kaufmann said. "They missed us by twenty-five yards."

"That was a warning shot. The U.S. Coast Guard doesn't miss—not at that distance. Stop all engines." Riviera turned to Kaufmann. "Lamar, you have five minutes before they board. I suggest you use it wisely."

The possibility of anyone boarding the *Chimera* had been considered remote. The ship had Panamanian registry and always remained in international waters. Other than the Panamanian government, which had no significant navy, no nation had such authority on open seas. It would have been considered an act of piracy. Still, there were contingency plans for such a mishap, should it occur. Measures could be taken to mitigate the damage. Five minutes would be all they needed.

The appearance of the Coast Guard with its beaming searchlights hadn't gone unnoticed. Aroused by curiosity and concern, senior staff officers gathered on the bridge. They whispered quietly among themselves. No one ventured to query

Kaufmann or the Spaniard about the proceedings, but observation of the on-going drama provided the gist of the situation.

Finally, a subdued Lamar Kaufmann turned to the small gathering. "Shred all correspondence. Toss all computers overboard. I want no hard drives left onboard the ship." He checked the depth gauge: They were in three hundred and forty feet of water. No one would be retrieving the computer data before the salt water had time to make them useless. "I want that baby thrown overboard. That Russian girl will never see it again."

23

Lt. Commander Raymond Connors wiped the salty spray from his face. The salt water burned his eyes, but he had endured worse punishment in life. Inactivity was more distasteful. He now bobbed in a light sea on *Zodiac One* waiting for the signal to proceed. With the sky overcast, darkness was absolute. Only the whites of their eyes betrayed the five other men in his inflatable boat. Like Connors, they had blackened their faces to match the body armor covering their fatigues. Stun grenades protruded from utility belts, and Uzi submachine guns were strapped across their chests. A pair of state-of-the-art night-vision goggles hung from their helmets. Boarding recalcitrant ships on the high seas was a procedure they had perfected over the years, although none of them had ever participated in a takeover of a hostile ship. The *Chimera* was small compared to the larger ocean-going ships they had commandeered in practice. That should shorten the execution time. Connors looked into the darkness in hopes of seeing the other inflatables under his command. There was no sign of *Zodiacs Two, Three,* and *Four.* They would be somewhere on the starboard side of the *Hamilton,* out of the *Chimera's* field of view—not that they could be seen in the darkness.

At forty-two, Connors was at the age when most men were cultivating beer bellies and switching from racquetball to golf. He knew that would happen someday. Keeping up with the men he commanded was more challenging every year. One wouldn't know that looking at his muscular six-foot-two frame. It was the product of daily weight lifting and a five-mile run. As long as he was leading men, he needed to adhere to their standards. He was a third generation Annapolis grad. Giving anything less than his best had never been a consideration. Next year would be different. In the fall, he would be up for promotion to full commander. After that they would confine him to a small office with a metal desk covered with papers and drab walls covered with maps. His connection to any military operations would be restricted to the pins stuck into his wall maps. That would require serious physical and mental adjustments to his life style.

Connors checked the luminous dial on his watch: They had been in a holding pattern for six minutes, far too long. Waiting dulled the senses. It provided time for the adrenaline rush to dissipate. His men were ready. It was time to push their plan into action.

The deck lights on the *Hamilton* flashed on moments later, invading Connors' darkness. It was the prearranged signal to begin. The other three Zodiacs, now clearly visible, bobbed on the open water not far from *Zodiac One*.

Connors spoke into the microphone attached to his helmet. "This is *Zodiac One*. Let's roll." His encrypted message was repeated in the earphones of twenty-four navy SEALs. Connors zeroed his stopwatch. The clock was now ticking. They had factored five minutes of confusion on board the *Chimera* into the assault plan. Anything beyond that was problematic.

Following Connors' command, *Zodiac One's* helmsman pushed forward on the throttle and the twin 150 horsepower outboards roared into action. More saltwater splashed on Connors' face. The boat banked sharply as the helmsman skidded the boat around the back of the *Hamilton* and headed toward the *Chimera's* stern where they were less likely to be seen. To cover their approach, the *Hamilton's* powerful searchlight flooded the *Chimera's* bridge. It would blind anyone in its wash. Three Zodiacs followed closely in *Zodiac One's* wake. As they approached the *Chimera,* the boats split, two to each side of the ship. *Zodiac One*, still in the lead, pulled alongside the *Chimera's* stern on the starboard side. Connors aimed the beam of his flashlight at the ship's hull near the water line searching for obstructions. For the most part, it was free of barnacles—the crew of the *Chimera* took good care of their ship. When the Zodiac was no more than a foot from the *Chimera*, Connors slapped an eight-inch diameter magnetic disc against a section void of barnacles. A seaman at the front of the Zodiac did likewise. The "O" rings on the magnets provided moorings to secure the Zodiac to the *Chimera*. Ropes were quickly attached.

As if resenting its confinement, the air-filled Zodiac bounced angrily against the *Chimera* like a twig caught in the eddy of a rapids. The two-foot swells were more random and chaotic next to the *Chimera's* hull where the waves ricocheting off the metal plate collided with oncoming waves. Sometimes the waves canceled, other times they converged into larger waves. *Zodiac One* now wallowed at the sea's pleasure. It could have been worse. They were in the lee of Tutuila. Even at nine miles out, it offered some protection. In training they had boarded ships in eight-foot swells. Connors foresaw no immediate problems.

Connors steadied the boat while men shot grappling hooks from two small mortars attached to plywood bases on the Zodiac's floor. The grappling hooks bounced noisily off the ship's hull just below the ship's lower deck and fell into the water. The rolling waves made aiming the mortars a matter of timing. This time their timing had been off. It could have been worse. The cast iron hooks could have fallen on the Zodiac inflicting serious injuries, or they could have punctured the boat. Still, it was a setback. Connors looked at his watch. They were squandering precious time. Without hesitating, the men retrieved the grappling hooks and recharged the mortars. The second attempt was more accurate, sending the grappling hooks over the railing of the lower deck. As they pulled the ropes taut, the grappling hooks caught on the upper rail.

Chief Petty Officer Carlos Rodriguez grabbed a rope and gave a tug—it seemed secure. Another seaman grabbed the second rope and did likewise. Then, placing their feet against the hull, they began scaling the side of the ship. The ropes had knots every two feet to provide better grip. It was still a difficult task requiring considerable upper body strength. In practice they used gloves to prevent rope burns, but Connors had decided to forgo gloves. Gloved fingers cannot fit inside a trigger guard or easily pull the pin on a flash grenade. Rope burns could be treated later. He heard no complaints from his men.

The two men climbing the wall were now on their own. As an afterthought, Connors pointed the barrel of his Uzi at the sky. He didn't expect trouble, but if someone were to peer over the side, a burst of gunfire over his head would discourage further curiosity. When the first two SEALs reached the top, Connors strapped his Uzi to his back and began his ascent. The climb was easier than he had anticipated—courtesy of excess adrenaline. The *Chimera's* deck was also lower than the ocean-going freighters they had scaled in practice.

Connors looked at the luminous dial on his watch as the last member of the team cleared the railing. They were two and a half minutes into the operation. The operation should have proceeded more quickly. What they had done so far was routine. There had been no opposition. That wouldn't last forever.

Connors spoke into his microphone. "This is *Zodiac one*. Our feet are dry. Proceeding to objective."

Connors scanned the walkway. Unlike its commercial counterparts, the *Chimera's* walkway was constructed of polished teak. Scattered along its length were mahogany benches where people could sit and admire the sea. At the moment there was nothing to admire, and the outside deck was deserted. He had expected that. It was approaching five o'clock in the morning and non-essential personnel would still be sleeping. Floodlights spaced every twenty yards along the walkway illuminated doors to the interior. According to the ship's floor plan in the cargo pocket of Connors' fatigues, they needed the second door from the stern. A draftsman had cobbled the plan from details provided by the Russian girl. It was quite detailed—too detailed to be realistic. Connors wondered how much was fact and how much was confabulation. The entire assault depended on its accuracy. It left Connors with doubts he didn't wish to share with others.

The outboards on the Zodiacs below were now in idle producing a soft, muffled noise. Connors tuned them out and listened for human sounds, hearing none. Above him he could hear the whopping sound of a helicopter. That would be the *Hamilton's* Jayhawk helicopter ferrying over additional troops. They were jumping the gun. They weren't to arrive until the ship was secured.

Connors looked up and saw the outline of a Bell 430, definitely not the Jayhawk. The delay was taking its toll. Someone was escaping. Whoever was onboard wouldn't get far. They were in the middle of the South Pacific with no place to go other than Tutuila. It was a small island. They could run, but not hide.

Connors led his men toward the second door, finding it unlocked. Given more time the *Chimera's* security personnel would have had it secured. Connors had plans for that possibility, although it would have been time consuming.

The door opened to a steep metal stairwell. A water hose and red-handled fire ax were mounted on the side wall. So far the Russian was batting a thousand. Connors led his team down two flights of stairs into the bowels of the ship. Another door opened into a long corridor. The corridor was narrow and utilitarian. This section of the ship wasn't designed for show. It was illuminated with overhead red lights, unusual for a non-warship. According to the Russian, the engine room would be behind the door at the end of the corridor. Connors and his men ran the length of the corridor, their rubber-soled shoes minimizing noise. Like most structures onboard, the door was constructed of metal to limit fires. It hung on three heavy hinges. Connors heard muffled voices through the metal door, but was unable to discern individual words. The inflection was casual, revealing no signs of anxiety. The element of surprise was intact.

Connors gave the door a shove, finding it locked. The setbacks were beginning to multiply. Stepping back, he nodded at Rodriguez who placed a plastic explosive charge over the lock and molded it around a detonator cannibalized from a claymore mine. He played out thirty feet of wire and attached the bare ends to an M-57 detonator. Thirty feet was pushing the edge of safety. Connors would have preferred fifty feet, but the size of the corridor had its limitations. The resulting explosion produced a six-inch hole in the door where the lock had been. The door swung freely. Rodriguez pushed the door open, tossed in two stun grenades, and covered his ears. The resultant noise, flash, and concussion momentarily incapacitated the three engine room workers. They were cuffed with disposable nylon handcuffs before they came to their senses.

"How do I shut down the diesel engines?" Connors asked a crewmember. He was greeted with silence. Time restraints precluded formal negotiations. There were ways to make him talk. Connors placed the barrel of his 9 mm against the man's head. He was bluffing of course, but the engine room worker didn't need to know that. "You have five seconds to tell me. One...two...three..."

"I think I found it." Rodriguez pulled a lever labeled *emergency shutdown*. The diesel engines went silent, and the twin propeller shafts came to a halt. The only remaining noise was the high-pitched whine from the electrical generator. This too ceased with a pull of a lever. Without electricity, a pall of darkness descended on the *Chimera*. Only the occasional battery-powered emergency lights remained.

***

"Let's go." Lt. Junior Grade Todd Bennett, leader of *Zodiac Two*, donned his night-vision goggles when the *Chimera* fell into darkness. It was the signal to begin his segment of the operation. Metal walls prevented electronic communication with those inside the *Chimera's* bowels. He could only assume by the sudden darkness that *Zodiac One* had secured the engine room.

According to the Russian girl, the ship's armory with its collection of M-16s and 9 mm pistols would be found in a forward compartment two floors down. Like the other team leaders, Bennett had a detailed map of the ship in his pocket. He hoped the Russian's assessment was accurate. If the weapons were distributed to crewmembers, the ensuing carnage would be substantial. It was assumed the power outage would stimulate confusion among the crew, if not panic. And the darkness would reduce mobility, a problem not shared by Bennett and his men with their night-vision goggles. That assumed everything went according to plan. In reality, events seldom progressed as planned. To add confusion, Bennett pulled the lever on a fire alarm. Nothing is more terrifying than a fire at sea. A loud wailing noise echoed through the darkened hallways. It was painful to the ears. If nothing more, the noise would make verbal communication between crewmembers difficult.

Bennett led his men down two flights of stairs and followed the corridor the Russian said would lead to the armory. They smashed any emergency lights they found along the way. The corridor opened into a small anteroom dimly illuminated by a solitary emergency light. An armory sign hung above an open doorway. There was no sign of human activity. Bennett peered into the interior beyond the doorway, seeing nothing but darkness. His night-vision goggles were useless in the presence of the emergency light and could cause blindness. Bennett raised his hand to halt the men following him. They silently crouched down awaiting further orders. Something wasn't right. Bennett expected the armory door to be closed and locked. He wasn't fond of the unexpected. Bennett saw the motion too late. Two men armed with M-16s moved into the doorway. The commandos dropped flat on the floor to reduce their silhouettes. But not before Bennett took three rounds to the chest, paying dearly for the honor of leading his men. He fell to the floor in pain. It was if he had been stabbed with a red-hot poker. It took maximum effort just to breath. His brain began to fog. He shook his head to clear his mind. When it did, it filled with guilt. He had failed. He led his men into an ambush, and they were now confined to a narrow corridor with no room to maneuver or retreat. A quick spray from the M-16s would finish them off. Despite his injury, Bennett rolled to his side and fired a short burst at the emergency light. The corridor went black. Inside the ship with no windows, darkness was absolute.

One of the security guards, having lost his orientation, fired several shots over the commandos' heads. They embedded in the anteroom wall two feet to the left of the corridor where Bennett's men hugged the floor. They were random shots, but even random shots eventually strike home. Petty Officer First Class John Cagney pulled down his night-vision goggles and surveyed the scene. The security guards, now appearing as green caricatures, remained in the doorway firing sporadically. He could see fear on their faces. Fear along with sensory deprivation was a bad combination. It made men unpredictable, and that made them more dangerous. Lt. Bennett, curled in a fetal position, lay in front of Cagney. Cagney couldn't tell if he were dead or alive. Breathing wasn't obvious, but such fine details aren't always evident with night-vision goggles. Assuming he was now team leader, Cagney crawled past Bennett's convoluted body. It was a blunt reminder that what Cagney and the others did for a living wasn't without risk. Close up Cagney could see shallow breathing—Bennett was alive, but no telling for how long. The grimace on Bennett's face evinced the severe pain he was enduring. Despite his pain, Bennett suppressed any moaning. Such noise was sure to draw fire. Cagney considered providing medical assistance, but rational thought trumped the urge to provide aid to a friend. Without first aid, Bennett could die. Even with first aid, he could die. The priority now was to eliminate the immediate danger.

Cagney crawled toward the armory door. He felt pain in his left shoulder. He reached over with his right hand and found blood dripping down his arm. He must have taken a stray slug or perhaps it was shrapnel ricocheting off the wall. His arm was painful, but functional. Although any use of the arm would increase bleeding. It was a risk he would have to take. Cagney continued crawling toward the armory door, stopping when he was within twenty feet. He could easily take out the two men with his Uzi. Instructions were to avoid personal injury if possible. Such orders were relative—at least in Cagney's opinion. If they pointed the M-16s at him or his men, he would waste them without guilt. They were now shooting only occasionally and none in Cagney's direction. Cagney pulled the pin on a stun grenade and gave it a toss. He had hoped to lob it through the armory door. That would provide maximum effect on the insurgents with minimal injury to his team. The grenade hit the doorjamb and fell in front of the doorway. That was too close for comfort. Cagney removed his night-vision goggles and placed his index fingers in his ears. He hoped his comrades had seen the stun grenade and were doing likewise. Even with his eyes closed, the light was blinding. The concussion reminded Cagney of being hit by a defensive lineman in high school football. He was prepared to toss in a second grenade, but it wasn't necessary. Intimidated by the darkness, the security guards had dropped their weapons and were holding their ears in obvious pain. The men of *Zodiac Two* rushed the two men. They offered no further resistance.

Bennett took a deep breath. It was painful, but the air came more readily. He reached under his fatigue shirt searching for sticky fluid leaking from holes in his chest and found none. The

Kevlar vest with ceramic inserts had served him well. He would have to send the manufacturer a thank you note. From the tenderness on his chest, he assumed he had a couple of broken ribs—perhaps three.

Zodiac Three experienced far less excitement, securing the bridge without incident. The captain was unarmed and recognized the futility of resistance.

***

FBI Agent Marshall Peterson climbed the steep metal stairs leading to the ship's bridge. Peterson and a few other key personnel had ferried over on the *Hamilton's* Jayhawk helicopter after return of electrical power. From what he had seen, it appeared the *Chimera* was now under military control.

He found Lt. Commander Connors on the ship's radio conferring with the captain of the *Hamilton*. "Any sign of the baby?" Peterson asked when Connors finished his conversation. Connors returned the microphone to its proper place on the radio console. Connors had secured the *Chimera* in under six minutes, a minor miracle in Peterson's book. An FBI SWAT team couldn't have done better, but there were no signs of satisfaction on Connors' face.

"*Zodiac Four* found a room filled with disposable diapers and a crib...but no baby. The crewmembers we've talked to either don't know the child's whereabouts or aren't willing to talk. Kaufmann pays them well for their loyalty."

The ship wasn't that large. There were only so many places to hide a baby. "I want this ship turned inside out," Peterson said. If the infant was on the ship, they would find him, but their intelligence could have been faulty. The infant could be in the States. It wouldn't be the first time Kaufmann had gotten the best of them.

"Yes, Sir. I'll have extra personnel sent over from the *Hamilton*." Connors wished he could be more optimistic. If the baby were onboard, the Seal teams would have found it. "We have the ship's company confined to the ballroom. They'll be interrogated. One of them might talk."

24

"The ship's under our control," Lieutenant Naikelekele said. A hand-held radio was pressed to his ear. "We should have more details shortly."

It was finally ending. Ana had been preparing herself for a letdown. The entire plan had seemed so incredible. Logic had dictated that something somewhere would go wrong. This was America where Murphy's Law was the law of the land. But her baby was on the *Chimera,* and the *Chimera* was under control of the American navy. The Americans had pulled off the impossible. The ship, still drifted in the light sea, but the electrical power was back on, and lights flooded the superstructure.

"There's a rope ladder hanging over the port side," Ana said. "Take us over there. I'm going aboard."

"That's not a good idea," Naikelekele replied. He made no effort to start the Zodiac's engines. Until told otherwise, his orders were to maintain a safe distance from the *Chimera*. The U.S. Navy frowned on civilian involvement, especially foreign civilians. The Russian and her friend would have to wait until the official all clear.

"I'll return your life vest later," Ana said. She stood up and prepared to jump into the water.

"Sit down!" Explaining to his superiors why one of his charges was free-swimming across the Pacific wasn't a pleasant thought. With or without a life vest, they wouldn't be happy. "Hang on. I'll take you over there."

"Thank you, I'm not a good swimmer."

Naikelekele restarted the engines and motored over to the *Chimera*. Without diesel engines, the *Chimera* drifted with the tide like a ghost ship. There appeared no sign of habitation. Naikelekele killed the Zodiac's engines and coasted up to the rope ladder. "You sure you want to do this?" he asked.

Ana's enthusiasm diminished when she looked up the side of the ship. The rope ladder hung down from the deck thirty feet above her. The rungs of the ladder were made of heavy-duty plastic with six-inch diameter flanges on the ends to keep the rungs away from the ship's sides.

"Let me go first," Dorek said. "I'll help you at the top."

Ana stepped back, allowing Dorek access to the ladder. She wasn't about to argue the point. He climbed the ladder with ease, not once pausing until reaching the top.

"Come on up," he said. "It's an easy climb."

Ana grabbed a rung and started up. She wasn't fond of heights, and the bobbing of the boat didn't help. A small wave slammed the Zodiac against the *Chimera* causing salt water to spray into Ana's face, stinging her eyes.

"Don't look down," Dorek said. It was an unneeded suggestion. Ana's eyes were closed, and she was climbing on feel alone. She only opened her eyes periodically to see how much higher she had to climb. To push the climb from her mind, she thought of Alek with his small fingers wrapped around her thumb. Alek looked back at her with his gray-green eyes. She was singing Russian lullabies when Dorek pulled her over the top.

"Piece of cake," Ana said when she opened her eyes. The Zodiac looked small floating on the water below her. "Thanks for everything, Keoni." Keoni gave her a military salute and powered the Zodiac toward the *Hamilton*. His work was done.

"Now we need to find the man in charge," Ana said.

"My guess would be the bridge," Dorek replied.

"Follow me. I spent nine months on this heap of scrap metal. I know my way around."

Ana led Dorek toward the bow and up three flights of stairs to the ship's bridge where several people were conversing. Marshall Peterson from the FBI was the only one she recognized. He was talking to one of the Navy SEALs. He had to be the SEAL team commander. They were scrutinizing the ship's floor plan but looked up when Ana stepped onto the bridge.

There was a moment of silence that hung ruefully in the air. "Ana, I'm so very sorry," Peterson finally said. His face, filled with pain, testified to the sincerity of his statement.

"My baby?"

"Kaufmann ordered the baby thrown overboard." There was no way Peterson could sugarcoat the truth. They had a good plan, but they had failed. He had failed. No one had envisioned Kaufmann stooping to such treachery. "We didn't get here in time. We searched the ship. The baby's gone. I'm very sorry," Peterson repeated.

Ana's eyes began to water as reality set in. Her baby was dead. The baby she had held ever so briefly was now gone. She should have let Kaufmann keep the baby. Then Alek would be alive. The thought flooded her mind with guilt. She had no one to blame but herself. Ana wiped the tears from her eyes. "What about Kaufmann? Did he get away on the helicopter?"

"Kaufmann's in custody," Peterson replied. "The man they call the Spaniard escaped in the helicopter. He didn't have a pilot's license, but apparently had some skills. In this case, it wasn't enough for night flying. The helicopter crashed just west of the runway on Tutuila. It had a full fuel tank. The fire department decided to let it burn itself out."

"Will Kaufmann be charged with murder?"

"Peterson paused. It was a question he preferred not to answer. "Unless we find the body, it'll be a tough call. Whoever threw the baby overboard isn't going to talk. We have little evidence of a murder other than some hearsay."

"You mean he might get away with this?"

"We hoped to find some of his records. With all his illegal activities, that would put him away for most of his life. But his computers were thrown overboard. We may not be able to charge him with anything. He could walk."

"If you need evidence, I have copies of his computer files."

Ana led them to her old room. It brought back somber memories. Her clothes still hung in her closet. A half stick of summer sausage vegetated in the refrigerator where she left it when they transferred her to the *Diamond Stud*. She had spent nine months on the *Chimera*, but it had seemed like a lifetime.

"I copied it to a CD and placed the label from Sally Rogers' *Unclaimed Pint* on it. It should be in my CD case." Ana found the CD case—it was right where she left it. She opened it and flipped thought the CD's. There were classical music CD's. There were several John Denver CD's. She found *We'll Pass Them On* and *Generations*—both Sally Rogers' CD's, but no *Unclaimed Pint*. It was missing. The Spaniard had found it. The only evidence that could put Kaufmann away, and it was gone. Her baby was gone. He had won again.

"It's not here," she said. Tears began to flow. They had outwitted her. They had blocked her every move. Now it was checkmate, game over. She had lost.

"Ana, let me again say how sorry we are," Peterson said. He had never been good at this part of his job. "I know that baby meant a lot to you—both of you. You're young and strong. You have a lot to live for." Ana didn't feel strong, and she had aged several years over the last nine months. "In a few minutes the coast guard helicopter will be leaving for the Pago Pago airport. There's nothing more you can do here. I want you to catch a ride on the chopper. From the airport you can take a taxi back to your van. It'll take us most of the day to sort out what we have here—if we have anything at all. I'll be taking to the Justice Department. If they think we have enough evidence to press charges, I'll call you at the Trade Winds Hotel. But I have to be honest with you. Unless we find some hard evidence, he may likely walk."

25

Ana rode in silence. With the steady roar of the helicopter's engines, any attempt at conversation would be futile—not that she cared to talk. Across from her in the crowded cabin were two navy commandos. Neither of them was willing to make eye contact, as if she were the cynosure of their shame. One had a bandage saturated with blood on his left shoulder. The other held his chest and grimaced in pain with each breath. The Americans had done their best. Two of them had paid a painful price. Ambulances would be waiting at the airport to take them to the LBJ Medical Center. Hopefully, they would fully recover. When noise level permitted, she would have to thank them—they cared.

The Jayhawk touched down on the runway close to the terminal building. It was now daylight, but only a limited portion of sunlight filtered through the overcast sky, providing the nidus for a gloomy day, at least for those individuals leaning toward despondency. On the tarmac, airport maintenance personnel were transporting luggage, refueling planes, or at least trying to look busy. West of the airport, smoke continued to rise from the site of the helicopter crash. It had stimulated idle conversation during coffee breaks, but for the most part, it was business as usual at the Pago Pago International Airport. The story behind the crash had yet to reach the rumor mill, although it was public knowledge that the pilot wasn't an Islander. It would be no one they knew. Due to the intense heat of the fire, it was assumed the next of kin—

whoever that might be—would have nothing but ashes to inter following the funeral service.

Ana and Dorek walked the fifty yards to the terminal entrance in silence. This was the day Ana was to be reunited with her baby, when she had hoped to cuddle him or rock him to sleep with softly sung lullabies. Instead, it was a day of bitter disappointment that no mathematical equation or high-tech apparatus could resolve. Despite her preternatural intelligence, she had been incapable of altering its outcome. It was inevitable that the days and months of torture and torment would eventually exact its toll causing Ana to reconsider the value of life itself. If Dorek hadn't been by her side, she might have done something foolish.

Inside the terminal, people were also trying to look busy. People talked in small groups, mostly in the native Samoan tongue. There was laughter, and people with carefree, buoyant faces. To them it was just another day on an island paradise. They were oblivious to the arrival of the somber European couple.

"Let's stop and get some breakfast." Dorek pointed to a small café at the far side of the terminal.

"I'm not really hungry."

"You at least need some coffee, and we need to sit down and decide where we go from here. According to Russia, Anastasia Petrova is dead. You no longer exist. Maybe now we can get married and have some other children. We're still young."

Ana sat down in a booth opposite Dorek. She knew Dorek was right; life had to go on. Life wouldn't stop because of her son's death. There had to have been other sons in other countries that died during the night. The world hadn't stopped for them. Did their mothers love their babies any less? Emotionally, Ana couldn't comprehend how life could go on, at least not for her, not without her Alek. But life was going on all around her. The waitress was busy fussing over customers, people in work clothes were eating breakfast, and overhead the ubiquitous announcer was warning passengers not to leave their luggage unattended.

Dorek ordered sausage and eggs with a large glass of orange juice. Ana ordered coffee and a sweet roll, although she wasn't sure she could eat it. She needed to move on. They had a rented van to return and luggage at the Tradewinds Hotel. Other than that, there was nothing to keep them in Samoa. She needed to leave

Samoa. She needed to put this behind her. But where was she to go?

The overhead announcer again admonished travelers not to leave their baggage unattended. Ana and Dorek pushed it back into their subconsciousness. It was one of many background noises. They resumed eating in silence. But the announcer continued, "Will Mr. & Mrs. Dolinski please come to the Hawaiian Airlines courtesy desk." Dolinski was a common name in Poland, but this wasn't Poland.

"You think they're referring to you?" Ana asked.

"You mean me and my wife? Last I knew, I wasn't married. Although I'd like to be if I could get a certain young woman to say yes. They're talking about someone else. Us Polacks are everywhere." Dorek finished the last of his sausage. "Why don't you come back to Poland with me? We can get married."

"Who would you marry? Anastasia Petrova is dead. The only I.D. I have is for Cordelia Kaufmann, and she's already married."

Dorek left some money on the counter including a generous tip while the overhead announcer continued his monotonous monologue. Again it was followed by, "Will Mr. & Mrs. Dolinski please come to the Hawaiian Airlines courtesy desk."

"Let's check it out," Ana said. "It could be Marshal Peterson from the FBI trying to reach us. Maybe they found some incriminating evidence." Even as she said it, Ana knew it wasn't true. Kaufmann would get off clean. He always did.

"The FBI would call us at the hotel, not the airport. Besides, they know we aren't married. They'd be paging Petrova, not Dolinski."

Ana had been hoping the FBI had discovered inculpating evidence that would incarcerate Kaufmann for life. He shouldn't get away with what he'd done. The crime had been committed in Samoan territorial waters. She wondered if Samoans had capital punishment. Even capital punishment would be inadequate for the likes of Lamar Kaufmann. But Dorek was right. The FBI would page Anastasia Petrova, not Dorek Dolinski.

"Dorek, we need to leave Samoa. I don't care where we go. I can't spend another night here. There're too many memories."

"This isn't a huge airport, Ana. They don't have flights every hour. We may not catch a flight today."

"I don't care. I have to get out of here. I'll swim if I have to."

"I suppose we can see what flights are available. We'll have to fly to Hawaii first and then catch a major flight from there."

Being a small airport the Hawaiian Airlines courtesy desk wasn't hard to find. It was on the second level. The ground floor was mostly baggage claims and car rental booths. Two Samoan women behind the courtesy desk were talking in their native language. Their conversation was interspersed with laughter. At least some people were in a good mood. It only made Ana more depressed.

"Can I help you?" one of them asked when Dorek approached their desk.

"My name is Dorek Dolinski. I would like to make reservations for two going to Hawaii. We would prefer the next flight."

"Do you have identification?"

Dorek handed her his passport. She looked at for a moment and then returned it. "And you must be Anastasia?" she asked, looking at Ana.

"Yes, that would be I."

The woman's pleasant disposition dissolved, the friendly smile replaced by a cold stare. "I'm not a bit happy about this," she said. "I never would have done it if your uncle hadn't been a priest. I probably let it carry more weight than I should have."

"A priest?" Ana asked.

"Father Ginatti. What did I do with that package he left?..." The lady looked under the counter and came up with a manila envelope. "Here it is." She opened the envelope and took out two sets of plane tickets. "Your uncle pre-paid your tickets to Warsaw."

Ana looked at the tickets. One was for Dorek Dolinski. The other was made out to Anastasia Dolinski.

"I also have your passports. You really should keep these with you. Don't give them to anyone. That includes your uncle even if he is a priest." The lady pulled two Polish passports from the envelope and gave them to Ana. Ana opened the first passport. Her picture was on the first page. It was the picture taken in Chelyabinsk. Below the picture was the name Anastasia Dolinski.

She opened the second passport. It had a picture of a small infant. Below his picture was the name Alek Dolinski.

"He's really been a doll." The airlines clerk picked up a baby carrier and passed it to Ana. The clerk's stern disposition rapidly melted away. "We enjoyed having him. He's very well mannered. Didn't cry once. I may be out of place, but…" The clerk returned to her stern look. "…you really need to take better care of him. You have no idea how quickly they can be stolen. Like I said, if your uncle hadn't been a priest, I might have reported this to social services. He seemed like such a nice man. I could tell by the way he cared for the baby that he's a very proud uncle. They give up a lot when they enter the priesthood. I hope he enjoys his retirement in Barcelona."

"Where is my uncle?"

"You just missed him. He should be boarding his plane now. You might see him from the window…Don't forget your diaper bag. He left some other personal items." The clerk gave the envelope to Dorek.

Dorek and Ana walked over to a bank of windows overlooking the runway. From their second-story vantage point they could see a small, twin-engine, Hawaiian Airlines jet parked on the tarmac. Servicemen were loading the bowels with boxes and suitcases. In the front, a steady stream of passengers queued up to board the plane. One of the passengers was dressed in black with a broad brimmed black hat.

"My new wife comes with a dowry."

"What do you mean?" Ana asked.

Dorek showed her a bankbook he had found in the manila envelope. It was from a Swiss bank. "If my conversion factor is correct, you have the equivalent of a half-million American dollars in this account."

Ana looked at the bankbook. The name on the account was Anastasia Dolinski. "What else is in the envelope?"

Dorek reached inside the envelope and pulled out a CD. It was *The Unclaimed Pint* by Sally Rogers.

"That's my missing CD with the files from Kaufmann's computer. There's enough evidence there to put Kaufmann up for a long time."

"There should be enough to put the Spaniard behind bars too. He only got religion, so to speak, after everything was falling apart," Dorek said. "That's not going to get my sympathy."

"He once told me it takes a month to make a good passport forgery. No, he was planning this before the baby was born. Let him go. There's a little good in everyone."

The Spaniard walked toward the waiting plane. He was feeling unusually tired. Perhaps age was catching up with him. It was time to retire—return to Barcelona. The line of people momentarily came to a stop. He looked back at the terminal. On the second floor, behind the pane of glass, was a young couple. The woman was holding a small child. The Spaniard gave them a nod. She had been a worthy adversary. Sometimes the adversary deserves to win. The line began to move. The Spaniard climbed up the ramp to the plane. It was time to go home.

ABOUT THE AUTHOR

Larry Buege is a former chemistry and physics teacher and a retired physician assistant. He currently lives with his wife in Marquette, Michigan along the southern shore of Lake Superior.

Made in the USA
Charleston, SC
06 June 2014